12/06

D0445159

Thanksgiving Night

Thanksgiving Night

A Novel

Richard Bausch

HarperCollins*Publishers*

THANKSGIVING NIGHT. Copyright © 2006 by Richard Bausch. All rights reserved. Printed in the United States of America. No part of this book may be used or reproduced in any manner whatsoever without written permission except in the case of brief quotations embodied in critical articles and reviews. For information, address HarperCollins Publishers, 10 East 53rd Street, New York, NY 10022.

HarperCollins books may be purchased for educational, business, or sales promotional use. For information, please write: Special Markets Department, HarperCollins Publishers, 10 East 53rd Street, New York, NY 10022.

FIRST EDITION

Designed by Sarah Maya Gubkin

Printed on acid-free paper

Library of Congress Cataloging-in-Publication Data

Bausch, Richard
Thanksgiving night : a novel / Richard Bausch.—1st ed.
   p. cm.

ISBN-13: 978-0-06-009443-0
ISBN-10: 0-06-009443-5
  1. Thanksgiving Day—Fiction. 2. Virginia—Fiction. 3. Domestic fiction. I. Title

PS3552.A846T48 2006
813'.54—dc22   2006041222

06 07 08 09 10 /RRD 10 9 8 7 6 5 4 3 2 1

FIC
BAUSCH

For Robert and Denise and David Bausch

"No matter what passions compose them, all private worlds are good, they are never vulgar places."

— TRUMAN CAPOTE

"The human heart could never pass the drunk test."

— TENNESSEE WILLIAMS

PART ONE

August–October

CRAZIES

I.

From the first overlook of the Sky Line Drive, heading south, you can only see the old part of Point Royal—washed in hazy distance, an intricately laced aggregate of antique houses and white steeples, set among many shades of blue and green and tawny summer. A sleepy, lovely, Virginia country setting.

Up close there are, of course, the complications of the age.

Antebellum porches mixed in with two-car garages and fast-food chains; an Internet café in a glass-front, low-slung building within a block of a town hall that is almost two hundred years old—all of this across from a parking lot and a red-brick radio station with flags out front and a skinny seventy-foot tower behind.

On the radio station lately there's mostly talk, and the subject is invariably the president and his recent troubles. The call-in shows are full of moral outrage. The news, even now, six months after the Senate's acquittal, is still full of the names: Starr, Hyde, and the women, Slick Willy's women, all the way from back when he was governor of Arkansas to the uneasy present, with its rumors of war and the threat of general shutdowns as a result of Y2K. Religionists are growing more strident, and there's apocalyptic zaniness all around, starting with the Hale-Bopp suicide crowd, who expected that there would be a turnstile on the spaceship taking them beyond the stars, and so each one carried a ten-dollar roll of quarters on his person. The news media character- izes these people as intelligent. (One caustic voice on the radio points out that certainly the Hale-Bopp fruitcakes *would* look intelligent to the *media*.)

On the other side of the radio station, on a small, red-clay rise of ground, a strip mall that was built ten years ago languishes in weeds and wild flowers, crabgrass and dandelions; it's shut down and boarded, with postings advertising commercial space. The postings are wearing away in the weather.

Beyond the strip mall is a small used-book shop called The Heart's Ease.

Take a look at it now: this charmingly derelict-looking place, its windows stacked with the sun-faded spines of volumes, one on top of another as if they had all been arrested in the act of crowding to the openings to breathe. The paint is peeling on the porch, and the color of the trim is the exact shade of old paper. If you were to characterize the store or make a simile out of it, you might say it's like an elderly man nodding off to sleep. It faces into the sunny lot across the way, the gravel road veering to the left, toward the century-old brick-making factory, with its five house-sized stacks of new red bricks, and its weirdly attendant-seeming next-door neighbor, the ancient clapboard relic of a church, white-steepled Saint Augustine's. This church is a historic land- mark, and is flanked by a shady lawn dotted with gravestones, carved dates and inscriptions going back to the eighteenth century. BELOVED MOTHER; WITH THE ANGELS; LOST TO US.

It was once said that two people could leave at the same time from main street, one heading for the wildest hollow in the Blue Ridge and the other for the Lincoln Memorial in Washington, DC, and both would arrive at their destination at about the same time.

Now, one travels only minutes to be in what feels like the tatters of the city, and the thin blue roads that wind up into the mountains are lined with apartment complexes.

The Shenandoah River runs along the town's western edge, and on some hot summer days, after a little rain, it's muddy and so slow-running as to seem calm. Because of the willows dipping their filamental branches at the edge, you can stand on the highway bridge that crosses there and swear, from the look of it, that there is nothing but woods all around. Signs along the bank warn against swimming or fishing.

On Main Street, just now, the sharp shadows make pretty angles. You feel, gazing upon the scene, that you saw it somewhere in a painting, if only you could remember which one. It's three o'clock in the afternoon. The end of August. Stillness. Not even an airplane in the sky. Some celestial creature landing here might think the whole world a quiet place, deserted or abandoned.

But now a little wind stirs; a scrap of paper rises in the street, and a camp bus full of altar boys from Saint Augustine's comes rumbling along, followed by an old Ford pickup, covered with dust, which turns off onto a side street. The radio is on loud in the truck, an evangelistic rant, a frantic baritone crying the terrors of a thousand years.

It's the dog days of summer nineteen ninety-nine. And God is coming.

2.

At an angle from the corner of the only intersecting street of this part of town is a small, white house, with a little porch, flanked by other houses of the same stripe, all of them built in nineteen fifty-nine and nineteen-sixty, when the country was not even ten years out of one undeclared war and already at the beginning of a new one. In the small window of the east-facing bedroom, an elderly woman sits turning the pages of a magazine with a sharp, swiping motion, as if each page contributes to a growing sense of an affront to her sensibilities. Behind her, another woman, also elderly, stands and folds laundry that she absently lifts from a basket in a chair. She puts the laundry on the bed. There's something about her apparent nonchalance that seems studied, done for effect—now and again, she monitors the page-turning of the other. She's dressed to go out. The other wears a blue bathrobe.

These two are surrounded by emblems of religion that seem to exist in an atmosphere of neglect, like bric-a-brac: Christ praying in the garden on one wall, and facing out, with radiating heart, on another; a rosary lying on the polished surface of the bureau; a crucifix on the wall above the door. One picture on the dresser sits propped upside down against a makeup box: two girls in sepia light, posing coquettishly before the gate of a white picket fence, clad in the fashionable attire of nineteen forty-two.

On the polished wooden floor under the side table in the room beyond this, in a pool of warm, dust-moted sunlight, the bottom part of a water glass lies in a scintillating circle of its shattered upper half. Several larger pieces, reflecting the light, are scattered along the baseboard. The radio is on here, too. News, worries about computer glitches, power failures.

The pickup truck stops in front of this house, and the driver gets out—a blocky, heavy-jawed, muscular man with hundreds of tiny freckles all over him, though his hair is dark brown, graying at the sides, and he has a deep-lined, clay-colored face. His name is Oliver Ward, and he's of that generation of Americans that came of age in the tumult of far-reaching material advances and civil unrest that was the sixties. War amid unprecedented bounty. Stupendous feats of technology involving everything from electron microscopy to journeys away from the Earth—coupled with appalling failures of spirit, the numbing repetition of burning cities and assassinations. He served in Vietnam, and was wounded in a firefight only two months after arriving in country. Two pieces of shrapnel hit him; one in his neck, injuring a nerve in his upper spine, and one in his upper leg, missing the femoral artery by a sixteenth of an inch. He spent the rest of his tour recuperating at the air-base hospital at Da Nang, typing orders for troop shipments home. He felt happy there, sending men home, alive, most of them unharmed.

It was someone else's job to type out the other orders.

But his life has been taxing enough. He's a widower. He looks older than fifty-five: heavy skin drooping under the eyes; deep lines and a settled look about the face. One of the aftereffects of his neck injury is that he's continually shaking his head "no." It's a back-and-forth motion exactly like denial, and when he's nervous, it becomes more pronounced. He's had to spend a lot of time retracting imagined rebuffs and refutations.

Now he reaches slowly back into the truck, making allowances for his arthritic shoulders and the old leg-wound, which still aches with the dull ache of memory. Bringing out a clipboard, he holds it before him like a hat, and approaches the house. As usual in such circumstances he feels as if someone is watching from the windows. Next to the door is a darkly smudged white button. He presses it and waits, and then presses again. Nothing. Listening at the door, he's poised to press the button one last time when the door opens suddenly, and an old woman strides quickly toward him. She looks to be about eighty, and is wearing a bathrobe. Hair white as pearls. She has a purse draped over her shoulder as if she's completely unaware that she isn't dressed for the outside. Oliver's so startled by this sight that he can't unplant his feet; he rears back, chin tucked into his chest. She stops, having nearly run into him, and says, "Oh." It's almost a cry of alarm. And then she gives forth exactly that: "Ah!"

Oliver Ward says, "I didn't mean to scare you. I've been ringing."

She stares for a moment. "That thing doesn't work. What do you want? I'm on my way out. I'm getting the hell out of here."

He stands there, dumbstruck.

She stares. "Well?"

"I rang the bell, ma'am." In moments of stress, his head-tic is more pronounced.

"Did you or didn't you?" she demands.

"I did," he tells her, and hurries to say, "I have a tic. Pay no attention to this." He points to his shaking head.

"What the hell are you talking about?" she says impatiently, one hand held over her chest.

There's nothing for him to do but explain: "Somebody called me to talk about doing some work here. I could leave a card. I have an old shrapnel wound in my neck. It makes my head do this."

"You don't want to talk to me," she says, with a look of incredulity.

Oliver waits, still stunned. But then he says, "Pardon?"

"Holly!" the woman shouts, without taking her eyes from him. The voice is piercing.

Startled again, he takes a step back, raising one arm.

"You want to talk to my insane niece."

He glances beyond her. The words are only now registering.

"How old are you?" she asks.

"Excuse me?"

"Never mind." And she shouts again: "Holly!"

He stares.

"My appalling niece," she says.

"Someone called—"

She raises a hand, nearly places it on his chest. "Hold your horses," she says. Then she shouts: "Holly!"

They wait. Oliver actually thinks of turning and running away. He's still feeling the startlement traveling along his nerves. Finally, the niece comes from one of the rooms of the house, and she's in a pantsuit. She looks scarily the same age as the first woman. Except she has dark hair in a tight little knot on top of her head, and cheeks the color of violets. "What?" she says. Blue eyes, a wide mouth, perfect, very white teeth. When she sees Oliver, she smiles, then seems to recall something unpleasant, frowning.

"I'll come back later," says Oliver. "Forgive me, ladies."

"You called this guy, didn't you?" says the white-haired woman.

He leans in to explain further. "You—somebody said you-all needed some work done around the house? Is this—" he steps back to look at the number next to the door, "Three-eleven? Yes. Temporary Road. This is—"

Now both women stare.

"I'll come back, you know, if there's—if you—if the time's not right. I'll come back."

"I did the work," says the niece, turning to her housemate. "And I didn't make the call, Fiona. You did. You nagged me about it and then you called this poor man, purely to get at me, and I did the work already—" She halts, and then addresses Oliver: "Really. She did. I know it sounds incredible but it's true. It was a simple matter of a faucet needing to be replaced, and you'll have to forgive this. I already did it. I did."

"I made no such call," says Fiona.

"Yes she did," Holly says to Oliver, shouldering past the other woman and stepping out onto the porch. Then she turns and stares at her. "What're you gonna do now, Fiona, walk out of here in a fucking bathrobe and slippers?"

"Please excuse her language," Fiona says to Oliver. "She's an apostate."

"I'd be happy to make some kind of payment for your time coming out here," says Holly. "But we really don't have a thing that needs doing. Really," she goes on, staring at him. "We don't. Unless you feel like cleaning up broken glass, because I'm certainly not going to touch it."

He says, "Broken glass?"

"We don't have a thing that needs doing, honest. Sorry for your trouble."

Oliver feels his blood rise a little. These women involved him in whatever squabble they're having, and he has driven out here, and been frightened, for nothing. He says, "Well, ma'am, I did say on the phone that there's a sixty-dollar minimum charge."

"You did *not* say that," Fiona says.

"Well, if I didn't, I meant to. And I'm pretty sure I did. It's my policy."

Holly turns and glares at Fiona, giving forth a small exasperated sigh. Then she faces him again. "Do you cut grass?"

"I don't want to do make-work either if it's all the same to you. I've got other accounts. I paint houses, and do carpentry, mostly. Some drywall and electric. You-all don't need anything like that done?"

"The place needs painting," Fiona says. "But you think she'd do anything about it."

"Well, I do good work, painting." Now he has the thought that this might turn out. He can paint for them, and keep to himself in the work, as is his habit anyway. He can keep far from them in the work.

"The house does not need painting," Holly says.

"Then I guess—well, I guess that's that. I wish you ladies would clear things with each other before involving the rest of the community."

"What the hell is that supposed to mean," says Fiona. "We're not paying you for doing nothing."

"I got a request to come out here," Oliver says. "One of you gave me directions on the telephone." He's feeling anger now. He's about to begin shouting, though he will also back down from the porch as he does so. These days, one can never tell. The white-haired lady might have a Glock 9 mm in her purse.

"My aunt is the one who gave you directions," says Holly, with a motion like waving something bothersome away from herself. "You poor man."

"I made the call," Fiona says proudly.

"Well, and I was pretty clear about the minimum charge," Oliver says. He half believes it himself now.

"You ever read Shakespeare?" Fiona says.

For a beat, he's simply too flabbergasted to speak. "I know who he was."

"Name one play. My niece here thinks he's only for elitists."

"Sixty dollars, ladies."

For a tense few seconds, they're all staring at each other, Oliver looking from Fiona to Holly and back again. He'll stand his ground now. He's decided, by God, he won't budge. He remains where he is, feeling his head make the repeated refutation, so pronounced now that they seem to be taking it as intended. The younger of the two ladies shakes her own head and looks down, and he sees something like sorrow in her face. Is she about to cry? He wants to go back in his mind and replay everything in an attempt to decide how to proceed.

"Look. Let's start over," he says. "I'm Oliver Ward. I guess it's on the card. Oliver's General Contracting. I do excellent work. General contracting work. Carpentry and house painting mostly. A little drywall and electric. I live with my daughter, who is a policewoman and someone I'm awful proud of, and her two children over on Drake Avenue. A mile or so that way." He points east. "I'm glad to make your acquaintance." When the two women do not react, he goes on. "Oliver's General Contracting, that's me. Carpentry. Drywall. Electric. House painting." He waits another moment. "*A Midsummer Night's Dream*," he says.

"Excuse me?" says Holly.

He indicates the other woman. "She said name one play. That's a Shakespeare play. My daughter played in it in high school. Shakespeare. Good play. I know it."

"Name another," Fiona says.

"I fix things, too," says Oliver, choosing to ignore her.

"There's some things nobody can fix," she says. "Are you a liberal? Do you think a man should get away with perjury and lying to the people?"

"I've told you and told you," Holly says. "I think he should resign."

Again, there's a silence, this time rather extended.

"Well?" Fiona demands.

"I never mix politics and business," Oliver says. Then: "I never mix politics with anything."

"Was there something else you wanted to tell us, then?"

"Ladies, it seems like we—looks like we've got some signals crossed. But I'm out here in good faith, and there's a charge for coming out. A minimum charge. Sixty dollars."

"One-track mind," Fiona says. And then the two women turn to each other and seem about to begin hitting and flailing. They speak at the same time, and their words mix, a tangle of "this is your fault" and "if you'd done as I asked in the first place," and "since when did you become such a prig and a reactionary." They scowl and breathe and sputter, and lean into each other in the doorway. It's astounding.

"Look," Oliver Ward says at last, loud, raising one hand to gain their attention. "This time—okay, this time—*this* time, let's just say I'll let it pass. I've got too much work without having to worry about it." As far as he's concerned, though he keeps this to himself, both women can rot.

The niece, Holly, reaches into the other woman's purse. Fiona tries to hold back, and they tussle a little. Oliver thinks it might be the gun he worried about earlier and takes another step back, nearly falling off the step. "Jesus Christ," he says, righting himself, trying to keep hold of reason.

Holly pulls a billfold from the purse—a checkbook-shaped one, leather, just like a man would use. She reaches into it and pulls out a twenty-dollar bill. "Here," she says, handing it to him.

"I need that money," says Fiona. "Have him get it from Will and

Elizabeth." She steps forward and takes Oliver surprisingly by his shirt. He hears a small cry come from the bottom of his throat. "You can get the full sixty from them. They'll pay it," she says, her face not one inch from his own. "And don't use the Lord's name in vain."

"Take your hands off me, madam!" Oliver says. "For God's sweet sake!" The absurdity of the words he has just spoken seems to glare at him from some reasonable quarter of his mind, and he's aware, in a strange, wordless way, that he'll repeat all this to someone purely for the laugh.

"I'm telling you they'll pay you the sixty," Fiona says, letting go.

"I can't believe you'd do that to Will and Elizabeth," Holly says.

"I need the twenty," says Fiona, snatching it back.

Oliver waits, smoothing the front of his shirt while they argue. Once more he thinks they might come to blows.

"It's just over there—two blocks," Fiona says to him. "Tanhauser Street. Second house on the left. It's got a big green awning. The only awning on the street. Tell them I sent you."

"She's cracked," Holly says. "Anybody can see that."

"Sixty. Take it or leave it," Fiona says.

"I apologize for her," says Holly, making the circling motion at her ear with her index finger.

He decides the best policy is to speak only with her. He says, "Good day," holding a hand up to wave good-bye and feeling the ridiculousness of it, all of it, wanting now only to get away.

"It's her son and daughter-in-law," Fiona says. "They'll pay it. He's too nice not to pay it. He won't even ask questions. Just tell him we sent you."

"If you would please not listen to her," the other says. "She's crazy."

"Try them, you'll see," says Fiona, as she's being moved aside by her niece.

"Thanks for your consideration," Holly says to Oliver.

He actually catches himself bowing slightly, then makes his backward-looking way down the sidewalk, while the two women mutter at each other, going in. The door to the house slams. He gets into his truck, starts the engine, and shifts out of neutral. The radio blasts at him and makes him jump. "Jesus Chr . . ." he begins but stops himself. Pulling into the driveway, he worries that they'll come out again. He backs into the road and starts down the street. The strangest thing. *The nuttiest five minutes in history*, he thinks.

Past the sun-burned and parched yard, the view of the mountains out toward the interstate is hazy blue, and the new mall in the foreground gleams in the bright, warm light. There are people, perfectly sane types, walking among the parked cars. On the other side of the expanse of asphalt parking lot are more houses, sizable ones, with wide, brown lawns, and he heads that way. He might as well see. He's lived long enough to know that even the advice of the mad can lead to some sort of gain, if one is alert enough. He'll need the money, with winter coming on. It's always a scramble in the cold months, and there is also the fact that he has the need of periodical liquid refreshments, enough to worry about not having the wherewithal to treat himself now and then. This is just something he knows without quite voicing it. Provide, provide.

The voice on the radio shudders and rises dramatically. He likes to hear it, though he seldom really listens to the words; there's a sense of harmless, even childish calamity about it that gives him pleasure. On Tanhauser Street, he goes slow, past one house with a SALE sign stuck down in tall weeds out front, and stops at the house with the green awning. He walks up to the door and, instead of ringing the bell, knocks, half-expecting a batty old lady to come bursting out at him. But music's coming from somewhere. Whoever lives here likes Van Morrison, and he does, too. This warms him. He knocks again, waits, listening, gazing at the next-door house—it's clear from the curtainless windows and the uncut grass that it's empty and has been on the market for some time. Oliver thinks of the homeless. He thinks first of people, but then he thinks of the condition itself—it's something he has narrowly avoided several times in life.

The door opens, and a tired-looking but lovely young woman stands there, wearing red shorts and a man's white shirt tied at the waist. Her hair is straight and brown, with the slightest tracings of gray in it. "Yes?" she says. There's an exquisite glow to her skin, the gleam of sweat on her brow.

"I'm sorry—Hello. Sorry to bother you—you don't know me—I—these ladies—"

She interrupts him. "Two of them, right? Old? Wild? Scary?"

He hesitates, then can't help a small, agreeing laugh. "Yes ma'am, the old wild scary ladies. They sent me. They—well, they contracted for some work. But didn't pay. Sixty dollars. I said we could call it even this one time, but they—the one—insisted I come here."

"Fiona," she says. Then: "The white-haired one."

He nods again. "I mean, to be honest with you they were arguing about it. I just thought—" he ceases, looking down, and then back up at her. The tic is even more pronounced now, because this is a lie he's telling and it's purely to get the sixty dollars and he knows why he wants it. Of course, he notices—as he always does—the look on her face, so, again, automatically but with a kindly reassuring tone, he explains, pointing at his neck.

"I'm sorry to hear that," she says. It's clear that she's puzzled as to why he bothered to tell her about it. Yet she could hardly have failed to see it.

"People think I'm saying no all the time." He smiles at her. "When my daughter was a teenager and wanted the car keys, I didn't even have to say anything."

"I see." She smiles back. He's certain she missed the joke. And now he sees that she's just gotten it. She actually chuckles, so sweetly, putting one lovely hand to her lips.

"An advantage," he says.

"I guess so."

"The silver lining of the cloud."

She nods, but she's gained control of herself.

"Anyway," he goes on. "These two ladies—"

"Just a minute," she sighs. "How much did you say?"

He repeats the amount. She leaves the door ajar, and, after a brief interval, he hears her talking to someone. A moment later, he realizes that she's talking on the phone. He decides to stick to his guns. A lot of people charge money just to show up. A sixty-dollar minimum fee is reasonable for his trouble. He's a businessman, by God, and, from now on, that's the policy.

The young woman comes back to the door and says, "Will you take a check?"

"Yes, ma'am."

"Will," she calls. "Where's the checkbook?"

Oliver waits. A man comes from the back of the house, carrying cuttings—roses, Oliver sees, at least a dozen of them, the stems wrapped in construction paper. The man is in his late forties, tall and rather gangly, as if not all his leg muscles want to work at the same time—there's a shambling glide to his gait, almost sleepy-seeming. He's got sandy hair, thinning at the front, and his face is rather babyish, smooth-cheeked, open; you can see what sort of child he was.

"Will," the woman calls.

"I'm right here," the man says, nodding at Oliver, coming up on the porch. He puts one flower on the railing, obviously intending it for Oliver, and then walks on into the house. "Look what I brought you from the woods," he says. The door closes partly, and then the man leans out, with that friendly boy's expression on his face. "Sorry. One second."

Oliver hears the woman say, "Oh, Will. They're beautiful. You sweetheart."

"Happy Wednesday, my love," Will says.

Oliver has the thought that he ought to sneak away and leave these people in their joyful pass. He thinks of his daughter, whose life is hard, and wishes with all his heart that she could have something like this with someone, anyone—something just like this. He starts to leave, and then hesitates and clears his throat. Worry about money is one of the things that makes his daughter unhappy. He clears his throat again. The door closes and then opens almost immediately. The man, Will, stands there. "I'm so sorry," he says. "You know—special occasion. Er, nonoccas—you know." He smiles sheepishly.

"I do know the feeling," Oliver tells him.

Will stares. "Can I help you?"

But then the woman steps out with the checkbook. The men watch her while she writes the check. She hands it to Oliver, and he thanks her. But she's already talking to her husband. "Holly and Fiona. Don't ask. I called them and Fiona's pitching a fit. You don't want to know."

"I'm sorry for it," Oliver tells her.

"Do me a favor," she says to her husband. "Let's take no calls from that house tonight."

"Yes, ma'am," says her husband.

She turns to Oliver. "Thank you." Her husband has already gone inside.

"I am sorry for it," Oliver tells her. "I just can't afford—you know. The time and the stop."

"It's fine," she tells him. "I'm sorry you got bothered."

"I hope you won't think this is—uh—rude," Oliver says. "But, the one is the—the niece of the other?"

"Fiona, the aunt, is a late-life child of Holly's grandfather. They're only a couple of years apart."

"That's something."

"Fiona's the older one. We've been calling them the Crazies." She smiles. "Self-explanatory."

"Yes, ma'am," Oliver says. "No offense."

Sometimes being stubborn works out, and, after all, upholding one's principles is invigorating. Now he can take the afternoon off, and drive into Manassas, where he'll cash the check and treat himself to an early dinner at a Mexican restaurant. Maybe he'll buy a pint bottle of bourbon, and have a little something of it, just a touch, to celebrate. It won't cost more than ten dollars. The rest of the money will go to his daughter, Alison. The bills. All that. Having collected his one rose from the porch, he drives on with a feeling of having left trouble behind. He turns the radio up loud. He's happy, listening to the fervent evangelistic voice in its harangue about a thousand years, the approaching end of everything.

BROTHER FIRE

I.

At seventy-two years of age, the pastor of Saint Augustine's, Father John Fire (pronounced *fear-ay*) has the fluidity of motion one might expect of a twenty-year-old. He's never suffered from stiffness in the joints or any of the other ailments of aging, except a small irregularity in his heartbeat, which is controlled by a pacemaker. He's bald as a stone; his teeth are strong and white. His eyes are light blue, shading to aquamarine, depending on what he's wearing. He weighs one hundred seventy-one pounds in his stocking feet, is six-feet-one-inch tall, has very skinny, spindly legs and very large feet. In his youth, he was a bit of a tough, and he carried that into his priesthood. For the first twelve years of his life as a religious, he was a brother in the order of Franciscans, and earned there the nickname Brother Fire (pronounced as the word for conflagration). The story has it that when they put flame to Saint Francis of Assisi's face, he turned and spoke to it. "Brother fire," he said. So, people called John Fire (pronounced *fear-ay*) Brother Fire (pronounced *fire*), and the name stuck.

Fact is, he likes the name.

He also likes mornings when the sun breaks through fog, wind that shakes leaves out of the trees, lightning forking across a summer sky, rivers—all waters, really—plants, animals, birdsong, the roar of lions, music of every type, drums, all the kinds of coffee and tea, cats, dogs, horses, paintings of people bustling by on city streets, paintings of flowers, all the sculptures of Bernini, flying buttresses, those great red sequoias in Northern California, Northern California itself (for the wines), wine, white and red but mostly the reds, especially Italian, the Shenandoah Valley, presidential politics, philosophy, the poetry of John Berryman and Gerard Manley Hopkins (he sees the affinity between them), and, of course, all of Shakespeare. But above everything, he likes people. He loves people. The sweetest music to him has always been the sound of another human voice. What for all others would be the most unattractive, nerve-grating accent pleases him for the fact of its contribution to the happy proliferation of human notes. He enjoys others, not in the abstract way of, say, a Lenin or a Trotsky—though he has always been decidedly leftward-leaning in his politics—but in a very specific and direct way. When you talk to him, you have an immediate sense that he is interested in your benefit, and that you can tell him everything, even when, as it is in the confessional, what you have to report is sordid and full of failure and contradiction. He will tell you—and mean it—that the sign of contradiction is the center of Christianity, that the cross itself is the first sign of contradiction, and that the human condition is in its way similar to that of Christ: the contradiction of being both God *and* man, and alive on the earth; of possessing an eternal soul yet living in a body that dies. It is all meaning. And meaning, for Brother Fire, is what gives a measure of majesty to ordinary lives. He's uncomplicatedly convinced of his own ordinariness, and so, when he speaks to his parishioners, this simple faith in that fact and in their charity convinces them, brings them forth in a welter of love, a sweet dependency. His gift, above all else—above the humor and the good nature with others and the charm—is acceptance.

A brief history:

Only child, born in Belgium. Mother Jewish. Father a fierce Catholic from a large Catholic family that included two nuns and two priests. His father was the youngest brother and spent his life trying to make up for a belief that, because he was the only son not to enter the priesthood, he was a disappointment to his parents. He also had to make up for the fact that he fell in love with and married a Jewish girl. John Fire grew up in a house where holidays were celebrated in tandem: Passover, Easter; Hanukkah, Christmas. All the others. It taught the boy that striving for goodness was inherently goodness itself. His father moved to America a year and a half before he and his mother followed. This had not been the plan. The Great Depression and the rise of Hitler and his gang had changed everything.

John Fire's early childhood years were spent in little towns in Tennessee and North Carolina, wherever his father could find work—itinerant labor, though the man had training in engineering. In nineteen thirty-three, the old man found permanent employment at the Navy Yard and moved his wife and son with him to Washington, DC. They lived in a big, old Victorian house with a porch and a small lawn, within sight of Catholic University. After the death of John's mother in nineteen forty-three—of the same heart condition with which he's now living—the old man began a slow decline, his health compromised, he would say, by the Depression, the stresses of wartime, and grief. He slipped away in the winter of nineteen forty-six. Young John entered the seminary that year. He did well. The work helped him through, kept him from looking inward too much, or thinking too much about his sorrow. He enjoyed words, the language, the prayers, the poetry, and he had a talent for remembering. He remembered names, lines, places, faces, concepts, the prayers of the mystics, the works of the church fathers, law, philosophy, and every last batting average of the Chicago Cubs from nineteen-thirty to nineteen forty-one, when he stopped following baseball.

His life has been simple, direct, and mostly good.

Of course, as we know, one seldom uses the word *good* anymore about anyone, except as that word relates to *skill*.

But we are not talking about skill. Where Brother Fire is concerned, *good* is the word that one can say is operative about the man: He has the gift of charity. He wants little for himself. A glass of wine in the evenings. A good book. A little music. Pleasing conversation. And there is his abiding love of his own kind. If, at times, something in his eyes gives forth a sense that he carries in his heart a great and sover-

SIMMS LIBRARY ALBUQUERQUE ACADEMY

eign weight of human misery—one thinks of such a compassionate soul
carrying around everything that has been unloaded on him in the dark
of the confessional; one imagines his personal sorrows, the loss of his
parents and of the other members of his family—if this darkness shows
in his gaze, it's fleeting. He has gone from being a young, devoted man
to being an old one without much change in the tenor of his days, and
it hasn't seemed nearly so long as it is. His own battles with himself,
and his own work against the despair in his blood ("Not, I'll not, carrion comfort, Despair, not feast on thee; not untwist—slack they may
be—these last strands of man in me") have cost him plenty, physically
and spiritually, but he considers all this the province of his own journey
and not a part of his real life, which is, simply, helping other souls on
their journey. All of it, to Brother Fire, has been a journey toward the
Godhead. The benevolent light at the heart of the universe. And he has
managed all his troubles by concentrating on his pastoral work. People
come to him not only to confess but to *complain*. Because there's nothing
judgmental in him, nothing of the prig. The sacrament of penance has
always lifted his spirit.

Until now.

The trouble now is that while he has always been strengthened by
the hope of those who come to him seeking the mystery of divine forbearance, lately, his spirits are weighted down with a morbid curiosity
about the confessions of his parishioners, as if it were all something being whispered to him as gossip. And Brother Fire is thinking seriously
about leaving the priesthood.

2.

Here are Holly Grey and Brother Fire at the local diner, having a late
cup of coffee together. They're old friends. They met through Fiona
many years ago, when Holly was still married to the father of her one
son. Holly and the priest worked together back in the early seventies,
organizing protests against Nixon. They appreciate each other, though

Holly doesn't attend church, has never practiced. She says her aunt Fiona attends enough church for both of them. Brother Fire counters that he worries about her immortal soul. Yet he also believes that Holly will probably go to heaven anyway, and he smiles. Like so many American clerics, he's far less rigid than his own church. It's true that he worries about everything in the nights—the nights lately have been long for him—and sometimes he thinks of friends like Holly, and tries to pray for them, friends who have never availed themselves of the strength of faith, never had that gift. His trouble now, of course, is that he's been having a little trouble in that vein himself. He has no real doubts about the tenets of his religion and practice, it's just that he hasn't been able at all to concentrate on the words of the prayers he says. This stems from the trouble he's having with confessions. There are sins his parishioners confess that interest him salaciously—weirdly—as if it has all come close to a form of entertainment. In the beginning, this was nothing more than a minor irritation, something he put aside in his usual manner, as one dismisses an importunate thought. But the fascination has begun to lead him away from concentration on the words of his office.

His reaction to the problem has been rather severe: he spends the hours after confession on his knees, in his room, saying his office and enduring the discomfort of the hard, wooden floor. He denies himself his evening meal and the glass of red wine, and he retires without drinking any water or juice, though the medicines he's taking for his heart give him dry mouth.

Then there's the problem of his curate, Father McFadden, a young man whose energies are difficult to respond to. Well, it's just that Brother Fire knows his reactions to Father McFadden's heartfelt enthusiasms are less than the younger man might hope for.

The new situation concerning confessions has shortened his patience and left some nerves jangled, a synapse broken, a line disconnected in his soul, like a phone left off the hook. The words go off, and his mind wanders. It's disconcerting and rather scary.

Now, he sips his espresso and drums his fingers on the table, trying to appreciate, for itself alone, in reference to nothing, the sunny day, the quality of the pleasant, half-shady light. He looks off at the street, at the

post office entrance on the other side, with its open patio where four ladies stand talking and smoking and laughing through the smoke. How
he would love a cigarette just now. He hasn't had one in about thirty
years.

Holly remarks that the coffee's proving to be too acid for her stomach. She has never been the type to worry about her health. She takes
a long drink of her water. "I don't know what to do," she says, talking
about Fiona. "This morning she threw a water glass at me. A tumbler.
Just hurled it, pitched it at me. It broke on the dining-room floor and
it's still lying there."

"I'll come clean it up," he says. He's serious. If it will solve anything, he's willing to try it. There's the dignity of working with one's
hands. This morning, in the rectory, he gave Mrs. Eddings the day off
and cleaned the whole house himself. At noon, he was down on all fours
in the kitchen, scrubbing the floor, wearing an apron belonging to the
lady—the one with the cartoon drawing of a cheery-eyed roasted pig
with an apple in its mouth—when Father McFadden came in from a
stint at the hospital. The curate was appalled and tried not to show it.
"Is there anything I can do, Father?" he asked in a quavering voice. It
was exactly as if he'd walked in on Brother Fire while the old priest was
performing some privy act.

"No," the Monsignor answered simply. "I'm almost done."

Now, he offers a slightly conspiratorial smile to Holly and says, "I *will*
come over and clean it up, you know. I wasn't speaking figuratively."

Holly says, "The woman should clean up her own mess."

"What caused her to throw it?" he asks in what he knows is a faintly
chiding tone.

"I don't remember. I really don't. Lately, she doesn't need a reason. I
never know how she's going to react to anything. Maybe she'll call you
in the middle of the night and tell you."

Fiona often does call him at night with one or more of her obsessions: he has tolerated it for Holly and because Fiona has always been
like a kind of moral barometer for him. Whatever else there is about
her, she's a woman who speaks the unvarnished truth. When, early in
his time in this parish, he first knew her, he thought she must be some
kind of savant about it all: he could never have believed anyone could

be so penetrating about what kinds of untruth were taking place around her. The trouble is that when she chooses to overindulge with wine, her discernment suffers, yet he has to listen to her in any case.

"I never knew our dear Fiona to be anything but direct," he says.

Holly shakes her head, giving forth a little smirking laugh. "By the way, she would kill me for telling you this, but she always thought you were a Socialist, and a terrible influence on me."

He leans back in his chair as if having heard something quite surprising. "Is that so?" But there's no real surprise in his tone. He's actually grinning slightly. He laces his fingers together in his lap, thinking about how Fiona might react to his leaving. Holly stares. "What?" she says.

"Pardon?" says the priest.

"What was that? Something crossed your mind. I saw it." Holly has a kind of radar of the emotions.

He says, "Actually, I'm thinking of leaving the priesthood."

She stares.

"Well, you know, retiring. Priests do retire sometimes."

"But this wouldn't be retiring, would it."

He looks at his hands, the veins there. "No, right. In fact, you've guessed it."

"Well, old friend," Holly says, "I won't say I'm not surprised."

"A function of my age," he tells her. "Perhaps it'll pass."

"I don't feel old, because I don't feel tired," Holly says.

Brother Fire ponders this for a moment. This morning, over breakfast, young Father McFadden wanted to discuss a recruiting idea for more altar boys. He was waiting for the thirteen present members to arrive, along with a camp bus, for a journey up to a monastery in the West Virginia mountains. Something he'd worked very hard to arrange— parents' permissions, insurance coverage, the rental of the bus, the tour of the monastery—and the old priest had felt remiss for not being of more help. "I thought I'd arrange more outings like today's if that meets with your approval," Father McFadden said, spooning oatmeal into his mouth. "When I was a boy, being an altar boy was a big prize. You got to go on field trips like today's, and there was a certain amount of status attached to it—you know, advancement."

Brother Fire reflected that his curate was still a boy. He smiled at him and said, "I think that might be fun. Anything I can do to help?"

Now, he glances over at Holly sipping her water, and feels the urge to unburden himself even more. He allows himself the statement of a truth he has, in fact, suspected for years: "I sometimes think I was meant to live alone."

"I'm sure Fiona was," says Holly. And so she has already left the subject of his possible exit from the priesthood.

"It's been strange, over this past year," he says. "Seeing her in her old place in the front pew. It's as if she never left. She seems to dote on my every word."

"Oh, she's always thought the world of you as her priest," Holly says. "Don't get me wrong. But she's also been convinced that politically, like me, you're only a couple of yards to the right of Trotsky." She chuckles at her own figure of speech.

They sit quietly for a while, a pleasant silence. The world goes on with its obsessions all around them. Across the way, the women are beginning to disperse. Two of them are starting off together. Holly takes another long swig of water, and then sets the glass down with a decided clunk. She's finished with it. "I think I can get some prominent people in the area to be involved," she tells him. "Especially if I have your help."

"What would you do?"

She stares, narrow-eyed.

"All right. What would *we* do?" he says.

"Letter-writing, maybe a little door-to-door. Maybe a little standing in doors. Maybe even a little sitting." She smiles. Twenty-nine years ago, they camped with a crowd of others for fifteen days in the downstairs lobby of the Bureau of Indian Affairs.

"I'm so old, dear. I have to say that the energy is flagging a little. I *am* tired, you see. And you know, to tell you the truth, just between you and me, Father McFadden is fairly exhausting to live with."

"So we're essentially contending with the same kind of problem."

He grins out of one side of his mouth, nodding slightly. It is such a pretty day, really. He wishes he felt better. He wishes he could tell her more about his present difficulty—part of the upset of it is simply that it could have such an unraveling effect on him, rob him of sleep as it has, depriving him of any kind of peace. But he knows it would worry her, and it isn't in his nature to trouble anyone. "Well," he says. "I'd better get back to the rectory. Young Father McFadden will be coming in from his field trip with the altar boys and he always needs bolstering after being with that particular group. Poor man. Black Irish, you know. Human foibles upset him." The priest is indeed dreading the afternoon with Father McFadden, who actually is afflicted not with melancholy, like the Black Irish, but with ebullience, a kind of wellspring of excited idealism that suffers whenever he's thrust among the rough and unidealistic—and perhaps there's no species on earth less idealistic than a fifteen-year-old boy.

Holly talks about Oliver Ward's visit, Fiona's behavior about the money. Brother Fire rubs his eyes, then sips the last of the espresso.

"I'm at the end of my rope," Holly says.

"I've been having trouble concentrating," he tells her, as if he's reporting a curiosity. He smiles, telling it. Some part of him would be relieved if she were to say that she's experiencing something similar. He goes on: "Lately, you know, my mind's a jumble of everything I've been told."

"Good Lord," says Holly, who understands his duties. "That must be some jumble. No wonder you're thinking of leaving."

They say nothing for another little space. A breeze kicks up a spiral of dust in the empty lot next door, where construction has begun on an IHOP.

"Do you ever look at something like this," Holly says, "and feel a sense of complete astonishment at human industry?"

"Well, no," the priest tells her.

"You want to talk about your trouble. And I'm making pompous observations."

"It's something I ought to be able to shoulder alone," he says. But he begins brooding about it, even as he shrugs it off to his friend.

The scary thing is how unexpectedly it arose, out of nothing he could name or discern. A man named Petit, who teaches math, and is an assistant principal at the local high school, was on the other side of the screen, confessing to having impure thoughts about one of his students.

Everybody loves Mr. Petit. Kindly. Softhearted. Resourceful Mr. Petit. Passionate about his work, a dedicated and devoted educator. He lives in an apartment not far from the church. A widower more than twelve years now, and childless.

I see myself reaching out and holding him. Just a hug. But I can't stop seeing it.

I'm not sure that qualifies as impure thoughts.

No, but I indulge in them. I go to sleep with them. Thinking about how it would be to have him with me.

Do you mean sexually?

No. Yes. No. Just to protect. Keep—keep warm.

Pray for strength, take a long walk each morning if you can, and say a Rosary each evening for the next nine weeks. I want you to call me if you experience any kind of crisis about this. The number's listed.

The nights are the worst, Father.

This does not surprise me.

I'm not a bad man, Father.

No. You wouldn't be here if you were.

When the priest pulled the little sliding door shut, he felt a surprising urge to remind the poor man not to forget to call, not from wanting to help but purely from the wish to know what might happen next. It stopped him. He had always felt, when he read or heard of others with this problem, that it was a matter of failed concentration, like losing the thread of meaning in a prayer. That evening of Petit's confession, he sat in the dark, both doors shut, hands in his lap, unable to turn away the sensation of hunger for the sordid details.

For some reason beyond knowing—age, or circumstance, or weariness, or undiagnosed illness—he has entered a zone of detachment. It frightens him. And, in the night, it haunts him.

Hearing confessions has become an ordeal.

Last night, he woke from some nightmare, the kind that wake you as they vanish, and he thought of poor Mr. Petit at the high school. The thought was now redolent of the scare of the dream, whatever it was, and he became rather distressingly agitated and sad-hearted—he could have said so many other things to the man—for instance, he could have said that affection, even when it is colored with longing, is only human, and not to be despised.

But then he stopped himself from the sin of being scrupulous, of expecting perfection, demanding more than God provides.

He labors to do that now, turning to his friend Holly and attempting to give her an untroubled smile.

"Well," she says. "I think I'll let you tell Fiona about these thoughts you're having about—um, retirement."

"Oh, please don't mention anything about this to her."

Holly gives him a look of friendly annoyance. "How long have we known each other?"

THE COMFORTS OF HOME

I.

Holly and her aunt Fiona Gerhin moved into the house on Temporary Road at the beginning of last winter, having spent the last several years in Scotland, where Holly had moved with her third husband, an elderly Scotsman named Michael Grey, the last name pronounced, by Mr. Grey, as *Gree*. He was the sort of man who insisted on that one thing, and about everything else was as tractable as a little boy looking for friends—a jolly man, large and round and generous, and he provided Holly with exactly the temper and passion she needed. He did, indeed, have a temper, and a highly developed sense of humor. Holly's letters home were full of reports of his tirades and escapades, which somehow managed to be both hilarious and disconcerting. She loved the edginess of it all, and the excitement. He was unpredictable, a gifted man in an argument, since his verbal resources seemed to increase in direct proportion to his displeasure. Injustice in all its forms—up to and including casual rudeness to waitresses and all the various populations of people in service, as he called them—sent him into towering rages, and he could be an adventure in a restaurant. Actually, Holly has always been like that, too. They were suited to each other. They both believed that there's a special place in hell reserved for the kind of person who sends a steak back to the kitchen if it is not cooked exactly to specification. (Of course, the fact that Fiona is one of those people is not lost on her niece, or anyone else. Only last week she got after the manager of a local steak house because her frijoles were, according to her, only a little past being resuscitatable, to use her expression.) After Michael Grey's demise of a stroke, at ninety-seven, Holly invited her aunt Fiona to join her in the big castle, as she called it (it was a stone cottage, actually, out in the country north of Edinburgh).

The two women had lived together for intermittent periods all their lives. They had grown up together, and they squabbled—still squabble—in the particular way of people who have grown up together. They stuck it out in the cottage for a winter and part of a spring, but Holly decided at last that she wanted to come back to her native Virginia. She wanted, she said, to live out her final years there. Fiona, not surprisingly, came with her. They sold the cottage for a load of money and came home, where they bought the place on Temporary Road. Holly liked the name of the street. She called it appropriate.

The house is small but expensive, as all American houses are expensive, but, for a time, things were fine: Holly had the money from the stone cottage and enough from her first marriage to live on interest. Years ago, she set up a trust fund for Will, whose income from that affords him the pleasure of running The Heart's Ease bookstore. Fiona has money of her own, too, but, in her own words, has always been along for the ride with Holly, having never married—having, Fiona would say, never found the right man. Something in her nature always refused to forgive the slightest variant from her ideal, which could be described as a somewhat rosy version of her father, a correct man in all ways, upright and high-minded, public-spirited—and sexless as a tree.

While it's clear that the two women wouldn't be able to function for five minutes without each other, it still happens that they'll disagree over how much garlic to put in a sauce, and with appalling rapidity this harmless difference will tumble into recriminations concerning offenses, imagined or real, that one or the other committed decades ago. This process happens with all the gathered force and inevitability of the pro-

verbial stone rolling down the hill. And since they have shared everything for most of their lives, really, even during Holly's marriages, they
do not quite know how to be separate. For a while they lived abroad,
and life in a foreign country does tend to strengthen the natural bonds
people have formed anyway over a lifetime: they were already like sisters. Fiona worked for a travel agency in Brussels, and then in Paris,
while Holly wrote travel articles for the *London Times*. When Holly married her first husband, Fiona moved with them to the U.S. Consulate
office in Bangkok; and when the marriage failed, she went along with
Holly to Egypt. The first husband, the foreign service official, whose
name was Nigel—Holly, telling this, would say, "No kidding"—wanted
no children, and in fact he was thirty-five years older than she, and
the marriage was doomed, Fiona said, from the start. In Egypt, Holly
worked as a foreign correspondent for the *Washington Star*. Fiona cooked
and kept house. Shortly after Holly began to see Tom Butterfield, Fiona
traveled alone back to the States and took up residence in a small apartment in Arlington, Virginia, with a view of the Lincoln Memorial across
the usually muddy swirl of the Potomac. As a child, Will spent time
there while his parents, who had returned one month and six days short
of his birth, worked on their fractious marriage. During the first nine
years of the boy's life, there was no chance of Fiona coming to live with
them, because Tom Butterfield couldn't abide her. The separation of the
two ladies lasted until Will's father rejoined the Navy, and set out for
Vietnam, though he never got there. He was killed in North Carolina,
in a freak accident involving an oxygen tank and a cigarette. He was on
guard duty in the oxygen storage barn, and there was a leak in one of
the tanks. He lighted a cigarette within five feet of a NO SMOKING sign
as tall as a horse.

Boom.

Holly remained single after that until Will was old enough to go
away to college, and so his adolescence was spent with the two women.

Indeed, the only other time the women were separated was the first
few months of Holly's marriage to Mr. Grey. At that time, Fiona was
in a brief relationship of her own, with a retired physician, who kept
exactly the distance she preferred. And when he stepped over the line,

as Fiona put it to Holly within Will Butterfield's hearing, that was the end of that. "Stepping over the line" for the unimaginative gentleman involved reaching over to put his hand on her breast while she showed him pictures of Holly and herself, schoolgirls at Sweet Briar. He had all the subtlety of a baboon, Holly said. Fiona is through with men, and, for that matter, so is Holly.

The two old women agree on this. But it seems that all other matters between them are in question. They grow more quarrelsome by the hour.

In Will and Elizabeth Butterfield's house, the level of comfort has dwindled through the weeks and days, in more or less direct proportion to the increasing requirements of the Crazies. Neither Holly nor Fiona is particularly adept at keeping a house or its grounds—indeed, with the notable exception of the cottage in Scotland, which stood in the middle of a tangled field of wild grasses and gorse, neither of them has lived anywhere but in apartments—and so, the little house on Temporary Road is looking run-down these days. Neither of the women can cook, and they're both rather forgetful. One day last summer, they took the car into town to have lunch. (It is usually their custom to take the bus on such occasions, so they can have a glass of wine if they wish to.) This time they took the Subaru, and they spent a fairly peaceful hour at the little café on Bower Street, across from Saint Augustine's, eating pasta and drinking tea. When they were finished, they took the bus home. They each had a pleasant little afternoon nap, then decided that it had been such a fine day that they would take a drive into the mountains to watch the sunset. They would have dinner in a small mountain restaurant they knew. Of course, there was no car in front of the house. For a few minutes, they were mystified, and then they were alarmed. Fiona had punched in the number of the police—the line on the other end was ringing—before, as Holly put it, they realized what they had done. This realization arrived to them both almost in the same instant, according to Holly. Fiona believes she realized it first (they have argued, also, about *that*).

2.

For Holly's son and daughter-in-law, the summer has been overbusy and too short. And now Labor Day is upon them. The new school year has already started. The nearness of the Crazies has opened a vein of instability and unrest in Will Butterfield, and in his wife, too. A shadow has come over everything. The sense not of an impending catastrophe, but of a catastrophe already accomplished.

The strangeness in this is that the catastrophe *has* already been accomplished.

Fourteen years ago, his first wife, also named Elizabeth, disappeared. That is, she decided to assume another identity and live someplace else.

What happened was this:

He had driven with her and the two children to New Haven to visit her parents, where they spent four apparently happy days, playing yard games in the summer sun, making good things to eat and drink, and telling stories late into the night. Gail was fourteen and Mark was eleven—two delightful, dark, early adolescents with brilliant, straight-toothed smiles and deep brown eyes. On the way home, they stopped at a fast-food restaurant on the interstate just south of New York. They ate cheeseburgers and French fries and they talked about what a good time it had been, and then Elizabeth quietly excused herself from the table, saying she had to use the bathroom. She had been laughing at something the boy, Mark, said, and touched the top of his head as she left the table. Butterfield would always remember watching her disappear into the crowded rows of doorways along the far wall, near where the restrooms were.

She never returned from the restroom, and when, after almost half an hour of waiting, he asked a waitress to go in and check on her, the waitress came out with a sad expression and said very gently that there was no one in there but there was a message. Will Butterfield walked in and saw the reflection of his own distressed, disbelieving face in the mirror through letters looping with a florid expressiveness in her bright-

red lipstick: I CAN'T DO IT ANYMORE GO ON WITHOUT ME LOVE ELIZA-
BETH. He went out and walked around the establishment, thinking it
must surely be some kind of bad joke, half expecting to find her buying
something in the convenience store or the service station. No one had
seen her. No one had witnessed her departure, and they all looked at
him, and at Mark and Gail, with a mixture of compassion and avoidance, a man with his children in tow, holding out a photograph—it was
actually an expired driver's license photo that he had liked and kept—of
the missing wife and mother. At another stop, farther south, a little soft-
faced balding man at the cash register of a convenience store said that he
saw her get into a beat-up Olds Cutlass with a man, and drive off after
buying some coffee to go. He was sure it was the same woman in the
photograph. She had come into the place as a passenger in a big semi.
He'd noticed it because he always thought it was illegal for truckers to
carry riders.

No one else knew anything, or had seen anything.

Butterfield and the children have never heard from her—or about
her—since, and, as far as they know, her poor parents haven't, either. At
least they hadn't as late as the summer of nineteen ninety-five, the last
time Butterfield spoke to them. So much has changed, and, of course,
the only reason for continuing to visit them, really, has been the children. But the first Elizabeth was an adopted child, and Gail and Mark
were old enough to grouse about the long drive from Virginia to Con-
necticut even before their mother left. As the months of her absence
wore on, Butterfield found it easy enough to let things lapse. The visits grew fewer and farther between. His first wife's sad adoptive parents
seemed resigned to their grandchildren's new lives, and to the fact that
Will never visited them anymore, though they retained an uncritical affection for him. The last time he talked with them, he expressed the
hope that they might all get together soon.

"That would be nice, Will," his former mother-in-law said. "Well,
you take care, now, and good-bye."

One afternoon several months later, he looked up from drowsing over
a book and realized that he hadn't called them or received a call from
them in all that time and that this good-bye had ended his last con-

versation with them. Feeling guilty, he tried to telephone and got no answer. He tried twice, then let it go. Things had settled this way, he decided. Gail and Mark were busy with their increasingly separate lives; they had their own concerns.

They are both coming to spend the holiday. They seldom miss one. Gail is twenty-eight now, and Mark is twenty-six. She lives in Philadelphia, where she went to school, and her brother has lived in Indianapolis for the past several years, having moved there for a job in public relations after college in Maryland. No one intends it, but the visits always cause tension. He has grown to feel a measure of irritability about family gatherings. When Gail and Mark are present, something seems to prey on their stepmother's sense of belonging. It's been ten years, and even so, when Mark and Gail visit, he often feels as if he must compensate for things that get said or don't get said in the passages of idle conversation, and in all those serviceable and apparently hospitable moments that seem—on the surface, at least—to contain anything but the seeds of discord and injured feelings.

He cut the roses for Elizabeth from an undomesticated bush that grew back in the woods, on state land. It's a watershed, and people with the county assured him when he bought the house that no one would ever build on it for that reason. The roses are lovely, full and round and fragrant, as if grown in a hothouse, and he has no idea how they got there, in this wild parcel of woods. It's a mystery, and he likes that about it. He discovered them during a walk, feeling this new turmoil, and, when he saw them, he knew exactly what he would do. This afternoon, he got a pair of scissors from the shed and walked back there to put together a bouquet—a dozen pink blooms, in a bunch, wrapped in paper from the school where she teaches.

The business with the handyman—caused, of course, by the Crazies—made the gesture seem diluted, or, worse, irrelevant. It went by in the need to be gracious and to make up for the difficulty the two women had obviously caused poor Oliver Ward by involving him in their squabbling.

And it cost Butterfield sixty dollars.

"Roses," he sings to Elizabeth now. "And roses and roses." He can't remember the rest of the song. He kisses her shoulder, standing behind her in the kitchen, where she's cutting the flowers and putting them in a clear vase.

"Do you want more credit than you deserve?" she says, turning to embrace him.

"Can't you call in sick tomorrow?" he asks.

She gives him a look expressing the futility of the suggestion. This is the first week of school.

Finished with the roses, she carries the vase into the living room, setting it first on the mantel, and then hesitating, one finger touching the corner of her pretty mouth.

He says, "They look great."

"No." She moves the vase to the end table opposite the front window. Then stands there, looking out. The house next door is for sale. The old man who lived there—someone with whom they never had a single conversation—moved into a nursing home five months ago, and while there have been several prospective buyers, it's been empty all that time. Looking out the window now, Elizabeth straightens and murmurs, "Somebody's looking at the house next door."

He stands at the window with her, and feels peculiarly disconcerted. There's something unpleasant about the contemplation of a change, not for desiring things to remain the same but for opposing reasons: he yearns for exactly that. Some change. It's confusing, and when he thinks about it at all, his anxiety becomes unreasonable. He steps away from the window and pretends to be concerned with the roses. She sits on the sofa and starts on her work from school. He enters the kitchen and opens the refrigerator, staring into it, aimlessly looking for something that might appeal to him. Nothing catches his eye. He returns to the entrance of the living room and watches her work for a time.

She looks up. "What?"

"Nothing. You look pretty sitting there in the light."

The telephone rings, and they pause.

She says. "Let the answering machine get it."

"They might kill each other." He picks up the receiver and hears a computer-generated voice, that voice of impersonal technology, say an important message is about to be played. He says, aloud, "Hello, Aunt Fiona." The voice goes on about a new, lower-interest bank card and announces that he, lucky lucky man, according to their records, is among the few who already qualify for it. He holds the phone as if he's listening to one of his great-aunt's rants, shaking his head. Elizabeth gives him a look of consternation tinged with exasperation. She mouths, "I told you so."

He says, "Fiona, please don't call here anymore. We've decided that we wish to break off relations with you and Mother entirely." He hangs the phone up.

His wife seems astonished for a second or two, but then frowns skeptically and shakes her head. "Who was it, really?"

"The Visa card of our dreams."

"I had a second's hope."

"You don't mean that."

She says nothing.

"Okay, you mean it."

"Oh, Will. They *are* driving me crazy."

"I think they may be getting that idea."

A moment later, she says, "It's Labor Day already and I don't feel like we had a summer. Gail and Mark are coming and I haven't done anything to prepare for them."

"Come on. They've been with you almost as long as they were with their mother. They don't need special treatment."

"They've *always* needed special treatment from me, Will. And you know it."

"I think you've built that up in your mind a little."

"That's not what I get from Gail," Elizabeth says. "Really."

Her own parents have been gone since she was twenty-three. Within a year of each other. "The king died," she told Will when they were first dating, "and then the queen died, of grief." This wasn't strictly true. Elizabeth's mother lost her life in a bus crash, twenty miles south of Atlanta, on Route 85. She was on a tour of Civil War battlefields. Elizabeth believes she would never have been on such a trip, would never have registered for such a trip, if her husband had been alive. Will would say that, for Elizabeth, the world is often a threatening place. His second wife sometimes has trouble holding on to any sort of cheerfulness. It requires effort, the expense of spirit. She's up to it, without quite feeling that this is so, and she's unaware of the resonance that this underlying darkness gives to her personality; it's a major aspect of her charm. It's as if the very timbre of her voice were slightly colored by it. People are captivated by her without quite realizing that it would not surprise them to learn that she'd been through something desperate or extreme.

All her depths are darker-shaded than her seeming brightness, and this has been true as long as he has known her.

She spent most of her childhood in a house whose central ethos was that of a kind of fortress or barricade against the outside, because her parents, though happy enough together, were rather bizarrely distrustful of everyone and everything else. Many summer evenings, Elizabeth sat out on the little porch purely for the air, purely in reaction to the suffocating atmosphere of the fastness behind her. Her parents loved her and each other, but their lives were mean and narrowly confined to suspicion, doubt, and misgiving about the simplest social dealings, and she felt this like a weight. Sitting on the stoop, looking at her street, she took to repeating the word *away—away, away,* like a prayer, wanting so badly to be able to go wherever *away* might be, as long as it wasn't the bastion of the house behind her.

So, of course, she left home at the first opportunity, eloping with an air force boy, who never got past being a boy and who thought she had been born to care for him in the way his mother had always cared for him—picking up after him, and tending to his every whim, and listening to his troubles, even, on occasion, rocking him to sleep at night. His name was Jimmy. That is, there was no proper name, no James. It was Jimmy on the birth certificate. Jimmy liked to call her Mommy, the way his father called his own mother. So, she answered to the name Mommy, for a time. Sex with him was hurried and loutish from the start, but after they were living together, he settled into a pattern of rehearsed actions and lines, all having to do with his sense of what domestic happiness must be—mirroring what he saw in his parents. He grew more and more steadily demanding, especially in the bedroom. Sex with him, which had been her first, began to feel creepily familiar as if she were breaking some ancient taboo merely allowing him to kiss her while murmuring "Mommy," over and over. Which, after the first weeks, was the only way he could become excited enough to make love. "Mommy," he would murmur. "Oh, Mommy, kiss me there."

She left him after six disastrous months and moved south, where she went to college, graduating in record time (only two and a half years, because she went in the summers, too—it was as though she were in flight, to get as far away from the marriage in mind and body as possible), and she became a high school teacher. She never spent more than a day or two in her parents' home after that first escape, at the age of seventeen. And they have been gone for a long time now.

When she met Will, she had, for several years, been seeing a man she was introduced to in college. It wasn't serious on her part, though everyone around her wondered why. He was handsome—pretty, actually—and accomplished, interesting, and wealthy, and about Elizabeth he was almost fanatical. But the bad marriage had made her wary, and perhaps this was part of the problem. Then, too, there was something about his very ardor that worked against him. His name was Andrew and he was always finding new ways to ask her to marry him. He started with the cliché of the diamond ring in a glass of champagne (she wept and told him she required time after the failed marriage to Jimmy), and, in following months, moved to other methods: a series of flower deliveries, singing telegrams, and finally stunts. He rented a billboard (ELIZABETH, PLEASE SAY YES), and then had a small plane fly over with a trail of smoke that said MARRY ME (the smoke got in the wind that came up, so very quickly the words thinned out to say MAR ME with tails of ragged smudges suspended from the letters). Andrew looked at her with a devoted, puppy-dog expression that made her feel weirdly uneasy, as if something in her makeup called up this kind of behavior in men. It reminded her too painfully of everything she had run away from.

When Will entered her life, he seemed refreshingly self-contained, and there was something sweetly relaxed about him—a man without urgency. She'd never seen anything like it—even her father, compared to Will, seemed afflicted with that peculiar hyperactivity of men, burdened somehow for competition, poised for some mental or psychological leap. Will simply went along in the hours of his day, amused, glad to be wherever he was, interested in things without wanting necessarily to possess them. She had accepted the first date with him out of a wish to separate finally from Andrew, and had discovered that she wanted more, wanted to see Will again. She spent the hours when she wasn't with him feeling an agreeable nostalgia for his presence. There was an evenness about him, a sense that he was only provisionally present, only looking around. It charmed her, because it appeared not quite to include her.

3.

"Do you really want me not to answer the phone?" he asks her now.

"I have a lot of work to do. I swear it's more every year. Stupid rote work, filling out names. It's ridiculous. Go ahead and answer it if you want. But leave me out of it." She leans over to the coffee table and brings back the stack of her work, sighing, shaking her head slightly. One of her tasks now is to decide which students get to be in an honors English group, and there are brief essays from the candidates. She reads the first one, puts it aside with a sharpness—the gesture she uses when the work is dead. With the second one, she seems faintly interested. "Oh," she says. "Listen to this: 'Shakespeare must have had a bad childhood because Macbeth shows how much I bet he hated his mother, and all women.'"

"Boy or girl?" he asks. Sometimes she reads him this sort of thing, and they laugh.

She looks back at the paper. "Boy. Seeking points with his feminist honors teacher."

"Are you a feminist?"

"Apparently."

"Let's go out and have a nice dinner somewhere."

"I've got all this to do, Will. I'm not hungry."

He's quiet. He had thought the roses would lighten her mood. She sits there working.

"I guess I'm not much fun," she says now, without looking up.

"It's okay." He takes up part of the newspaper on the table, and snaps it to straighten the page. He sees that she has turned to him with a start.

"Are you mad?" she says.

"No," he says. "Why?"

She returns to her work. He reads for a time, then gets up and goes into the bedroom. In the closet is a coffee tin with dope in it. He rolls himself a joint and brings it with him back to the living room.

"Want some?" he says, lighting it.

She only glances at him. But smiles and nods. "I thought of it an hour ago."

NIGHT HOURS

I.

The sun is going from the sky and the day is cooling and fall is coming. Oliver Ward drives along uncertainly in his truck, full of tequila and merriment. He's thinking about the coming season. It's almost joy that he feels now—what he has always considered to be joy: that combination of happiness mingled with the knowledge of its frailty with which he has always experienced gladness, any happy pass.

This particular gladness is laced with Mexican firewater, and he's aware of the ephemeral nature of it. For the moment, though, this is fine with him. He thinks a little sadly about the fact that he'll have to stop sitting on the porch, playing guitar in the evenings. Another winter, another slacking off of opportunities for his kind of work. But it'll be all right. He feels certain things will, as they always have, take care of themselves.

When the car with its flashing red and blue lights pulls quickly in behind him, he has a moment of alarm, but he pulls over and waits, smiling. It'll still be all right. Things are sweet. He knows most of the police, because of his daughter. The policeman is a young man, chiseled, clean as this morning's fresh shirt. He has a hat with a flat bill and a chin strap. His bearing is military. "License and registration, please," he says crisply, not making eye contact.

Oliver says, "One second." Then: "Is everything all right?"

"You were weaving. Sir, I'm gonna have to ask you to get out of the car."

Oliver does so, and stands there for the young man's inspection. "I did have one margarita with my dinner."

The young man looks like a high school kid, and Oliver doesn't recognize him. "Hello," he says.

"One minute, sir."

Presently, the officer says, "Can you take a few steps for me, sir?" Then, gazing at him with puzzlement, "Are you telling me you can't?"

Oliver explains patiently, as he has always done, about the tic in his neck. Then obligingly walks a few paces away. He concentrates and manages it, feels himself managing it and is proud, is even sure of himself now. He turns and waits. The officer seems to be waiting, too. The lights from the squad car circle in the long shadows of the street.

"Walk back, please," the young man says.

Oliver accommodates him. And he almost laughs when his stride falters a second. But he rights himself and comes on.

"I don't think you should drive, sir."

"I understand," he says quickly. Though now he's worrying about how his daughter will take this. "Is it a problem if I call my daughter and tell her I won't make it home? She works for the force, you know. Alison Ward Lawrence?"

"Alison?"

"That's her."

The young man shifts slightly. "Look. How far is home?"

"It's just down the street actually. A left turn about a mile up."

"Go straight there?"

"Yes, sir."

"I'll follow you to the turn," says the officer.

"Thank you."

They get back into their respective vehicles, and Oliver pulls out. He's extra careful, looking back down the empty prospect of the street, with the distant lights wavering in it. Perhaps he himself might've said no to this. Of course, with the tic in his neck that is his constant expression anyway: always no. The thought makes him smile again. Well, it's a pretty world, anyway, he thinks. Great Mother of Big Apples, yes. He can't remember where he heard that or read it, and then he can: Kenneth Patchen. Of course. Oliver used to carry the poet's book around with him when he was in the war. Kenneth Patchen. A little City Lights paperback, *Poems of Humor & Protest*. Oliver's favorite poet, Kenneth Patchen, mostly for the love poems, and he does know some things, he's not illiterate, and the one Shakespeare play he has seen pleased him very much. He's read plenty of books, back in the day, as they all say now. Men his age, so many, who have prospered where he has not but whose lives nevertheless seem strangely unsatisfactory to them. It isn't the tequila that makes Oliver smile now, though it helps. It does help. In a funny way, it reminds him of his own good fortune, while he rides along, naggingly also aware of the repeating negative gesture.

The police car follows closely. And now the lights come on again. Oliver realizes that he has drifted toward the curb. He parks the truck and gets out.

The ride to the police station is pleasant. They talk a little about Oliver's evening. He mentions the crazy ladies he visited, and the sixty dollars, thirty-six of which he still has in his pocket. He tells the young man that it was happy hour and he did have two or three margaritas—ice-cold and tasting so wonderful. Has the officer ever had a margarita? Yes. The two men agree, it's a marvelous drink, but not while one is driving. "No," Oliver tells him. "I know that. I don't know what I was thinking. I was just going to buy a bottle and take it home."

"People don't think," says the officer.

"I'm Oliver," he says. "My daughter's probably told you about me."

"No, sir. I've never actually spoken to her. But I know who she is."

"I'm so sorry to have caused any trouble."

"Is there someone you can have come and get you?"

"Well, my daughter works so hard."

"You'll have to come to the courthouse tomorrow to be arraigned, and there'll be a bond. Can she pay it?"

Oliver hears these words and comes crashing down out of the clouds of good feeling through which he has been sailing. He sits back and looks out the window at the passing desolation of the street—this part of Point Royal is particularly rundown and dilapidated—and with all his heart he wishes he were someone other than who he is. "Like I said, she works so hard," he says, "I don't want to bother her on her days off. I'll stay the night. If—I mean, we can't really afford the bond."

They ride along in silence. Oliver folds his hands in his lap and bows his head, then looks again out at the boarded-up shops, the mostly empty lots, and the occasional restaurant facades, with their blinking neon and cartoon shapes, and blazing words EAT. ABC ON & OFF. DANCING. COCKTAILS. All the appeals to night appetites. This fellow in the front seat has decided about him, no doubt. And, no doubt, he's near enough to being right.

At the station, they book him, and then an older man with a big belly and tufts of black hair in his ears walks him down to a cell. The drunk tank, though he doesn't call it that. There are two others in the room, already sleeping the sleep of the guilty—one of them, not much beyond being a teenager, smells of vomit and cleanser, a badness that makes the air almost too heavy to breathe. It stings the lungs. Oliver sits in the farthest corner, away from the others, whose agitated sleep seems on the point of breaking, yet doesn't. They sleep on. Oliver's awake. The tequila's wearing off. He won't sleep. He'll sit here and think about the course of his evening, the counterfeit cheer of the end of it, the comedown. Poor Alison. He has failed her yet again, and this is not the time, with her best friend and next-door neighbor getting set to leave for an extended time away. Alison has been worried about it for weeks, and, in the harsh, sobering minutes of the next hour, he comes to the fact, evident though unspoken, that she is mostly afraid of having no one now to turn to, no one on whom she can depend. His divorced girl, with her two children and her worries about money, and her deadbeat husband.

Deadbeat husband.

He murmurs the phrase aloud. Then murmurs another: "Deadbeat father, too." When Oliver is down, as he is presently down, he mutters out loud, becoming the voice of his own dispassionate judgment of himself: a complete malfunction in everything, a loss, one of the many troubles life has visited upon his lovely daughter. "Alison," he says, low, as if she's sitting right there with him. "I was so happy, I just didn't think."

But no. He won't allow himself this conceit. A child's excuse for bad behavior. If only he were different; if only he weren't always vaguely lonely and filled with a sense of something missing, something left undone, something frail and aching at his center, waiting for light, relief, balm.

He wipes his eyes, sitting against the plastic sculpted seat-back, looking at the sleeping shapes in the enclosure that isn't like a jail cell so much as a hospital waiting room without a television. There's a couple of other cots in the room, but he stays where he is. It's going to be a long, bad, cold, cold wait for morning.

2.

Brother Fire, this evening, sits in the den of the rectory, trying to read his newspaper. Father McFadden lounges on the sofa across from him, with a notebook open in his lap, pondering over something he has written. The old priest has recently learned that Father McFadden desires to become proficient at the reading and writing of poetry. He thinks of it in this way, as a form of learned dexterity. He has discovered that he can figure out the scansion of different poems and then try to reproduce the rhythms and rhymes of those poems. The trouble is, he has no ear at all and no gift for metaphor. The poems are excruciating, and at times unwittingly hilarious. Tonight, he reads two of them to Brother Fire. The first is called "Romancing the Cross." The old priest can't help tuning it out after the first two lines—"There were no smiles on Calvary that day/ No one could even begin thinking what they ought to say."

"What do you think?" Father McFadden asks, staring. "Something's not right. The rhythm, maybe. Something."

"Wasn't there a movie by the name of *Romancing the Something?*"

Father McFadden pauses, frowns, then lifts his chin slightly. "Oh," he says. "No. That would be *Romancing the Stone.*"

"I see."

"Did you hear the sprung rhythms in this, though—after Hopkins?"

There are lies of kindness. "Yes," says Brother Fire. He's suffering a little heartburn, which is lately rather frequent. He desires nothing more than to listen to the music that's playing—Mozart's clarinet quintet. But Father McFadden wants, in his enthusiasm, to talk. And to read his poems. Brother Fire thinks of it as a small penance. And then, very soon, it becomes a great penance. The other man reads his second poem; this one, he says, to John Donne. Brother Fire loses track of it, too, after the second line: "The battering of God outshined the sun/And battered your heart as you said he did, Donne." This is followed by six other rhymes of the name Donne. Gun. Run. Bun. Spun. Pun. Stun. And a slant rhyme using the word *wonton*.

It's almost more than can be borne, even for a penance. It goes on for some time, because Father McFadden likes to sound the dramatic notes he hears in the lines. Brother Fire tries to keep his face from showing his increasing discomfort.

Earlier, they had a meal of lamb chops and fresh kale with garlic and olive oil, and it's the garlic that's bothering the Monsignor.

"I've always liked good rhyming," Father McFadden says. "Do you think this sounds a little singsongy? Maybe I should put some other rhymes in."

"Well, I don't know."

"I think it sounded a little singsongy. Especially when I say 'The bright sinews of your heart could be tied up in a bun/And brushed like a girl's long locks so long and spun.' What do you think?"

"I don't know anything about poetry." Brother Fire inwardly asks pardon for the lie. He has the slightest urge to teach the other man, and then thinks better of it. Such a tack would upset Father McFadden's equilibrium. The old priest understands, without having to voice it to himself, that his curate rides happily on a very thin web of warm feeling: the slightest negative note can derail him. Black Irish. Father McFadden's greatest battle with himself involves his temper, which plagues him. At the religion classes one evening, Brother Fire was walking by the curate's class—a group of high school students, who were apparently talking and not paying attention. "I am *not*," Father McFadden said—and this was when Brother Fire came to the entrance of the room and

saw the curate with the pointer raised high, as if he might strike someone with it. But he said, very slowly, as if each word were a separate
paragraph, with a tremendous, scary tightness in the muscles along the
side of his face: "Going . . . . to. . . . .
lose. . . . . my. . . . . temper." And he
brought the pointer down slowly, incrementally with each word, until it
was pressed against the desk in front of him. The students stared, wide-
eyed, several of them in midspeech, frozen—some, it seemed, trying to
call back words already spoken, sounds that had left their lips and were
still traveling in the air. Managing that kind of temper, working with it,
keeping a calm, in the middle of the frustrations of a busy parish—well,
the old priest admires his curate's bravery in the struggle, knows what it
costs him to maintain his cheerful demeanor.

Now, though, he's about to excuse himself and risk agitating his curate's brittle threads of good feeling. He has a call he promised to make,
he tells the younger man. Another lie. But then he decides he does want
to talk to Holly Grey.

She answers on the first ring. And is very quick to dispense with the
amenities. "I was about to call you. I was *threatening* to call you. Let me
ask you something, Father. Drunkenness *is* a sin, is it not?"

"It's also a sin to judge another," the old man says gently.

"All right. But I have to deal with it when she does this."

"Why don't you put her on."

He hears a muffled discussion, a back and forth that sounds almost
like bantering. He thinks he hears a laugh. Perhaps they're both realizing, as Brother Fire would say it, how much they love each other.

"She won't come to the phone."

"It was pleasant seeing you today," the Monsignor says.

"I'm sorry to bring it up to you, like this. I really am."

Brother Fire hears the other woman shout something in the background. It sounds as though it comes from another room.

"Yes I *am* talking to him, and if you don't believe me you can come
over here and see for yourself."

A silence. Behind him, in the room, Father McFadden murmurs, "Is
everything all right?"

The Monsignor raises one hand to reassure him.

"Well, I'm truly sorry, Father. She's not coming to the phone. Is stubbornness a sin?"

"It depends on the circumstances," Brother Fire tells her. Turning from the telephone table, he observes Father McFadden rise and stretch, and start upstairs with his book. He's faintly shamed by the wave of relief that comes over him.

3.

Later, joking about having the munchies, the Butterfields decide to order a pizza. He gets up and makes the call.

"Thirty minutes," he says. Then he seems to staighten, standing there gazing at her. An idea has occurred to him in his happy state. "Let's make love," he says.

"You *are* stoned," she says.

"I'm fine. I'm still young. Only—*only*—forty-eight. And the pizza's on its way and I want to make love."

"You're cute."

"Come on. Let's run the risks of love together while the forces of pizza delivery are in motion." His own figure of speech makes him chuckle.

"I don't know if I can concentrate if I'm worrying about somebody knocking on the door."

"But that's why it's perfect. Somebody's rolling the dough right now, and it'll go in the oven soon, and it'll cook, and then be boxed and speeding toward us in the dark, and we'll be meanwhile, um, occupied, coupled and risking getting caught." He walks over to her, dropping his shirt. "For the roses."

"Were they a bribe?"

He shakes his head and attempts to keep the exasperation from his voice. "Oh, darling, I'm really not all that calculating. Surely by now you've figured that out about me."

She shrugs, and rises, and begins to unbutton her blouse.

The two of them move through the house to their bedroom. She leaves the light off and stands in the dim window, removing her blouse. Butterfield's laughing hard, struggling to get out of his pants.

"What if the delivery boy's one of my former students?" she says. "I didn't think of that."

"How long ago did I call them?" he asks, laughing. "You want some music? Wait. I'll hurry."

Some of her work papers are piled on the stereo in the living room. It's part of her nature to be in disarray when she's working. He removes the papers and opens the cabinet of the stereo.

She comes to the entrance of the hallway in her bra and panties, leans against the frame there, smiling at him. Completely, uncomplicatedly beautiful.

He rummages among the CDs, trying to decide what to play.

"Find something soft," she says, "so we can hear the door." Then she giggles. "I feel naughty."

"Baby," he says.

"This is fun. What can we call to have delivered tomorrow night?"

Things don't go well.

Aunt Fiona calls, drunk as a skunk. They hear her slurring on the answering machine about Holly having some sort of breakdown—that's the word she splutters into the tape. She uses the word *emergency* and, in fact, she sounds rather terrified. "Fiona," Elizabeth says, picking up the receiver, "what is it? What's happened?" She's straddling Butterfield, who is half-sitting, kissing her left breast.

Fiona shouts something he can't distinguish.

"Oh, for God's sake," Elizabeth says.

Butterfield makes a sign of exasperation that she has answered the phone, even under these circumstances. She shrugs at him, and listens. He can hear the voice, voluble and high-pitched, going on, but he can't quite distinguish words. He's inside his dear wife, the long, lovely column of her body atop his own, the soft, warm bed so comfortable beneath him. He lies back and observes her with the phone held to her ear and wonders at the incongruity of the picture. In the next instant, he discovers something wildly erotic about it, too, lying here in the middle of sex while someone rattles on the telephone. But it's his great-aunt on the phone. Jesus. Putting Fiona far from his mind, he follows the soft beauty of Elizabeth's abdomen to the place where her legs are spread, and he thinks about the whole principle of femininity—what a glorious creation, perfectly divine, the most beauteous gift, the greatest, primal, blessed reason for existence—and he reaches up to touch her breasts.

"You called who?" Elizabeth says, lifting herself from him, disengaging. There's the exquisite open lusciousness of her legs, and then they close and she has gotten around to a sitting position. Gazing at the faint suggestion of the bones of her long spine, he runs his hand up the very center of it, and she reaches back and takes his wrist. "Slow down, Aunt Fiona. Please. Can you speak a little slower? You called the police?"

She stands, looks back at Butterfield, and frowns, signaling for him to get up. Then she holds one hand over the speaker part of the phone and says, "Hurry and get dressed. Your mother's on the roof."

"Fiona's playing a joke."

Elizabeth waves this away. "Listen, Fiona—will you stop yelling and call them back? Tell them it's a false alarm. Tell them you made a mistake. But will you please do what I said? I'm going to hang up now."

Butterfield steps to the closet, opens the door and stands there, naked. For the moment, he can't decide where to begin. Elizabeth talks to Fiona, trying to calm her. He stirs at last, strides over to his bureau and puts on a clean pair of underwear.

"Blotto," Elizabeth says, putting the phone down, still naked, sitting on the side of the bed. "But your mother's on the roof. And she refuses to come down. Fiona says she's just sitting there. And she's called the police."

"I say let her sit."

Elizabeth's face registers incredulity. It's such a pretty face, and Butterfield finds himself merely standing there appreciating it. This annoys her. She gathers the blankets around herself. "Come on, Will. She might fall. The police are coming."

"She climbed up there, didn't she? She's done this kind of thing before."

"Climbed roofs?"

"Remember that first night they were here, and she got mad at Fiona and locked herself in the bathroom and wouldn't come out?"

"She went up on the roof that night?"

"She talked about getting away from Fiona in her mood. She locked herself away. It's the same thing isn't it?"

"Stop it, Will."

"Well, that's how they get. You know it. She isn't going anywhere. She's where everyone can see her. At least she won't disappear. She did that once, too. Three days. I thought it was the first Elizabeth all over again. Turns out she slept in her office and bought new clothes every lunch hour so she wouldn't have to come home. Fiona was frantic. *I* was frantic because I was alone with Fiona."

"I can't believe this," Elizabeth says. "So you're just going to stand there and not do anything? Your mother's up on the roof of the house, Will. And there are police on their way."

"I was so happy," he tells her, turning, abruptly feeling that he ought to cover himself.

On the way out of the house, they run into the pizza deliveryman. Elizabeth pushes past him, and starts along the sidewalk, calling back that she'll walk over there and for Butterfield to catch up. Butterfield fishes around in his pockets for the money. The deliveryman holds the pizza in its box and stares at him with an expression that gives forth all sorts of irritability and questioning. When the phone rings, the man actually shifts a little, as if startled. Something about the urgency of Elizabeth's exit has upset him. Butterfield offers him the money and says, "Keep it."

"The change?"

"The pizza. Keep the pizza," Butterfield says.

"You didn't order pizza?"

"No—yes. We don't want it."

"Well, I don't want it. Your phone's ringing."

"I paid for it," Butterfield says. "But you can keep it. I know about the phone."

"I can't keep the pizza, bud."

The phone rings with an insistence, that edge of crisis always created by an unanswered phone. Its jangling grates on his nerves. He hears the exasperation in his own voice. "But we don't want it. We can't eat it now."

"You couldn't put it in the refrigerator or something?"

"I don't want the fucking pizza," Butterfield says. "Take the money."

The man takes the money, then sets the pizza down on the porch step and walks off.

Butterfield calls after him. "Hey."

Nothing.

He lifts the pizza in its box, carries it into the kitchen, and puts it on the counter. The phone is still clamoring. He picks up the receiver. "What?" It's Fiona.

"Thas' how you answer your phone?"

"I knew who it was, Fiona. I had no trouble guessing who it would be."

"Your mother's gone off th'deep end."

Something stirs in his stomach. "She fell off the roof?"

"She's sitt'n up there an' says she's gonna stay all night. Watch th'stars, she says. Purity of the universe. Crazy."

"Fiona, we're coming right over. Don't call here again. No one will be here."

"I called th' p'lice," she says. "Tell Elizabeth. The p'lice are coming."

"You were supposed to call them and tell them *not* to come. Remember?"

"Coming. Hear the sirens now."

"Jesus. Elizabeth's on her way over there."

"Woman's crazy, s'what she is. You should see'er. Sitt'n up there like it's not crazy to be sitt'n on a roof in your pajamas."

"Fiona, she's in her pajamas?"

"Sitt'n there to spite me. Drawing attention to herself. I wouldn't clean up th'glass and I call th'radio to put in my two cents, so she went and got th'step ladder and climbed up on th'roof and pulled the goddamn ladder up after her an' I called th' police. So she can deal with that. They'll be here any minute."

"How much have you had to drink?" Butterfield asks her.

"She says she wants t'look at th'stars. Imagine'at." The line clicks shut.

"Fiona?"

Nothing. He stands there with a profound urge to walk out the door and head in the opposite direction, anywhere. It actually occurs to him to let Elizabeth handle it—or, more accurately, he feels that his abandonment of the two old women in this particular episode would be mitigated by the fact that Elizabeth is already dealing with it. He's aware of this as a form of cowardice, and so he rejects it, and even so he can't bring himself to start.

The aroma of the baked cheese and tomato rises to his nostrils. Exquisitely appetizing, even in this distress. After all, he hasn't eaten since two o'clock in the afternoon. Opening the box, he takes out a slice and begins gingerly to eat it. A small bite. A little something to tide him over. He'll carry a slice in a folded napkin to Elizabeth. It's a God-given right to eat when hungry if there's food. It's a sin to let food go to waste. The pizza, something about which he has been little more than indifferent since he was fifteen years old, tastes better than he can ever remember. It's as if he's lost all the years between his first experience of it and now. The whole of his palate is trembling with the enjoyment of it, that wonderful layer of melted cheese, moist with tomato and oil, and the crisp little round lozenges of pepperoni. It fills his whole mouth. Somewhere out in the night, he hears sirens, and he starts out, but then comes back, agitated now, wrapping a piece for Elizabeth, and then deciding to eat it himself. He wolfs it down, breathing back through his mouth to cool it, standing guiltily in the entrance to the living room. His mother is sitting on the roof of the house on Temporary Road, and he has the nearly petulant sense that this crisis can wait the one minute it will take him to wolf down another small slice of pizza. Reaching hurriedly into the refrigerator, he brings out a can of beer and opens that, gulping down most of it. Beer has never tasted so good, either. He washes down the rest of the second slice.

Holly and Fiona's house is only a five-minute walk away. The two old women have worked the little flower garden in the front all summer, though the lawn is in disrepair, the grass overgrown and patchy. The only time the two women seem in concord—and it always seems to be perfect concord—is working that little oasis of order in the tangle of the yard, while music plays on the small transistor radio they keep on the little porch. They talk about happy things—being girls together down at Sweet Briar College; living in Brussels, Paris, and Cairo. You would never dream from seeing them in this pastoral harmony that in an hour or two they might be at each other's throats over the Middle East, or the impeachment, or even something as inconsequential as whether to use dry or fresh-cut parsley, or whether the air conditioning is at the right setting.

Butterfield makes his way over there at a slow trot, still hearing sirens. Like most people who don't use their time well, he has misjudged how much has elapsed since the pizza man walked away from the door. As he approaches along the street, he sees people standing out on their lawns, and Elizabeth just below where his mother sits with elbows clasping raised knees, at the edge of the roof. Everybody's watching the show. There's been enough time for all these people to gather. He makes his way to Elizabeth, saying her name softly. Elizabeth only glances at him.

"Holly please listen," she says.

"Mother," Butterfield says. "What're you doing?"

No answer. The old woman stares at him, squinting slightly.

Elizabeth turns and takes his sleeve. "What took you so long? It's been almost twenty minutes."

"No it hasn't." He remembers that he had planned to bring her a slice of the pizza. "Has it?" he says. "Fiona called. I had to deal with Fiona."

She steps back from him. "Hey. Is that—did you—?"

"I wolfed a little of the pizza, yes. I was going to bring you a slice. It's an inalienable right to eat when hungry, Elizabeth."

"I smell inalienable beer, too."

"Had to wash it down with something." He looks around for the emergency vehicles, the sirens of which are nearing. He looks up at his mother. "This is ridiculous. Mother, come down from there. You're upsetting the whole neighborhood."

"For God's sake," Elizabeth says, hands on hips. "For God's—sweet Jesus Christ's—sake."

"I had to deal with the pizza man," he says to her, low. "You left me there."

"What did you—have a beer together? Watch part of a ball game? This is your mother, Will, not mine."

He says nothing to this.

"If you two are finished with your marital spat," Holly says from the roof, "I'm still up here. I'm still sitting high up on the roof."

He looks up at her again. "Oh, and it's important to you, is it, that we have to contend with that. Is that right, Mom? And what age would that be most like, speaking purely on an emotional level? What grade in the elementary school is that?"

She looks off at the night sky. "I think I'll stay here all night."

"Happy now?" Butterfield says to her. "You have our full attention. You've got a crowd gathering. Happy? We'll all be in the funny papers."

"Go home," Holly mutters. "Leave me in peace." She gestures to the people on the lawn across the street. "All of you. There's nothing to see here. An old lady in pajamas looking at the sky. Fuck off."

"Holly," says Elizabeth. "This is a neighborhood. Please."

"Tell us what Fiona did," Butterfield says.

"We've already been through that," Elizabeth tells him.

But Holly speaks: "I have no idea what you're talking about. I wanted to look at the moon."

Fiona calls to them in a slurred stage whisper from the front door. "I've got th' cops com'n. They'll be here moment-ari-ly."

"You think I'm deaf?" Holly yells from the roof. "You unreconstructed, cruel-hearted . . ." She doesn't finish, but scowls and makes a sputtering sound of dismissal.

"The p'lice," Fiona says, holding on to the door frame.

"They'll arrest you for public drunk," Holly says. "I'm going to watch them do it."

"I'm inside my house."

"It's *my* house."

"I'm inside *this* house."

"Both of you," Butterfield interjects. "Cut this out, now. You know you love each other."

"I don't hate anyone," Holly says. Then: "I hate Kenneth Starr, I

guess. I'm not too fond of Henry Hyde or Newt Gingrich. And the television news people. I hated Nixon. Everyone down there, listen to me,
I don't think Nixon redeemed himself at all. I think he was a bastard to
the end."

"Holly," says Elizabeth, "please. Please come down."

The next-door neighbor now walks over, carrying a stick. He looks
like a vigilante, eyes wild with conclusions, mind made up; he's had suspicions about these women, and his suspicions have been borne out. It's
in the way he looks at Holly, approaching, holding the stick like a club.
"Someone stop her using that language," he says. "I've got little kids."

"Yes," Holly says from the roof, "and you cuss at them, I've heard
you."

Someone else, another man, comes from the other side. He's in a
bathrobe. Elderly-looking, back slightly bent. "This has gone too far,"
he says. "This is pathology."

"Top-flight detective work," Holly says from the roof. She looks bad.
The wind has picked up, and her hair is a tangled, wiry fright wig now.
Her bony knees are too white in the moonlight, as if the skin has been
peeled away from them. "Go away," she says, putting her head down on
her knees. "Stop cluttering the yard. Stop killing my crabgrass."

"Mom," says Butterfield. "I swear I'll lose it. Right here."

"Should I call the police?" the second neighbor asks.

"Mind your own business," says Holly. "You never voted anything
but Republican in your life. You're a dupe of the corporations."

"Excuse me?" he says. "Excuse me?"

"You heard me. I see you watching everything and everybody out
your window. How many alarms you got on that dump anyway? I bet
you spend all night listening to a police scanner."

The man stalks off, muttering about language and vowing to call the
authorities.

"Will," Butterfield's wife says. "She's going to get arrested."

He addresses his mother: "Holly, you know if the police come—you
know what a mess that'll be. Those sirens are for you. Now come on
down from there."

She mutters back, staring off: "They are not for me. There was an accident over on the highway. Fiona and I heard it on the scanner. I've got

a right to sit on my own roof if I want to and no one can stop me." Now she looks at him. "I'm not threatening to jump, you know. I'm looking at the sky. I've developed a sudden interest in Orion, and all the other constellations—okay?"

"She'll jump. Jus' t'spite me. You jus' watch."

"What did she say?"

"She's crazy, too," Butterfield says, his exasperation turning to anger.

Elizabeth takes him by the arm. "Don't, Will. Jesus." Then she addresses Holly again. "Fiona did call the police, you know. This is not going to end well if you keep it up."

In the next instant, a police car does pull up, no siren, lights flashing. A man and a woman get out. The woman walks over to them first. The man leans back into the car and mutters something into the radio. The woman's solid and evenly built, neither slender nor fat, with square shoulders and a beautiful Italianate face. She introduces herself as Sergeant Alison Ward Lawrence. Gazing up at Holly, she says, "You can call me Alison." Butterfield sees her dark eyes. She steps closer and says "Hello, there" to Holly, as if there is nothing uncommon about finding a woman sitting on a roof. "Would you like to come down and talk for a spell?"

Holly says, "Hi. I'm Holly. Pleasure to meet you. Would you like to come up? I mean, I'm not breaking any law, you know. And it's pretty up here. A lot more peaceful than down there, no kidding."

Alison murmurs to Butterfield: "What're we dealing with here?"

For a second, he's unable to speak. There's something so inconsistent about the way her face makes him feel. Its very softness seems to call up an urge to protect; yet she's staring at him, demanding an answer by her matter-of-fact silence. He's abruptly heartsick along with his anger, and the anger goes toward all the authorities, the furor over this dispute between two old women. He can't express this feeling to such a friendly, attractive face.

"That's his mother," Elizabeth says to Alison, almost crying.

"Did you make the call?"

"I made th'call," says Fiona joyfully from the door. "I called you. Woman's crazy. She'll do something terr'ble, you'll see. And s'not high enough. She'll break her legs and I'll have t'take care of her. Fetch'n and carryin, listenin to her complain . . ." Fiona continues talking, but her voice trails off, so the words are lost.

The policewoman peers at her. "I think I get the picture here." She gazes up at Holly. "You need help coming down? You have to come down, you know."

"Not till I want to. You need help coming up? The stars are perfect from here."

She turns to Butterfield. "How did she get up there?"

"You can ask me that, Alison," Holly says. "I'm not deaf, you know. And *I'm* sober, too."

"All right." Alison waits.

"I was levitated by a desire for higher things. And my housemate is batshit."

Butterfield almost laughs at the use of the one word he's used most often in thinking about both women. *Batshit.* He can smell the beer on his own breath, holding one hand over his mouth and turning away from his wife, who again starts pleading with her mother-in-law. But Holly continues talking to Alison.

"Now and then," she says with a grandiose gesture of taking in the surrounding beauty, "I seek the ethereal company of the air. And if that's against the law, arrest me. But you'll have to climb up here to do it. I've been arrested before. It's nothing new."

"Look," Alison says. "It may not be against the law to sit on your own roof, but you've created a disturbance. And that is against the law."

Holly says, "You're the ones raising all the disturbance. I'm sitting here peaceably watching the fucking universe."

Alison turns to her partner, who has walked around the house and come back. He's very big and lumbering, with a round face and eyes that seem too close together. He says, "There's a ladder pulled up onto the roof in back. That's how she accessed the roof."

"Hey," Holly calls to him. "Accessed? Jesus. Accessed? Am I the individual that accessed the roof? Where's your thesaurus?"

The partner says, "Ma'am, my name is Roy."

"Hello, Roy," says Holly. "Come on up."

"I'd need your help."

"Aw, a big strong man like you?"

Alison takes Butterfield and his wife aside. "How old is she?"

"Seventy-five," Butterfield says. "She's never done anything like this." Elizabeth gives him a look. "Well, she hasn't. Not like this."

"Tell us about her."

"I'm a retired union organizer," Holly says from the roof. "Do you know Brother Fire, the monsignor at Saint Augustine's?"

"Yes," Alison says. "As a matter of fact I do."

"I got arrested with him in nineteen-seventy. On the Key Bridge in Washington, DC. You can look it up. We were protesting the war in Vietnam."

"I won't need to look it up," Alison says. "Thank you anyway."

She pulls Butterfield and Elizabeth farther away, toward the street, while her partner moves closer to the house, talking softly at Holly, who evidently isn't listening. She stares at the sky and loudly hums something that sounds like a hymn. Below her, still clinging to the frame of the open front door, Fiona simply watches.

"Okay," says Alison. "Talk to me."

"She's not senile, if that's what you mean," Butterfield tells her.

"Does she have some other form of mental trouble?"

He looks at his wife, who shrugs. Alison waits for one of them to answer.

"She's always been—well, a little eccentric," Elizabeth gets out. "I mean, as long as I've known her."

"And how long is that?"

She shakes her head. "Since we were married." She indicates Butterfield. "Ten years—ten and a half years."

"Since forever," Butterfield says. "She's my mother for God's sake."

"Is she armed? Are there any firearms or other weapons on the premises?"

"Of course she's not armed."

"I have to ask the question, you know. And you'd ask it too if you were me."

"Well, she's not armed."

"Then the question is, do we compel her to get down? Do we go up there and get her, or leave her there?" Alison surveys the street. The people who have come out of their homes are standing along the curb on the other side, an audience. Evidently, Holly understands this in the same instant that Alison notes it. She comes to her feet, slowly, creak-ingly, and raises her arms to the sky.

"Now, Holly," the policewoman calls, running toward the house.

Butterfield and his wife follow.

"As I have already indicated, I wish for everyone to leave me alone in my heavenly pursuit of a little peace," Holly says calmly. "Fuck off, please, all of you." She brings her arms down and folds them, looking right at Butterfield. "What is it, Will, fifteen feet? How bad could a person hurt herself. I just want a little quiet under the stars, Son."

They're all silent for a moment. The only sound is the sputter of voices on the police radio. Another police car pulls up, and two more policemen get out. Butterfield watches his mother settle herself again, putting her knees up and clasping them, gazing at everything with a stubborn, chin-high haughtiness. He can't help admiring her, even in this blaze of exasperation and helpless rage. Lights are going on every-where now, more people gathering.

"If I sent someone to get Brother Fire, will you come down for him?"

"I'd stay here for certain. He's an old man. Don't you dare disturb his peace."

"What if I tell you that we'll go get him if you *don't* come down," Alison says.

"I'd like to think that we're above that sort of vulgar threatful nego-tiation," says Holly.

Alison begins beseeching her to please make it easier on herself and come down. There isn't going to be any peace tonight. That's clear. If she'll come down, they might reach an agreement whereby she can get back up there if all she wants to do is look at the sky. But the town's involved now, and a lot of money's being spent and employees occupied by this situation, and it's the responsible thing to come down and put an end to all that.

During this, Elizabeth begs her in a low, half-crying murmur: "Please, Holly. Can't you see what you're doing? Please. This isn't you."

"Talk to my drunken aunt," Holly says. "She's the one that called you."

Aunt Fiona is lying on the small hammock on the front porch, snoring softly, completely gone. For a brief moment, everyone seems to contemplate this fact. It's as if this turn of events is so bizarre that they are all struck dumb, like people staring at a sudden manifestation of phenomena from outer space. No one saw her lie down, and no one can say when in the course of this trouble she did so. It is a moment of complete, dumbfounded concentration.

"She's asleep," Elizabeth says in an astounded tone.

"In that case," says Holly, "I'll come down."

This is also amazing to everyone. They watch silently as she stands, turns, again slowly, with effort, and makes her way up to the peak of the roof and down the other side. Everyone moves around there.

They reach the backyard in time to see the ladder come down. Holly manages it all quite well, stepping down into Roy's arms and then turning to glare at him. "I don't need your help, young man."

She huffs away from them and onto the screened back porch. The whole crowd follows her: Butterfield, Elizabeth, all of the police. They go up into the dark of the back porch, and she turns a light on and faces them from the open door, holding the screen open. "Anybody want something to drink or eat?" she says.

With the police who remain behind—Alison and Roy—Holly's very well-spoken and direct: The problem is Fiona. She tells them that she climbed up on the roof for a little tranquility, and that Fiona overreacted because she was drunk. It was Fiona who called them. Fiona threw a water glass at her first thing this morning. "And look," she tells them, pointing an accusatory finger at the place on the dining-room floor, "there it is. I was damned if I was going to clean it up and it'll be there next week if I don't. That's what it's been like. I tried to get her to clean it up, and she had too much to drink and ended up calling the police."

"Then she called us," Butterfield says. "She always calls us. No matter what we're doing and no matter what time of the night it is or what plans we might have, you, both of you, always call us."

"There," Holly says to the officers. "You see how it is? Hysterical overreactions all around. The fact is, I called Brother Fire first."

"I think I still have to cite you for disturbing the peace," says Alison.

"Go ahead," Holly tells her. "Cite me. I'm quite used to it. I used to be a union organizer. I protested the war. I fought the battle of civil rights."

Alison shakes her head with something like grudging admiration and begins writing out the citation. While she does so, Holly engages the other officer in conversation.

"You got a family, Roy?"

"Yes, ma'am."

"How many kids?"

"Two—boy and girl. Twins."

"Identical?"

"Well, no. Identical are always the same sex."

"That's right. Sorry."

Butterfield tries to get his wife's attention. But Elizabeth's concentrating on the piece of paper and Alison's smooth, wide-fingered hand writing out the ticket.

"Do I go to jail?" Holly says evenly, not even quite curious. "As I told you, I've done that, too."

Alison tears the ticket out of the book. "No. I don't think that's necessary, but there's a court date. You can waive trial and pay the fine." She sets the ticket down and stands.

"Thank you," Butterfield says. "I'm sorry for all this." He holds the door for them. When they've gone, he closes the door and turns.

"Somebody help me with Fiona," Holly says.

They all go out onto the front porch and stand over the shape of Fiona in the hammock. One thin arm is dangling over the side. Holly says, "Wait a minute," and goes with alacrity back into the house, as though she has just realized that she left the coffee on. Butterfield and Elizabeth stand apart in the small snoring sound the sleeping woman makes.

"She's regressing," he murmurs to Elizabeth. "I swear."

Holly comes back, moving now, incongruously, with stealth, carrying a saucepan full of water. She puts it under Fiona's drooping hand and brings it up slowly, so that the other woman's fingers go in.

"Holly, what the hell—?" Elizabeth says.

"I heard it'll make you wet your pants," says Holly. "Leave her here."

"We can't do that. It's supposed to get down in the fifties tonight."

"Good. She'll be wet and cold."

"Mom, stop this," says Butterfield. "Christ. Stop this right now." He stoops and reaches under Fiona, lifting. She's much heavier than she looks. He almost drops her, staggering with her in the doorway, hitting her ankle against the frame. She wakes, looks up at him, and gives forth a high-pitched, whispering cry of terror.

"Take it easy, Fiona. It's just me."

"Will. She wants me dead."

"Nobody wants any such thing," he tells her. He carries her into the house and eases her down on the sofa.

"Where is she?"

"Stop it, Fiona," Elizabeth says. "You're drunk."

"Everyone's against me."

"Settle down and try to get some sleep," says Butterfield, seeking to keep a reassuring tone.

Apparently, she hears condescension. "Don't talk to me like I'm crazy. I'm not crazy. I'm a victim."

"Shut up," says Holly, having come in from the bathroom. "Shut up and go to sleep or I swear to God something will happen."

"Nothing's going to happen," Butterfield says. "Come on, guys."

"You smell like a brewery," Fiona says. "And you talk about me."

"Okay," says Butterfield. "I've had it. I'm heading back to the house. I don't want to spend another minute in this chaos."

He moves to the door.

"Will," Elizabeth says.

"No, I'm gone."

"Go ahead," Fiona says. "That's just like a man. The slightest sign of trouble."

He's out and on the sidewalk and then crossing the lawn, and Fiona screams from the yellow windows of the house.

"Slightest sign of trouble!"

He's going along the sidewalk, muttering to himself about his great-aunt, and when the sidewalk gives way to grass and weeds, he steps down into the street. The trees along the road whisper in the summer breeze, and he stops a moment, shakes her out of his thoughts. He stands here and reflects that it is indeed the kind of night one might want to watch the stars. He goes on, listening to the leaf-murmuring on either side of the street, and finally he comes to the empty next-door house. Lying down on the lawn, he remembers having done so with Elizabeth on just such a summer night, full of pasta and wine, happily anticipating the rest of a weekend. He looks up, recalls enjoying the summer stars—the clarity of the light and sparkle, all those immeasurable spaces, and the breeze moving across his face like a soft cloth wielded by a loving hand. When was that? Earlier this summer? For a moment, he can't place it. And then the urge to call it back is swallowed by the sound of Elizabeth coming along. Perplexed, irritable, unhappy. He keeps silent, feeling dimly guilty, as if he has spied on her. And so he has—unless, just as she is opening the door to go inside, he speaks, says her name, shows her where he is, lying here in the dark of the neighboring yard, in the long moonshade of a sycamore. But he doesn't do so. Instead, he whistles. A wolf's whistle, and he feels momentarily like a character in a movie. She whirls around, startled.

"It's just me," he says.

"What're you doing there?"

"Waiting for you."

He rises and crosses the space of grass to the door. She has already gone inside. She's in the kitchen, standing at the counter with a slice of the pizza, chewing. She doesn't look at him. And then she does. He's surprised to see sympathy in her eyes. "They're my family," he says. "I shouldn't've left you there."

She shrugs.

"We're gonna have to do something," he says. "They're both completely bonkers and we can't keep going on like this with them."

"That's a helpful way of putting it, Will." She stares at the room, not really seeing anything, crying quietly, one tear making its way down her left cheek.

He touches her shoulder, realizing the seriousness of the situation, completely unready for it and appalled at his own denseness: how could he have missed seeing what a sorrow this has been for her, too? At the precise moment he has this thought, the beer he had drunk causes him to belch.

"Excuse me," he tells her, and she gives him a look. "Baby," he says, "I should've—" But he can't finish the thought.

She takes another bite of the cold pizza and shakes her head. There's something else on her mind.

"Baby," he says. "What is it?"

She shifts slightly, but says nothing.

"Elizabeth?"

She only glances at him, closing the pizza box and then seeking a place for it in the refrigerator. "I don't know what we can do. There isn't really anything." Then she seems suddenly to be searching for some answer to the question she hasn't even asked yet. "Is there?"

COST OF LIVING

I.

In the predawn, having turned down anything to eat, Oliver Ward is put in leg chains with five other men (he must have slept, because he has no memory of the three new prisoners), and they all ride in a van over to the courthouse, to be arraigned. It's going to be sunny and cool, with little fresh breezes out of the north. Two of the men are together, arrested only an hour ago for sleeping in the street and public drunkenness. The police know one of them, and call him by name: Mickey. Mickey introduces his companion, Stanley. The police call Oliver Mr. Ward, because they know Alison; they assume, too, that Alison is aware of Oliver's fate for the night. Mickey and Stanley are in their late twenties. They joke about sleeping on a sidewalk—Stanley says he went into a phone booth to call his cousin and fell asleep there. "I remember trying to make a date with an operator in, I think, Peoria, Illinois, no kidding—said she was based in Peoria. Figure that. And I ended up going to sleep. I wasn't exactly in the street or on the sidewalk. It could've rained and I'd've kept dry." He turns to Oliver and says, "Remember me? About fifteen summers ago?" Oliver does remember him. Oliver's suffering a terrible headache and dry mouth, and desires nothing more just now than to be on his way home, but he does remember Stanley, and now he has a bad sense of belonging in this company, though, intellectually, he's certain that he doesn't know Stanley from this sort of thing, since he's never been arrested before. Over the years of doing contract work, he has occasionally hired part-time help, and, often enough, the help has turned out to be undependable, erratic, irresponsible. Like this boy, who stands chained to him now with the others: Stanley. Young Stanley, not long out of high school then, hired fifteen—yes, fifteen—summers ago. His hair is cut off now, and he doesn't even look like the boy Oliver knew. Stanley's gotten heavier around the face. He looks rugged, roughed up, in a way.

"Has it been that long?" Oliver asks him, merely to be polite.

"I liked working for you," Stanley says, smiling. "What'd you do to get in trouble?"

"I got pulled over last night. DUI."

"I fell asleep trying to call somebody to come get me," Stanley says. "I don't even drink. I had two glasses of beer at a bachelor party for a buddy of mine and I was scared to try driving home. I hadn't slept in two days because I already did drive here from Knoxville—didn't want to miss the wedding."

The other one, Mickey, says almost proudly: "I lost my driver's license for repeated DUI."

They are led out of the building and asked to get into another van. Their chains rattle; it's absurd. Oliver glares at the police, as if to say he'll tell on them. The cuff of the chains abrades the skin of his ankles. "This is just a little ridiculous," he says to Stanley. "Chains? They know us."

"It gets your attention," says Stanley.

"State law," one of the officers says. "Sorry, Mr. Ward."

The ride to the courthouse is quiet. Light is coming to the sky. Alison will wake and find that her father hasn't been home; the children will worry. This is the day her best friend and neighbor, Marge, leaves for Montana to have her baby at home. Oliver won't be there for Alison.

He won't be there to say good-bye to Marge. He has an appointment at seven a.m. with a couple named Gilman—at their insistence—about painting their house and adding a sunroom. He'll be late for that, too, if he doesn't miss it altogether. Everything is fucked up. No, he, Oliver Ward, is fucked up. Has fucked up. As usual, he thinks, clasping his hands tight in his lap.

The arraignment amounts to the assignment of a court date. Stanley and Mickey go first. It turns out that Mickey is in violation of parole, and will have to go back to jail. Stanley is let go, and then it's Oliver's turn. It's all cut-and-dried: court date, the signing of the release form. A woman in a gray pantsuit hands him his truck keys. The truck has been impounded, is parked in the police garage. Oliver's chains come off; he's released. The morning is brightening. It turns out that Stanley has waited for him outside. In the new sun, his skin looks smooth and healthy. "Can you give me a lift?"

"Where to?"

The young man falls into step with him, assuming that his question is agreement.

"I'm in a hurry," Oliver says. "I've got to get home."

"I think I'm on your way."

They go through getting Oliver's truck out of the police garage, and soon they're riding along in the first light, with nothing whatever to say to each other. Oliver decides that anything is better than the silence, and he is a little curious, so he asks Stanley what he's been doing with himself. The young man says he just left a job with a contractor in Knoxville and is looking for work. He's staying for the time being with a cousin and his wife and two children. He's been doing spot work to stay ahead of bills—electrical, drywall, general carpentry, and even some plumbing. It pays to get as proficient as possible with all the various jobs there are. But the winter's coming, and things are about to get thin. This is all very familiar to the older man, who nods and searches his mind for something encouraging to say.

It turns out that the cousin lives only a couple of blocks from him. He pulls the truck next to the curb and looks at the litter of toys in the yard. "I do some babysitting for them, too," Stanley says. "They pay me for it. I do worry about this winter—first one in a while I'm not with a contractor. Anyway, somebody somewhere'll need some things done. And I'm pretty good, so there should be some demand."

Oliver, who believes in doing business without regard to personal feelings, recollects that Stanley was indeed very good at a lot of the tasks involved. And he remembers liking him, too—for all the times he didn't show, or was late, or knocked off early. Like so many young men who have come and gone over the years.

"Well," he says. "I know where you are anyway. I can't afford to hire any help right now, but if things change—you know."

"Thanks," Stanley says, getting out of the truck. "I really wasn't asking you for work."

"Nevertheless," says Oliver. "If things change."

Stanley smiles and waves, turning to go on to the house and in. Oliver taps the horn, pulling away.

Five blocks past the turn to his own house is the Gilmans' place. It's a low rambler, L-shaped, tucked into thick shrubbery and in the shade of a giant chinaberry tree. Past seven-thirty now. Oliver notices the car is gone from the driveway. He was going to tell the Gilmans that materials are often slow arriving, and it's time to decide about things: the Gilmans have been going back and forth; the wife can't settle on a color for the outside. Mr. Gilman keeps waffling about the size of the sunroom, how far across the rear of the house it should extend. They both work in the town and are gone into the nights. Oliver gets out of his truck and approaches—he sees Mr. Gilman standing in the front door, behind the screen.

"It's late," Mr. Gilman says. "I've had to call the office." The Gilmans have an oblique way of putting things. Oliver knows that what is meant by this is "You're shiftless and lazy."

So, he apologizes and makes up an excuse—car trouble. He looks back at the parked truck and talks about how old it is. "One thing after another," he says.

"Dorothy already left," Mr. Gilman says. What this means is: *I can't talk to you now. I can't decide anything without Dorothy. I never do anything without Dorothy.* Oliver's familiar with the pattern.

"I could come back tomorrow morning if that's better," he says.

But, in fact, Mr. Gilman and his wife have already decided something. "I don't think we'll do this until the spring, now. She and I discussed it before she left, actually."

"Oh, well—I could get it all done in a couple of weeks."

"That'll be fine in the spring."

Oliver says, "If you're sure."

Mr. Gilman nods at him, looking him up and down. "We'll need our deposit back," he says.

2.

Not quite a mile away (a left turn at the end of one street, a straight-away for eight-tenths of a mile through the splashed shade of lovely black locust trees), Oliver Ward's daughter, Alison, stands outside her rental house with her friend Marge Creighton, soon to be Myers again. Because they're in the cool shade, and it's so early in the morning, Alison has a sweater draped over her shoulders, tied with the sleeves; she's off duty today, too. Marge wears a turtleneck and a light sweat-shirt. This day's hard for both of them, each with trouble that is ongoing and separate from this problem of Marge leaving for Montana for six months. Her mother is a midwife, and her mother's husband is an asshole. That's how Marge has expressed it. She and Greg are splitting up. Because Greg is indeed the number-one all-time champion asshole (again, Marge's phrase). They haven't been able to sell their house, but Marge can't stay there anymore, with him moving through the rooms, a bad presence, a heavy worry, a selfish emotional infant unable to see beyond the next moment, the next physical need, the next opportunity to bask in a mirror admiring himself. A vain, self-satisfied nullity. A bully and a bore. The champion. They're going to have to keep the house for a time, because they don't have the money or the credit to buy two separate places. He's seen to that with his bad habits. So, she's going to her mother's to have the baby and start over, and he's staying, at least until someone buys the house. Eventually, he'll head north, to start over in his hometown, Albany. A job in his father's bank. The old man's been a loan officer there since Christ was a zygote. Greg's been running from the job in the bank for ten years, and now, at thirty-five, it's time, Marge says, to give up the fight. She and Greg spent a lot of time drunk or stoned in their first years together. Last year, they got married and moved to Point Royal, where they met Alison and her father. Greg had a job with a radio station, doing the graveyard shift. The marriage hasn't even lasted out the year. If Greg wasn't such an asshole, Marge says, he'd be a dick, and, in fact, he cannot think beyond the end of that particular organ. It's her pregnancy that has snapped everything. So, he's going to go home and she's heading west. She'll drive as far as the Indiana line today.

For a little while, the two women have talked only about the specifics of the journey. Alison holds her youngest, Kalie, on her hip, while Jonathan, her fourteen-year-old, sits on the little rise of grass and red dirt a few feet away, under the mailbox. He looks like someone waiting sadly for something bad to happen. And, since the divorce, he's become rather heavily bookish, more so than Alison herself. He spends hours every day turning the pages of big tomes: biographies and histories and books about science and anthropology. His vocabulary's laden with four- and five-syllable words, as if he's trying to impress everyone with his intellectual acumen.

He has one of those end-of-summer colds, and is sniffling now, though that could just as well be attributed to this farewell. He comes to his feet and offers to take Kalie from her.

"She's okay here," Alison says.

He turns to Marge. "It's going to be quite difficult not having you next door."

"I know, sweetie," Marge says, "I'll miss you, too."

Alison thinks how Marge, in the space of this one year, has become her closest friend. Other friends are childless, or have no immediate plans to have children, and the ones with children are in stable relationships. They appear to be, anyway. Nobody seems quite comfortable with her anymore, and, in fact, many of them were more her ex-husband Teddy's friends than hers. Her partner on the job, Roy, is a young father, and he's completely flummoxed by the fact that it's twins. He's scared, and seems always after her for reassurance (and so even her conversations at work are about babies). Then there's the job itself, the odd hours, and her father and Marge have been so good about seeing to the children, though Jonathan is old enough to take care of his sister, and often does. "Please," she tells Marge, standing out by the packed jeep. "Call me a lot?"

"I will," Marge tells her. "I'm gonna want to know how to do this." She indicates her abdomen. "It scares me to death."

"I don't know how to do it," says Alison. "And you *have* been doing it, with mine."

"I'm talking about that little matter of the passage through the birth canal, darling."

"Oh."

"And you've done it twice."

"I still don't know."

Marge smiles, pushing her blond hair from her forehead—a nervous, appealing gesture of hers. Her hair is luxuriant, thickly shining in the brightness. "I thought I'd get to say so long to Oliver."

They look up the street, shaded by these giant spreading trees that are still as a picture. For this moment, it's almost supernaturally quiet. Alison says, softly, "He called and said he had some luck yesterday and ended up with sixty dollars without doing any work. So I bet he went on a little toot last night. I didn't hear him come in, and I went to bed after midnight. He was gone when I got up this morning."

"Well, tell him I'll miss him."

Now Kalie has begun fighting to get down. Alison hoists the child, jutting her hip out to support her.

Jonathan says, "Why don't you allow me to take her, Mom." Such a sensitive boy, always thinking, always looking out at the world with that sorrowful, troubled gaze. His father has left him alone and rarely comes to see him. "I've got her," Alison says, jostling Kalie again. All the child wants is movement. She's four years old, and, since the divorce, she's become very quiet and needy. Some nights, when Alison's off duty, the girl sleeps with her (as does Jonathan, too, now and then; a thing they keep to themselves), and she still likes being carried and held. She almost never says anything, and when you try to get her to, she becomes moody and even more introverted. Alison bounces her slightly and reaches with her other hand to hug Marge one last time. Both women are fighting back tears. "I'll keep in touch," says Marge. "It'll go fast, and I'll be back here with this kid."

It's hard to imagine. They exchange a look that expresses this. Marge touches Kalie's cheek.

"Bye," Kalie says, and puts her face in the little hollow of Alison's neck. Marge kisses the little curls, hugs Jonathan, and gets into the jeep. "Bye," Kalie says again, not quite looking up from her hiding place. It occurs to Alison that this is another leave-taking in the child's life. She's clinging tight.

"I'm not going anywhere," Alison tells her. "Ever."

Marge starts the engine, and Kalie squeezes even tighter. Marge's big St. Bernard begins to bark, sticking his large, floppy head out the passenger window. As Marge shifts the gears, grinding them slightly, Oliver pulls up behind her in the truck, honking his horn. He gets out and hurries to the driver's side door of the jeep and leans in to hug her. His dusty black shirt rides up, and his lower back is visible—the wiry black hair there. It makes him look so vulnerable, and he has put on a lot of weight in the last two years. He steps back and seems faintly out of balance, but then rights himself. "I'm gonna miss you, kid," he says. His hypothalamic tic is more pronounced than normal, and his eyes are glazed. The tic is always worse when he's tired or stressed, the head shaking back and forth, back and forth. He looks terrible.

Marge is crying. "I'll be back. Do me a favor and kill Gregory for me."

"I told you I'd take the rap for you. But you have to do it, honey."

Marge blows him a kiss, waves the small handkerchief in her hand, and drives off, honking the horn. The dog stares dumbly back, wind displacing his large, soft ears.

Alison's father is still in the street, wiping his eyes and sniffling a little.

She again lifts Kalie, who complains and seems about to cry, so she lets her down and turns to Jonathan. "Honey, watch her for a little while, do you mind?"

"I requested that, not two minutes ago."

"Will you please take her out back and let her swing?"

He takes his sister's hand with a motion expressing faintly parental exasperation and walks her around the side of the house. Kalie's quiet again, her face down-turning, and there's an aspect of patience about her, as if she understands her brother's mood. They go out back, where he'll watch her swing.

Alison turns from this vision of her children to find that her father has come to the curb and is observing her.

"I tell you I'm proud of you today?" he says. There's something hang-dog about his expression. She notices that he's wearing the same clothes he had on yesterday, which is unlike him.

"What'd you do this morning, Dad? Where'd you go so early?"

He steps up into the lawn and puts his arm across the top of her shoulders. "Honey, I've misbehaved. I spent the night over at Justice Hall." He shakes his head.

"Oh, no, Oliver."

"Stupid, I know," he says. "I had a couple margaritas."

The phone rings inside. For a moment, they hesitate, and then he steps away from her and starts toward the house. "I'll get that."

She watches him hurry on in, and then walks back through the complicated shade to the front of the house, with its single step leading onto the porch—the best feature of the place. Here are boxes of the baby's toys, and Jonathan's old ones, too, because the boy is sentimental and can't part with anything. Plastic trucks, model planes (one with a broken wing), dolls, rubber food, action figures, paint sets. Along with the boxes, there are five lawn chairs and a small tea table with toy tea-things that Kalie got from her father last Christmas. Clutter. She wonders what someone might think coming upon these things a thousand years from now; this doll with its asinine grin and its eyes that roll open on a weighted metal rod in the head. Her father's talking on the phone, and she doesn't want to hear it—it's either someone he drinks with or someone about a job for him. His arrangements trouble her, precisely because she's afraid it's someone he drinks with.

"Morbid," she says to herself, going in. The light in the house is gray; the white walls look gray. The pictures she has hung on them, her own bright paintings and some of Jonathan's drawings—he makes blueprint-like sketches of buildings, cathedral shapes, or modernistic, sleek complexes of angle and wall and roof. She can hear the little protest of the chains on the swing outside.

Oliver's just put the receiver back in its cradle. "Did you say *morbid*?"

"My thoughts. Me." She picks up the newspaper that's strewn across the couch, stacks the sections, and drops it in the magazine rack.

He sits down in his chair with a sigh, reaches for his guitar, and, leaning back with it, plays a couple of soft chords. He's really quite comfortable with the instrument, and good enough so that people notice. "Anything go wrong last night?" This is his usual question about her work hours.

She tells him about Holly and Fiona, and the episode of the roof.

"I'll be goddamned," he says.

"What?"

"Temporary Road?" he says.

"Yes."

"Got to be them." And he tells her about his visit to the Crazies. He uses the word, because Will Butterfield and his wife used it. "That was one of them—Holly—just now on the phone."

"I got a kick out of her. She was the one on the roof."

"I think I might've guessed the other one."

She stands at the window looking out on the side yard and the neighboring house. Greg has come out and is sitting in a lawn chair on his back stoop, watering the backyard with a hose. The water arcs in the sun like a bending stream of light. Sometimes, when she can't sleep at night, she listens to him on the radio. There's something entertaining about knowing the person behind the voice—and knowing that for all his cool on the air waves, he's pretty unhappy all the time. He begged Marge not to leave.

"Tell me what happened last night," she says to her father.

He shrugs. "I had too much to drink. I'll have to go to traffic school. There's a court date."

"What would we do if you lost your license?"

"It's almost ten years since I got a ticket, honey." He sighs and plays a blues progression, watching his fingers on the fret board. "It's a miracle, I know, that I've made it this far. I saw Stanley there. You remember Stanley?"

She sighs "No," and, moving from the window, flops down on the sofa. "Should I?" She feels as if she could sleep for months.

"Guess not. Good kid, I remember. Nice guy."

"Are you thinking of setting me up with somebody you met in the drunk tank?"

He says nothing, playing the guitar, not looking at her.

"Sorry," she tells him.

"Nothing to be sorry about."

But she has hurt him, she can tell. And just now she lacks the energy to do anything about it. She closes her eyes and feels the drowsiness that comes from stress, the haziness of an overactive mind. How good it might be to go under and stay there until all the problems melt away, and to wake up fresh, in a new situation.

Oliver puts the guitar down and stretches back, crossing his legs at the ankle. "I've got an appointment in a little while. Our nutty ladies. I got them to agree to sixty more dollars. They want to consult me about a job."

"You should take a nap or something," she tells him.

"You ought to see if *you* can take a nap. I'm okay. I'll watch Kalie awhile. I don't have to go over there right away."

"What about the Gilman house? Don't you have to do that?"

"I—I stopped and talked to them briefly before I came here. Talked to them about it a little."

"They're not doing it and they want their deposit back," Alison says.

Oliver's eyes answer.

More strain on her about money, the rent, the bills, which she takes care of. Occasionally, she fields calls from people she has taken to calling kindly collectors—those gentle, affectionate, warm voices promising eviction, talking of affidavits and lawsuits and jail, even jail. She imagines their faces, because she can't help it, though mostly she tries not even to think about it. The mail is depressing, filled with demands and notifications, along with the usual enticements, the usual presorted junk telling her she's eligible, or in need of something, or in possession of something that can quickly be turned into big savings or earnings.

Now she gives forth a small, involuntary groan, sitting forward. He holds one hand up, palm toward her. "I know, I know. But I think our crazy ladies are going to be good money—with what she talked about."

She knows that he'll eventually get around to the Gilman house, too, and when he does, it'll be good work. Excellent work. It's his pattern. Delay, procrastination, and then furious work, continuously, until it is done. He has a perfectionist's eye for detail, once the work is under way. She wonders if he doesn't put these jobs off because of some worry about leaving her alone for the long hours with the children, though, in fact, it has always been the story, as long as she can remember. Her father in his work clothes, coming home in dawn light, after finishing a job on time, no matter how late it was begun.

He puts the guitar down carefully and then crosses his arms over his chest, lying back. They say nothing for a spell. Often they sit quietly like this while the children sleep. She'll read her books, and he'll look at the paper or play the guitar softly or work a crossword puzzle. They'll watch a baseball game together. Sometimes Jonathan stays up to watch. Jonathan does so with a curious detachment: he doesn't really care about sports. His gestures are those of vague curiosity, as though the real matter of interest is the passion with which his mother and grandfather watch it. Oliver has tried to teach him how to throw and catch, but the boy seems genuinely appalled at the prospect of trying to manipulate something as hard as a baseball. It frightens him, and he shies away from the softest lob; he cringes, bat in hand, and swings wildly as if to fend off a hornet or a wasp. His discouragement shows, and Oliver is very patient with him, as he was with Alison when he taught her to play, all those years ago, in what she remembers as a happier time than it must have been—because Oliver, by his own admission, has always had this fault line about the bottle. "Your mother put up with a lot," he says often enough for her to feel the truth of his words.

And it is indeed true that Alison, when off-duty, spends too much time alone. She and the children and the bills and waiting for Oliver. It's all she knows these days. The shifts of work—two nights on, one night off, three nights on, two nights off, and back again—and now, with Marge having left, this is all going to be that much harder.

One evening last month, she and Marge split a bottle of chardonnay and then decided to open a bottle of red. They drank merlot and ate cheese and crackers, sitting on the couch, the children asleep, a movie playing that neither of them much liked. Marge lay over and put her head in Alison's lap, and let her hand play along the ridge of Alison's collarbone. Alison closed her eyes, astonished at the excitement this tactile contact caused in her. Abruptly, the other woman sat up and put her mouth on Alison's, and Alison found herself returning the kiss. It felt simple and rather innocent; it felt, in fact, utterly, miraculously good, too. Calming and deeply restorative and nourishing. They went to Alison's room and locked the door, and soon they were out of their clothes and engaged in acts neither of them would've believed possible, given who they were and how they had always lived their lives. It went on and on, and when it was at last over, they got dressed and had another drink—from another bottle of chardonnay—and agreed, rather shyly, not to refer to it again. Alison went to bed that night and couldn't sleep, wondering at herself, and wondering, too, what lay ahead. For her, sex had always meant some sort of commitment. She wouldn't have believed that she could get so starved-feeling for physical contact. Except that it felt more like a discovery involving her deepest nature.

When she saw Marge again, the following afternoon, the other woman's eyes gave nothing back about what had transpired the night before. It seemed that, more than wanting to keep to the agreement they had made, Marge had forgotten everything. And, in fact, they had been very drunk. So, Alison was left with the memory adrift inside, faintly tinged with guilt and puzzlement, and more important for its revelation of the depths of her loneliness than for anything else.

Now, Jonathan comes in with Kalie. He walks with her into the kitchen to make a bowl of cereal for her. Alison gets up, moves to the doorway, and looks out at the houses across the street, the man there, going off to work.

The day's starting, the first without her friend to talk to and worry with. She makes her way downstairs and busies herself with putting in a load of laundry. Her father catnaps over the newspaper. Standing in the downstairs hall, folding clothes from the dryer, she sobs suddenly and puts her hand to her mouth, listening for movement on the stairs. In a little alcove-like space off the main room of the basement is a table laden with the materials of an old hobby: tools and various dolls in different stages of completion. She goes in there and sits down, sniffling softly, and picks up the nearest doll, an Indian girl with braided hair, carrying a child. The whole condition of the living universe, understood in the viscera and bone, is the feeling of something carved, by courage and necessity, out of fear. Alison thinks of the rabbit foraging in a field, one eye on heaven and what wheels and circles there among the fleecy clouds in the wide, bright blue. She fears loneliness with that same wrenching of the nerves and heart. It has made her run to these different crafts and hobbies—photography, knitting, doll-making, watercolors. Holding the doll with its wide-cheeked, clay-colored, Asian face, she decides that this hobby can be rekindled. She recalls losing herself in it. So, she stays here for a while, sanding the edges where the knife has left marks, concentrating only on the motion of her hands.

FORCE OF GRAVITY

I.

If, in the beginning, Elizabeth was troubled by Will's calling the old women the Crazies, recently she has taken to calling them that to their faces. Lately, she doesn't wish to spend time in their society at all. And if Holly and the roof haven't sealed it for her, what happens the following Wednesday evening does. She gets trapped into going to Kmart with Fiona, to get some charcoal for the grill. Will says he'll cook a big filet of salmon. Elizabeth volunteers to go get the charcoal, because she wishes to go off by herself for a little respite; but Fiona insists on coming along.

All the way to the store, the old woman talks about the curse of materialism. She sees it everywhere. She's been thinking about it.

Of course, Elizabeth knows what this means.

By the time they get to the store, Fiona has fairly well worked herself into a state. One can see it in her walk—a certain headlong aspect to her gait. Elizabeth follows her on her march through the aisles of the Kmart, to the lawn-and-garden section. Fiona chooses a big bag of charcoal, muttering about consumerism. Even so, Elizabeth begins to hope that her companion will simply purchase the bag and they'll get out of the store and the only discomfort she'll have to endure is Fiona her-self, going on, in escalating volume, about the decline of values in her native land. But there's a line at the checkout: other people patiently waiting with their purchases. The man directly in front of them has a television, a combination VCR and DVD player, and three tall CD racks in his cart, along with a sack of crabgrass-killer. Fiona stands with her charcoal, gazing at him, and then gazing beyond him at another man, this one with a fifty-foot garden hose, a garage-door opener, and a weed-whacker. At the register, a heavy woman in a tank top is getting her order rung up: a tremendous number of lawn ornaments and five electric clocks.

"Would you look at that," Fiona abruptly says to the man in front of her. "That lady will never be late anywhere ever again."

The man, who is also quite heavy, and very hirsute, looks at Fiona and then looks down.

"That's a hell of a lot of clocks," Fiona says, to no one in particular.

The woman only glances at her.

"What would a person do with all those?"

Elizabeth says, "Fiona, please."

"This is what I'm talking about, though," says Fiona. "Look at it. Look at this. It's just consumption. Rapaciousness." She indicates the TV and the player. "I bet this gentleman's already got a couple each of these at home." She reaches over and touches the man's heavy elbow. "Excuse me, there, sir. Do you have a television set at home?"

He's startled by her touch—he was obviously daydreaming—and now he seems puzzled and maybe even a little annoyed. But he answers, "Yeah. So?"

Fiona indicates his purchases. "Are these for somebody else?"

"No, ma'am."

"Do you really need this, then? Any of this?"

He hesitates, seems about to respond with anger, but then shifts slightly and grins, hanging his head. "Oh, well, all right. I'll put every-thing back."

"But, seriously, sir," Fiona says. "Think about it. Do you need these things?"

Now he shows some indignation. "No, I don't. I don't need one damn bit of it. But I got the money for it and I'm taking it out of here."

"Do you know that there are children in this town who go to bed hungry every night?"

"Yeah? Well, they ain't mine, though. You know?"

"A society's responsible for its children, sir."

"Look, I'm sure you're a nice little old lady, but I'm not in the mood, okay?"

The woman with the clocks has finished paying and is leaving, hurrying, like someone moving away with stolen goods.

"Well, but do you ever think of the hungry children?" Fiona says.

"Excuse us," says Elizabeth. "Excuse her."

"Hey, lady," the man says to Fiona. "I work hard. I've earned everything I've got. If I don't buy this and everybody else doesn't buy these things, then this big store shuts down and has to close and this big fat terrible corporation has to start laying people off and a lot of innocent children end up going hungry, you know what I'm saying?"

"That's a rationalization. And you just said you've got one at home."

"I've got four of them at home. This one's for the bedroom. It makes five. I'm thinking of getting one for the garage. And if you keep talking this crap to me I just might get one for each of the four bathrooms. Kapeesh?"

"But all this is just running you into debt. You won't be able to pay it all off. Do you want to owe more money than you can pay in old age?"

He looks at Elizabeth. "Can you control her or something? God."

"There's no need for you to take the Lord's name in vain," Fiona says. "Do you know what Jesus did with the money changers in the temple?"

"This ain't no temple, lady. And I ain't no money changer. And you sure ain't Jesus. This is a Kmart. Where I happen to be buying me a few things. Now shut up and leave me alone." He turns his back.

Fiona's undaunted. She moves a little to one side and reaches for the man in front of him. This one is not so heavy, but he also has a big beard and long hair. "You, sir," Fiona says. "What about you? Aren't those Prada shoes?"

"Pardon me?"

"I thought those were only for women," Elizabeth hears herself say.

"No, men, too," says Fiona. "I saw it in the *New Yorker*. Men, too, and they're extremely expensive."

The man has turned away again.

"You, there, sir. You can't afford those shoes. Is that an Armani blazer you're wearing? You shop at Kmart. You spend money like that on a pair of shoes and look at you, shopping at Kmart."

"Are you talking to me?" His incredulousness shows in his face, almost as a kind of admiration: he cannot believe this old lady who now fixes him with her gaze and stands too close, actually leaning into him with a combination of challenge and familiarity; it's as if they're old friends and she's with him in his effort to better himself.

"You must've heard us," Fiona says. "You're not deaf, right?" She pronounces the word as *deef*—as if it's a joke between them.

He rests his hands on the back of his cart and regards her, like some sort of phenomenon that he can't quite believe and yet is entertained by. "Why don't you tell me what it is you want me to do?" he says. "And I'll see if I can accommodate you."

"Well," Fiona says. "Look at you."

Elizabeth says, "Fiona, I swear I'll leave you standing here."

"Hold this," says Fiona and hands her the bag of charcoal. It's either take it or let it fall, so Elizabeth takes it. Fiona moves around the first man to this new one, who takes a step back at her approach. "Do you really need all this? Can't you weed your own garden without using up valuable electricity and taxing the power companies on hot days? Do you know how many brownouts there are in this area every summer because of the profligate use of power? And if you shop here, then you probably went into debt to buy those shoes. Look at you—you've got your card out. You're only going to get deeper in debt. They charge twenty-four percent interest every month. In the end it'll cost you five times what you paid for it and you don't need the debt."

"The what?" says the man. "What the hell? Are you on something?" He looks past her at Elizabeth. "Is she on something? This your grandmother, right, and she's on something?"

Elizabeth sets the bag down and walks out of the store, away from the sound of Fiona explaining. She moves across the parking lot to the car, and waits there, leaning against it, arms folded across her chest over a burning. It's this kind of stress that she can't stand anymore, this sense of constantly unfolding confrontation. She can see Fiona and the others through the wide windows next to the door. They all seem now to be engaged in some sort of general chaos. But then the man with the lawn tools and appliances comes out, shaking his head and smiling, and then the heavy man, closely followed by Fiona. They're laughing and smiling. The man actually waves at her as he moves off with his merchandise.

Fiona lugs the bag of charcoal over and stops. "Where'd you go?" she says.

"Oh, Fiona, what was that?" Elizabeth says.

"What was what? We made friends. We had a friendly discussion and we made friends."

They say almost nothing on the way home. Elizabeth decides she doesn't want to hear it. At the house, she walks into the living room, goes to her husband, kisses him on the cheek, and murmurs, "I'm going to bed with a headache, and if you question me about it I'll scream."

"What happened?" he says.

"I'm sure Fiona will tell you."

And, in fact, Fiona is already talking to Holly about the nice men she met at the Kmart and how she opened their eyes to the plight of the hungry children.

2.

No one has ever permanently come between the Crazies, through all the years, and they share a measure of pride in this. They like to describe themselves as the world travelers they are. Indeed, they're a little vain about what they consider to be the sophistication that comes of experience. Sophistication can be founded on many things, but a certain openness is required, and there are people whose knowledge of the world is vast but who hold to certain attitudes and restrictions concerning all that knowledge—usually having to do with religion. In the case of Butterfield's mother and great-aunt, in spite of the religious décor of their house, these restrictions are indeed not overly religious, but they amount to the same thing, since the two ladies would defend them to the death. They are the kind of women who are happy to voice their opinions in all situations, and frequently enough their opinions are far from reasonable.

Aunt Fiona, for instance, believes that not only are there alien space-ships in Roswell, New Mexico, but that the government has been hoard-ing physical evidence of thousands of visiting interplanetary soldiers, and a battle is being fought for the survival of the species under our very noses. It's all going to end, this war of species, with human be-ings on the losing side. We'll all be food, kept in cages, harvested. Her occasional excess with liquid pursuits has always been a feature of life. Lately, when she goes too far, she's apt to say that she's trying to relax from the expected apocalypse.

There are people for whom the consumption of alcohol is obviously a sickness, but Aunt Fiona isn't one of those. She can go for weeks without a drop, and she can sit at a table and have one half-glass of wine. There is no aspect of addiction in the way she drinks. She's as moderate as an Amish grandmother in all circumstances except those when she decides, quite willfully, to go over the line. How she squares this behavior with her still daily practiced Catholicism is a source of continual puzzlement to her niece, who has her own set of what Elizabeth gloomily calls deliri-ous notions. Holly, a self-described leftist, believes that TV is a plot by the corporations and the politicians and the medical profession to distract the people from the truth by bombarding them with trivia and false alarms. One passage implicitly berates you for not having the right dish detergent or for buying the wrong deodorant, and the next heats you up with the evil possibilities contained in faulty automobile design, the rape of the wilderness, or the increasing incidence of violence in the cities.

It's the paranoia of older people, Elizabeth used to say, trying at first to excuse her. For Elizabeth, the differences seemed generational. At first.

More recently, she has seen each difference simply in light of the lu-nacy of the two women.

Will's father, before he abandoned them for the Navy, was quite prosperous, owned his own real estate company. Will was supposed to be the first of several children. But of course no other children came. Will never really knew the man in the pictures on the upright piano in the parlor: Nine years is so young. Holly has kept the pictures because the man was, after all, the father of her one son. To Will, the person in the photos looks like a corrupt politician, with his black fedora and his double-breasted suit, and the dark circles under his eyes. There's something vaguely seedy about the whole makeup of the face, it seems, as if the smile is harboring shameful secrets.

The marriages he saw growing up among the people his parents knew seemed to be bad ones.

So, he entered his own first one—with Elizabeth Jane—finding it difficult to believe fully in the possibility of long-term love. It seemed to him that these relationships all became antagonistic, though people clung to them, suffering each other out of habit, or some need neither could explain or understand. When Elizabeth Jane went away, she confirmed his unhappy conviction.

The second Elizabeth—Elizabeth Marie—has changed all that. When the subject of faith comes up, Butterfield utters the phrase "I believe in love." Simple as that. Easy as a song title, which it probably is. Except he must admit to himself that it is not quite as easy as it sounds. It's simple in the same way that virtue is simple, and difficult in that same way, too, requiring from him the same spiritual energy and sometimes seeming as frangible. When the doubts come, they come in the middle of the night, and, as the saying goes, at that hour, they come in battalions.

3.

In the middle of this night, Brother Fire awakens from a dream of a snow desert stretching far into a distance, with rising clouds in it, blown by wind. The sound of the wind is what wakes him, and then that becomes his cell phone ringing. He thinks he knows who it is.

He gets out of bed in the chilly room and reaches for the phone on the dresser. The book he was reading—a biography of FDR—falls from his lap and makes a terrible thump on the hardwood floor, bringing a small, shuddering cry from the bottom of his throat. He waits a moment, expecting to hear Father McFadden stirring on the other side of the wall. But there's only the murmur of his window fan. When he clicks the answer button, he almost says "Fiona?" Instead, he simply murmurs, "Yes?"

"You said to call, Father." Mr. Petit's voice, a whisper, exactly as if he were on the other side of the little screen in the confessional.

"Oh, yes," the old priest gets out.

Silence.

"Hello?"

"I shouldn't bother you. I woke you."

"What is it, two o'clock in the morning?"

"You said to call."

Brother Fire rubs his eyes, yawns, but then, he hopes, manages to speak clearly, his voice only slightly laced with sleep. "What happened today?" The weird interest again. It makes him momentarily dizzy.

"Nothing. I went to school. I taught my classes. I kept my thoughts clear. But I had a bad dream tonight."

"You can't commit a sin in your sleep," he says and realizes that it sounds rather irritable. Softening his tone, he adds, "That's a mercy, too."

"But I can't stop thinking about the dream."

"Dreams can be that way. I've got several myself. In one, I'm ice-skating. You tell me." He has always found that reporting his own idiosyncrasies helps his parishioners forgive themselves for theirs.

"I never once ever had a homosexual thought, Father. Not ever. I was married for almost twenty years."

"Remember that God is merciful, and He loves you."

"God is no respecter of persons, Father."

"That's Episcopalian, you know. We don't believe that. We believe that the hairs of your head are numbered."

"I wish I could touch him."

"You can. He's all around you."

"I'm not talking about God!" There's a strand of impatience in the voice. "God!" A sigh comes now. And then a level tone. "I don't want to do anything but put my hand on his shoulder without shaking inside."

The old priest sits in the chair by his bed and feels the cold wood on the back of his legs, just above his knees. The question rises in his heart, and he can't keep from asking it, though he knows it is only the infernal curiosity surfacing. "Can you tell me about the dream?" he says.

"I'm trying not to think about it, Father."

"Talk to me, then. Tell me what's in your heart."

"I'm afraid of what's there, Father. It terrifies me."

"You've come this far."

"No."

"But you have."

"You're not helping."

"You're not listening," says the priest.

"I don't want to argue."

There's a silence.

"I'm sorry I woke you, Father," Mr. Petit says and seems about to hang up.

"Tell me about your wife."

Again, silence. A sigh on the other end. "Maybe later, Father. She was a nice woman. A sweet woman. I made her mostly happy. We made each other mostly happy. It wasn't all that much fire in the heart, though. It was friendly."

"Yes."

"I never even thought about boys. Men."

"No."

"Good night, Father."

"Don't go," Brother Fire says. But the connection is broken.

He gets up, dresses for the day, though the day is still hours from now, and goes quietly downstairs, to make coffee. Father McFadden is in the kitchen, writing under the one lamp at the kitchen table. He looks up, his eyes made sad-looking by the glasses he's wearing. "Oh, I'll make more coffee."

"No, never mind."

"It's no trouble at all, Father. Really."

The old priest prevails on the younger one to keep his place, and he makes the coffee himself. Father McFadden is writing furiously in his notebook, and it becomes a sort of unspoken race, a race only the Monsignor is aware of as such—to get his coffee made and himself back in his room before his curate finishes his latest literary effort.

"Almost finished with this one," the younger man says as Brother Fire starts upstairs with his coffee.

"Well, I've got to use the bathroom," says the old priest. A lie, for which he's immediately sorry, asking inwardly for God's pardon. But, while making the coffee, he saw the phrase "warm bags" in the frantic lines the curate is scribbling, and he knows he will not be able to sit for this one, whatever it is. "Later," he says with the definiteness of authority. And he makes his escape.

He drinks the coffee for a time alone in his room. Then, remembering his lie, he flushes the upstairs toilet and closes the door to his room. He won't be able to go back to sleep, though he's tired, weary down in his bones. He sits at his desk, composing letters: to Fiona, to Mr. Petit, and, finally, to Father McFadden, saying that, unfortunately, talent is far from him—oh, many distant light-years from him—as a poet, but that he can still be a fine priest. He folds this letter up and puts it far in the back of the top drawer of his desk. It's going to be a long, sleepless end of the night, cooped up here. With a kind of disconsolate tentativeness, he picks among the books on the small shelf across from his bed, looking for something to take him away and perhaps to make him sleepy. Tomorrow, Labor Day, he can get away early, and there's an invitation, which he's accepted, to go to dinner with Holly and Fiona.

FAITH AND LOGIC

I.

For Elizabeth Butterfield, waking each morning is complicated by the sense of crisis engendered by the Crazies. Everything's in question now. She has dreams, busy dreams, that are dissimilar on the surface—that is, they are lived in different places, in odd circumstances, in wildly disparate weathers—but in all of them she's searching for something, rummaging through tangles of clothes, among objects, bric-a-brac, books, papers, for something ineffably important, for which she has no name and no sense of its shape or texture. These dreams wake her, and the aftereffects leave her restless and scared. Lately, she has no appetite. Anxieties plague her. It's all so wearisome. And now school has begun.

Gail and Mark arrive late Friday afternoon. Mark flew to Philadelphia from Indiana, and the two of them drove down in Gail's ratty little green Honda with the rusted undercarriage and the duct-taped right rear window. It's a hot, sticky, windless day. Gail wears a tank top, no bra; she's stopped shaving under her arms. There's a mannish sort of abruptness about her now, a kind of studied, unfeminine pitch in her talk. She's bigger about the hips, and her face, always her best feature as a child, with its soft, oval sweep and the round eyes, has flattened and squared, the chin widening, the new width of her cheeks giving her a look of faint distrust. There's something glowering about it. Mark, on the other hand, is thinner than he ever was, too thin. With the lean musculature of his arms, the once-weight-lifter's definition of bicep and forearm—those thick veins forking down the bone—and with the sad little goatee actually graying at his long chin, he looks a little as though he might've walked out of an El Greco. He seems depleted, more from Gail's company than from the heat. They've been squabbling. Will helps with the suitcases—Gail has packed as if for weeks—and Mark goes directly to the kitchen to put away the foods he's brought. He's on a special new diet: fish and eggs, mostly. Low carb, but with this twist, his own, about eating only fish. Fish oil is supposed to lower cholesterol. He has packed sea bass, trout, and salmon. He'll cook for everyone, he tells them. Gail is strictly vegan, so there are also her requirements to worry about.

Mark tries a joke, asking Gail if vegans give up their sense of humor with meat.

"Oh, Christ," Gail says. And the weekend can be said to have begun.

In the kitchen, Elizabeth prepares iced tea, and Butterfield joins her. "There're some interesting pamphlets in the front seat of the Honda," he says.

She gives him a puzzled look.

"Gay rights. Lesbian activism."

"Why don't you ask her about it?"

"I don't think I want to know," he says.

The Crazies pull in with Brother Fire, and there's a lot of commotion. Greetings and offers of food and drink, chatter about the road, the weather, Mark's flight from Indiana. The Crazies are going to have the house on Temporary Road partitioned—made into a duplex. It's decided. They've hired the contractor: Mr. Oliver Ward. A very kindly gentleman. Holly introduces the priest, though everyone already knows him. "You remember Brother Fire," she says. Elizabeth shakes his proffered hand and looks into his warm, blue gaze.

Mark and Gail complain about the heat and about the fact that they had to drive without air-conditioning, because the radiator in the Honda kept overheating.

"Why don't you fix it?" Fiona asks them. "You're like a dog sitting on a nail and howling because he's too lazy to get up off of the nail."

There's a silence.

"Count on Fiona," says Holly and stops there, as if nothing else needs saying.

The afternoon is tense, ruined by a brittle politeness. And then, at dinner—spinach salad, broiled salmon, and corn—Gail announces that she's been searching for her mother. For a moment, no one says anything. The exasperation shows in Mark's face: he's known about this for some time. Perhaps they argued about it in the car, driving down from Philadelphia.

"You think she wants you to find her?" Butterfield says.

"I guess I'll know that soon enough."

"Any leads?" He pours more of the chardonnay Holly and Fiona brought, which Fiona is not drinking.

"Grandma and Grandpa," Gail says.

"*They've* heard from her?"

"They haven't heard from *anybody.*"

This is aimed at the whole family. "Well, they've heard from you," Butterfield says. "Haven't they?"

Gail ignores this. "Grandpa gave me the name of a girlfriend she had in school. I tracked her down in Florida, and she told me she got a post-card from Mom only a few years ago."

"How many years?"

"Three."

"That's an age, kid."

"Maybe. I've got a woman working on it for me. From an agency that helps people find loved ones. She says three years is closing in on locating somebody."

Butterfield looks across the table at his wife who can't decide what the look means. He turns to Mark. "You in on this?"

"I found out about it on the way down here," Mark says. "I found out in spades, if you know what I mean."

And then everyone seems at a loss.

Gail goes on, talking of a book she read about missing persons. According to the authors of this book—a pair of psychological counselors from San Francisco—there are more than three million people in the country who are "disappeared."

"A verb turned into a noun," says Brother Fire. "It's usually the other way around these days. People talk about 'gifting,' for instance, and 'parenting.'"

"Could make a person think of 'suiciding,'" says Butterfield.

The priest grins and nods. "Well, if he couldn't find someone to 'solace' him."

Gail interrupts crisply to say that the book offers solace for those in her situation. Fiona declares that if she herself wanted to disappear—and she has indeed wanted to, from time to time—she would make it so no one could ever find her.

"That might be just the thing," Holly says. "One lives on hope, doesn't one?"

"What do you think will happen if you find her, Gail?" Butterfield asks abruptly.

Gail hesitates only a second. "I don't have the slightest idea. I plan to find out."

"Maybe she's dead," says Fiona.

"Then I'll find *that* out."

Elizabeth notices that Holly's gazing at her from the end of the table. She knows what's coming. Holly doesn't disappoint her: "How does this make you feel?"

"I'm neutral," Elizabeth tells her and feels a displeasing sense of having lied. Holly seems to think so; she gives a little shrug, smiling out of one side of her mouth.

"I damn sure wouldn't be," Holly says.

"Well," says Will, "I'm not neutral for sure." He fixes Gail with a stare. "You find her, missy, I don't want to know about it. Okay? I don't care about it, you know?"

"You mean you wouldn't even be curious?"

"Not remotely."

"Me, too," Mark says. "I don't want to know."

"That's so like men," Gail says. "All tied up in their injured egos."

"That's me," says Mark. "Help yourself to the sweeping generality."

"God is in the particulars," says Fiona brightly. "Isn't that right, Father?"

"Yes," says the priest. "Exactly."

"Well, I think I'd be curious," says Holly. And takes a slow sip of the wine. Her enjoyment of it seems subtly enhanced by the fact that Fiona has refused any. She glances at her aunt with each sip, almost as if to taunt her.

"Yes," says Brother Fire. "The thought comes from Aquinas. 'It would seem that God is simple.' I remember reading that when I was eighteen and being appalled. How could the creator of so much complex reality be simple? It seemed insulting to the majesty of God. But the particulars—the simplicity of that. And the devil, evil, is of course understood as the spirit of sophistry and rationalization."

"What's the name of the book?" Mark asks.

"The *Summa Theologica*. Saint Thomas Aquinas. He spent twenty years writing it, and after it was done, he had some sort of revelation and renounced all of it. Called it straw. And spent the rest of his life living quietly on faith. Wouldn't even talk about his great book."

"There's an online group called Finding Mom," Gail says, "that adopted people use. I've joined them, too, and I'm going to find her."

"I don't think your father wants to talk about this," Elizabeth says.

"I don't either," says Mark. "It got talked about anyway. All the way from Philadelphia to here. Incessantly. In spades."

"Poor baby," Gail says. "What's that mean anyway. In spades?"

"It means incessantly. Until I can't stand it. I'm sorry, I should've explained it to you."

There's another silence. Elizabeth shifts slightly and offers the priest more wine. He demurs, holding up one thin hand. Will holds his glass over, and she pours some for him.

"We have a real missing person in our family," Fiona says to Brother Fire.

The priest seems faintly at sea. He nods, frowning with interest, but you can see that he hopes this is enough. There's a very slight tremor in his hands as he folds them. Elizabeth looks at his light blue eyes, the network of wrinkles around them. It's a weathered, humorous, like-able face—with tufted dark brows and an imposing forehead, a sculpted, long nose, under which part of the thin mouth disappears when he smiles. The face seems rather sad just now. She leans toward him a little and says, "Tell us more about Aquinas, Father."

"We were on the subject of our missing person," says Gail.

"No, we were *not* on that subject," Elizabeth says. "We had left it to talk about Aquinas."

"Well, I just want everyone to know—"

"You've made your noise," says Will. "Now let it alone. Christ." He turns quickly to the priest. "I'm sorry."

"I always follow the profane use of the name with a prayer," the priest says.

"You'd spend all your time praying in *this* family," Fiona puts in, not quite under her breath.

"I'm going back to Philadelphia," says Gail. And then, without look-ing at anyone, she rises from the table, collects her plate, wine glass, salad bowl, and napkin, and starts toward the kitchen.

"Don't let the door hit you in the ass," says Butterfield, before turn-ing to the priest and saying again, "Sorry. That's something we all used to say in my family. It's not as bad as it sounds."

"You ought to be ashamed," Fiona says.

"It's been apologized for, Aunt Fiona. And now's the time for you to practice some Christian forbearance. Right, Father?"

The priest nods and looks to one side, toward Fiona, so that it's as if he has acceded to and denied the thought at the same time.

"I'm sorry," Will says again.

2.

Elizabeth talks Gail out of leaving by reiterating softly the litany of Will's reasons for not wanting to talk about his ex-wife. Gail listens. It's one of the good qualities she possesses: Even when adamant about something, she will patiently listen to opposing views—there's a kind of intellectual pride in it for her. But nothing deters her once her mind is made up. And, in this instance, she's committed to the search. "It's my mother, after all," she says. "And I want to talk to her."

"Do you want to ask her why she did what she did?"

Gail considers for a moment. "No. I really just want to have a normal conversation, woman to woman." And her eyes suddenly brim over with tears. "What's wrong with that?"

"There's nothing at all wrong with it," Elizabeth tells her, putting a hand on her shoulder.

The evening ends with Fiona and Holly arguing about plans to partition their house on Temporary Road. They try to involve the poor priest, who speaks generally and kindly about the push and pull of family love.

When they've left, and Gail and Mark have gone upstairs to their respective rooms, Elizabeth puts her arms around Will's neck and kisses his cheek. "Don't be so hard on Gail," she says.

"I wish we were alone," he tells her. Through the wall, they hear Gail's music—Indigo Girls.

"We can be quiet."

"You all right?" he asks.

"Sure," she says. "Even the Crazies weren't so bad."

"You think so, do you?"

"I felt sorry for poor Brother Fire, being between them."

"*Everybody's* always between them," says Will. "Everywhere they go."

Through the rest of the weekend, Gail keeps bringing up aspects of her search for the first Elizabeth. It's as if she can't help it, thinking aloud. It's on her mind. It worries her. Will grows quiet or finds some neutral reason to leave the room. But, several times, she and Mark exchange bitter words about it. The whole holiday is weighted with this tension. The Crazies come over for dinner each night, and Holly comments on the bad electricity between Mark and his sister. "They always argued," Will says. "It's probably a primal need for the young. You're an only child, and you had an only child, and so you didn't see a lot of it."

Sunday night, Gail begins talking about gay rights, and Will breaks in to ask her point-blank: "Missy, are you telling us something?"

"I'm telling you what I'm telling you."

"Which is—"

"Oh, Jesus, Dad. Have I frightened you?"

"I'm just trying to figure out the boundaries here, kiddo."

"Don't call me kiddo."

"Kiddo," Will says, staring into her. "Okay, there, kiddo? Kiddo. Kiddo."

Elizabeth steps in. "Can we please stop harrowing each other?" She's worn out with it, has felt several times like throwing something. Sunday morning, she almost poured water on their heads, going past them to water houseplants while the arguing went on about how important or absurd it was or wasn't, concerning what the first Elizabeth might've seen or done or been through, and if she'd had other husbands, other children. All that, back and forth. And Gail's brand of feminism has been threaded through it all—the depredations of male-dominated society having, Gail bothers to point out, produced the pressures that must've made the first Elizabeth abandon everything and run.

Now Will says, "Kiddo is a term of endearment, I believe. Even when you're twenty-eight years old and absolutely cocksure of your own opinions about everything."

"Cocksure?"

"Yes, cocksure. Cocksure. Cocksure. Look it up."

"I find 'kiddo' and 'cocksure' offensive."

"You *find* those things offensive. Are you *looking*? What've you—got radar or something? Turning slow on the world, looking for offenses?"

"Can we all please stop?" Elizabeth says. "Please? Can we? Please? Please?"

When brother and sister leave, Monday afternoon, they're barely civil with each other. "That'll be a long, hard ride back," Will says.

"It was a long, hard weekend," says Elizabeth. "It was like dealing with my high school kids. And now I have to do just that."

"I'm sorry," he says. "Baby. I really am."

WILL AND THE ELIZABETHS

I.

Several nights in the first year after the first Elizabeth left, he found both children up, talking. Sometimes he had drunk a little too much scotch, intentionally, so he would sleep—sleep having become a thing he had to chase through the nights, and there were times when it did feel precisely as if he were pursuing it through an arid landscape of feverish half-dreams that broke down slumber and left him anxious, staring into the dark, listening to the sounds of the sleeping house. So, he would drink a good deal of scotch, for the narcotic effect, and come stumbling in his stocking feet to the top of the stairs, and he would find Gail and Mark, awake talking. They stopped when they saw him, and the heavy concentration in their faces shifted to forced smiles and artificial casualness: they evidently thought that he would, as he had done often enough, remain downstairs on the couch. They waited for him to speak. And he waited for something to occur to him to say. He knew they were in pain, and he was in pain—he knew they worried about him. And, of course, he was worried about them but they couldn't really speak of it. They seemed at times to be like other children—they bickered and got cross at little things, but they also laughed and were silly, too; Gail also had problems sleeping, and would be up late, reading, or simply lying in the light, looking at her ceiling. When he questioned her about it, she would say that she wasn't sleepy. One night, he sat on the edge of the bed and took her hands.

"Are you thinking about your mother?"

"No."

"You're sure."

"Daddy." There was a certain elliptical slant to her cheekbones that made it seem always that she was about to smile, and when the smile didn't come, there was a little surprise about it. It never failed to charm him, and at times, in those first months, he thought it might break his heart.

"*Do* you think about her?"

"Sometimes."

"Do you and Mark talk about her?"

"Sometimes."

"You can tell me, sweetie. Really."

She looked down at her own hands on the blanket covering her knees.

"Can you tell me what you talk about?"

Now she gave him a look. "*Her*."

"But what, though," he said. "You know."

She turned from him and fluffed her pillow. "I don't know."

It was clear that this was something so private for her—something about which, for whatever reasons, she could not talk to her father. So he tried to let her know that he was there for her if she ever did want to. There wasn't anything else he could think of to do. He went on with the daily matters—the household, the meals, school. Twice he attended a meeting of single parents, one that was actually for the parents of abandoned children. The participants in this group happened to be women, and it seemed to him that they all looked at him with eyes that wondered why. He never went back.

His chief worry was that the children blamed themselves. Mark, of course, was the tough one; well, he was working at being tough, anyway—he wanted weights for his twelfth birthday and he spent an hour every day lifting them. At twelve and a half, for his height and small-boned compactness, he looked buff. It was worrisome. Butterfield had waking horrors imagining the boy bulking up like those freaks in the weightlifting magazines, with their roils of muscle, those outlandish bulges forking with veins; caricatures, disproportionate combinations of knotted shapes, walking overstatements of the human form.

But, quickly enough, the boy shifted to other enthusiasms: basketball, football, wrestling. About his absent mother he was even less forthcoming than Gail. His night problem was sleepwalking. He would get out of bed and come downstairs and stand in the front hallway as if waiting for someone to come through the door. His aspect was exactly that expectant look of a person who has heard the doorknob turn and is responding to the sound: the front door of the house opening. Coming home. This happened often enough for Butterfield to seek some explanation of it from a psychiatrist, who told him that traumatized children often develop patterns of sleepwalking, and that it would pass. But it kept happening. And the boy had no memory of it after waking, and would not talk about his dreams or his worries or anything much else. He was outwardly all boy—rough-and-tumble, headlong, prone to minor cuts and bruises. One summer evening, he broke his arm from a fall while running. He had gone to a neighbor's yard to play hide-and-seek with some boys who lived in the neighborhood. Mark had come upon an unevenness in the ground and tumbled forward; he just hit wrong. Butterfield drove his son to the emergency room, Mark bracing his injured arm with the good one. The broken arm was elongated unnaturally by the injury, which was just above the wrist, and the forearm went off at a terrible angle.

"It's okay to cry, if it hurts," Butterfield told him.

"It hurts like a bitch," the boy said through his teeth.

But he didn't cry until they hooked him up to an IV and the anesthetic dripped into him. Then, losing consciousness, he closed his eyes tight, and the tears ran out of the corners of them, as if the relaxation of nerves had allowed to flow at last what he had been so bravely keeping back. *Then* was when Butterfield might've been able to speak to him about his mother. He thought this, sitting on a bench in the waiting room, with Gail, who slept, head resting on the seat back, mouth open, looking stricken, years older than fifteen, and she wasn't old enough, really, to see this as anything but life. Her life. He patted her shoulder, lifted her slightly, and leaned down to kiss her hair.

Later, when she was awake, she worried aloud about her brother. "Will he be able to come home, do you think?"

"Of course," Butterfield said. "That's why we're waiting."

"They won't keep him overnight."

"No."

"Don't go to The Heart's Ease."

"No, of course not."

"Good."

The television in the room was on, and the newspeople were rattling on about a coal fire in a mountain somewhere, which had been burning for twenty years. She watched it intently.

"Do you want to change the channel?" Butterfield asked her.

"No," she said simply. "Unless you want to."

"Maybe there's something funny on."

She shrugged.

His children, he realized, were unreachable. They were clearly suffering the loss of their mother, and he couldn't find the way to be everything that they needed. In fact, it seemed that they were faring better than he. Nights were long and restless. Disbelief kept him awake for weeks; and then it was belief that did so. He watched the children for signs, and then realized one morning while he made breakfast for them that *they* were watching *him*. It stunned him. He looked up from slipping pancakes onto a platter on the dining-room table, to see that they were both staring. And, of course, they looked away immediately.

"Everything okay?" he asked.

"Sure," Mark said after a pause.

Butterfield realized that he had been whistling, and that it had surprised them to hear this coming from him. "Hey," he said. "It's a beautiful morning."

"Whatever," Gail said.

"Do you want to talk about anything?"

"Like what, Dad."

"Well, your mother."

She looked at him as if he had asked her to remove her blouse; there was truly something outraged and appalled about it. "No," she said.

They ate in silence for a time, and then Mark, still wearing a cast on his right arm, began talking about trying to get the arm healed enough to go out for baseball.

Through the months, they navigated the strange, depthless waters of their unexpected journey together. Butterfield sought to encourage them whenever they seemed lighthearted. He took them places and spent time with them.

And then he was himself involved in another life, thinking of getting married again.

For a little while after the first Elizabeth disappeared, he entertained the idea that she'd been forced to write her message across the mirror, those sweeping strokes in the letters notwithstanding; she'd been kidnapped and maybe subsequently killed. He saw her lying in a ditch somewhere, a victim of the random violence of America during the last of its supposed best century. But the police didn't take very long to conclude that this was a case of someone wanting to vanish: she'd used her credit cards to build up a store of cash and canceled accounts or paid them off weeks in advance of the day she walked away. Clearly, she'd planned it all out, and the scribbled message on the restroom mirror had certainty and determination, and even happiness in it, rather than any distress. Her very silence now seemed to say get on with it, get on with your lives and never think of me again.

This was never exactly possible, of course.

There were bad, bad days of trying to get used to her absence while attempting to assuage, in his own bafflement and hurt, the uncomprehending pain of the children. He would never have believed that he, a grown man, could lie, despairing and tearful, alone in his bed at night, suffering while they slept, ashamed of himself for all of it, feeling somehow as though he were at fault, but lacking the slightest insinuation of an idea as to why, and powerless to stop it or to change it. Sometimes he even woke up crying—and how disconcerting, how deeply confidence-shattering it was to find himself coming out of unconsciousness weeping. For a time, when he was with friends, he caught himself hauling out photographs of himself with the absent wife, unable to keep from seeking reassurance against the suspicion that another man, someone with a finer sensibility perhaps, would have seen it coming; this other, more capable man might've been able to prevent it, head it off, by perceiving something, some shade of it all, in her face. "Does she look happy, there? She's smiling, isn't she? You see anything wrong? Would you say that's a happy woman?"

Of course, Mark and Gail, being children, attributed the whole matter to something they had done. He had to find ways to make them believe that it had been aimed at him and not really the children; that their mother's leaving had come from the extreme of what she felt toward him. But this wasn't quite true, and the children knew it. She had left them, too, had found her life with them to be too much, too.

No one had seen it coming. As the months and years wore on, and the three of them had the usual troubles with setting boundaries during adolescence, the abdication on her part seemed all the more directed at each of them. Gail especially had trouble with it, and her one marriage—her o'er hasty marriage, as Butterfield then called it—was probably an unconscious reaction to the whole thing: she had been abandoned, her father was someone whose failure to understand her was painful and complete, and so she sought affection in the arms of the boys who came along. And she married young, at nineteen. Her choice was unfortunate, to put it kindly. An over-tall, thin-faced wretch with pretty, black hair and a fearful case of the shies. Literal-minded, and usually mute as a stump. A basketball hero with no other skill, and with half her brains. His name was Phil, and he's long gone.

Mark, too, has had his troubles with relationships over the years— the main feature of his personality being the belief that no one will stay, that he himself is not lovable *as* himself (while most of us have subscribed to this view in company, inwardly we have also been taught to believe that we are, in fact, our own reward; it is a common enough notion, isn't it? to believe that if we end a relationship, the one left behind will not survive the loss). The sorrowful thing for Butterfield is that poor Mark lacks Gail's stridency and toughness. Whereas Gail got angry and is evidently planning a lifetime of getting even, Mark sleeps much of the time when he visits, watches too much television, and drinks too much wine.

On Memorial Day of this past year, he had too much shiraz and ended up sitting in a bathtub of cold water with a headache, while everyone else ate grilled burgers and hot dogs. And that night, late, he explained to Butterfield that his present relationship, which had looked for all the world like the real, true thing, was ending. The woman in question was downstairs, sleeping on the living-room floor with her children, who had gone a good distance toward wrecking that room and the front porch. One of them, a girl, had run through the house with a lighted sparkler, and when Butterfield took it away from her, she kicked him in the shin. Butterfield bounced around in his living room with a sparkler shooting fire from him, trying to take hold of his hurt leg. The girl waited a beat, adjusted her angle, and kicked him again, this time in the other shin. Elizabeth and Holly pulled her away. Holly took the still-burning sparkler, and Butterfield sat on the sofa to hold his shins, both of which were already showing the welts that would turn into bruises. Nothing could've pleased him more than to throw the child, burning, out a window overlooking rocks and pounding surf. And knowing that this woman and her children would not be joining the family made him very happy, sorry as he was for Mark—who was, indeed, grieving the loss, and believing, again, that no one would ever settle on him or find him.

But he makes his way, too. He has never been unemployed for more than a week, and he's evidently very good at designing Web sites. If he spends a large part of his salary paying for visits to one psychologist or another, and if his bookshelves are full of self-help volumes and diet cookbooks (sometimes Butterfield wonders if he's not anorexic, though he knows this is a disease of young women), it's no one's business but his own.

In his son's estimation of things—and this is with the help of several doctors of psychiatric medicine—he has and always will have abandonment issues (his expression, or, rather, that of the doctors), as do Butterfield and Gail. The hard thing to accept gracefully is the assumption on Mark's part that any conflict arising between them comes from there. This has also angered Gail, whose anger is probably too steady to be healthy. Elizabeth has told Butterfield that she pictures Gail with an IV, except that the thing dripping into her veins isn't plasma or sucrose but bile. "She's on a bile drip," Elizabeth will say. "It's what keeps her going."

He met her—the good Elizabeth, as he sometimes teasingly calls her—during parents night at Mark's middle school, his ninth-grade year. She spoke to him about how bright Mark was, how much fun he was to have in class, and something about the faintly crooked shape of her mouth made him think of touching her lips. It was plain tactile curiosity at first, not sexual, like wanting to run one's hands over the back of a cat.

"Are you seeing anyone?" he said and was surprised at his own forwardness.

She said, turning, "Well, yes there are still several sets of parents—"

"No," he said. "I meant—you know. As in dating." His voice shook.

It was this tremor, she told him later, that had moved her to say, with a slightly sardonic smile, what was at the time an outright lie. "No, as a matter of fact, I'm not seeing anyone as in dating."

Over these mostly sweet years together, their complications have always felt like matters they could see through or beyond, some solution or relief awaiting them, like the proverbial clearing in the woods or the light at the end of the tunnel. And then the Crazies moved into the house on Temporary Road.

2.

For Elizabeth, the first part of the school year is always the hardest. The paperwork is roughly what it might be for the creation of a small independent state. The meetings go on and on, and, during all of this, there are, surrounding her—each one demanding individual attention and

assuming she has no life or purpose except to supply it—the hundred
and thirty-odd nascent salesmen, Rotary Club presidents, truck drivers,
bums, homemakers, mechanics, secretaries, doctors, lawyers, soldiers, ac-
countants, artists, broadcasters, adulterers, victims, and criminals, whose
heaped frustrations and hormonal frenzies constitute all of life in these
rooms: the prodigious, outlandish energy for which no outlet is quite as
alluring as all the forms of mischief, not to say devastation.

The school itself is housed mostly in the new wing, which appears to
be close to the ground, because the back wall of it is partially submerged
in the side of a hill. It looks to Elizabeth like a brick-and-aluminum
bunker or redoubt, a postmodern stronghold with a ribbed, dark brown
metal roof. Over the door is a long, narrow rectangular panel inscribed
with large letters in bas-relief: WE ARE STRONGEST WHEN WE ARE
SEEKING TO KNOW. Beneath this is a cloth banner, showing a black
horse rearing—it's the silhouette of a horse, really—and the words THE
MUSTANGS in bright red letters suggesting English heraldry.

The main building, the original building, is a tall, gabled, nineteenth-
century manse flanked by a gigantic spreading oak and a small, fenced
graveyard where the victims of an eighteen-seventy-eight cholera epi-
demic are buried. This was a teacher and his entire family, apparently—
three little boys, two girls, a wife, and the wife's elderly parents, all of
whom died within weeks and sometimes hours of each other. The school,
back then, was in this one building, and all the classes were taught by
the same stern-looking, morally assured gentleman whose picture is
engraved in the wall of the entrance, and whose mortal remains lie in
eternal peace with his family under the shade of the oak tree. It is always eternal peace, and it is always acceptable with the passage of time.
It doesn't seem tragic or wrong or even quite so terrible—there seems
nothing particularly unjust or unbearable about it now, because it was
a hundred years ago, awful as it must have been, and is accomplished,
and now the unfortunate lot of them are buried in the quiet shade of the
yard. The man's name was Briarly, and the building is now called the
Briarly Building. Elizabeth likes the old place better than the new wing,
and her classroom is off the big hall upstairs, where a leaded window
overlooks the lawn and the little graveyard. She has her own desk and

computer. In the desk is a drawer full of over-the-counter medicines, papers, makeup and combs, and mementos from former students—letters and cards, mostly—all of this under lock and key, because she has to vacate the room in the middle of the day for the traveling teacher, or floater, whose name, oddity of oddities, is James Christ. He pronounces the last name as the first syllable of Christmas is pronounced, but the spelling is there. Elizabeth imagines his parents deciding on a first name beginning with the letter *J*. What can they have been thinking? James Christ never talks about his name, other than to point out its proper pronunciation, and Elizabeth has yet to gather the courage to ask him about it: he's so direct and immediate about the pronunciation (Elizabeth can't help but pronounce it in her mind as it is spelled). Mr. Christ arrives punctually at one o'clock with a cart and his own lesson plans and materials. His manner is hesitant and humble, and there's the look about him of general discouragement that comes to the faces of the itinerant and the rootless—especially (Elizabeth has had the thought) when they carry the stigma of being named for the redeemer of all humankind. The fact is, she often feels fairly rootless, too, for she has to make space for him and take her work with her down to the library to sit and grade, or prepare lesson plans, or answer memos.

She's allowed less than thirty minutes for lunch, the administrators long ago having understood that children in the throes of changing into adults require constant busyness to protect them from themselves. There's enough pure human electricity in a room full of these changelings to solve all the hemisphere's energy problems.

After lunch, she has to do STOP duty (Student Time Out Place). This is a room with stalls for individuals to sit in and study, and it's where they're sent as a last resort before being suspended from school. Here is where she must watch over the defiant, the troubled, the sleepy, the alienated, the unfortunate—the intellectually, emotionally, and, at times, spiritually, halt and lame. Many of these particular students, given the circumstances of their lives and the conditions of daily life in a public school, have her best sympathy, which is, doubtless, more sympathy than they get anywhere else in their lives, and they know it.

Today, she has forms to fill out, questions that need answering so even more forms can be filled out. She goes through homeroom, where the intramural television student newscast is played to a chattering group of nonparticipants in the civil life of the school, and then starts her morning class with a writing exercise, so she can see how far she has to go—how desperate will be the climb, scaling the alp of nonunderstanding in the room before her. This affords her a little time to go over the massive load of paperwork. Along with the forms for upcoming parent conferences, there are reports to legal authorities about her juvies, as they are called. These are children who have been in trouble with the law—which is fairly common these days, nothing new.

Once, a couple of years ago, she had a boy, Jerry Bergenstein (she's learned to remember names, hundreds of names), who ended up taking part in a heist where weapons were brandished. He was tried and sentenced as an adult and is now spending the first part of fifteen years at the state correctional facility in Norfolk. Elizabeth sometimes still receives letters from him. The kid was never really such a bad boy: he had a sense of humor, and she believes that no one with a sense of humor is ever unredeemable. Long before the heist, when he was only fifteen, he got in trouble with the authorities at school. At an all-classes assembly about sexual hygiene, where a film was shown about the dangers of AIDS and other sexually transmitted diseases, a man gave a lecture about puberty and the changes attendant upon it, and, when asked about masturbation, explained that it was perfectly normal, nothing to be ashamed of, but that if the urge came too often, one should think about taking a cold shower to help keep it to a minimum. As the session ended, Jerry Bergenstein yelled out, "Last one to the showers is a rotten egg," and for this harmless joke was suspended from school. Elizabeth still believes he would not be in prison now if it weren't for the fact that this minor transgression was so severely punished—by the assistant principal at that time, Mr. Sellars, who went on to the school board in one of those trajectories reserved for the coldhearted, the efficient, the humorless, and the tireless.

In her first-period class, a boy named Calvin Reed throttles another boy, named Jonathan Lawrence. Reed is a juvie, in school to avoid being sent to the county's juvenile detention center. But it's not the kid's circumstances that are particularly unusual. It is, instead, Calvin Reed himself.

Tolerance, that happy but complicated matter, dictates the confidence that treasures are hiding inside a painfully unappealing countenance, and, of course, Elizabeth believes this. In any case, she has to.

Unfortunately, Calvin Reed is epically unattractive, and it just so happens that sometimes, regrettably, ugly is as ugly looks.

She had Calvin all last year, and progress was glacial. He took up way too much of her time. There were arguments with his parents about it—two people of such enormous, grasping, busy selfishness that several of Elizabeth's conferences with them became like wrangling at the marriage counselor's office, with Elizabeth in the unwanted role of the counselor. The father described himself as an independent entrepreneur. He was bald to the crown of his head, and wore a long, graying pigtail, so that it looked as though his hair had simply begun to slide off to the back. His independent entrepreneurship, it turned out, was the transporting and sale of marijuana. Over the summer, Elizabeth read about his arrest and incarceration. He's serving a two-year sentence in Norfolk for possession of an enormous cache of dope, which he attempted to sell out of the trunk of his car to an undercover agent. Calvin himself has possession and assault charges pending. Elizabeth knows this from the student affairs office.

She knows also that the boy's mother is gone, too, now—spending her time in a Buddhist commune somewhere in Texas. Mrs. Reed, apparently, still lives the hippie lifestyle, an exemplar of how certain faddish developments in the cultural landscape can hang on in the lives of the pathetic and the uninspired.

Calvin's uncle, according to the information on his forms, has been the responsible party since the middle of August.

The law requires that children in the schools be given whatever they seem to require for their education, and what Calvin has required, in nearly every instance, is constant attention. The boy exudes that air of gloom that makes one fear that his soul is as misshapen as his body. He's a couple of fractions over six feet ten inches tall, and breathtakingly thick through the hips and legs. His whole form suggests one of those orange traffic cones the Department of Motor Vehicles uses to close off a lane. His eyes are so small that they look like dull, facetless, hazel-colored stones, flat and cold. And, during the summer, in some unconscionable lapse of discipline or sense, his parents or his uncle allowed him to dye his hair a terrible shade of green. It's the hue of the bottom of a very dirty fish tank. And he has it done up in stiff, polished-looking spikes that add another six inches to his height. He could be some kind of pre-historic creature. Calvinosaurus.

As if all this were not enough, there's the matter of his voice: when poor Calvin opens his mouth to speak, what comes out is a squeak more girlish than Betty Boop's, and his small, uneven teeth are something like the algae shade of his hair. He has a terrible overbite, bad, splotched, pocked, too pale, pasty skin, a weak jaw, and a small, unattractively up-turned, large-nostriled, piggy nose.

Mostly, though, it's those hard, dull, pebble-like eyes.

One of the exercises she has devised for her own sense of the per-sonalities behind the facades of ignorant savagery in the room is to have them think about themselves metaphorically: she writes on the board, "People think I'm . . ." and "But really I'm . . ." and tells them to fill in the answers. Because the exercise is fairly simple and short, she breaks them all into groups of four or five and spends some time talk-ing to each group. She joins Calvin Reed's group last. In barely readable scrawl, he has written: "People think I'm a pig. But really I'm a hog." When he reads this aloud in that group, the other three—Jonathan Lawrence and two girls in identical shades of blood-dark lipstick—break into laughter. It's unclear whether they are laughing at the expression or the voice. Calvin looks at them, obviously surprised, and then surly and suspicious; the little squeaky voice comes: "Don't laugh at me." And he reaches across the small space between the desks and grasps Jonathan's throat. The boy's eyes bug out; he immediately turns blue. Elizabeth has to work to get the bigger boy to let go, and when he does, he glowers at her. A familiar look. It all comes back to her, as if for the first time—the whole strain of last year.

"Oh, Calvin, not already," she says.

He folds his arms and hunches down in the seat.

Elizabeth goes on, "Don't do that again." It occurs to her, the memory of a curse, that in a way she's already been forced to put herself among those who have brought this huge, unappealing boy to his present state of social maladjustment. The school year isn't even five minutes old. Quickly, she adds, "And Calvin has shown confidence in us by letting us hear what he wrote. So we're going to respect that. Right?"

Jonathan presses his hands to his throat, staring with terror at Calvin. The others have gained some control, because of the threat Calvin now poses, sitting there with his scowling, doughy, mottled face. They've put their collusion into hiding, exchanging frightened looks, and putting their hands over their mouths.

"Let's just do the assignment," Elizabeth says.

Calvin turns his attention to the paper on which he has expressed the terms of his self-loathing. Elizabeth takes him aside.

"Do you understand the exercise?" she asks him.

"Yes," he squeaks. "They can't laugh at me."

"Maybe they think you meant it as a joke."

He stares. Those little eyes. It's hard not to turn away from him. She holds what he's written toward him and says, "Is this what you really feel?"

He looks at her. "Huh?"

"It isn't a trick question, Calvin. I really want to know. This exercise makes it so I can be a better teacher."

He simply gapes at what he has written. "I get it—the exercise."

"I'm talking about what you said."

"I said I get it."

"I mean, what you wrote."

He looks at it again.

"Calvin?"

He shrugs. "I don't know. I don't like it."

"I'm not trying to give you a hard time," she says to him. "Why don't you try the exercise again."

He looks at the paper, picks up one corner of it, as though it is something under which he might find a worm or an insect.

"What do you think?"

He takes the pencil and holds it and seems to concentrate, and she rises, thinking to move on to one of the other groups, but then pauses, because he has begun to write, and she's curious. He writes: People think I'm a jerk. But really I'm a pig.

"No," she says. "You don't think that."

And she's suddenly seized by a feeling of such exasperation that she nearly gasps. It comes to her that she lacks the energy for even one day of trying to penetrate the leaden exterior of distrust and unawareness in which this lumbering boy is encased. She has the rest of the day to get through, the rest of the year. All the other fragmented or incomplete personalities await her attention. She says, "Try again. No pigs or jerks or hogs this time." And she moves off, to Jonathan, who's staring at Calvin with a kind of astonishment.

"Are you going to be all right?" she asks Jonathan.

"Indubitably," he says.

She waits a moment while he writes. "People think I'm shy, but really I'm gregarious and outgoing. When I enter a room, I'm always looking for a friend. I live with my mother and little sister, and grandfather and he's going to teach me how to play guitar. The terpsichorean muse interests me greatly." Elizabeth thinks of reading this about the terpsichorean muse to Will. The boy pauses, one hand going lightly to his throat again. He's ruddy and freckled around the eyes, which are dark blue and rather sad. "Some people think I'm a bit stand-offish but it's really that I'm reserved. I like conversing with others. I like to draw. Cliffs and rocks and buildings pique my interest."

She visits the other groups, and then has to take a few minutes resolving one more tussle: Calvin Reed and another boy, over something that the other boy said about basketball. Calvin, she remembers, is sensitive about his height. The other boy brandishes a cuticle knife. It's about to be a knife fight. She writes referrals for them both to the present assistant principal, Mr. Petit, who will, of course, do little—beyond an hour or two in the STOP room and the confiscation of the makeshift weapon. Mr. Petit's failing is that while he's an excellent teacher of math and a gentle, accepting soul, he is also far too lenient.

She sends the two boys off to him, and then returns to Jonathan, who's tapping the end of his pencil against his front teeth, staring out the window.

"You're through with the assignment?"

"Indubitably."

"That's a yes?"

He looks at her. There's now something caught-out in his expression. She has embarrassed him about his choice of words.

"Write me something else," she says to him. "Just for the fun of it."

By one o'clock, when James The-Savior-of-Humankind (one of her secret pet names for him) comes with his cart and his neatly stacked lessons and mimeographed sheets, she's gotten into the flow of things. Though there's something nagging at her in the back of her mind, a sense of something crowding her. She knows perfectly well what it is, of course, and she tries to put the Crazies away from her thoughts. Mr. J. Christ (another of her pet names for him) approaches, and she has the thought that he is indeed a dour, gloomy man, without a trace of humor or lightheartedness anywhere in his countenance, and it isn't just his last name. She has seen him in restaurants in the town, with the same stern, mirthless, stonily miserable expression, chewing on a sandwich or swallowing spoonfuls of soup. Sometimes she sees him in the cafeteria during lunch, eating something whitish—chicken salad? tuna fish? coleslaw? potato salad?—out of a Tupperware container. He's deeply secular—in what seems to Elizabeth to be a nearly fanatical and studied reverse of what anyone might expect from someone with his name.

"I'm not staying through the semester," he tells her. This is something he has talked about so frequently over the last couple of years that she almost fails to hear it. "I've got another job lined up. They'll have to get somebody else."

"It's the beginning of the year, J.C."

"I'm getting another job. I just applied at the Census Bureau. The government. Better benefits and better pay. I'm gone. You'll see. And I've told you not to call me that."

"Well, and I've told you I don't want to hear any more about your frustrations on the job."

She stands there, waiting for him to respond to this if he wishes to.

But he folds his arms and turns slightly, facing the door. Students are filing in, chattering, pushing and shoving one another, throwing pieces of balled-up paper and straws from the cafeteria. Elizabeth raises her voice in the usual manner, calling for everyone to settle down, feeling the sameness of it, and realizing that, whereas she had once felt this very sameness as a kind of refuge or respite in the middle of the various crises that were always arising, now even the crises have achieved a sameness. It's discouraging, but, for some reason also weirdly exhilarating, as if something in her expectations has been vindicated and the vindication is satisfying. She looks at James Christ, whose class in mathematics this is, and decides to let him control the disorder erupting through the door.

"I don't even like math anymore sometimes," Christ says. He's very thin and has trouble keeping weight on. He has told Elizabeth he has a condition that makes it hard for him to digest anything. He's always having to run to the bathroom. Nervous lower abdomen, he calls it. There's often the faintest redolence of stomach acid about him, like the fumes of colic in an infant.

Elizabeth wonders why he wouldn't simply change the spelling of his name, take the *h* out of it. There's something obstinate about it, as if he secretly likes the circumstance and only complains about it to draw attention to it and to himself.

Christ goes on: "Will you miss me when I go?" This is another familiar tack. He asks her this nearly every day. It would be like a running joke between them if he didn't ask it in complete earnestness.

"We'll all miss you," she tells him. This is what she always tells him. Then she goes on to say, "But you're not leaving yet, right?"

"Soon," he says portentously. He'll be here ten years from now. Twenty. Forty. He'll never change a thing, because he enjoys his misery. His days are spent in the delectation of his status as a victim. He'll avidly tell you that when he was a child, he was abused. It's hampered him, he'll say, his whole life. Crippled him. Lazy parents. Bad priests, sexual pillage, bungling school authorities, the cruelty of other students. The full gamut of offenders. Especially, of course, the parents and the priests. It's all one story of his walking sorrows, and she has grown progressively more annoyed by it every time he brings it up.

But, then, a lot of what she has to do in a day annoys her now.

She thinks of Will, sitting in the peace and quiet of the bookstore, tending to the accounts, talking to the customers who come by, some of whom are there simply to visit with him. He has his life arranged quite well.

When they were first married, the arrangements—her teaching, his tending the bookstore—seemed natural; it was the way things were in the first place and there seemed to be no reason to change anything. Now she has to work to dispel the sense of being depleted by it all. It's the Crazies, she knows. But she feels that there's a kind of leveling going on in her heart.

It's become difficult not to see Will as someone who's simply drifting, not really doing much of anything except coasting through the days in that little store. Because she's always having to evaluate students, she finds herself evaluating him—and it has occurred to her that he lacks ambition or very much in the way of initiative. He's oddly passive with her, malleable and sweet, but also rather lackluster and stolid. Nothing seems particularly to engage him, as if he has reached some plateau in himself and wishes not to move from it, not to make waves or disturb the calm. Conflict or confrontation of any kind always distresses him; he'll do anything to avoid a scene. At night, she's been visited by a recurring dream that the first Elizabeth returns and wishes to claim her rightful place at the table. That is the phrase the other woman uses in the dream. And, in the dream, rightful place seems quite logical and just.

A moment later, like a stirring of the world to teach her about the connectedness of everything, her cell phone vibrates. It's Will. She presses the little button and says, "I can't really talk now."

"Just wondering how your day's going."

"Fine," she says, though she doesn't really feel fine at all.

LONG DIVISION

I.

In the first week of October, Oliver meets with the old ladies about their plans for the house. He drives over there in the truck, in a rainstorm. For a time, he has to wait outside, while the two ladies gesture at him from the house. Fiona starts toward him with an umbrella, but a gust of wind blows it backward, after nearly pulling her with it across the drenched lawn. She hurries back inside, having dropped the umbrella on the sidewalk. The rain comes down in sheets. Oliver takes a section of the day's newspaper and sits, reading it for a minute, then, holding it over his head, hurries to the doorway and in. They bustle around him, offering a towel and wiping up the water that spills from him where he stands in the foyer. He accepts their ministrations, noting with a little shock that the broken glass still lies in its area of dust in the dining room. It seems to him that they've forgotten it altogether.

They give him a deposit check for materials, in the amount of nine thousand dollars. They've drawn up detailed plans—Holly has experience with this sort of thing, having worked for a time with an architectural firm, just out of high school. There has been a rather lengthy discussion between the two women about whose side would get more windows. The argument is not what you'd expect: each wants to give what would be the side with more windows to the other. Their disagreement is the result of attempted sacrifice. Fiona says she'll offer it up to Jesus, living in the part of the divided house that has one less window. Oliver stares for a moment, wondering if she can be serious.

"You'll give it to me in expiation for your sins," Holly says to her.

"I'd hoped not to find myself belittled for it," says Fiona, with a wounded expression.

"I want you to have it purely because I want you to have it," Holly tells her. "So that's the end of it. I thought we'd settled this before Mr. Ward got here."

"I'd like to revisit it," says Fiona.

"No," Oliver breaks forth. "Please, ladies."

And they look at him as if he has just uttered an oath, or emitted some impolite sound.

"Can I show you what I've got?" he asks gently as he can. It's as if he's talking to Jonathan and Kalie. He thinks about this, and then goes on in the same tone: "I've got some very good things to show you."

"Well," Fiona says to her niece. "All right, then."

"Now, the biggest problem," Oliver says, sitting on their sofa and opening his plans, "is going to be the kitchen."

"One of us will have to have a whole new kitchen," says Holly.

"You take it," Fiona says. "If I'm getting the extra window you should get the brand-spanking-new kitchen with all the best newfangled appliances and conveniences."

Oliver listens to them argue about that. He sits there looking from one to the other. It's actually fascinating—the ways in which they communicate through their indirection and denial what they really feel. "No," Fiona tells Holly, "I wouldn't think of it. You take the kitchen and the extra window."

And Holly shakes her head. "Nonsense. I don't need the window or the kitchen. We decided on the window. You get that. You take the kitchen too. You like to cook more than I do."

"Now that's a complete mystery—that you could think I like to cook more than you do. I'm not half the cook you are."

It goes on while Oliver waits for some semblance of agreement to fall upon them. It's indeed almost as if agreement would be like a form of natural fate, something neither of them expects.

They agree finally to wait until Oliver has drawn up more specific plans for the kitchen—they want him to suggest what might be best for it. Holly says she'll spare no expense to have the best of everything for Fiona's kitchen. Fiona grapples with this, harrumphing and seeming to falter, shaking her head, but she says nothing. The two women are willing to let the thing go for a while. Oliver has a rush of gratitude about this that surprises him, and he thinks about the effect these two odd old ladies can have upon him. Between the two of them, he rather likes Holly—there's a fluidity to her motions that is complemented by her speech and by the alto music of her voice; the liveliness of her expressed thoughts has impressed him. He likes Fiona's bluntness, but—he admits it to himself—he also fears her. There's always the urge to take a step back when she starts to talk. Some of this is the result of the way she approaches anything: with a suddenness, a forward tilt, as if she means to walk into whomever she's addressing—no, as if she means to collide with him. And her speech is so weirdly abrupt, as if she was born without the organs of reserve or anything like a sense of the boundaries that normally exist between people.

After the question of the kitchen has been settled, they sit down to sandwiches Holly made, in the kitchen that she says she's quite used to and doesn't mind keeping, and Fiona opens a bottle of burgundy. They all have a glass. Fiona looks at Oliver as she sips hers and says, "You must get tired of explaining that you're not saying no to everything all the time."

"I'm used to it," he tells her, then uses this invasion of his old trouble to brazen out pouring himself another glass of the wine. It's very fruity and thick-feeling on his tongue, and he doesn't like it much, but the effect of it is pleasant. It's been a long, uncomfortable, rainy morning, and he decides that he has earned a little liquid refreshment. He thinks of Alison, who must work an afternoon shift, into the night hours. He's supposed to watch Kalie today while Jonathan is at school. Alison won't be home until midnight.

"The thing that amazes me," Holly's saying, "is that they kept going even when they knew it was a lost cause."

Oliver has lost the subject. He looks at Fiona, who seems still to be watching his head. It makes him uncomfortable, which, of course, makes the tic even worse. "What were we talking about?" he says.

"The war," says Holly.

"The Gulf War?" he asks.

"No," Holly says. "Yours."

"Oh." For a moment, he can't say anything. "Actually, you know—it wasn't my war."

Fiona laughs. "Have some more of this wine."

"Don't mind if I will," he says.

They laugh about his odd phrase, and then, out of nowhere, Fiona introduces the subject of Brother Fire. She's worried about him. Something's eating at him. She's never seen him so sad and distracted. And why doesn't anyone notice it? Why is it always left to Fiona to perceive these things that are happening right under everyone's nose?

"I noticed it, too," Holly says. "And furthermore, he's talked with me about it. Because I'm not religious, like other people he knows, I can talk to him on a level he's more at ease with."

"He talks to me, too," Fiona says and then quickly adds, "but he's more relaxed, I'm sure, with people he doesn't have to be a priest for."

"Do you mean moral cripples?" Holly asks.

Oliver has the disconcerting thought that this is a reference to an earlier conflict, about to be revisited. He'd like more wine, but he doesn't want involvement in another argument between these two. He stands so suddenly that he almost has to sit down again. "Ladies, I really have to leave, I'm afraid."

"We'll look forward to finalizing everything," Holly says in the same instant that Fiona says, "Why don't you stay and help us finish this wine?"

He pretends not to have heard Fiona. As he takes his leave, feeling the wine, a pleasant yielding heaviness behind his eyes, he again notes the broken glass on the dining-room floor. He almost asks if it's all right for him to clean it up. But then he rejects the thought. He goes out into

the lessening rain, hurrying, and climbs into the truck. He has five minutes to get home, so Alison can leave for her shift, and he's ten minutes
away. If he makes up for it by speeding, he might get pulled over by one
of her colleagues, and certainly the Breathalyzer test will show that he's
had more to drink than he should have. Well, in fact, he *has* had more to
drink than he should have. That's the simple truth. And he is speeding.
That, also, is true. "God damn," Oliver says. "I wish I had one goddamn
ounce of self-control sometimes."

2.

Brother Fire has taken to reading in *The Summa Theologica* again, after all
these years. Something in him feels drawn to the spirit of this youthful
enthusiasm of his—and it is indeed enthusiasm that he feels, wandering in its genial provinces once more. Such fun. An aspect of his earliest
training tells him that the spiritual quest is not supposed to be so much
fun. And what about that? Surely Aquinas must have found tremendous
enjoyment, great delight, high spirits, jolly hours, in exercising his powers of mind, his gift for phrasing, for the ladders of meaning in words,
the subtle shadings of thought that come from merely rattling the language and letting it run with one's perceptions until the surprises are
complete. Nothing like it. Brother Fire has experienced this very thing,
working out the simple progression of ideas in his weekly homily, and
he knows something of the sublime pleasures of writing. He asks himself, what is it about the spiritual life that precludes enjoyment—plain,
human, earthly gladness of one's own gifts? Aren't the gifts from God?
And isn't it blessed to make a joyful noise? And why does the joyful
noise have to be shepherd-simple? Why couldn't the *Summa Theologica*
itself be taken as a vast joyful noise? *Fun?*

He's thinking these things, sitting in a chair with the book, when
Father McFadden walks in from the soaked afternoon, carrying a bag of
football helmets. He's tired but undaunted, braving his own darknesses
to seem lighthearted. Brother Fire cannot find in himself the words or
the gestures, or the prayerful thoughts, to express for himself the blaze

of admiration that surges in him at the sight of the other priest with his sharp, hawklike face, those black brows forming a single shelf across the bridge of his nose, the brown eyes set back in deep, narrow sockets.

Courage is so rife in the world, and it is mostly invisible, unappreciated as the miracle of a sunrise.

Father McFadden puts the bag of helmets down with a clatter, next to the umbrella stand. He turns and gives forth a sigh of weary relief. "I found them at a flea market. I had to act. I think we should have a football team in the CYO league."

"But it's October," Brother Fire says. "Hasn't the season started?"

"I think there's still a window—if we get started right away."

"Isn't it just a matter of announcing in the Sunday bulletin that we want to put together a team? Say, boys from twelve to sixteen? Something like that? Seems to me that was how it worked when I was at Saint Catherine's, in the city."

"Yes," Father McFadden says. "But that's the city." He holds one hand up, almost as if to shush the older priest. "I've got something else outside."

Brother Fire watches him go out, then closes the book with a mild sense of loss.

The other priest returns, carrying a bag of shoulder pads and another full of pants. He also has a football and still another bag, in which there are shoes with cleats.

"You've certainly got all you need for everything, there, Father."

"Well, uniforms. And a name."

"We can ask for those things from our parishioners, I'd expect."

"I was thinking, how about The Confessions?"

"I don't think so," says Brother Fire.

"Guess not."

"How much did this cost?"

"Only twenty-eight dollars. I got it all for one price."

"And where was this?"

"Oh, by the way, Father, a Mr. Petit called while you were gone this morning. He left a number."

Brother Fire waits for the young priest to find the piece of paper with the number on it. When, finally, he produces it, his embarrassment is so acute that he hiccups. Poor Father McFadden often has this gastric tic, brought on by nerves—by worries as well as excitements: that is, he's as inclined to hiccups in response to happiness as he is inclined to them in reaction to trouble.

"He left the number but then said you shouldn't call him."

"I don't understand."

"Neither do I."

Climbing the stairs to make the call anyway, Brother Fire has a moment of realizing how pleasurable it was reading Aquinas's book, how for those moments he forgot his own increasing sense of having come upon some trouble for which he is ill equipped.

There isn't any answer when he tries to call.

3.

Several days after his midday-wine visit with the two old ladies, and one day after a night spent sleeping in the truck with too much to drink, Oliver wakes from a late-morning nap with a dull headache and an increase in the tic in his neck. He finds Kalie sitting on the floor in front of the television, watching a large Slavic woman do exercises. He recognizes the sound of the language and, for a moment, wonders if he isn't dreaming it all. Alison's off today. He recalls waking earlier and fearing that he was alone in the house, wondering where she and Kalie might've gone, and then Kalie came in from the bedroom, carrying one of her rag dolls. He thought of rising, and then dreamed he had risen, and now here he is, awake again, listening to a heavy female voice count in the language, trying to lessen the shaking back and forth of his head. Kalie has happened on some cable channel and is watching this, hands clasping her small knees, fascinated.

Alison is probably downstairs, working on the laundry, in the basement that Oliver finished after many delays, when his Mary was alive.

He reaches over, picks up his guitar, and plays a few notes that he always plays for Kalie when he wants her to come to him—a little bluesy riff with which he used to play her to sleep when she was younger.

Then, he played it slowly. Since then, he's added a little to it and made the tempo more sprightly, and she loves it. She turns and looks at him with the glazed eyes of having been engrossed in the television, and then comes to her feet and strides, smiling, over to him. He puts the guitar down and brings her up on his lap.

They remain like that for a time, without speaking.

"Where's your mother?" he asks.

"Basement."

It's a good sign, to get even this from her. He has treated her reticence as if it's normal, and he talks to her as if she'll answer him, and sometimes she surprises him. "I've gotta go visit my new lady friends in a little while."

She just nods, toying with the buttons of her dress, looking down. She's almost weightless in his lap. He can't believe the lightness of her little body.

The lack of progress on plans for partitioning the house on Temporary Road has been a source of anxiety—the ladies have new complications all the time. Recently, over the telephone, Holly proposed that he build another floor, an addition. And he looked at the expense, the necessary equipment, the buttressing and reframing that it would require, and how long it would take to do it. He drew up some alternate plans, and, of course, Holly decided to drop the idea, because she and her aunt couldn't agree on who would have to climb stairs each day. Last night, he went to the Mexican restaurant and had too much tequila, and slept in the cab of the truck. One of Alison's colleagues woke him and was kind enough not to take him in. He did the little walk, the Breathalyzer. It had been long enough; the alcohol had worn off. He drove home, shivering, hungover, and full of regret.

Now, he brings Kalie to his chest and squeezes her. "What're you watching there, little girl?"

She shrugs, not looking at him.

He breathes the sweet shampoo-fragrance of her hair, the strands of which are silky and soft, dark blond, and so perfect they cause a turning in his soul. The long night he spent in the truck is laced across his back, a reminder, an accusation. He feels the ghost pressure of the door handle in his side. It seems to him that he's not a man this little girl can benefit from knowing. He rocks her gently and then when she decides she wants down, he lets go. It seems to him that so much of family life is fraught with the sorrow of parting, and that love is rounded with grief, like something lying in the folds of a blanket. Love and sorrow, mingled in all the tender moments. Mary knew that. Well, no time to think these somber thoughts. He has to get going now. There's so much to do, keeping afloat. He moves to the top of the basement stairs, those curves and angles of wall that he built himself, after all the stops and starts, though it no longer feels quite like his. It is part of the country of his failures. He comes to the first step. "Alison?" he calls. "I've got to go."

She calls something back that he can't hear, so he waits, and here she is, hurrying up the stairs. "Can we come with you?"

"I don't know how long I'll need to be," Oliver says. But she looks so sorry to hear this that he goes on: "If you don't mind waiting around. I'd love to have you along."

They have accompanied him a couple of times. The ladies entertain Kalie, and Alison likes being away from the house now that Marge is gone. Marge has only called twice, and both times she seemed oddly distracted, not wanting really to talk. Absorbed in her new life far away, and Alison fully expected it, and it still wounds her each time.

They get into the truck, taking a little trouble to get Kalie safely in the seat belt in the middle. And Oliver drives over to Temporary Road. It's a sunny, hot, breezy, pretty day. Kalie sits staring out, and seems calm, not terribly unhappy. She appears to like the going-by of the houses on either side of them.

They pull onto Temporary Road, and Oliver sees that Fiona's making her way along the sidewalk with a wagon full of what looks like packages of food. He slows and says out the window, "Need a ride?"

"Where would I go—in the bed of that thing?"

"I can take your groceries."

"She wouldn't let me drive my own car. Wouldn't say where the keys are. And I wouldn't ask."

Oliver pulls over to the curb, stops, and gets out. "Here," he says. He picks the wagon up and puts it in the truck bed.

"I had to buy the wagon," she tells him. "Imagine that. Walk down to the strip mall, buy the wagon, fill it with groceries and haul it home."

She huffs at the thought, then looks in at Alison and Kalie. "You both look tired. You tired?"

"We're fine," Alison says.

"My niece is batty," says Fiona. Then she turns and marches on toward the house, only a few yards away. She crosses the lawn as Oliver pulls up to the curb and gets out again.

Inside, they find Holly sitting on the sofa, reading a book, Benjamin Thomas's biography of Abraham Lincoln. Fiona says, "I bought a wagon. Hah!" Then she strides into the kitchen, followed by Oliver, who can't help but mark again the fact that the broken glass still lies in its area of dust under the side table in the dining room. He thinks of archeological digs. What would some future anthropologist make of this array of broken glass under a wooden table in what these ancient Americans called a dining room?

Holly says she wants to revisit the idea of building onto the existing structure, though it would cost twice the original amount of money and necessitate the hiring of subcontractors. Kalie stands between Alison's legs and sucks her thumb, swaying slightly and staring at Holly. Oliver unfolds his latest plans, experiencing the full fury of his hangover and trying to tamp down the conviction that there's something wrong with taking these ladies' money.

Fiona has gone into the kitchen. Holly calls for her to come back into the room. "You should be in on this," she says. "We're talking about the house."

"You decide everything," says Fiona from the kitchen. "I'm tired of wrangling about it. I'm making something here."

So, it's Holly who settles finally on the partition and agrees to a start date for the work. She says, "Done." Then: "Decided."

A drinking glass rolls with a little rumbling sound across the space of the wood floor, from the entrance to the kitchen into the dining room. It comes to rest against a shard of the broken one. For an extended, embarrassed moment, no one says anything.

Holly rolls her finger in the air around her ear, but, when she speaks, her voice is full of honey and pleasantness. "You dropped something, sweetheart."

"Don't anybody even think of leaving," Fiona says sweetly. "I've poured iced tea and fixed some snacks."

So they stay and partake of the cheeses and different crackers that Fiona has arranged on a big platter, and they drink iced tea. The two old ladies talk in loving tones about how sweet life will be when there's a wall between them. They don't put it that way, but Oliver knows the subtext. How fine it will be, Fiona says, to get up when she wants to without worrying about waking anyone or disturbing anyone. How pleasant to fix her own breakfast her way, whenever she likes. Yes, Holly says, and how good she'll feel knowing that she can leave the television on into the early-morning hours, for the sound of it, while she reads in bed. She has always loved reading in bed, and that has been denied her of late, since the light keeps others awake. Fiona says she'll sleep so peacefully in her dark bedroom. It goes on like that for a time, and then Alison asks, "Will you have different phone numbers?"

No one seems to have the answer.

But then Holly says, "Well, of course."

"That might be hard to arrange," Oliver says. "At least where payment of the bill is concerned."

"You take the phone," says Fiona. "You talk on it more anyway."

"No, you," Holly says, but with an edge of sarcasm. Then: "I think we'll find a way to put two phone lines in."

"I was talking about the bill," Oliver puts in.

"Oh, well, I pay the bills."

Holly's son, Will Butterfield, comes to the house with some home-improvement books that Holly asked for. Oliver recognizes him immediately, with his shambling walk, and he remembers the roses, the pretty wife making out the check. He notices that Butterfield doesn't seem to recall meeting him. The two men shake hands, and Oliver is about to move to one side when Butterfield pats his shoulder and says, "I'm so damn glad you got the call that day." It makes Oliver smile. And over the next few seconds, he watches the way the younger man frowns as the two old ladies speak about their project, and as Fiona begins talking about Elizabeth, who hasn't come to visit in weeks.

"School's started," Will Butterfield says. "You know how that is."

"She seems tense every time I see her now."

"She reacts that way to fall," says Will. "The change of seasons."

Butterfield obviously wants to say more—it's in the vague restiveness of his stance, the way his hands move to his face and down the front of his white shirt.

"My Jonathan is in her English class," Alison says to the room. "He loves her."

"Well," says Fiona. "She has a headache every time I see her."

"You noticed that, did you?" Butterfield says.

"Amazing," Holly says. "Fiona noticed something. Isn't it amazing?"

Oliver looks across at Alison, who busies herself with Kalie, making no eye contact with anyone else. "We ought to go," he says, understanding his daughter's fretfulness.

Butterfield says, "You all don't have to leave on my account."

"Well," says Oliver. "Kalie needs her nap." They shake hands again. He covers Butterfield's hand with his left, wanting to express his liking for the other man. "I gave the rose to Alison," he says.

Butterfield seems momentarily at a loss, but then he remembers. "Oh, good," he says. "That's great."

"Thanks again," Oliver tells him. Then he and Alison and Kalie make their way to the truck and climb in. Abruptly, when he sees the weary, sweat-shining countenance of his granddaughter, it seems to him that this going back and forth in a pickup truck is actually a kind of indignity he's put upon them. Something they endure because they want to be with him. "Are you all right?" he says to Alison.

"Sure," she says, arranging herself, buckling in. "Why?"

HALF A STOLEN CAR

I.

Toward the end of October, Gail calls to say that she's uncovered a strong lead as to the whereabouts of her mother. She's pretty sure her mother lives in Newark, New Jersey. The woman she has been working with at the agency has been very helpful. She has managed to gain access to the missing woman's credit history. It's not good. There have been several judgments, which is fortunate, since they contain contact information, year by year. There's one from Portland, Oregon, another from Santa Cruz, California. One more from Milwaukee, Wisconsin. The trail disappears after this for several years. But this new lead is a strong one: a woman who worked with Elizabeth for a time wrote to say that she's pretty sure Elizabeth moved to Newark last year with a boyfriend.

Butterfield listens to all this in silence, and when Gail pauses and waits for him to speak, he keeps silent.

"Well?" Gail says.

"Amazing," he says.

"I told you I'd find her."

"No, it's amazing that you called me with this, Gail. Are you on something?"

"What?"

"Are you taking something?"

"Yes. Prozac, if you must know."

"What're the side effects? Does it take away your sensitivity to the feelings of others? Don't call me with this shit. Okay? Is that clear enough? Don't call me with anything like it again." He starts to say more but then realizes that she has broken the connection.

That evening, he mentions the call to Elizabeth, who, an hour later, develops a migraine. There's a slow rain outside, leaves dropping heavily from the wet trees. She tells Butterfield that it's just the weather. He doesn't believe her. "I wish we could go somewhere for a few days," she says. And then she covers her eyes. He determines to settle Gail once and for all about this business of finding her biological mother.

But there's also the Crazies. The work on their house has commenced now, and they've already run into unexpected costs. They enlisted Butterfield to accompany them to the bank, where Fiona frightened a poor teller into calling his superior over. The superior hashed it all out and, because the ladies have capital and Fiona has a trust fund she has never used, they get the money they need. Elizabeth knows this means that he'll be kept busy with these worries, along with the inevitable disputes. "Oh, God," she says. "I can see it now. One blind headache after another for three months."

He rubs the muscles of her upper back and shoulders, and then goes into the kitchen and fixes her a bowl of soup. But the headache has made her nauseous, and she can't eat. Nor can she read her student work. She can't lie still, and, finally, the headache won't let her do anything else. He pads back and forth in bare feet, shirtless, bringing her water and heavy doses of aspirin, feeling elderly and halting, dull. Maybe they should think about having a child. The thought discourages him in some elemental way, at the blood level, and he supposes it has to do with his specific history: the first Elizabeth leaving that way. Mother of his children. Even now, after all these years, the strangeness of it can surge through him like a spell. He doesn't want to go back there.

He avoids looking at his own reflection in the mirror when he crosses the living room. Toward dark, the phone rings. He decides not to answer it. Elizabeth has fallen asleep on the couch, a cold washcloth folded across her forehead. The phone stops, then starts again. She stirs, moans softly, and sighs. He decides to go ahead and pick it up before one of the Crazies appears on his doorstep. The voice on the other end is female, familiar, dimly impatient and weary. It takes him a moment, even as she explains it to him, to realize that this is Oliver Ward's daughter. Quite quickly, he understands that she's calling in an official capacity. "Yes?" he says. "Alison. Yes—what is it?" Something tips over under his heart. She clears her throat and explains, in that drained voice, that she's been on the phone with Holly for the last twenty minutes, trying to convince her that there is no provision in the law of any land, no practical way provided for in the statutes of one civilized society anywhere—not to mention the Third World—for a person to report half a stolen car. There is no workable concept of a car being stealable by halves, or divided in such a way as to make it possible for one to report it as such. "I know they're dividing the house," she says. "But this. It isn't doable, not even in the case of somebody with Holly's strength of personality, and not even for the sake of friendship. No one can steal half a car, and therefore—I'm sorry, I don't mean to sound official—no one can report such a thing. I like your mother, Mr. Butterfield. I do. Or I would've told her to call whoever the car is registered to. Well—and exactly who is it registered to, if you don't mind my asking?"

"They were coming over from England and I put the money down for them."

"You're saying it's registered in your name, then."

"I guess so, yes." It's an admission he feels is painful enough.

"Well, your mother assures me that Fiona is at least sober."

"But she's somewhere out there in the car. They share the car. They both drive it."

"So Fiona took the car and Holly wants to report her half of it as stolen."

"That must be it."

He's glad, for the moment, even in his embarrassment, that it's Alison Holly spoke to. Because, to Alison's colleagues, his mother and great-aunt are characters, comic figures. "I think that Fiona, if she's in one of her snits, is a danger in that car or any car and for all I know her license has expired."

"Do you think we should bring her in, then?"

Butterfield waits a beat. Elizabeth stirs on the couch, moans low; she's suffering the migraine even in her sleep, dreaming pain. It's in her features, and in the way she turns, face into the cushions, trying to shut out sound and light. "No," he says. "No, I'll settle it. Or they will. I'm sorry they bothered you."

"Oh," Alison says. "It's no bother at all, really. Slow night here, you know."

He can't help saying, "Must be pretty funny down there."

"I know it's no picnic for you and your wife." The kindness in her voice unnerves him. He feels chastised by default.

"I'll get to the bottom of it," he tells her and is aware of the words' other meaning—the bottom indeed. And where would the bottom of his troubles with the Crazies be?

"Do you have an idea where she might go?"

"She probably just went to a movie," Butterfield says. "She's done that before." He doesn't go on to say that back in April, in one of her tantrums, she went to a bar and grill called Macbeth's, got stinking, and talked an out-of-work furniture salesman into driving her home in her car. The salesman, it turned out, was as impaired as she was, and he drove off the road, through a thick hedge. The car vaulted a small hill, taking to the air like a rocket, and landed upside-down nine feet off the ground, wedged in the forking trunk of a very large old oak tree, with sprigs of the hedge trailing from it like green flags. Fiona and her new transient friend were found an hour later peacefully asleep upside-down in their seat belts, suspended, happily secure, and, no doubt, half-consciously enjoying the sense of weightlessness. The driver who found them thought they must be dead. And, although the car required new door panels on both sides and it took two road crews and most of a night to get it extricated from the tree, neither of them had received a scratch.

"She might've just wanted to drive around," Butterfield says now to Alison, and he hears the note of prevarication in his voice. He strives to seem unconcerned. "Or she's already back home. Could've gone out to buy a bottle of wine. She likes wine. Wine is usually her drink of choice."

"Mine, too," says Alison.

Now there seems nothing at all left to say. He wonders if she knows about the tree incident. Certainly there must have been talk about it at the police station—a red Subaru in a tree, nine feet off the ground. He has the sense that if he mentions it, she'll remember it, and then put together the fact that the woman involved was Fiona. "I wish Fiona didn't like it so much," he says.

"Did you say her license has expired?"

"I think I said that for all I *know* it has."

"But you did say you think she's a danger whether or not. If she's in a snit."

"Well, yes."

Silence.

"So where does that leave us?" he asks.

"The car's in your name. That means you probably ought to try locating her. I think I'll put something out on the radio, too."

"You're going to arrest her?"

"Not if she has a license and is obeying the traffic laws and isn't under the influence."

"I wouldn't want to be the one that stops her if she isn't breaking any laws."

"I'll keep that in mind. I'll make certain it's not me."

Butterfield hears the note of concern—after all, the woman's father is working for Fiona.

"Meanwhile, if you need us for anything," Alison goes on, "—well."

"I hope I don't," he says.

"It'll probably be fine," she says.

He thanks her. It's mechanical, and, oddly, rather forlorn. He feels unpleasantly inauthentic, a man striking false notes out of some elemental dishonesty. She tells him again that she knows this is no picnic. When he hangs up, Elizabeth lifts her head and stares at him. "Well?"

"I'll be back," he says. "Fiona took the Subaru."

She buries her face in the cushions. And she doesn't move when, a minute later, he comes past her with the car keys, wearing his running shoes and a T-shirt.

2.

Macbeth's is a stylized English pub in a newer quarter of Point Royal, tucked into a line of upscale shops and antique stores, at the edge of a parking lot far too expansive for the amount of traffic it ever receives. Butterfield has only been in the place a couple of times, but he has driven by it at night, when the few cars outside it are the only ones in the parking lot. As now. The Subaru is there, an invitation to trouble. That's how it strikes him. He parks his own car next to it and sits there for a few minutes, feeling like a policeman on a stakeout. Macbeth's looks closed, even for the group of parked cars. No one arrives, and no one comes out. When he steps out of the car, he hears bagpipes and remembers that on the occasions he visited the place, an enormous, barrel-chested, red-headed man wearing a kilt came out every few minutes, playing the thing, while everyone looked on in the enforced silence the instrument always produced. He waits until the music stops, leaning against the side of the car. The night air is balmy, cool, even pleasant, though it contains the redolence of exhaust and gasoline. There's a filling station at the far end of the street, sending its harsh luster, the pale shape of a chalice, up into the moonless dark. Butterfield looks at the stars.

When he's fairly certain the music has stopped, he makes his way to the entrance of the pub, opens the door, and peers in. It's surprisingly crowded and loud, and the smell of cigarette smoke and beer is strong; he glances back at the clutch of cars, momentarily confused about how that small number could translate into so many people—he has an image of each car arriving packed with riders. Fiona's at the bar, flanked by two young men. She's talking to them, disputing, it seems. Butterfield walks over and puts his hand on her shoulder. She's startled by this and nearly drops her glass—it's whiskey.

"Fiona?" he says. "What're you doing now?"

On the bar next to her wrist is a twenty-dollar bill. She says his name to the two young men, and then recites their names without indicating clearly which is which. They are Abe and Ronny. Butterfield doesn't want to be confrontational. He shakes hands.

"What happened to you and wine?"

No response. She speaks to Ronny or Abe. "My niece's son is here to collect me."

"Buy me a drink?" Butterfield says.

Her gaze is dismissive, yet she holds up one hand to get the bartender's attention. The bartender is a slender, dark-haired woman with deep, black eyes and a full, sensuous mouth that she seems quite aware of; she draws one side of it back in a crooked smile as she approaches. There's something oddly forward and even scheming about it, as though she and Fiona are old friends in on a joke. Her features remind Butterfield of those wiry, tough, fierce-eyed women one sees on TV newscasts. High cheekbones, luxuriantly black brows, long neck, sharp chin. Striking without being quite beautiful, and so much of a type as to produce a blur. Butterfield steps to the bar and asks her for whatever Fiona's drinking.

The woman nods and pours a malt scotch. "The McCallum," she says, putting the glass down. "It's eight dollars a glass." Her voice is richly sensuous and changes his mind. She does have beauty. This thought comes to him, and he examines it with a form of puzzlement. What in the world—? Why is he in this state of mind at all, looking in this evaluative way at a woman behind the bar of a place like Macbeth's?

"Here," Fiona says, pushing the twenty toward her.

"Expensive whiskey," Butterfield says.

"Very," says the bartender.

Fiona finishes hers, opens her purse, and brings out another twenty. The beautiful bartender puts five on the counter and starts to turn away.

"Ariana," Fiona says. "One more here."

"Fiona, let's finish our drinks," Butterfield says. "Let's go home. I'll take you home."

"Take a cab," she says. Then she and the two young men go on talking. The subject is hockey. One of the men played in high school. He's from Minnesota. They're also talking about the far north. This turns out to be Ronny, who says he loves Canada and all things Canadian. His favorite hockey team, he says, is the Montreal Maple Leafs. Fiona says, "You ass. It's the Montreal Canadiens. Or Habs, for Habitant. It's Toronto that has the Maple Leafs. How much do you love all things Canadian?"

"I was testing you," Ronny says.

His friend Abe says, "He was lying." And, as Ronny tries to explain how he likes to test people's knowledge by pretending ignorance, Abe keeps repeating, "He's lying. He's lying."

Ronny stops and looks to be fuming a little now, his jaw muscles tightening.

"He likes people to buy him drinks."

"I don't mind," Fiona says.

"I like hockey and all things Canadian and anyone who doesn't believe me ought to watch himself."

"Ronny's creative," Abe says. "Right, Ron?"

It's all rattling in a bar, and Butterfield sips his whiskey, feeling his own migraine coming on. "Fiona," he says. And then has to repeat it, loudly. "Fiona."

"Well, I know you're lying," Fiona says to Ronny. "You're drunk. Can't you hold your liquor?"

Ronny laughs good-naturedly, and then moves off. It turns out that the two young men aren't together at all. They're just the men to whom Fiona was talking.

Now Abe moves off, too, after giving Fiona a kiss on the cheek. Butterfield has a sense—he almost feels it as his own—of the mortification awaiting poor Fiona in the morning, after having spent time arguing in this way among others under the influence. He sips the whiskey and watches as the barkeep named Ariana puts another one down on the bar. Fiona lifts the glass and peers into the amber light of it, then takes a small sip, beginning to mutter something. Butterfield leans in to hear.

"I taught'er to drive a car. Me. Taught'er about boys an' men and books. Like a older sister, an' what do I get. What do I get for th' years when she was hurting and unhappy and the boy was a baby, all th' hard times I went through with'er. Sisters. An' she repays me with dis'r'spect, sarcasm. Sarcasm."

"Fiona, do you want to spend the night with us?"

She ignores him, muttering, cataloging again the slights and ingratitudes she imagines Holly has heaped on her. Years of abuse, she mutters, dark jealousies and failures to appreciate happiness, loyalty, love—all the generosity of heart that Fiona remembers providing over the decades—everything, of course, exaggerated by the overwrought and besotted state she's in. Butterfield knows it will continue until she goes to sleep. The thing is to get her home before this happens. No one seems really to be with anyone here. It's just Butterfield and his greataunt at this end of the bar now. He leans his elbows on it and sips the whiskey and waits for her to pause.

"Fiona," he says. "Fiona?"

At last she stops, whiskey held to her mouth, and regards him. In that instant, the big man with the bagpipes comes from a door on the other side of the room and begins the suspiring whine of the instrument, walking around the room with a swagger and the slightest tipsy hesitation when he turns. Fiona raises one hand as if to wave at him. She turns to Butterfield and seems surprised to find him there. She shouts, "What the hell are you doing here?"

"I came to take you home," he shouts back.

"Not goin' back there until he's finished dividing th'place up."

"Come on, Aunt Fiona. This is childish."

"What'a you know about it? You don't know."

He finishes the whiskey and watches the red-haired man blast away on the bagpipes to the glassy expressions on the faces of the clientele. The onslaught lasts for what seems a terribly long time. At length, the man retreats, with a great amount of leaning and twisting, making adjustments for the bulky instrument he's carrying through the narrow door. After the door closes, the silence is almost solid-feeling to the ears. Aunt Fiona moves down the bar and begins a conversation with the man there—a man closer to her age. She says bluntly that he's wearing the ugliest shirt she ever saw—it *is* rather startlingly loud, with what looks in this light like all the wrong colors—and the man seems entertained.

She asks how much it cost him. He says he doesn't remember. She asks if he has a lot of money to throw away on ugly shirts. He says, "Yes," smiling.

The bartender, Ariana, comes down to Butterfield and leans on the bar across from him. "She's fun," she says about Fiona.

"She's drunk," Butterfield says.

"You want another McCallum?"

He nods. She pours it while he watches. When she sets it in front of him, she says, "Do you come here a lot?"

"Couple times in the last year."

She smiles. "Not a regular."

"No."

"I'm new here." She offers her hand. "Ariana."

Her handshake is firm. When he lets go, she leans on the bar again.

"We're in the process of moving in," she says.

Butterfield nods, sipping the whiskey. She tips her head slightly, regarding him. "That your mom?"

"Great-aunt."

"That's kind of sweet. She live with you?"

He begins telling her about the Crazies. Others come to the bar for refills, and she takes care of it all, returning each time to hear more. She leans close, chin on one hand, staring deeply at him while he talks. It's oddly conspiratorial feeling. Butterfield talks on, not criticizing Holly and Fiona—there's, of course, plenty to say just confining oneself to the history. He has two more whiskeys, and the evening goes on, Fiona ordering hers and having her own conversation with the man at the other end of the bar. The word *Watergate* comes to Butterfield, and he knows she's going on about the present scandal. He tries to tune it out. Twice more, the bagpipe man comes in with his ruckus. Butterfield finds himself glad of it. He watches Ariana and is troubled by the strange light in her black eyes when she talks to him. She says she and her husband have lived in nine different towns and never been quite happy in any of them, that she never watches television, that she grew up in France at the American embassy, that they've rented a house here in Point Royal but she's already restless. "Do you ever get restless?" she asks.

He nods. "Sure." The whiskey has loosened his inhibitions. He's enjoying this.

"Look at me," she says, and he is, and so he has a split second's surprise before she continues: "I'm telling you all this. You're supposed to be telling me all your bad stuff." Her smile has the most candidly conniving sort of expression, as if they have just decided upon a secret place to meet. It makes Butterfield's blood rise. He looks down into the pale whiskey in his glass, wondering if he has imagined everything. She's pouring a refill for the young man, and Butterfield watches her, unable to look away.

Fiona comes unsteadily back down the bar and looks at him. "I'll come home with you. To your house."

"All right," he tells her.

"Stay with you 'til he's finished the work."

He decides not to argue with her now. He knows that, as all the books and pamphlets say, he would only be arguing with the whiskey. He pays the bill, giving Ariana a large tip. He watches her move to the cash register, gazing at her legs and then taking his eyes away. He has never been the type. The whole thing makes him uneasy.

"Take care," she says as he and Fiona move to the door.

Outside, the old woman sings softly, walking along, head-down, apparently no longer aware that she's accompanied. She walks to the Subaru, and then turns. "My purse."

It's on her arm, hanging from her elbow.

"Come on," he says to her, taking hold of her other arm. "Remember? You're coming with me."

She lets him lead her to his car, and then stops, resists. When she speaks, it is unintelligible: "I'm not g'n d'ba."

He opens the door, gets her in and seated. She sighs and begins to mutter again. "Never loved me."

From inside Macbeth's, the bagpipes moan again. From here, it sounds like some sort of calamity. Butterfield walks around the car in the cooling night and gets in behind the wheel. His great-aunt is asleep on the passenger side, her head leaning against the closed window. When he shuts the door, she stirs, looks around. "Where's Holly?"

"Go on back to sleep," he tells her.

"Have t'talk t'Holly."

"We'll go there."

A little later, as he's pulling out of the lot, she says, "If I ask you to stop, will you stop?"

"If you ask me," he says, annoyed with her.

"Will?"

"Go to sleep," he says.

"Please can you stop?"

He pulls to the side of the road, and she sits there for a time. Then she sighs. "Think you can come around here and open the door?"

He gets out and makes his way around the car, realizing that he's probably a little over the line himself now. He opens her door, and barely catches her by the arms. They stagger to the grass, where she sits down in her dress and looks around as if surprised. "Damn," she says. "I thought I was gon' be sick. Not sick. Help me up." He does so, again having to hold her under the arms. Carefully, he drags her back to the car and gets her in and settled again. "Na' sick," she says. "Good."

He drives to his own house, where Elizabeth is waiting, sitting at the window in the living room, holding a wet rag on her forehead and looking worried. She frowns through the glass, watching Butterfield bring the old woman up the walk. The fact that she doesn't get up to open the door is noteworthy. She wants nothing to do with this, what this is: Fiona on the rampage, the Crazies fighting again. He helps his great-aunt inside, and she walks unsteadily over to Elizabeth, badly affecting surprise and gladness to see her. "Well, look'a you. Wait'n up for us, sweetie." She offers a hug, cooing, as if Elizabeth is a very small child. Elizabeth takes the hug and glares over Fiona's narrow shoulder at her husband.

"Where do I sleep?" Fiona asks. "Let's have a li'l drinky-poo."

"I'll take you home," Elizabeth says. "Holly's been calling. She's frantic."

Fiona appears rather stunned for a second, then begins again her low, muttering tirade from the bar.

Elizabeth says to Butterfield, in a brittle voice just this side of song, "Take care of this. I'm not going to stand for this."

"What do you want me to do?" he sings back.

"Fiona," Elizabeth says. "I'm going to take you home now. Holly's waiting up for you."

Butterfield has the old woman by the arms again, because she appears about to keel over. But she's turning, as if looking around for her antagonist.

"Not go'in anywhere I don' want to," she says. "Right, Will?"

Elizabeth looks at her husband. "If you don't do something about this I'm going to scream bloody murder I swear."

"Don't scream," Fiona says. "S'not ladylike. I used to teach in finishing school. Not p'lite to scream. Frowned on. Believe me, I'm certain of it."

"Will," Elizabeth says, sings.

"I had too much to drink," says Fiona. "I'm sorry. Holly's worried." All of this is spoken with a precision that seems like an affectation after the slurring of only a second ago. The speculation arrives in Butterfield's mind: an instant's integrated thought: she has sobered up enough to do this, or she has been affecting the drunkenness in the first place, or has reached some zone of intoxication beyond the normal patterns and come to a kind of full circle. There is no telling with Fiona. She goes limp now, eyes closed, head down, either unconscious or feigning unconsciousness.

Both Butterfield and his wife drag her to the car and work together to get her into it. She lies across the back seat, silent, eyes shut, mouth open, looking almost harmless. Elizabeth points this out.

"Be quiet," Butterfield says. "She'll hear you."

"I don't care if she does."

They both drive the two blocks to the other house and work together to get her up the walk and onto the porch. Holly's standing there, holding the door. She's in a nightgown and slippers, and her hair is pulled up into a knot on the crown of her head. There are combs in the knot, which look like chopsticks. She's wearing her glasses and has a book under her arm. "Where the hell is the car?" she says. "I'm gonna need that car in the morning."

"Elizabeth'll take me to Macbeth's and I'll bring it back," Butterfield tells her.

"Tonight," Holly says definitely. "You poor man."

3.

Neither of them says a word on the way to Macbeth's. Elizabeth drives. The night is clouding over, cold now. The moon seems to be flying among the dark-edged clouds. At Macbeth's, she pulls next to the little red car and stops. The side doors and two front fenders are, in fact, slightly lighter in color than the rest of the car; it shows in this parking-lot light. For a little while, they sit there in the sound of the idling engine. With the first Elizabeth, there were often these moments of a kind of pained waiting for one of them to speak—whenever there was any kind of tension between them, he always sought to find fault with himself, being naturally disinclined to self-justification. Something about the gestures of self-justification put him off, as if the people who had fallen into the habit of it were doomed to repeat other failings—lies and cheating and dullness of mind. Now, he feels something of this, and wishes to put it aside, since it calls up unpleasant memories and is part of what he perceives as his general failure with the first Elizabeth. He says, "Listen. I'm really sorry, you know. But I don't really have much choice here."

She almost moans, "I hate this."

He sighs, gets out of the car, and pauses, feeling the need to say something more, though nothing specific comes to mind. It's all so much like the other times, and he has an image of this wife also driving away and never coming back. She does drive off, of course, tires squealing when she makes the turn out of the lot. He watches until the lights disappear beyond the far row of buildings. She's headed home. He's alone in the quiet, desolate, sensing himself to be less than any of them require—any of the women in his life. All the complications seem like aspects of one overriding problem: himself. And yet he hates such self-absorbed thoughts, and, as if in reaction to this brief indulgence in them, he shivers slightly. The chill in the air contributes to the feeling.

The wind has a bite to it now, is a good ten degrees colder. There's the sound of his shoes on the asphalt, and now he hears again the muffled notes of the bagpipes in Macbeth's, something vaguely less brisk about it, as if the player has reached the end of his endurance. It fades on a bad series of squawks.

He thinks of Ariana and walks to the entrance and in, telling himself that he should probably apologize to her for anything rude Fiona might've said. A part of him is perfectly aware of the rationalization that this inescapably is, but he puts this away as a negative thought. The action of pulling the door toward himself and stepping through it shuts down any hesitation or introspection. She's at the cash register; the bagpipe man is struggling through the entrance of the little side room at that end. The place is almost empty now. Butterfield walks over to the bar and sits down. Ariana sees him, a glance and a smile, going about counting change and then wiping down the surface. He can't help staring. But it's a flirtation, nothing less. He wants more of her, more talk, more watching her movements.

She walks over with a shot of the McCallum. "On the house," she says. "Good to see you again."

"I had to pick up Fiona's car."

"Interesting lady." That smile.

"So you grew up in France?"

"*Oui,*" she says with an ironic little twist of her mouth. "My father worked at the embassy when I was little. He was in what I believe they still call service. You know?"

"You mean—"

She nods. "Butler. Right. I went to a school for the American children. But he left that business. He's got his own business now. Did you ever see the movie *Sabrina*?"

"No."

"They made it twice, too."

"I missed it both times."

"Well, I used to pretend that was me. When I was small and inno-cent."

He sips the whiskey, and she goes to the other side of the bar, where a woman in a gray work shirt waits to pay a bar tab.

The bagpipe man starts out of the little side room, gets caught in the door with his unwieldy instrument, blows a couple of terrible notes, then gives up and goes back in and slams the door.

"He's drunk," Ariana says. "Poor bastard."

"I never liked bagpipes," says Butterfield, finishing his whiskey. She takes the glass and fills it again. He watches her. He can't take his eyes from her. She comes back to where he is. When she remarks that he'll be hungover for work in the morning, he tells her about running the book-store, about being his own boss, and she gazes at him. "I do get up early, though," he says. "My wife teaches school."

"I've done a little of that, too."

"What'd you teach?"

"Everything but science or math." She laughs softly, shaking her head. Then she begins talking about the other places she has lived: Italy, for a year on a scholarship. She was an art history major, and then she was a student of Renaissance literature. She never finished college. She met her husband. This year, she'll turn thirty, and the idea has her thinking about starting over elsewhere.

All of this is offered in that confiding, nearly intimate way. It's thrilling. There's a deep, sensual, melodic something in her voice. He orders a cup of coffee now, to offset the whiskey, which he can feel behind his eyes. She brings it, and then has to be busy again for a time, settling accounts with an older couple and with a man in a FedEx uniform. There are only three other people in the bar now, two men and a woman, all separate, all drinking beer. She comes back to Butterfield and asks, in that confabulatory way, if he likes living so close to mountains.

"I never thought about it," he says. "But I guess I do, yes. It's nice up there."

"We came from Indiana to here," she tells him. "Country flat as a table. And we lived in Mississippi, too. The delta. Renting. That's us.

Same thing. And in Delaware. And Arkansas. The same. Flat, flat, flat. I haven't driven up into these mountains yet but I'm itching to."

He drinks his coffee, staring as she closes down the cappuccino machine and takes the last of the night's tabs. If he stays much longer, they'll be alone. He looks at his watch—it's almost two o'clock in the morning. Abruptly, he feels the need to get away—it's almost the impulse to flee. He puts another twenty on the bar, and she sings at him from the other end, in that rich alto, "On the house, remember?"

"You're sure?"

She doesn't answer. The bagpipe man comes, sans bagpipe, from the side room, takes a seat at the bar and puts his head in his hands. She pours a cup of coffee and sets it before him. Butterfield waves at her and makes his way out. The temperature has dropped considerably now.

He gets into Fiona's perfume-smelling car and then sits there, watching the entrance to Macbeth's. Any minute, she'll come from there and walk over to this car and get in. They'll ride up into the mountains and find a meadow where it's warm, and, under the starlight, they'll answer the call of their blood. He sits there, entertaining this fantasy for a minute or two, and then he catches himself in it and is aghast. Breathing like a runner, he starts the car and drives out of the lot without looking back, willing himself not to look back where, in his mind, the beautiful Ariana comes out the door looking for him. He drives to Holly's. The lights are out, but his mother opens the front door when he comes up on the porch. Behind her are plastic curtains, shards of wallboard, nails, the mess of work on the division of the house. He hands her the keys.

"You want me to take you home now?" she says. "Where the hell have you been?"

"I'll walk."

Holly steps out and, reaching for him, kisses him on the cheek. "Is something the matter? You were gone so long. Elizabeth's worried."

"I had a drink. I wanted to calm down. I'm fine."

"You don't seem fine."

"If you want to ask me about this, I'll tell you. If you want to tell me about it, I have nothing to say."

She kisses him again. "It's okay."

"Been a long night," he manages.

"You know how Fiona is when she does this. She doesn't mean any of it. She'll be so contrite in the morning. And I'll forgive her, I suppose." Without waiting for a response, she murmurs good-night, enters the house, and closes the door. He turns and starts down the walk. The wind is really getting up now. It must be close to freezing. The leaves are flying from the trees, fluttering high in the streetlight.

Elizabeth has gone to bed. The lights are off in the bedroom. He stands in the kitchen and eats a granola bar and drinks a glass of milk. There's a singular kind of aloneness loose in him, a forlorn sense of having failed at something for which he has no name. Elizabeth comes to stand in the doorway. Her eyes are not accustomed to the light and she squints at him.

"Don't be mad at me," he says. "I stayed and had a drink."

"I'm so mad at *them*," she tells him, "I can't tell you."

He drinks the milk. On the wall of the kitchen, there's a woodcut of an Indian on a horse, a gift from his mother. He stares at it.

"I'm not mad at you," Elizabeth says.

4.

Brother Fire lies still in bed, hearing the house settle into the hours of the night and also marking the little creaking sounds made by Father McFadden, who is moving around in his room. The old priest knows that if he makes a sound, Father McFadden will come out and want to talk or show poems. How sweet it would've been if he had remembered to take the Aquinas with him upstairs instead of putting it back into the bookcase in the living room this afternoon. He has had such solace from the pages, turning them, savoring the stately progression of reason. The stairs will protest with his weight on the way down; he'll be discovered. It's failure of a kind, not to give the other man the benefit of the doubt, and there's a guilty sense of having judged him. But Brother Fire can't bear the thought of any more poems, or any more of the other

man's sincere exuberance. It fatigues him, makes him feel vaguely un-
charitable. Father McFadden's very presence these days makes the old
priest feel mean.

Reaching over for his bedside telephone, he dials the number again.
Somewhere in him is the conviction that Mr. Petit's trouble is a window
out of his own lived life. Yet he doesn't feel spiritually dry or dull. He
can still pray, with enough effort. The Lord hasn't abandoned him entirely. It's just that something else has come in, some new element of his
being, some hitherto sleeping gene that has awakened in him and made
him an avid watcher of everything. No matter how hard he prays or tries
to concentrate on the words of his prayers, this element of watching is
always there, always attending to everything with mortal concentration.

"Hello?"

"Mr. Petit. I know you said not to call—"

"Father?"

"Is everything all right?"

"No, Father. It is not all right. Nothing is all right."

"Do you want to talk about it?"

"It didn't help, Father. I thought divine grace was supposed to help.
Nothing helps."

"Pray with me, Son."

"You don't understand, Father."

"Pray with me."

"Who do we pray to?"

"Mr. Petit," the priest begins. But the line clicks. He hears this and
says the name again, waits, and when the dial tone starts, he redials the
number. He does this four or five times in the course of the night. The
line is busy the first few times. When it rings, he has a moment's anticipation, but it goes on ringing.

5.

In the predawn, the Butterfields rise together, simply find that they are both awake and in no need of her alarm. She turns it off, then sighs and stretches. "Morning," she says, as if she's reporting a result. All night they've gone in and out of sleep, and her migraine persisted. He rubbed her shoulders again and talked about Fiona's amazing ability to draw people into arguments with her. Through it all, he felt as if he were lying, since he couldn't think about Fiona or Holly but only about last night's strange minutes with Ariana. Finally, Elizabeth drifted off to sleep—dreaming, he hoped, of a life free of scenes and upsets.

Now the gray beginning of dawn comes through the window, and he says, "Hey."

She says, "Hey, yourself."

He makes coffee while she goes through some student work—a series of essays she has been putting off looking at. At one point, she says, "Oh, listen. This is in response to a question about what they've been reading. Ready?"

"Ready," he says.

She reads: "'I devour books. I'm a bookworm. It's hard to say who I like best but this summer I've been rereading one of my favorite authors, Epscot Fitzgerald.'" They laugh.

"Boy?" he says.

"Girl, this time. Arlene Gutterman. A sweetheart with a roll of baby fat and sad blue watery eyes."

"She'll grow up to be a CEO."

"It's so cute," she says. "And then you think about it and it's sad. She's the one who wrote the book report about Don Quixote and called him Donald all through it because it was a formal paper and she didn't feel it was proper to call him Don. Remember?"

"Oh, yes," Butterfield says. "I've told it around."

"I hate so to embarrass the poor dear again. Maybe I'll lose this one."

"Maybe it'll have a salutary effect," says Butterfield. But he's already left the subject, thinking about Macbeth's, and already wondering how he'll get over there tonight. The realization of this upsets him, and he tries to shake it off. He's standing at the living-room window, and he sees a truck and a small compact car pull up outside the empty house. A man and a woman get out of each, respectively. The sun is on the other side of the street, making shadows out of them. "Looky looky sugar cookie," he says.

She comes to the window and puts her arm around his middle. "Do you think?" she says.

"Somebody finally bought it."

"Should we go out and say something?"

The man and woman appear to be teasing each other, playing. There's something about it that seems rather too personal to be interrupted. For a while, Butterfield and his wife watch them, then decide to let them alone for now. Elizabeth has to get to school, and Will has to open the bookstore. They go out together, and he turns and locks the door. The new neighbors are talking low, jostling one another. "Hey," the man calls to them. "Hello."

"Hello," Elizabeth says and waves.

The woman waves back. Butterfield sees, with a shock, that it's Ariana. She and her husband hesitate for a moment, and then decide to come over and introduce themselves. Everyone shakes hands. As it was last night, Butterfield can't help staring. Ariana's husband is talking. He's Geoffrey Shostakovich, with a *G*, he emphasizes, and no relation to the great Russian composer. Are the Butterfields by any chance aware of the great Russian composer? Yes, Butterfield tells him. Quite so. Mr. Shostakovich goes on to point out that not many people are. He introduces his wife, Ariana Bromberg of the Kentucky Brombergs. Are the Butterfields aware of the Kentucky Brombergs? Well, no, Butterfield tells them. Geoffrey Shostakovich laughs and says that it would be an enormous surprise if they were, since the Kentucky Brombergs are a family of nonpracticing Jews who run a stereo store in Lexington, and no one's ever heard of them, except Geoffrey Shostakovich and his wife. His laughter is faintly forced-feeling, but his face reddens with it and the veins stand out on the side of his neck. The joke is apparently something Mrs. Shostakovich has heard repeated often enough to tire of it and to do a poor job of hiding her displeasure. She shakes her head and apologizes for Geoffrey's stupidity. That's the word she uses, turning to Elizabeth and asking if she might have a glass of water.

They all go into the house. Elizabeth wonders if orange juice would be more to Mrs. Shostakovich's liking.

"No," Ariana says with a definiteness. "I'll have some water. And I go by Bromberg."

"Of the Kentucky Brombergs," Elizabeth says.

"Right." Ariana's black hair is combed so that it frames the sides of her dark face. She wears jeans and a muslin blouse open in front down to the curve of her breasts. Her husband is thick through the neck and jaws, and his eyes appear to bulge slightly; they're a washed-out greenish color, and they give him a look of permanent surprise.

Elizabeth pours the water, and, as Ariana takes it, Butterfield sees the softness of the backs of her hands. "I'm sorry," Elizabeth says. "But we can't really stay. I have to go—I've got a homeroom starting in fifteen minutes."

"You teach?" Ariana asks.

"At the high school, yes."

Geoffrey explains that he's an architect, new with a firm in DC. They've come here from Richmond, Indiana. A one-year lease on the next-door house. They never stay very long anywhere; they're nomads. Ariana has worked several kinds of clerical jobs, and is bartending now.

"Which basically means I'm unemployed in my field," she says. She gives Butterfield a slight smile. The very smile.

He says, "You work at Macbeth's."

She nods. "I didn't know whether to say." When Elizabeth turns to her, smiling, she goes on: "Bartender's confidence. Some men go to bars and their wives think they're working late."

"Not this man," Elizabeth says. "So you were there for his crazy aunt Fiona."

Ariana hesitates. "The old lady did seem a little awry, yes."

"Ariana's done some substitute teaching, too," Geoffrey Shostakovich puts in as if to cover something. "Mostly high school, too."

"An awful job," Ariana says.

"Oh, I like teaching," Elizabeth tells her. "Most of the time, anyway."

"I'm talking about substituting."

"That is hard. But I do like the kids. I really have to go."

Ariana gulps her water down. Her husband moves to the door, and she joins him there. "I bet you teach school, too," he says to Butterfield.

"No," Ariana says, and then stops. For a moment, everyone is at a loss. Ariana goes on. "I think your aunt—I believe she said you have a business?"

Butterfield tells Shostakovich about the bookstore. "Elizabeth's my ride," he goes on. "She drops me off."

"I see that store when I head into work," says Ariana. "It looks so cozy."

"Well."

Now it seems they're all waiting for someone to do something. Perhaps half a minute goes by. At last, Elizabeth steps to where Ariana stands in the doorway, and says, "Gotta go."

"I'm sorry we kept you," Ariana says. "Really."

"No, it's fine. As long as we leave now."

"Can we take you out to dinner with us this evening?" Geoffrey asks. They still haven't moved from the door.

"We have plans," Elizabeth says in the same instant that Butterfield says, "Sure."

Again, there's a pause.

Butterfield glances at Elizabeth, then feels constrained to offer an explanation: "I never get the dates right."

"I'm sorry. Remember, Will? Holly and Fiona are coming over tonight."

"Oh."

"Well, tomorrow maybe?" Ariana says.

"Okay. I really have to—" Elizabeth makes a gesture of frustration, hands going up to the sides of her head and back down.

Shostakovich and his wife go out and turn, and are still in the way. Elizabeth skirts around them, excusing herself, and moves to the car.

The sun is just above the line of low hills to the east, on the other side of the car. The lights from it catch the strands of her brown hair as she hurries across the lawn.

"Sorry," says Butterfield, closing and locking the door. He quickly shakes Geoffrey's hand. "Welcome to the neighborhood."

"Thanks. Tomorrow then?"

"Don't let my husband railroad you. He likes to think that's charming, don't you, Geoff."

"Did you hear something?" Geoff says to Butterfield. "Could've sworn I heard something. A crow, maybe."

Ariana stands with arms folded, as if waiting for Butterfield's response.

"Moving's tough on everybody, I know," he says.

She says, "You're a very considerate gentleman," and she smiles— that same direct, just-between-you-and-me expression.

"Your wife's going to be late," Shostakovich says.

Butterfield hastens to the car and gets in. The new neighbors are standing on the front stoop, as if they'll simply wait the rest of the day there. But then, as Elizabeth backs out and Butterfield waves, they start across to the empty house. Elizabeth pulls down the street and on, speeding a little. They come to the first light, and she stops with a little more of a jolt than is her habit.

"What was that all about?"

He gives her an uncomprehending look.

"I felt like you were—as if there was—what did you do last night?"

"I talked to her a little. Yeah," he says. "Waiting for Fiona—you know."

"If I didn't know better I'd swear you and she had been together before."

"Together."

"Like you knew each other, Will. More than polite bartender-customer talk."

"Well, they say the things you tell your bartender, you know."

"No, what do they say about that?"

"That was a joke," Butterfield says. "Come on."

She pulls out into traffic, and, for a moment, neither of them speaks.

"Well," he says, trying to keep the tone light. "We're committed to socializing with them, I guess."

"Thanks to you."

"I'm sorry."

No answer. He wonders why he should feel guilty, but he does. He looks out at the sunny street, the cool morning, and the light on the blue mountains in the near distance.

"Maybe they'll turn out to be good friends," he says.

Elizabeth looks at him with a perplexed frown that she takes some effort to turn into a smile. But the smile is sarcastic. "You know what I think?" she says. "I think they are going to be a perfect nightmare."

A MATTER OF SMALL
HISTORICAL CONSEQUENCE

1.

Alison leaves Kalie with her grandfather and drives to the school for parent-teacher conferences. She meets with Mr. Petit, Jonathan's math teacher, first. She comes to his door and finds that he's still with someone, a man in a straw hat, whom she has seen before though she can't remember where or when. Out here in the hallway, seated on the floor with his long legs stuck out, is the big, hulking boy who lives across the street from her—and now she remembers where she has seen the man who's talking to Mr. Petit. It's the boy's uncle. She knows it's school policy that students are not allowed to loiter in the halls.

"Hi," Alison says to the boy.

He turns a playing card in one hand, making a clicking noise with it.

"Excuse me," she says.

And now he glares at her. She's in uniform and is used to people staring—but this is aggression. The unfriendly look, like a leer on his heavy face, makes her think of finding the strongest possible terms of speech to use with him. He's someone who's up to no good; she tries not to feel this, and, even so, she addresses him again.

"Do you have some place to be?"

He appears faintly surprised. He puts one knee up and folds his hands over it. "Right here," he says in a voice that she would not have believed came from him.

"You have an appointment with Mr. Petit?"

He answers with a sullen shrug.

"Well?" Alison says.

"You live across the street from us," the boy says.

"Yes."

The man in the straw hat comes out of Mr. Petit's office and barely looks at her, moving across the hall to stand over the boy. "You're not supposed to be here. You're supposed to be in the STOP room. Get up."

The boy rises slowly, as if he had been thinking of getting up all along and his action has nothing to do with the man standing over him. When he's at full height, he towers over the other.

"Go on," the man says.

"Bye, now," the boy says to Alison in that girl-high voice.

The man takes him by the arm and pushes him. "You want more trouble?" he says. They go on, and Mr. Petit comes to the door of his room.

"I've got an appointment as vice principal," he says. "We'll have to move quickly."

She wants to say that she didn't want to do this at all right now. But she follows him into the room, where he sits at the desk and shuffles papers. His hands shake. He seems more nervous than anyone ought to be in this situation.

"Did something happen?" she asks him.

"I'm looking for Jonathan's work."

"He's not very enthusiastic about math, I know."

"But he's working hard."

"I know you've been helping him—spending extra time with him."

Petit stops and looks up at her, apparently distracted by something, a perplexed frown creasing his forehead, but then he simply seems to be waiting for her to go on.

So she does: "He says he feels good about it."

"Yes. He's working hard. He's a good young man and you should be proud."

"I am proud."

"Good." Mr. Petit shuffles the pages again.

"Is something the matter?" Alison says. "I went through a separation and a divorce a while back—it's had its effect on all of us."

"I just can't find the work—I had a folder of his work. I wanted to show you . . ."

She waits while he looks through the confusion on his desk. It's evident that he doesn't want to talk about the personal reasons for whatever failures there are in Jonathan's performance. Finally, he sits back, folds his shaky hands under his chin, and begins to talk about the boy's troubles with math. It isn't anything so complicated that a little extra work can't solve. He has some exercises he wants her to try with the boy at home. He hands her a few papers in a small folder, his hands still shaking. And then he stands and thanks her for coming in. She has the feeling that he wants to be rid of her. She says, "How is my son in class?"

"Oh, completely sweet."

"Docile."

"Pliable, you know. Not docile. But he never causes me any trouble."

"I should have him do these exercises at home?"

"Yes, and we'll just—go along the way we've been going."

"His father's no help, you know."

"Oh, I'll help him—I'll keep helping him."

Alison takes his offered handshake—a soft, clammy nongrip—and then walks down the hall to the English room and Mrs. Butterfield, whom she finds sitting at one of the student desks in the front of the room. Mrs. Butterfield looks busy, tired, even discouraged, but she brightens when Alison walks in. The two women recognize each other, of course, and through the whole conference—which is all about how wonderfully Jonathan is doing in her class—Mrs. Butterfield seems confiding and even, in some ways, conspiratorial about how Jonathan might be further encouraged to develop his gifts.

"You've done very well with him at home," Elizabeth Butterfield says. "It shows. And now I hope you don't mind if I change the subject.

But you were so helpful that night. You know. My mother-in-law. On the roof."

"I've been over to see them, you know. My father's doing that work for them."

"Yes, I knew that," Mrs. Butterfield says.

They're gazing at each other, and abruptly they begin to laugh. Alison hadn't seen it coming, and this makes her reaction to it all the more pronounced; it becomes a jag. Elizabeth closes the door and they sit there in the student desks, laughing.

"I don't know," Alison says, coughing and trying to blow her nose, "what came over me."

"Well," says Elizabeth. "They're dividing the house. They're having it demarcated."

Alison talks about the broken glass that lies collecting dust in the dining room. And Elizabeth puts her hands to her eyes, nodding.

"I know, I know."

"But I like them both," Alison says. "I do. I like them a lot. And Oliver likes them."

"Well," says Elizabeth, wiping her eyes. "I've got to get ready for my next conference."

"I'm sorry."

"Oh, don't apologize. I needed that. I did. Thanks for it."

Alison touches her shoulder. "Thank you for being so good to my son."

2.

Saturday morning, a man comes into The Heart's Ease bookstore and spends almost seven hundred dollars, buying mostly novels but there's also history and biography, all of it very serious and literary. He purchases an entire set of Dickens; another set, fourteen volumes, of O. Henry; all the Joseph novels of Thomas Mann; several first editions, including an edition of Henry Fielding's *Tom Jones* with French newspaper print showing where the binder has peeled away; a seven-volume biography of George Washington; and a series of texts about the Civil War. The Washington biography alone is more than seventy-five dollars. He walks among the stacks, holding a sheet of paper before him and marking on it with a pencil as he chooses the books he wants.

Butterfield says, "Are you a dealer?"

"Just decided I like books," the man says with a small shrug, looking at one of them. "Never owned any before, and I want to leave some for my son."

"Did you say—" Butterfield halts. He can't get it out, can't quite believe what he's just heard.

"That's right," the man says. "Never owned any. This will be my new library."

Butterfield stares.

"I guess from the look on your face that you've already got a library."

He nods, feeling rather dull, unable to think of a word.

"I met a man the other day, has over eight thousand books. Amazing. I never would've believed it. Interesting man, too. Good talker. He gave me a list of these names."

Butterfield says, "Maybe I know him."

"This was in New York. Up near Buffalo. Guy claimed he was a poet."

"What was his name?"

"Hell, I don't remember. I just remember he had a hell of a lot of books and he was going to leave them all to his son. Thought I'd do something like that, too. He gave me a list of authors. These pretty good are they?"

"Yes."

"I need this book by this Joyce woman. Joyce something or something Joyce. Guy couldn't say enough about it, and I asked him for a list and then he didn't write that one down. Joyce something. Supposed to be the best novel of the twentieth century according to some list he was talking about."

"James Joyce," Butterfield tells him. "*Ulysses.*"

"Oh, shit. I got *that* one wrong. *Ulysses*, huh? And it's a guy. Jesus. You got any other recommendations?"

"Tolstoy," Butterfield says.

The man runs a crooked finger down his list. "Who wrote it?"

"Tolstoy's the name of the writer."

"I want to leave a wealth of intellectual riches for my son. Don't have much else to leave him. A lot of money." He smiles. "Loads of money. Rivers of it. Hell, the fucking Indian Ocean of dough. You know? Material things. A shall we say pleth-ora of material things. A lot of stuff."

Butterfield nods, looking at him. A wide, long-jawed face, small mouth pulled back in a crooked grin, round, hazel eyes, wild, uncombed gray hair through which the soon-to-be bald pate shows, with its freckles and imperfections.

"You know what?" the man says. "You know all that crap about being there for your kids and making sure you spend time listening to them? That business about how they don't want what you can buy them, they want your love and emotional support, and the talking to them and appreciating them and all that. Right?"

"Sure," Butterfield says, thinking of Gail and Mark. "With my own children I—"

"Yeah, well it's not true. The truth is they want you to buy them stuff. Lots of it. Oodles of stuff. The more the better. I'm here to tell you from experience. I've got a great relationship with my son and it's because I buy him things. Things. He doesn't know me from Adam's house cat. Wouldn't recognize a single thought I had as mine, not even this one about the material things. But he loves me deep—I'm the source of all his toys. And so, well, I want him to take something from the world of books, too, because I understand that's where all the wisdom is. That's what they all keep telling me, anyway. Kid has no education except in his possessions, if you know what I mean, and he just turned forty. And I won't be here forever."

Butterfield stacks the piles of books in boxes, and the other man watches him in silence. The books fill six big boxes. The man pays with cash, and then Butterfield and he move the boxes out to his car, the man letting Butterfield carry the heaviest of them, which he does without complaining or showing that he's noticed this. The whole thing's rather amusing, actually. They get all the boxes into the trunk, and, while they're accomplishing this, Ariana Bromberg pulls up. Butterfield sees that it's Ariana and feels a tightening in the muscles across his lower abdomen. She sits behind the wheel of the car and seems to ponder both men. Finally, she steps out of it and says, "Are you closing?"

"Not yet," says Butterfield.

She slams the car door and walks on into the shop, jingling her car keys. She's wearing a print skirt that comes to just below midthigh of her long, tan, perfectly smooth legs, and a white blouse; the skirt reminds Butterfield of the line from Herrick: "The liquefaction of her clothes." He puts the last box of books into the back seat of the man's car.

"I might be back, tomorrow," the man says. "I saw a few other things I thought might do."

"Have you really not read any of these?" Butterfield can't help but ask.

"Well, I don't say I haven't done any of them. Some, I guess. I mean I must've. I went to college."

Butterfield ponders this.

The man smiles. "Ain't it a bitch?" It's as if he's enjoying a joke at Butterfield's expense.

"Hey," Butterfield tells him. "As long as you're paying for the merchandise."

"Right-o."

"And they say a book *is* like a mirror."

"Whatever, sport. Bye." The man gets into the car—it's a beat-up little compact, nothing like what one would expect a rich man to drive—and pulls away with a little honk of his horn.

Butterfield stares after him and says the rest of the line: "If an ass looks in, you can't expect a saint to look back out."

3.

From behind him comes the now weirdly familiar-feeling, scheming laugh. Ariana leans against the frame of the open door. "I've never heard that one before," she says.

"Mrs.—um, Ms. Bromberg," he says. "What can I do for you?"

"So formal," she says, jingling the car keys. "Thank you for remembering in time that I don't go by the other name. And you might as well know I don't like the music, either. The Shostakovich. I'm not what you would call a classical-music person."

He steps toward the entrance, and she backs inside, out of the light, half-turning, looking over her shoulder. The expression on her face makes him hesitate; it's unsettlingly as if she's leading him into somewhere secret or private, a bedroom. The thought brings him to a complete stop. And so she stops, too. It's all in her facial expression—that strange, devious ease.

"Well?" she says. "I came to look at your store. Aren't you going to help me buy some books?"

"Sure," he says, and swallows.

He walks with her into the central bay of the place, among the shelves stocked with history and historical biography—the troubles and triumphs of the famous dead. Accounts of migration and war. Descriptions of the heroisms, sorrows, depredations, monstrosities, and folly of the politically powerful. His favorite section.

"What do you like to read?" he asks her.

"What're you selling?"

It strikes him that the strangeness of this question requires a literal response. "I've got a little bit of everything."

"I like biographies. I like reading about people's tortured inner lives and sufferings. That way I find out I'm not the only neurotic who ever drew breath."

He says, "Well, there's political biographies here. There's also a section of literary biography, too, and celebrity stuff. The usual. If you need anything, let me know."

"What do *you* like to read?" she asks.

"History. Art history, too. And some fiction."

"That covers pretty much everything, doesn't it." There is no hint of a question in her tone.

He says, "Well, no."

"What about your wife?"

"Elizabeth? Well she does read everything. She teaches—"

"Right, she said that."

"And you do too," Butterfield says. "Sometimes."

"Sometimes." She takes a book down, an academic biography of Lincoln published by a university press. It happens to be one that Butterfield knows, one of those exercises in intellectual fantasizing, every line of which reveals the stubborn refusal on the part of the writer to give the slightest nod to reality whenever that reality tends to be a stumbling block to his unstated agenda.

"I've read that one," he tells her.

But she was speaking. She stops herself. "What?"

"No, go ahead."

"You've read this?"

"Yes, and I'm afraid it's a bit dull and uninspired."

"How will you sell it if you talk like that about it?"

He shrugs. "I'd rather my customers trust me."

"And do they?" she says. And here's that expression again, that smile as if there is a subtext, something entirely *else* that they are talking about.

"I like to believe they do."

She flips the pages of the book, then closes it and holds it up, looking at the spine. She puts it back in its slot and makes sure it's even with the others, talking as she does so. "I was saying that my husband doesn't like to read. Or I was starting to say that." She folds her hands in front and turns to him. "I believe I was starting to tell you something."

Butterfield swallows again and finds that he can't speak.

"My husband," she goes on, "is always talking about buying a bookstore. You ever think of selling a bookstore?"

"Not me."

"Does *she?*"

"She who?"

"Your wife."

"What about her?"

"Does she ever think of selling?"

"No."

"The way you said not me I thought you were saying she would."

"No. She wouldn't. I just meant it rhetorically, you know. *Not me.* Like that."

"I see."

A small silence deeds him the chance to take a breath and to move a step away from her. He adjusts a heavy volume on the shelf a few feet closer to the back of the store.

"Now is when we move to a subject you won't want to talk about."

"Excuse me?" he says, though he has heard her.

"Do Shostakovich and I look like a strange pair to you?"

He shakes his head—it is equal parts answer and request. She's right: he doesn't want to talk about this.

"The truth is, he's calm and steady, usually, and very nice to me. But he bores me. This is like the twelfth house we've rented in the last nine years. I hate it. I feel rootless and agitated and—well, bored. And there's nothing more destructive than a bored neurotic."

Butterfield says, "I thought the term *neurotic* wasn't in use anymore in the psychological community."

"Maybe so, but it's plenty current to us neurotics."

He nods and starts to say "Well, I have some work to do," but he can't get it out. The part of him that willed going back into Macbeth's the other night now compels him to keep silent. He's a man who has been quite glad in his life and his marriage, and life is becoming complicated in ways that he can't allow himself to look upon with any detachment. It is all just happening, as if there's some aromatic drug emanating from this stunning woman's body.

"You're a neurotic, too, aren't you," she says, breathing it.

His own breath catching, he says, "I guess that depends on your— your definition of the term." He can't quite breathe out all the way.

"I'd define it as somebody carrying an unruly mind around."

"I guess that qualifies most of us, then. I mean isn't everyone's mind unruly?"

"Not so you'd notice." That infernal smile again.

"Well," he says, gathering himself to say the politely extricating phrase. Remembering, just in time, who he is. "I've got a lot of paperwork."

"Oh, don't let me keep you. I wouldn't dream of getting in your way." Once more, the smile. He chooses to ignore it, returning to the counter and pretending to work through the account receipts. Because of the rich man's overlarge purchase, he'll have to go to the bank this morning. He's nervous having that amount of cash around. She wanders among the stacks without taking anything down, pausing to stare at titles, and then moving on. Now and then, her right hand goes up to move the black wealth of her hair back behind that ear. Her beauty has a nervous kind of frail sensuality, skittery and faintly sad, and yet somehow opulent, too, almost rank with sex. No, that isn't quite it, either. He can't quite describe it to himself, but it *is* beauty of a very different kind than that of Elizabeth, or any other woman he has known before. It disturbs him to be thinking this way, and yet her face and shape and presence stir him, too, seem to drop down into him like something shimmering and burning, and, so, he keeps his eyes trained on the work at hand. A trio of elderly ladies come in for a few minutes and buy several postcards, a memoir book, and a night reading lamp. Their age looks to him awfully like an affliction—something avoidable, like a form of disgrace. Their very appearance seems like the wages of sin, their iniquities laced into flesh and bone; these shapeless, pale, faltering bodies are the price of indulgence. He can't believe his own thoughts, ringing up their purchases, thinking of Holly and Fiona. They leave, haltingly, helping each other, so gentle and so mutually diminished-seeming, chattering about going to Harper's Ferry.

Ariana comes to the counter, jingling her keys. "Are you afraid of getting old?" she asks.

He stares.

"I feel drawn to you," she says. "Is that too forward?"

For an instant, he's not sure he could've heard her correctly. He's completely at sea.

"You know?" she murmurs sweetly.

"I don't—I can't—I mean I—"

"I thought I'd be honest with you," she says. "Maybe I shouldn't have."

He hasn't the shred of an idea what would be polite to say in the circumstance. "I don't know," he gets out. "I mean—I don't know what to say."

She comes around the counter and stands close, her attitude exactly that of someone looking at an exhibit. He actually takes a step back. She says, "Do you know what Napoleon used to do when he approved of someone? So silly. He'd tug their earlobe." She reaches up to take hold of his left ear. "Like this." Then she steps closer, and he feels the warmth of her breath on his cheek. "Nice. What is it?"

"Listen—you—we—I don't—" he stops.

"The aftershave."

"I don't know. I don't remember."

"You should wear it all the time." She takes one more breath, so close that he could simply turn and kiss her. He has the thought.

It must show in his face. "You want to kiss me, don't you."

"Yes." He can't believe himself. But he does indeed want very much to kiss her.

"Well?" she says.

He leans only slightly toward her, and in the next moment she's pressing him against the wall, arms tight around his shoulders. Her mouth is amazingly soft, and she opens it so wide. A small moan rises from the back of her throat. It's a long, long kiss, and he thinks of the open front door in the same instant that he thinks the words *Christ Almighty*. "Wait," he says aloud. Too loud. Now he murmurs: "Wait. Let me—"

"Can you close this place?" she breathes.

In some respects, the centuries have yielded up nothing new in the world. This is the end of the terrible twentieth, and Butterfield finds himself thinking of the horrors of history—the plagues in Europe, the depredations of the Counter-Reformation and the Spanish Inquisition, the terrors of the bloody lane at Antietam, the mass graves of Treblinka,

the bombing of Dresden, the killing fields of Rwanda and Cambo-
dia. It's all there in his mind, disordered, by turns general and utterly
specific, yet all eerily present—a kind of vast, shifting mural of death
against which his present transgression might be played out, nothing
more than a shadow-puppet's dance, a small thing, a little taste of the
forbidden, momentary and no more momentous than gazing at a pornographic picture. He has trouble concentrating. Ariana is definite and
very focused.

It's all over in a matter of a couple of minutes.

PART TWO

October–November

INCIDENTAL FINDING

I.

Afternoon, now. Bright, warm. Not a cloud in the sky. More like a mild, cool day in July than the middle of October. Oliver Ward turns onto Temporary Road and parks the truck. The two old ladies are out in the leaf-littered, ragged, dirt-patched yard, working in the one little space of order in it, the garden along the front porch. They seem remarkably peaceful. Stepping down out of the truck, he takes a handkerchief from his pocket and wipes his brow, then reaches back into the cab for his clipboard. They appear not to have any idea that he has arrived. He's come to tell them that he's going to have to hire someone to help him with the electric wiring and the drywall, not to mention the new kitchen and bathroom. He has installed a separate fuse box; he has done the framing and some of the wiring and laid in new heat ducts, rerouted some of the others. But there is still too much to do, more than a man can do alone.

He clears his throat to announce himself, approaching them, and Fiona, nearest to him, straightens with an aching slowness, putting both hands at the small of her back and then pulling one forearm across her face. "Glad you could make it, Oliver," she says, smiling. Then she indicates Holly. "She bet me you'd be late. I win. Thank you."

"Nothing personal," Holly says. "I'm always a little late myself."

They talk briefly about Alison and the children, and the unseasonably warm weather. Fiona says she herself has only just arrived, having spent her morning substituting in the Saturday religion classes at Saint Augustine. Holly drove her and picked her up. Both women spent a pleasant few minutes with Brother Fire. They seem quite comfortable together, and Oliver has the thought that the old priest might be having an effect on them; maybe everything will fall through now. But Holly says she's anxious to talk about the plans for dividing the house, and Fiona nods enthusiastically.

His capacity for the appreciation of marvels is highly developed, and, even so, the complexity of human relations sometimes has the flavor of something exotic to him. While most people move through life with a sense of the ordinariness of their daily transactions, he's continually filled with wonder.

Mary, before she died—in the last week of her life, in fact—told him that she believed he had kept some capacity for emotional freshness that children usually outgrow. But there were other instances when she spoke of that aspect of his personality as a terrible innocence, nothing less than irresponsibility, charming but ultimately harmful.

He possesses no way of deciding such a thing with any finality, but there seems enough truth in it. He doesn't feel that he can help who he is anymore. The difference between who he might've been had she been able to change him, and who he *is* belongs finally to the province of regret—that realm of misplaced hopes. He doesn't like to think about any of it. And yet, these days, getting toward sixty years of age, he thinks about it more and more.

As he does now, while they all file into the house and through the hanging plastic, to what will be Fiona's part of the present living room. She opens a gallon bottle of Dr Pepper while Holly gets ice and glasses. Oliver hasn't said he'd like anything to drink. He looks at the broken glass with its companion lying, still untouched, under the side table in the dining room, dust so thick on it now that the glass looks as though it is made of solid wood or plastic. Several times while putting the frame up for the dividing wall, he thought of removing them; but decided against it. Lately, it makes him feel as though he's part of the stubborn game.

Fiona pours three tumblers, then picks two of them up and holds them out. Oliver takes his carefully and murmurs, "Thank you." Holly takes hers and says, "Ah, energy."

They sit on the couch, side by side, and sip the cold drink. Oliver has never liked soda pop, not even when he was a boy, and so he manages to keep a small smile, trying not to grimace through the syrupy sweetness. He tells them about the separate fuse box and about rewiring the original one.

"I think we should revisit the windows," Fiona says to Holly.

"No, we settled that, dear."

"Yes, but after all it's yours."

"What's mine, dear?"

"You chose it, is what I meant."

"I chose what? The windows?"

"The house."

"We both did that, sweetie."

"Both sides will have windows," Oliver says. "It's just that one will have a couple more."

"Well, but we already settled that Fiona gets the windows," says Holly.

"I won't argue, darling. But I did think you picked the house. I'm only along for the ride, remember."

"Well, I appreciate that but—"

"Ladies," Oliver says. "I'm gonna have to hire some help."

"Well," says Fiona. "But let her have the side with the most windows."

"I don't want the bloody fucking windows," says Holly. "In fact, I don't want any windows at all. I want total darkness. Complete, utter darkness. The outer darkness. That's what I want."

"Really, ladies," Oliver says, rising and then, with a heavy-feeling brutal thudding under his skull, sitting down suddenly. Knocked down, it seems, in a bell-like space of sharp burning. He has fallen onto Holly's right leg. This hot, blunt-instrument pain spreads to the back of his head, and he thinks momentarily that he's been hit with something. To his horror, he finds that he can't move.

"Oliver," says Holly. "Lord, what're you doing."

He can't speak, either. The air seems to solidify around him, encasing him in it, an ice; though—even shivering, cold, sinking into a cave of frost—he still feels the white heat burning under the flesh of his forehead. She pushes him from herself and stands, and he realizes he's lying on their couch, in this ice block of unbreathable air. The pain in his head is like a blackness now, coming over him. He looks up at her and sees the increasing alarm and concern in her face. Fiona seems to speak from some far, watery distance. "What's wrong?"

"Oliver?" Holly says, fading from him. "Say something."

The blackness covers her, the room, memory. Oliver turns in a little space and tries to ask for more light, tries to speak his own name, tries to hear or see or listen. There is only the roar of the ice now and cold darkness, night coming on with a rush, and the thudding pain, the clamor of his own heart.

2.

In a corner of Alison's living room is a small practice amp, with paperback books piled on it. Alison's ex-husband, Teddy, wanted to learn how to play guitar, so he could jam with Oliver, and he did take lessons for a while. Oliver plays an old Guild concert acoustic guitar, and Teddy's electric would've drowned it out. But no amount of explaining could dissuade Teddy, who believed that Oliver would eventually buy his own electric, once he saw how much easier it was to play than his old beat-up Guild. When Teddy wanted something, he believed in it so completely that you couldn't get through to him with the facts. This was also true of him when he *didn't* want something.

Marge's Greg—the champion asshole—bought the guitar from her a few months after Teddy moved out, and subsequently sold it. She keeps the amp out of a kind of inertia, really; though there is something vaguely talismanic about it, too. Teddy was never so happy as when trying to play the guitar, though he never got any good at it. Poor Teddy couldn't tell when the thing was out of tune, and he had no sense of timing. The few times he tried to play along with Oliver were embarrassing.

She looks at the amp now and recalls when life seemed happy. Since the divorce—and he granted her full custody—he has come to take the children out with him on only three occasions. Easter, the fourth of July a year ago, and one Sunday in early August. Each time, he had very specific things in mind to do, and, in each instance, he ended up dressing Jonathan down for some minor—or imagined—failure, mostly having to do with Jonathan's responsibility for watching the baby. Teddy's impatience with Jonathan is mirrored, perhaps not so strangely, by her impatience with Teddy. The sound of his voice grates on her nerves now, and it's hard to be civil, though she manages it.

She's off today. She stands at the window again, watching Greg water his lawn.

"What're you looking at?" Jonathan asks. He's sniffling with another series of sinus symptoms. Everything around him, it seems, gives him these psychosomatic episodes, stress-related, the doctor says, because they clear up when he plays, or reads, or watches television.

"Greg's out on Marge's porch, hosing down the backyard like it's the middle of summer."

He sniffles again. "It's supposed to be better if you do it early in the morning or at night. In summer. We could have a frost tonight. The grass is going to die anyway. What's he doing? It's insane isn't it?"

"I believe clueless is the word," Alison says.

A moment later, the boy sighs. "I miss Marge."

Her sensitive boy.

She learned young that voicing one's troubles only seems to make them worse. And she knows all the various theories about therapy and talking things out—she has even read some Freud—but, for herself, such delving only seems to make her feel tired, more beset.

No. She's not a person who puts much stock in digging around in one's soul. She believes that there are beautiful things to look at all around, if one only learns to see them. Being acquainted with most of the world's troubling ideas, she's cognizant of the essential homilic nature of the thought that one must teach oneself to see surrounding miracles. Nevertheless, the fact that such sentiments are used loosely by people who never think to follow them, and the fact that they are as familiar as the names of the weekdays on a calendar—well, none of this makes them less true. The secret heart of experience, for Alison, involves the quality of attention. One learns to appreciate; one struggles to be good enough for it, strong enough, awake enough. You raise your head out of the dark and look around. And if there's luck, and you persist, elements of your own ragged, hard-to-live life begin to reveal their indispensable shimmer.

For instance, there's her doll-making.

She has recently returned to it. Since earliest childhood, dolls have fascinated her, and she always enjoyed combining the shapes and the colors of the miniature clothes. She can't draw or sculpt, can't reproduce a single recognizable worldly shape, really, other than the cone of a dress and the naturally pinched features that come from sewing the cloth over the head-shape of a doll. Last spring, she spent a week sitting at a flea market in the valley, with other craftspeople, selling her dolls. She sold most of them. The ones she didn't sell are like projects for her, for the future; she'll get them into shape. She keeps several half-finished ones on a shelf in her workroom, a lot of silent witnesses to her work.

And the most hands-on aspect of her present involvement with the world is these dolls she works so assiduously to perfect in the late-night hours, when sleep is an evasive ghost, just gliding away across the next acre of night.

"How was school yesterday?" She was on shift last afternoon and night.

"In English, we had to write about weather. I was a bit dubious about it, but it turned out to be rather exhilarating."

It's as if he sits up nights searching the dictionary for words and planning how to bring about the contexts in which to use them. The simple fact is that he loves to read, and his reading finds its way directly into all his thoughts and expressions. She's always very careful not to show any awkwardness with him when, serious and in gentle earnestness, he spouts some ornate phrase, her sweet, odd boy. "How is it generally this year?" she asks him.

"I'm liking math a little better."

"You and math getting along now?" She's quite pleased now that she spoke to Mr. Petit.

"I've been staying after class for a half hour each day instead of going to study hall, and Mr. Petit helps me with it. It's actually fun when you understand it."

"Most things are better when you understand, yes."

The boy shakes his head. "You don't have to turn it into a life lesson, Ma."

"I wasn't doing that." Now and then, he reminds her unpleasantly of his father.

"I think Mrs. Butterfield's rather engaging."

"You mean nice? I like her too, by the way. We had a good talk."

"I think she's engaging," the boy insists. Then he goes on into his room.

3.

The night she told Teddy she was pregnant with Kalie, he went out and didn't come back for several hours. He told her that he felt like taking a walk to clear his head. But the next morning, he said he didn't want another child, and asked her politely, as if this were a thing that could be negotiated like a redistribution of tasks, to do something about it. She threw a dish at his head, and the dish broke on the wall. They laughed about this incident later in her pregnancy, but there was always the sense that it could ignite another quarrel. He left the first time shortly after Kalie was born. That lasted three months. He came back; he tried. He went to work and came home and he was polite to Oliver and he played with the children. Something was missing all the time. The days went by in a kind of haze for Alison, and the nights were long. She took the job with the police force, went through the training, and

Teddy drifted farther and farther away. The children were able to recognize the feeling, of course, even if they couldn't name it. Something was bothering Daddy. Daddy was always distracted and quiet around them, and his forbearance for noise and confusion shrank. It became harder and harder for Alison to find anything of the humorous man with whom she had fallen in love. And his distraction extended to the bedroom. From the beginning, she had delighted in making love, having discovered in herself a surprising enthusiasm for it. But as the year of Kalie's infancy wore on, and Teddy's unease in the house increased, her joyous feelings began to wane. Lovemaking began to feel like something they were doing by rote, without much thought or attention to any element of it. The whole performance was demoralizing, and the tension grew. They began quarreling over things far away from their intimacy, and there were times when she was quite happy to have him out of the house. And quite happy, herself, to have shift work at night.

Finally, almost two years ago now, he left again, this time for good. Even so, she feels no animosity toward him—he's a boy, like Gregory, and, for that matter, like Jonathan and, she has to admit to herself, Oliver, too. And while she has often laughed at Marge's funny tirades about Gregory, and added her own comments about her husband, she has always been tolerant of the boyishness in men, since it has been the largest element of her own experience with Oliver. Moreover, she half-believes men are simply not equipped with the necessary organs of understanding the practical requirements of life. She sees in this an explication of all sorts of bright accomplishment in the world: men lead adventurous lives out of a failure to perceive what sensible matters oppose their schemes and plans. She knows it's far more complicated than this, of course. Yet it helps her keep an inner truce with herself concerning her ex-husband's failures.

Now she goes to the bedroom door to check on the children. Kalie's rocking happily, sleepily, in the easy chair under the window, her favorite, a big, wine-colored anchor of a chair. Her hands are closed on the arms of it, and a small line of drool has come down from her perfect mouth. Jonathan's sitting cross-legged on her bed, paging through one of her *Animorphs* books.

"Honey," she says. "You want some relief?"

"I'm fine," he says. "I like to watch her."

She walks over to him and stands for a moment. When he looks up, he smiles, but there's something forced about it. "You seem sad, lately," she says.

"No." His tone is flat and simple. Perhaps there's the faintest question in it.

"Jonathan, you can tell me how you are. You don't have to keep everything to yourself."

"I'm fine," he says. But his gaze travels away from her.

"Is it something at school?"

"Mother, please."

She bends down and kisses his forehead, then goes over and kisses Kalie on her cheek. "I'll be in the other room," she says.

She paints for a few minutes, then puts everything away and washes her hands. Standing at the bathroom sink, she pulls a brush through her hair, noting the shadows under her eyes and the fatigued cast of her face. "Gorgeous," she says sardonically, because, like most lovely women, she can't see her own best qualities. There's no vanity in her, nor any duplicity, either. She sees what she sees, and the problem is that what she sees is a wide mouth and a too-rounded chin, and eyes the color of old wood.

She's in the living room when Greg comes to the door. He knocks and waits, hands folded in front. This is the first time since Marge left, and, even so, Alison's unsurprised. When she opens the door, she breathes the cologne he has put on his cheeks. He's the sort of man who wears monogrammed shirts and always has four or five silver pens with his name on them. Wiry, small, and lean, with a hook nose and black hair that he never combs, as a matter of style; his small eyes are a pretty green. The eyes were what drew Marge to him in the first place.

"I wanted to see how you're doing," he says.

"I'm doing just dandy," she says.

"I've been thinking about you," he tells her. It's as if he's bestowing this on her. "So, you know, if you feel you need anything."

"And what would I need, Gregory?"

He smiles. "Whatever."

"I don't need a thing."

"Well, I'm here."

She waits for him to leave. And when he doesn't, she starts to close the door. "I'm just concerned for you," he says. "Really. I know it gets lonely. Boy do I know."

"I can't believe you," she says. "Go away before I find some pretext to arrest you. Your wife's pregnant, remember?"

"She's in another time zone."

"Go away, Gregory," she says. "Go home and water your lawn."

He's about to say something else, but she closes the door quietly in his face. Not five minutes later, the telephone rings. It crosses her mind that Gregory has gone home and decided to try her over the telephone.

It's Fiona, quite shaky-sounding. "Alison, something's happened."

"Fiona?" Alison says, thinking: *Not now, oh, God. Please. Not now.* Then she says: "It's Oliver, isn't it."

"You need somebody to come get you?" Fiona says.

4.

Brother Fire is called to the hospital to administer the last rites to Oliver Ward. It's Fiona who calls him. Fiona indicates that time is of the essence. The hospital chaplain is not there, she says, and Oliver Ward may already be gone. The old priest is close by, can he please come? Yes. Of course. He hurries out to the car and barks his left knee getting into it. He drives himself to the hospital in a welter of pain. There's traffic; a minor accident, a fender bender, gawkers slowing to look at it. No one is hurt, and Brother Fire has an unpleasant sense of the precariousness of everything, going by, as if the whole edifice of his faith might collapse in the next instant, the world pressing in on him with its remorselessness, like a terrible, blank wall. He murmurs a prayer and can't feel the words; they are sounds issuing from his lips, from the mouth of a thing brought forth out of chaos and randomness. He tries to pray again. *Our Father who art in Heaven.* It's no use. Waiting behind a truck with its dirty backside and one broken taillight, he repeats the words, says the prayer anyway, tries to empty his mind, tries to call up the old joy, thinks of Aquinas, and receives an image of himself enjoying a peaceful night with wine; oh, if he could find something now, here, to cut this darkness that has descended upon him. *Lord, I believe. Help thou my unbelief.*

At the hospital, he heads toward the emergency-room entrance, where he encounters Holly and a young woman he has seen before, whom Holly introduces as Alison; and also Alison's children, coming from the opposite side of the parking lot. Alison has been crying. "I'm so sorry," he says to her.

"Is he gone?" Alison says in fright, staring at the cruet of oil and the book he's carrying.

"I'm just arriving myself," says the priest. "Fiona called me."

They go inside. Fiona's sitting in one of the vinyl chairs along the wall. She rises and approaches.

"No news," she says. "But it's a stroke."

"Oh, God," says Alison.

"All we can do is wait."

Alison moves to one of the chairs, turns, and seems to collapse there, putting her hands to her face, rocking slowly. "Mommy," says Kalie, "is Granddaddy dead?"

"No," Alison says to her. "Please, baby. Sit here for Mommy and be quiet."

Fiona sits down and extends one thin arm over Alison's shoulder, leaning in, murmuring something.

Holly takes the priest by the elbow. "We don't know a thing, John. You know Fiona."

"I'm not needed?"

"Not in the way you must've thought."

He limps back out to the car and puts the sacramental oil and the book on the front seat. The car feels to him like a chamber, the place where he was set upon by those black thoughts. He closes the door and turns from it, braces himself for what will be needed. Back in the waiting room, he sits with Alison for a few minutes. The boy Jonathan has a coughing fit, and Kalie, restless, begins to cry and protest being held. The two old ladies try to help. Brother Fire thinks of the confusions and muddle of family life, and feels like a fugitive, someone in hiding. There's this badness in his soul that causes him to rise and walk over to the water fountain, where he drinks and tries to tamp down the fright, the dark. A numbness has begun to spread in the center of him, in his bones. There's now, inside him, only the sense of having failed these people and everyone, and himself. Then he sees the selfishness of the concern, and his own recoiling mind makes him wince. *If I contend with thee, oh Lord.*

Holly walks over to him. "You all right?"

"I'm a bit shaky," he tells her, because she's his friend and will understand.

5.

On her way to The Heart's Ease bookstore, Elizabeth sees six-foot-ten-inch Calvin Reed walking along the side of the road, head down, everything about him sagging, as if the force of gravity were twice as strong for him and him alone. She slows the car and gives a light tap to the horn, which he either ignores or doesn't hear. So, she stops and stands out of the car, and calls to him: "Calvin."

No response.

She calls louder: "Calvin."

Now he stops and turns and seems to peer doubtfully at her. "What?"

"Where're you headed?"

"Home."

She wants to tell him to pull his pants up. Stand straight. Stop walking around like someone half-awake; stop being so strange. Stride through the world with some sense of his uniqueness, with some self-regard. In an age when the whole culture is in thrall to that very idea, when people are encouraged to be as grasping and selfish and vain as their most fugitive greedy whim, she finds his hangdog inferiority-complex annoying. There seems something almost willful about it. But she says none of this. Instead, she asks if he needs a lift.

He shrugs.

"It's not a complicated question, Calvin."

He ambles over, looking down—someone being compelled to do something he wishes not to do. He opens the car door and scrunches down in the seat, getting his long legs in, and closes the door with a quiet click, as though he's afraid of making too much noise. She pulls her own door shut and looks back to check oncoming traffic, talking over her shoulder. "How far is it?"

"Mile," he says. "Mile and a half."

"Do I go straight?"

"I'll tell you when to turn."

She pulls out, and, for a minute or so, they're quiet. He's very still; big, flat-fingered hands lying open in his lap. Out of the corner of her eye, his floppy apparel makes him look like a mountainous sack of dirty laundry. And, indeed, an odor of overripe fruit rises from him. "How long have you been with your uncle?"

"Not long."

She glances over at him. He's looking at his fingers. The world outside the window holds no interest for him.

"Have you been to see a friend? Or down at the recreation center?"

"The mall."

"Fairfield?"

"The Arcade."

"What's your favorite video game?"

"*Commando*. You get to shoot everything in sight."

"I used to be good at *Pac-Man*."

He shrugs. "Turn right at the light."

She comes to the light and does so, and he says, "Third house on the right."

She stops in front of the house. The uncle is out in the yard, wearing a wide-brimmed straw hat and gloves, wielding a weed trimmer, cutting the crabgrass along the border of the sidewalk. During the parent-teacher conference, he just stared as she spoke of Calvin's difficulties. It's going to be another long year with Calvin. He gets out of the car, muttering "Thank you," and crosses to the door of the house and goes in. He doesn't look back. He seems unaware of the uncle, who appears equally unaware of him—they might as well be shadows crossing in two different realms.

Elizabeth waits a moment, intending to wave at the uncle, but he never does look over at her, and so she pulls away, drives down to the end of the street and turns around. Coming back, she slows, and he's still working along—and in the house, she knows, is Calvin, alone.

The Heart's Ease bookstore is only a couple miles farther on, and she drives there in a funk, a restlessness that she can't quite understand or explain to herself.

When she and Butterfield were first together, and Mark and Gail were still children, she tried to give them whatever they needed most, which, often enough, seemed to be a sort of benign neglect. That is, they communicated by word and deed, and sometimes by plain omission of these things, that they wished to be left to their own devices. Elizabeth found herself acting as a referee now and then when conflicts arose—a go-between, for both of the children and for their father. This turned out to be especially so when Gail married so young; Elizabeth, half-consciously seeing it as an opportunity to get closer to the girl, sided with her against Will's determination that the marriage was a mistake. But Gail let it be known that she could fight her own battles. "I don't need permission from you," she said to her father. "I don't need anybody's approval about it." This was said at the top of her voice in the kitchen, the night before the wedding. Elizabeth took a step back then, as she would later explain it to Will, who claimed that the statement had nothing to do with her. But Elizabeth heard the notes in her stepdaughter's voice. Notes she sometimes believes only another woman can hear.

At any rate, when she expressed to Will her wish not to be placed between him and his children, not to be utilized in this fashion, things settled into the phase they have mostly been in since Gail left to study English at Temple. Guardedly cordial. And she hates it without being able to see the slightest window of a way through it to something more.

It's all perfectly understandable, though, and she has never been the type to require more than people seem able to give: back then, neither of the children wanted reminders of what had happened in their young lives; they had their memories of their mother. They were close to their father. The world they lived in happened to them, and Elizabeth, at first—she knows this now, and she sensed it painfully then—amounted to another change. Back then, she was troubled by the idea that they already were a family: Will and Gail and the moody boy. There were so many passes with Mark and his sleepwalking—night terrors, the doctor called it; Elizabeth had never heard the term used before—and this poor boy's fractured sense of dependable reality. He trusted nothing. Nothing. A school bus ride, a walk across a little field, a friend waving from the other side of a street—none of it had any kind of solidness to him.

Gail, by contrast, seemed at times almost too bright—a cheerleader, a member of the drama club, the chess club, the literary magazine and school newspaper staff, the yearbook committee. The girl appeared to experience everything like a cat walking in weather, as Elizabeth put it once to Will; it was all outside her somehow. Of course, most of this was a front, a way of being brave, pushing through deep fears.

So much has changed now for Gail, with her disastrous early marriage— and even that similarity between them has done nothing to deepen the connection. Gail's angry all the time at something or somebody, these days.

Well. Both offspring have suffered losses. Mark went with the same girl through high school and the first three years of college. The girl quit school and moved with her parents to the Midwest, and immediately after he graduated, he moved there to be near her. Three months after he arrived, she ran off and married a member of the Indianapolis Colts football team, a practice squad player (he's now coaching high school in Seattle, where they live). Mark began dating the divorced woman with three children last year, but that hasn't gone too well, either, and Elizabeth hears about it all from him, calling in his unexpressed bitterness, drunk, from his little apartment in Indianapolis.

At least, with Mark, there has been some kind of bond. Though his

voice over the phone, slurring, with its injured tone, its bafflement, often leaves her exhausted and wanting sleep, even if it's the middle of the
afternoon.

All she has wanted is to be what they need.

Will would say that she possesses an acute sense of the sufferings and
troubles of others. Starving orphans on distant continents are not her direct responsibility, he has told her, only half-joking.

For the worrying that she's beset with often enough, her remedy
has always been to lose herself in the society of others: when she suffers
the dark, she desires company, finds herself healing inside simply from
watching people talk. For Elizabeth, going out in the world and being
with friendly others makes the melancholy give way the ineffable fraction of ground necessary for surviving it.

At the bookstore, she finds Will talking to two men he sometimes
plays poker with, Tom and Amos, both of whom work at the local
travel agency. They're cousins. The three men have poured drinks from
a pitcher. Vodka and orange juice. They offer her one, and she decides
to join them. Will has been telling them about the Crazies, and their
present business of bifurcating their house. There's something vaguely
manic about him. He keeps glancing at her, talking about walls inside
walls. There's a strange, hard light in his eyes, and she thinks it's because he's had too much to drink so early in the day.

Amos refuses to believe it about the house. This is a trait the cousins share, this tendency toward skepticism, no matter the subject. Now
Amos's cousin doesn't go along—he's skeptical about Amos's skepticism. Elizabeth realizes that all three of them are crocked. She takes a
last sip of her drink and excuses herself, saying she's got work to do at
home; she'll come by in an hour or so. And, to her pleasant surprise,
Will says he wants to close the store and come with her.

"But you're having drinks," she says.

"I want to come with you now, darling." There's something almost
worried in his tone. She stares at him.

"Whoa," Amos says. "I guess we're getting kicked out."

"You can stay," Will tells them quickly. "Just take whatever sales come up, and close up when you leave."

But they all leave. The cousins get into a little Yugo and pull away, and, watching them go, Elizabeth thinks there's something unsteady about the car's shocks. It's as if the car, too, has been swilling vodka and is reeling. They go very slowly down the block and out of sight.

"I hope they don't get pulled over," she says.

Will shrugs, a gesture that reminds her disagreeably of Calvin Reed. She takes his arm and murmurs, "Let's not go home."

"Where do you want to go?" There's that odd light in his eyes. It worries her.

"Are you okay?"

"Sure. Where do you want to go."

"A hotel?"

He stares at her, searching her face.

"What's wrong, Will."

He says, "Nothing. You tell me."

She sighs. "I want to go somewhere the Crazies can't call us."

"Oh, I see," he says. Apparently, he's chosen not to take her seriously.

"Will," she says.

"It'll be all right," he tells her.

They get into the car, and he drives. Twice he heaves a deep sigh, as if he's experiencing some queasiness.

"Are you drunk?" she asks.

"No."

She looks out the window at the street, thinking of places they might go. But then he turns up their street, and, in another moment, they're home.

Inside, she unplugs the phone, and he smiles. She thinks of this smile as the first thing she recognizes about him this afternoon. But then it goes away, and he looks down at his hands, shifting slightly. He puts his hands on her shoulders and draws her to himself. She receives the unsettling notion that he wants to keep from looking directly into her eyes. But then he pulls back slightly and does exactly that.

"I love you," he says. "So much."

"Oh, baby," she says.

Now and then, even living through the shocks and horrors of a terrible century, people find themselves blessed with a perfectly glorious time, when it's easy to believe that hunger will be assuaged forever, or political prisoners will be released after decades of captivity; a sweet turn of the clock hands brings tests that come back negative; a widowed mother of three wins an all-expenses-paid trip to sunny islands; a lottery ticket yields untold wealth for the local elementary-school janitor, who bought the ticket on a whim; and blissful, married love happens in unlooked-for circumstances and with unexpected abundance, while a whole evening passes in the city without a single incidence of human depredation or sorrow.

This Saturday evening in Point Royal is like that. Or, at least, it seems so to Elizabeth.

The phone stays unplugged. The Crazies don't come over. The new neighbors keep to themselves. Elizabeth lies in her husband's arms in bed, in the soft afterheat of their lovemaking, listening to the breezes murmuring in the eves of the house. A charming sound in the soft evening light though in the darkness it would seem scary, the echo of a haunting, ghosts in the gloomy angles of roof and wall. There's a wonderful, time-frozen feeling about this charming, low-howling, windy dusk, as if the summer that has ended has been granted a permanent reprieve. It's a lovely, stolen season, armor against the winter that is arriving.

6.

Alison sits in the waiting room of the Point Royal Hospital, with Kalie sleeping on her lap and Jonathan at her side. Across from her, Holly and Fiona sit, Holly knitting, Fiona reading a magazine. Fiona has her hair in a knot on the very top of her head. Her eyes are fierce-looking, and Alison thinks it's probably the brows, sharply curved like those of an eagle or a hawk. The green irises are a dark shade, like lake water after a rain. Holly has the same sharp brows, but something of the blue in her eyes softens the effect. Neither woman seems even slightly tired. Alison told them hours ago that it was all right to leave her, but they remain. They talk to Jonathan about what's on television—not the waiting-room television but the world of television. Fiona knows all the sitcoms and talk shows well. Alison finds herself a little surprised at the amount of TV Jonathan has watched. He's up to speed on most of it. Fiona exhibits an ability to slip into Jonathan's world. It's strange. At times, it's as if the two of them are exact contemporaries. When Fiona excuses herself to go use the restroom and to call her great-nephew, Alison says to Holly, "She's so good with them."

"That's because she never got past the age of nine herself." Holly's voice seems lighthearted and full of affection. It's as if she's boasting about her aunt. "Believe me, I know."

Alison says, "My mother used to say that about my father." She thinks about Oliver—it's eerily almost as if she has to remember him from a distance. It frightens her. He's in surgery, and has been for almost an hour. The MRI showed what the doctors called an incidental finding: Oliver's carotid artery is almost completely blocked. They're performing the surgery to correct this. Alison sits straight-backed, waiting, almost as if the powers of fate in the universe might help Oliver if she keeps her posture correct and is sure to keep everything else correct, too—there's something propitiating about all of it. She adjusts the weight of Kalie in her lap. A little earlier, she called Marge to tell her about Oliver, and couldn't get it all out. Marge broke down crying, believing that this was death news. It took a while to make her understand, and, in explaining everything, Alison began to feel as if this talk about full recovery was a kind of whistling in the dark; it was as if she might effect a bad outcome by talking about it so reassuringly to her friend. Marge's unhappy where she is, and wants to come back, and can't. Gregory has been almost impossible to get a hold of. Alison explained that she hasn't seen him, and then said she had to go. Marge was still crying when she hung up.

The waiting room is small and painted an odd, ceramic-yellow color, dark, like congealed egg yolk. The television is suspended from an apparatus bolted to the ceiling; it hangs in front of a row of windows, so that anyone walking by in the hall outside can see the upturned faces of the people watching it.

"Here," Holly says, standing and leaning over Alison, reaching. "Let me take the baby for a while. You look tired."

Alison gives Kalie up.

Fiona comes back, and she's bought candy for the young folk, as she calls them, meaning Alison, too. Fiona bites into a Clark bar, and begins talking about her plans for living alone in a demarcated house. The completion of the division will have to be put off now. Fiona glides right past this, as if there is no question about Oliver eventually being able to finish. Holly nods encouragingly, holding Kalie and rocking slightly.

"You're both so kind," Alison says.

"Well," says Holly. "We don't have a lot to do. It's good to be of help."

"I always thought that," Fiona says.

"I know you did, dear. Right from the start."

"Since I was a baby."

"She did," Holly says to Alison. "She was a very helpful baby, weren't you, Fiona? Fed herself. Changed her own diapers. Ran the vacuum. Made house calls to the sick. Everyone talked about it all the time."

Fiona says nothing.

"Never cried or asked for anything. You could go for days without even noticing her, they said. Rotated everybody's tires—like that, you know."

"I'll try to call Will and Elizabeth again," says Fiona in an even tone. She rises with exaggerated dignity and trundles on out of the room.

"Sometimes she teases back," Holly says.

Jonathan turns on the television. There's been an explosion and a fire at a plant in Detroit. The television news teams are swarming, helicopters, vans, men and women standing in the foreground with microphones held up to their mouths. Every channel's the same. A spectacular fire and no injuries. For once, the lead story isn't the president's troubles, and Jonathan mentions this.

"I've said this before and I'll say it again," Holly says. "You're a very advanced young man."

"I keep up," says Jonathan in a tone that Alison finds a little supercilious. She gives him a look, but he doesn't notice. He's watching the television. They all watch for a while.

"Do you sense that these news types are disappointed no one was hurt?" Holly asks.

"My father hates them," Alison says. "But I guess people have to make a living."

Fiona comes back. "Something must be wrong with the line. It rings and rings."

Kalie stirs and fusses a little, sleepily, twisting in Holly's lap. Alison takes her, and she settles down again. They all watch the television, with its aerial view of the blaze.

"It's actually rather beautiful from a distance," Fiona says.

They talk about this phenomenon. Holly mentions that under a microscope, some of the world's worst organisms and toxins are quite exquisite to look at.

Alison says, "Oh, could we change the subject, Holly?"

Holly reaches over and touches the back of her hand. "I'm sorry."

They're quiet. Others come in. The television racket changes to early-morning infomercials. Jonathan and Fiona watch it, eating more candy. Alison and Holly talk about Holly's years working for the government and for the railroads as a secretary, and how it was back then, trying to form a union. Alison tells her about Teddy, and some about Marge and Gregory, and a lot about growing up, mostly alone with Oliver, who was always a little sad, and like a boy in so many ways, and such a wonderful lot of fun to be with. When Teddy left, it was all she could do to keep Oliver from doing some damage to him. Yet, when he understood that she wanted to try keeping a relationship with Teddy for the sake of the children, he became the picture of familial calm and amity. Even now, in Teddy's absence, he refrains from talking about him. Holly relates the story of her Scottish husband and a tirade he threw in a restaurant in defense of a waiter who had been fired for dropping a tray of food. "A sense of justice," she says. "That was the thing about him. I liked it in him, too. It wasn't a pose." She seems to ponder this, and something flickers in her eyes, a pang. She sighs and looks down at her hands. "Haven't thought of him for a while," she murmurs. "It's surprising what stays with you."

"I've heard my father say that," Alison tells her.

At some point in the long night the doctor, a short, very thin, stooped man with black hair and dark eyes, comes in to tell Alison that her father is in recovery and is doing well. The stroke was mild, and the damage is slight—there'll be a very mild aphasia, some small motor difficulties, all of which should fairly well correct themselves, some of it within hours or days. The discovery of the carotid-artery blockage was fortuitous, and that's been corrected. All the other arteries are clear. Oliver can return home in a couple of days, if there are no further complications and if recovery proceeds as expected. The operation was a complete success, and the prognosis is excellent. Alison has come to her feet, and now she sits down again and begins to cry. Jonathan hurries to her side, as do Holly and Fiona.

"When can I see him?"

"Be a while," says the doctor. "He's sleeping now. And the sleep is restorative. And speaking of sleep, you might go home and get some yourself. I'm going to."

"I'm afraid to leave here."

"It's going to be morning before you can see him."

Alison says nothing for a moment.

"He'll be fine," says Holly. "You should get some rest, honey."

When Alison was small, and her mother had the aneurysm, she left the hospital with her father without talking to her. That afternoon, Mary slipped quietly away. It's all happening again, and Alison can't leave, won't leave. "I'm staying," she says.

So, the waiting continues until well toward morning. The two ladies keep her company. Holly talks again about her last husband and the stone cottage in Scotland. But she's cheerful now, clearly aiming to distract the younger woman. Fiona and Jonathan play tic-tac-toe. Before first light, they all slip into little noddings-off. Kalie sleeps soundly through it all.

"Did I ever sleep that uncomplicatedly?" Fiona asks no one in particular. Then she sits forward and says, quite as if she's just now discovering it: "I feel very good this morning. I feel useful. I don't mean this in a bad way, but I like the feeling."

FAULT

I.

While Elizabeth sleeps more peacefully than she has in years, Butterfield tosses and turns. She sleeps without dreams—or if she has dreams, say they are visions of abundance, a feast enjoyed on a brilliantly flowered veranda overlooking a tranquil emerald coastline, in the calming rush of white-topped waves rolling in from the sparkling, far-darkening, blue-green horizon; a gathering, by that same dream sea, of all the people she has ever loved, and everyone loving her back with the kind of perfection and uncomplicated profusion that is only possible, alas, in dreams.

Butterfield does sleep a little, and then wakes up and remembers Ariana. *No one will ever know. If you don't tell anyone, then no one will ever ever know. It was wonderful and no one will ever know.*

Now, his beloved wife rolls over onto him and kisses him, and jokes about morning breath. For Butterfield, the joke contains a terribly distressing sense of the worm in the apple, but this is an old trait of his, now deepened, made worse by his present difficulty. Even when he was a boy—oh, so many years before he was an adulterer—the sight of a resplendently lovely natural scene never failed to make him think about how that loveliness concealed decay and desperate struggles, every acre of exquisite forest teeming with predation. Nature itself has always appalled him. He used to imagine how it would be to stumble onto Earth from some other reality, another home in the stars, only to find a world where creatures must eat other creatures in order to survive. Seeing the world from this imaginary sensibility always made him acutely aware of the relentless particulars of existence.

He kisses Elizabeth on this summery, bright early morning and attempts to put down the blackness in his mind. *No one will ever know.*

Years ago, during his first marriage, he drove up into the mountains alone—it was after some conflict involving the first Elizabeth and Mark and Gail—and, stopping to get out and breathe the air, he discovered a little place just past the nine-mile post, along Sky Line drive. It was at the end of a long declivity paved in loose gravel and then unpaved, a dirt path, leading by steady degrees downward to a trickle of a waterfall, a steep cliff, and a flat rock where he could sit and gaze through the top branches of trees at the other line of mountains across the Shenandoah Valley. He walked here simply to see where the gravel path led, since it seemed to lead toward the steep edge of nowhere. Finding the waterfall, he sat on the rock and waited for his equilibrium to return, somehow realizing that this was what would happen—that the scene itself, with its green silence broken only by birdsong and the small splashing of the water down the rocks, would calm his blood and return him to himself.

He has gone back there several times since, and for exactly the same reason—to seek the sweet calm it has always yielded.

Perhaps today he'll make some excuse and drive up there. He thinks of meeting Ariana in that sun-dappled remoteness, and his stomach seizes up. He never told anyone about the little waterfall—not the first Elizabeth, nor this one, who now yawns, stretches, rises in her lovely nudity, and—oh, such pretty long legs, such a wondrously swaying stride—goes into the bathroom.

Yesterday, in The Heart's Ease bookstore, for some damnable reason, he told Ariana Bromberg about the path down to the waterfall, the nine-mile post.

"Jesus Christ Almighty," he murmurs.

He hears Elizabeth start the shower and listens for a while, thinking of the sleepy sound of a summer daybreak in the rain, the once-restfulness of that seasonal music. At length, he rises and, still naked, makes his way down to the kitchen, where he puts coffee on, then stands at the window over the sink, looking out at the dim lawn with its uncut grass and its bare patches of dirt and tree root and stone. Bells sound in the distance, Sunday morning in his valley town. He scratches himself, a humble movement as ancient as walking upright, first the top of his head, then his backside, and then his groin, shuddering with the knowledge of the lies he will have to tell and go on telling. He looks down. Here is the equipment with which he has betrayed everything. It's so humble, so harmless-looking, so insignificant. Oh, the hour is early, still. There's a merciless quality to the way the day is beginning, as if nothing has changed at all. Light hasn't even quite reached past the mountains in their autumnal spatters of color—burnished red, stark yellow, and brown. He pours himself a glass of milk, wanting to settle his stomach, waiting for the coffee to drip. He stands at the sink, swallowing the milk, remarking to himself the cold sweetness of it and the way it slakes his dry mouth, the pleasantness of it even in his disturbed state. The world's sensations are not fundamentally changed by one's failures. Well. Such an odd thought. The mind going on, presenting him with its own little suddennesses of image and motion. Back upstairs, he kisses his wife's cheek and begins dressing himself. She goes downstairs, humming softly. It's a lovely morning for her. He dresses and follows her down. As he reaches the bottom of the stairs, the doorbell rings, startling as death news. It's like the tolling of the Last Judgment. Who in God's name at this hour but someone with bad news, someone coming to tell everything? *No one will ever know*

He thinks irrationally of the car in the driveway and hurries soundlessly back up the stairs. He hears Elizabeth call for him to open the door and remains quiet. And now he hears her come into the foyer.

"Oh," she says, rather too brightly, opening the door. "Good morning."

"Wanna have some coffee?" Ariana's voice.

He waits for her to go on and tell the rest. *Your husband and I got naked on the floor behind the counter in the Heart's Ease. He locked the door and put the gone to lunch sign up. We fucked like two people who've been denied it for centuries and were storing it all up. I told him no one would ever know.*

"I know it's early," Ariana goes on. "But I thought you might like to come over for a mimosa. A Sunday coffee."

Oh, Christ.

"Um, I guess, sure. I think my husband may have gone back to bed."

The two women step out onto the porch. They're talking. Words that he can't distinguish. And then there are other voices, too.

He moves to the bedroom window and looks out. The red Subaru is parked out front. They've all come to confront him, the women in his life. He hurries downstairs, blood rising, a pressure under his eyes. Pulling the door open, he comes upon a scene of simple sociability. Elizabeth seems fine, is busy introducing Ariana to Fiona and Holly, both of whom, he sees now, do appear a bit ragged and the worse for wear. They have two children with them—the contractor Oliver Ward's grandchildren—they hang back, the boy keeping his arm around the younger girl. Butterfield smiles at the boy, who can't seem to decide what to do with his hands. They're all gathered in the cool, slanting shade from the awning over the window to the right of the door. It's a bright, cloudless day, with quick, cold breezes.

"Where'd you go?" Elizabeth asks him.

But now Fiona's telling about the night she and Holly spent in the emergency room. "Full recovery, though," Holly says. "It's turned out to be a good thing because they caught something else that might've been trouble down the road."

Elizabeth says, "Hello, Jonathan."

"Hello."

"Jonathan's in my first-period English class, aren't you Jonathan."

"Quite so," says Jonathan, smiling embarrassedly.

"We're going to spend the day," Holly says, "so Alison can have the time at the hospital."

"It's going to be just fine," says Fiona, though her eyes betray her. Fiona can't believe the good news, even as she repeats it. Being close to any kind of physical ailment exaggerates her already highly tuned belief in the fragility of life. Now she talks about going to church to make a visit and light a candle. Her religious feeling has often seemed rather like something she keeps in case a need arises. Butterfield thinks she's been scared back to her religious childhood by the long night she's just been through. He understands the feeling while trying to dismiss the notion, for its unkindness.

"We're taking them to get some ice cream," Fiona says, "and then I thought we'd come to The Heart's Ease to look at the books." She leans down to Kalie. "Don't you worry, sweetie. It's gonna be fine."

"We didn't want you to wonder what happened to us," Holly says to Butterfield. "We tried and tried to call you. Last night and this morning. Is something wrong with your phone?"

Elizabeth gives her husband a look and says, "Let me go check." She steps quickly into the house and closes the door.

Fiona stares at Butterfield. "You look a little rumpled. You gonna wear that to the store?"

"We tried to call," Holly says.

Elizabeth comes back and raises her eyebrows as if to express puzzlement. "Nothing wrong with the phone. I mean there's a dial tone and everything." Again, she sends a look Butterfield's way.

Holly walks with Jonathan and the little girl back to the car, and Fiona trails along behind them. "We'll be at that ice cream parlor up the street from you," Holly says over her shoulder. "Then we'll bring them down. You're heading out to the store, right?"

"He looks rumpled to be going to The Heart's Ease," says Fiona.

"Shouldn't they have something like breakfast?" Butterfield asks.

"Try not to think like a parent all the time," Holly smiles back. "They've been through a rough night. It's just this once."

They get into the car and pull away—Holly driving.

"Guess you don't feel like coffee now," says Ariana to Elizabeth.

Elizabeth answers, "Sorry." And there is in her voice the sorrow for other things, for the fact that a wonderful evening and night like the one she has just spent must end in new complications involving the Crazies. Though, when she passes close to Butterfield, she takes his arm above the elbow and leans into him. A nudge, gentle and, under the circumstances, harrowing.

"Well, let's get together sometime," says Ariana.

"Yes," Elizabeth says without much feeling. "Let's."

She and Butterfield are inside the house before he can find the strength to say anything at all. "Poor Mr. Ward," he says.

She looks at him. "Are you all right? Your color's not good." She puts her hand on his forehead.

"I'm fine," he says, feeling sick to his stomach. "Really."

She says something in a vaguely flirtatious way about the fact that there's time for a little more frolicking. But she doesn't act on it. He can't clear his mind. His sense of calamity unfolding increases as she follows him upstairs. "Come here," she says. "Cuddle me." So he holds her, lying on the made bed. It's hard to believe that she doesn't feel the throbbing in his head, the culpable shuddering at the heart of him. Finally, she props herself on one elbow and looks down at him, so lovely. "I guess we should go," she says. Sunday is usually a busy day in the bookstore. The sliver of light from the window illuminates her exquisite brown hair. The heel of her hand is against the side of her face, pulling the perfect skin next to her eye up slightly. Gazing at this does something wonderful to him, deep—her eyes are so dark, so depthless, almost Asian-looking. Everything about her pleases him. And the knowledge of this sends him into an inward spiral of self-loathing and fright.

"It's been a lovely time," he manages.

She frowns. "I swear there's something—are you sure everything's okay?"

"Yes," he tells her, though he can't look her in the eye.

"Fiona surprised me. I've never seen her so—tentative."

"Maybe it's just lack of sleep."

"Will." Elizabeth suppresses a laugh. "She was positively grandmotherly." Then her face changes, a shadow crosses. She sighs.

"What is it?" he says.

She moves to get up. "I'm thinking about last night. I wish all our nights could be like that."

Sometimes it seems to him that the only true simplicity is far outside himself—the view from two thousand feet, near a little waterfall in the mountains.

"I might go for a drive this afternoon," he says.

She appears to consider this. Then she shrugs and moves into the bathroom. "Maybe we'll both go." She closes the door.

He opens the door and walks in to where she's standing before the sink, brushing her hair. He cleans his teeth again, brushes his own hair. He tells her about the little waterfall, the path down to it through the trees, through leaf shade and sun. It brings about a refinement of his guilt, like an invisible hand turning a knife blade under his breastbone. He almost chokes on the words.

She drives him to the store. He kisses her good-bye and watches as the car goes on down the street and through the blinking yellow light there. It's as if she's driving straight to the bottom of the mountain at the end of the road, but then the road takes her down and out of sight to the left, past the row of buildings at that end of the street.

He opens the store, walks past the guilty space, breathing deeply, thinking about being up in the mountains, in that secluded little spot, and then thinking intentionally about the slaughter of the innocents in fifteenth-century Europe. He makes himself keep moving through the rows of shelves, dusting the surfaces. He's always been proud of this place, and now it's changed forever; and he wishes he could've taken the car and headed up to the nine-mile post, to walk the path to the falls, alone, he tells himself, no one else there, not Elizabeth, not Ariana, not anyone—just to look at the valley, his home, in the bright, clear morning. The leaves at altitude will be such a profusion of color, that miracle of death and transfiguration.

Opening the blinds of the front windows, he sees Holly and Fiona pull up, with the two children in the car.

Fiona leads them through the store, pointing out likely candidates for them to get—she'll buy whatever they like—and Holly stands with Butterfield at the counter, Butterfield watching it all and trying to pretend an interest. He turns to his mother at one point, as Fiona chatters with the little girl about the book *Goodnight Moon*, and murmurs, "Did you know this about her?"

Holly stares. "What?"

"The way she is with kids."

"We both love them. These are sweet kids, too. Very well trained and brave."

He wishes he had some bravery. He feels utterly craven and alone and even cowardly, not to say black-hearted. Leaning across the counter, he kisses his mother on the side of the face, while Fiona reads to the little girl, sitting on a small stool, the girl standing between her knees, head back on Fiona's heavy chest, staring wide-eyed at the book. He would never have believed this of the old woman, and this incredulity must show in his face, because his mother leans over to him and murmurs, "She used to do that with you, you know."

He shakes his head. He doesn't remember.

"She did. You were this girl's age, too. And it was that book."

Butterfield watches his great-aunt read to the little girl, and the scene takes on an aspect of lightheartedness that he wishes he could feel. It comes to him with something like a shuddering in the connective tissues on either side of his chest that he was once, in spite of a tendency to a dark frame of mind, a very happy man.

2.

Alison tries several more times to call Teddy, and she leaves several messages, trying to control her anger. She takes time to put the house in order, before going over to the hospital. She thinks Teddy might call. She wants him to call. It occurs to her that some part of her actually desires to curl up in his arms and sleep. It's only, she realizes, that she wishes to be held. She's about to leave the house at last, when Teddy does call. Somehow she gets everything out without crying. He's in Atlantic City. He's sorry about Oliver; he'll come by as soon as he gets back to Point Royal. He'll wire her some money.

"Forget it," she says. "I wasn't calling you about money."

"I know that," he says impatiently. "Why do you always have to turn things around on me like that?"

"There's someone at the door," she tells him. "I have to go."

"See who it is. I'll wait."

"Bye, Teddy," Alison says, and hangs up.

It turns out there is indeed someone at the door. The knock startles her, and she feels as if she's been caught in a lie. She moves to the window and looks out. A sandy-haired man in a T-shirt and jeans, standing there with hands folded in front. He looks vaguely familiar. She opens the door.

"Hi," he says. "I was wondering if Oliver was around?"

Alison tells him what has happened. "I'm on my way over to the hospital right now."

His face drains of color. She notices that his freckled hands shake as he pushes them through his hair. One of Oliver's drinking buddies, no doubt. "I'm awful sorry," he says. "I worked for him a few years back. My name's Stanley."

She nods, and she remembers him now. He offers his hand, so she takes it. "Alison," she says. "I've got to go."

"I'm sorry." He steps back. "I had a possibility for some work he might want to do. I'm really sorry."

"The doctors say he'll be fine. It was minor."

"Well, please give him my best. Tell him Stanley, you know, if you don't mind. I ran into him—" He pauses, looking down. "I—we bumped into each other, you know, a while back."

"The county jail?" Alison says. She can't help herself.

"Yeah. I fell asleep in a phone booth." His smile is shamefaced. He shuffles slightly, looking off. "Ridiculous."

"I'm not going to argue with you," she tells him.

"Well," he says. "Of course not. Tell Oliver—well, yeah. You know, give him my best."

"Do you want him to call you?"

"If he's up to it. Or I could stop by and say hello."

"I'll tell him," she says.

Later, she sits next to her father in the small hospital room, watching the football game. Usually, when they watch, they make fun of the announcers, and, at first, her father, even with his slightly halt speech patterns, seems much like himself—funny, noting the failures of expression, the malapropisms and unconscious revelations of an astounding poverty of values, the hypocrisies inherent in the sport. How empty the highly touted values it supposedly teaches actually are: if you don't get caught, no penalty; if you get a chance to hit someone beyond the rules, take it; build on intimidation, dominance, fear, pain, gang action, violence that is purely designed to make mayhem. They love it. Oliver calls it "watching the millionaires."

Now, after the first few minutes, he seems to grow sleepy. He squeezes her hand and mutters: "Watch. They'll—call—somebody—a wa—water—bug. If he's black. If he's—wh—white, it'll be something—ph—physical, inanimate, like a—a machine."

She smiles, and he smiles back. He's already made a little progress toward recovery. But, of course, this trouble has brought home to her in the most potent way how much she depends on him and how wobbly everything is. She moves her chair closer and tries to keep the spirit of things cheerful. She holds his hand, here, in the little room, and, on the television, men in bright colors pummel each other in the roar of the stadium crowd.

"The kids?" he says.

"Holly and Fiona have them."

"Imagine—that."

"I know. I never would've believed it from those first times. They've been so good, though. They stayed with me that whole night, when it happened. I don't know what I would've done."

"What about—tomorrow? Will—you—be able to visit me—" he has to strain now, and the frustration shows in his face, the tic working, the hypothalamic denial going on, more pronounced because of his anger. Finally, he gets it out. "Tomorrow?"

"Jonathan has school. Kalie will stay with them. You know I will."

He squeezes again. There are plastic tubes running into his nose and along his wrist, an apparatus next to the bed, a structure of ill health. All part of the badness of her father being here.

They watch the game. In the next bed, partly obscured by a hanging curtain that ought to be more privacy-making, is a man with some sort of trouble in his legs—he's had surgery, too, and is also hooked to an IV. He sleeps fitfully, saying names. His chin descends into his neck, a single slack fold of gray-stubbled flesh. He looks helpless and too inert, until he utters the names, and then he seems dimly pathetic. There's something exasperated and anxious in his voice. "Lillian," he murmurs. "Georgia. Belle—Belle, honey?"

An elderly woman nods off in a chair by his bed. When she opens her gray eyes, dazed and sleepy, she looks at Alison through the open space in the curtain and nods with a seriousness that seems faintly censorious, as if the opening is Alison's fault.

"Elaine?" the man mutters, and then mumbles something indistinguishable. "Lydia," he says.

The woman looks at Alison. "People who work for him," she says. "He runs a sheet-glass store." This seems oddly flimsy as an explanation: there's something too familiar in the way he says the names.

"Marie, you sweetie."

"Shut up, Drew," the woman says. She looks at Alison. "He's had phlebitis. He's going to be okay."

Alison nods and looks away.

"Oh," the man mumbles, seeming about to laugh. "Agnes, for Christ's sweet sake."

The woman turns a bright violet color and gets up to close the curtain. "You're talking in your sleep, Drew. Shut up."

"Oh, Martha. I got a headache."

"It's the medicine. Shut up."

Alison stands and kisses the side of her father's face, and then sits down again. Oliver winks at her. "Gonna be—fine," he says.

In the first hour, he was angry at the doctors and nurses, cursing them, a man frustrated to the point of rage at the nonunderstanding of everyone around him. The doctors told Alison that this was normal, that this was all part of the attack, and was probably healthy. In any case, it was unavoidable. So, the wink, now, is especially charming, and it is intended, she's certain, knowing him as she does, to communicate to her his understanding that the worst is over; he will be himself again. He is already showing that, squeezing her hand once more and then patting the back of it.

The game goes on in a blaze of scoring. Washington and Dallas, neither side playing much defense—it seems at first that the thing must surely be decided by who has the ball last. But then, shortly after the start of the second half, Dallas begins to pull away. They're up by twenty-four points as the fourth quarter begins, and they have the ball again. Oliver has watched and dozed and waked, teasing *her* about sleeping through it, and now he stirs, gives her hand another soft pat.

"Hell," he says. "Let's go. The Redskins—don't stand a—a—chance now."

"Go?" Alison says.

"We'll miss the—traffic." The phrase seems momentarily to have confused him. He looks at her and then slowly gazes at the curtains surrounding the bed. It's as if he decides that his first impression is indeed right: they can get up and leave now. They can miss the traffic. But, then, another glance around convinces him otherwise. His mouth tightens, and it's clear that he wants to keep from her what has just happened.

"You should go get the kids. And—don't—worry—"

"Daddy," she says, fighting back tears.

He nods at her and smiles. It's a little conspiracy they act out, to keep from herself her own perception that this might actually be the beginning of something they have both dreaded. His eyes well up.

"They said you're going to make a full recovery," she tells him.

The voice on the speaker system announces that visiting hours are over. She stands, leans over him, and kisses his cool, dry forehead, then steps back. His eyes follow her.

"You look so much like your mother."

She bows. It's the old exchange between them. She kisses him again, and then asks if he wants the television off.

"I like the noise." He gestures with his head toward the hanging curtain and the other bed. "I think they might want it on."

"Okay."

At the door, she pauses. The elderly woman is still beyond the curtain. Alison starts back to Oliver—she won't leave until the hospital enforces the end of visiting hours. But then, the elderly woman makes her way across the foot of Oliver's bed. She's carrying a paper bag and a heavy-looking purse, and she looks at Alison with concern that Alison knows is a reluctance to get tangled at the door with leave-taking. Alison blows Oliver a kiss, and walks out into the hall and, along it, to the exit.

3.

Monday, at the high school, Elizabeth goes through the long morning, giving writing assignments, filling out forms, spending time in the library. She works with Calvin Reed for a few minutes, just before the lunch hour, and the boy seems to have drawn even further down into himself. She says, "Do you think you could meet me halfway a little?"

He stares dumbly at her.

"Just make the slightest effort."

"No." On his assignment, which is supposed to be a narrative, he has written: "Got arrested summer. B & E. Distruckshun of goods. Nobody home. Got plasted. Thru up all over."

She looks at it. She has learned that the best kind of response to writing is always specific and involving not the expression—at least, in the beginning—but the subject matter, to earn the student's trust. She says, "Is this *your* home you're talking about?"

He shrugs. "It says B & E."

"Can you tell me more about it?"

"No."

"I want to help you, Calvin. But you have to let me." The words feel stale in her mouth.

His expression is of complete nonunderstanding. But there's something else, too—a kind of blank coldness, as though she's something made of metal, about which he feels only the mildest curiosity. She thinks of the cold eyes of cats, the dead stare of a snake.

When James Christ comes in, he wants to tell her about a disturbance out in the hall. He had to break up a fight between two girls. "There's three groups in this school," he tells her. "The leaders, the mob, and the sufferers."

"It's like that in every school," Elizabeth says, barely listening to him.

"Yeah, well I got ganged up on. I was one of the sufferers. Can you imagine what I went through with my name? I'm still going through it. But you're right. It's the world. And I guess I better get used to it."

"But it isn't supposed to be about you, now, is it?"

"Oh, well pardon me all to hell."

Sometimes it seems to Elizabeth that, in his small way, James Christ, by the very fact of his namesake, underscores the sense of Christ as historical: a man, with a man's temperament and a man's frailties, whatever else he was. It's abysmal to think of the son of God being, even for a moment, petulant or irritable. Annoyed by a sound. Last spring, a bird outside her window seemed to repeat the same five syllables over and over, like a high-pitched cackle in the back of the throat of a very old witch. On and on it went, and she, who loves birds and birdsong, would gladly have shot it if she could've located it.

Now, in the early afternoon, she heads to the STOP room where, confirming her own unpleasant expectations, she finds Calvin, sitting in the first stall with a pencil in his hands, legs straight out under the table, down-slanting shoulders slumped, a little nervous motion of the hands with the pencil the only motion at all. He's staring at the shiny surface of the desk, polished black slate.

There's no one else in the room. Usually, there are at least three or four others. She takes her seat at the front of this classroom with dark paint over the window in the door, and the rows of stalls, each with its chair and its table. As she takes her seat, she watches Calvin, who doesn't look up, seems not to have heard her come in. "Did you sign in?" she asks him.

He nods without turning.

On the sheet before her is the paper with lines for students to write their names and the time they arrived. He hasn't put the time down. She writes it in for him, then sits back and brings *The Great Gatsby* out of her bag. "Do you have something to do?" she asks him.

"No."

"Your teacher didn't give you anything?"

"Math. Fuck it."

"You know what the rules are about that kind of talk, Calvin."

"Fuck it," he says.

How much a part of her would like to stand and say, "Well, you know, all right. And fuck *you*, Calvin. Fuck *you* and everybody that looks like you." But she holds her temper, opens the drawer of the desk, brings out a piece of paper, and stands to take it to him. Now he does

look at her—at the front of her. There's something so measuring, so na-
kedly lubricious about it that she almost stops and turns from him. It
requires a kind of dismissal of her own doubts to keep coming toward
him. She hands him the paper. "Draw me something."

His eyes have trailed up her body to her face. There is nothing at all
in his expression.

"Go on," she says. "I know you can draw. Draw me anything."

He shrugs and moves the pencil, holding the paper she's given him
and gazing at it as if he expects it to begin speaking to him.

She returns to the desk, sits, and reads for a time, purely for the
pleasure of it, though she will be teaching it soon enough. Then, because she has to, she takes out her work folder with its hundred essays
in it. She hears the pencil moving on the page, and so she watches him
a little, surreptitiously. His intentness grows. He's soon lost in whatever he's drawing, his knuckles showing white where his fingers grip
the pencil. The pencil makes a scratching sound, and she wonders why
the point doesn't break on it. She tries to read a little. She recalls Saturday night with Will, how perfect it was and peaceful. But then she remembers that, on Saturday, Oliver Ward had a stroke and poor Jonathan
Lawrence spent the night in a hospital waiting room. She glances up at
Calvin, who's still moving the pencil point hard back and forth on the
page, concentrating so heavily, staring down. Her own sensitivity to the
troubles of others often makes her feel susceptible, exposed, and there
is always the urge to look for some way to help. Before her are all these
student essays to evaluate, and she begins doing that.

Calvin makes a small, child-voiced, throat-clearing sound. It amazes
her, the notes his larynx can reach, coming from that big body. She looks
up and sees that he's holding the paper toward her. She stands, reaches
for it, but he draws it back.

"Just want to show it first," he says.

She comes around the desk and approaches him. She can see from
here that he's filled the page with something dark, a lot of shading and
dark lines. Before she can get to him, the door opens and another boy is
there, with Mr. Petit. The boy is all slouch and swagger. "This young
man will be spending the next hour here," says Mr. Petit. "His name is
Roger Stillman."

The boy stares hatefully, but is silent.

Elizabeth hands Mr. Petit a referral sheet.

"Can you please fill it out for me?" he says. The look on his face stops her.

"Of course."

"I have work to do. It was Mrs. Terrence who sent him to me in the first place."

The boy walks to a chair opposite Calvin and sits down, still glaring.

Mr. Petit leaves, and Elizabeth writes out the referral.

"You know why he won't suspend me?" the boy says.

Calvin's staring at his drawing and makes no response.

"Because I know something."

Elizabeth says, "Quiet please."

And there is quiet. A long, freighted silence. Time comes for Calvin to go to his next class, a gym class, though Elizabeth supposes that the gym teacher will send him right back here. He'll no doubt spend many days this year in this room. Now he scratches his name on the sign-out sheet, his drawing folded and stuffed into his ratty notebook.

"May I see the drawing, Calvin?"

He looks at her and then at the boy. "No."

"I can insist, you know."

Reluctantly, he takes the drawing out and holds it toward her. It's a nude, perfectly rendered. A woman lying back on a bed, legs slightly spread, staring. The face is startlingly, very disturbingly, like Elizabeth's, as is the shape of the body. She works to ignore this, though she feels as if this is a form of aggression. Of course, to show him that he has upset her would give him exactly what he wants. "You have talent," she tells him, handing the drawing back.

"I can make more."

"That would be boring, though."

He actually smiles—a thin, loutish grin. "Not really."

"Why aren't you in the art classes here?"

"Color-blind."

"Do you know the drawings of M. C. Escher?"

"I've got to go," he says.

She walks with him to the door, and when she steps out into the hall, he walks past her and on, not looking back. "Calvin?" she says.

He stops. The bulk of him in the hallway is almost frightful; four other kids walk by him, not even coming up to his waist. His hips are so wide, his legs are like thick stumps, and he's wearing his pants the way all the boys wear them now—halfway down his ass.

"Stay out of trouble?" she makes herself say. "Don't come back?"

He nods again, more definitely this time, and walks—lurches, it seems—away. When she starts back into the STOP room, she nearly collides with James Christ, coming from the other direction. It's like one of those comic passes in the movies: they move one way and then the other in tandem, and then she reaches over and takes his arms above the elbow and moves him. "I'm getting another job," he says. "I'm already gone."

4.

Alison drives to Holly and Fiona's house. There's no haze at all in the air now, and the mountains in the distance are a crisp, bright palette of color. How tired and depleted she is. Today, Oliver was mostly sleepy and unresponsive, so she simply held his hand and read a magazine article about global warming. Now, pulling up to the curb, she sees Kalie out on the sidewalk in front of the house. Kalie's drawing with chalk on the concrete, and Holly stands with her, watching. Alison gets out of the car, and, as she approaches, realizes that Fiona is sitting on the roof of the house, a blanket over her shoulders, wearing a wide-brimmed straw hat against the sun. She has her arms resting on her upraised knees, and sips something out of a cup. Alison looks at her and waves. But Fiona is gazing off at the distance.

"Pay no attention to that man behind the curtain," Holly says, smiling.

Alison stares.

"Fiona's having one of her fits."

Fiona sips whatever's in the cup and then holds it up as if to toast them.

"She wants me to call your colleagues, you know. But I'm not obliging, so she's a bit stuck. You never saw anyone stubborn as that lady."

"It must be cold up there," Alison says. Then, to Fiona: "You know you ought to come down from there. You might fall."

"Are you on duty, dear?" Fiona asks.

"Do I look it?"

"Shouldn't you do something?"

"Why don't you come down. I've got an impressionable somebody to think about, you know? And a good example means a lot, don't you think?"

"I'm enjoying the finer things up high. It's quite safe."

Holly laughs. "One card less than a deck," she murmurs. Then she bends, with hands on knees, admiring Kalie's drawing, which is of a big cartoon face, a line mouth drawn in a long, thin smile, enormous, floppy-looking ears. She has colored the eyes a strange, deep pond green. Next to that is another figure—something like a dinosaur, wearing a derby hat, with a bright yellow mane jutting from it. The mane, Kalie says proudly, was her idea. Alison kneels and kisses the side of Kalie's face, admiring with her the work she has done, wanting to hold on.

"It's such a nice view of the sky from up here," Fiona calls from the roof. "I don't think anyone could make me come down."

"I don't think anyone's going to try," Holly calls to her, "sweetheart."

"It won't matter. I'm staying. I like it."

"You do that, lovie. You must be a little chilly, though."

"Nothing I can't stand. I can always jump down if I get too cold, you know."

Alison walks to the spot of ground just beneath where the old woman is sitting and says, "You have to not talk like that around my child."

"Sweetie," Holly says to Kalie, "let's go in the house, what do you say?"

"Okay," says Kalie, rising, smacking herself on the backside to remove dust.

"I think it's best," Holly says to Alison, "if we pretend that the crank on the roof isn't there."

"That's not easy to do," Alison says, "given my job, and I'm talking about both of you. Please."

"How's Oliver today?"

Alison manages to tell the other woman about the morning.

"That's common with strokes, honey. Sleepiness. It goes away. They've got it in hand. He's still young."

Alison thinks of the long hours in the waiting room, the talk, and the feeling that she wanted to collapse in the arms of the two old ladies and be taken care of by them. She feels it now, though one of them is perched on the roof of the house, quietly peeling the paper away from the label of a Coke bottle she's produced from a fold of her blanket.

"How did she get all that up there with her?" Alison asks.

"She made three trips." Holly smiles. "You have to admire that, I guess."

"What are you talking about down there?" Fiona asks.

"Not you," says Holly, smiling. "Sorry."

"I hope not." Fiona smiles back. "Lord. What a bad subject."

"Let's go in and see about getting something to eat," Holly says to Alison, approaching her with Kalie, holding Kalie's hand.

"I'll be down in a little while," Fiona says.

Alison, Holly, and the little girl step into the apparent disarray of Oliver's work on the house. Holly moves the plastic tarp aside like a curtain.

She asks what she should make for them to eat, and Alison presses her not to worry about it. "We should go," she says. But Kalie wants to stay a little longer, and so Alison takes a seat on the sofa, with its view of the stacked wallboard in the hall.

"Pay no attention to that man behind the curtain," Holly says again, smiling.

As if this speech were some sort of off-handed cue, a police car pulls onto the street and speeds to the curb in front of the house, lights flashing, no siren. Holly shakes her head. "Oh, Lord. Fiona's got a cell phone." She starts out of the house. Alison follows, remembering to turn and tell Kalie to stay where she is in the house.

The police are Harvey and Eddie from the precinct, and Eddie will be trouble, because he's rigid and narrow, unable to look to one side or the other; he goes by the book and is proud of it. Harv is too heavy for his own good, gentle and friendly and generally incapable of making a real decision on his own. Alison has, in fact, spent time advising him about his hapless love life. Now Eddie's saying to Holly, "You mean *she* made the call? *She* made it?"

"I'm afraid so," Holly says. "I'm so sorry."

"That's breaking the law," Eddie says. "I've got to arrest her for it." Then he sees Alison.

"Hey."

"No arrest this time, Eddie, really."

Eddie moves toward the house a little and looks up at the old woman sitting there in the bright sun. "You know it's a felony to call a false alarm in. You know that."

"I don't know what I'm likely to do," Fiona says. "So I don't think it's a false alarm. Although I know some people do. I really am feeling a little desperate. I think I might do something awful."

"Will you please come down from there?"

Fiona says nothing.

"We can talk about it," Harv says.

"There's no telling what might happen," Fiona answers with great seriousness.

"Did you pull the ladder up after you?" Alison asks her.

"I didn't mean to cause trouble. I felt so good being *useful*. Ask her what she did."

"We don't have time for this," Eddie says. "You come down now or I'm going to take you to jail. I mean it. I'll book you. I'm going to write you a citation."

"She said I was in the way. I only wanted to help."

Alison looks back at the house, Kalie standing there in the screen door, her thumb in her mouth. She moves to Eddie's side. "Really," she says. "I've got this one, Eddie. I'll owe you one."

"It's on the manifest," he says. "The call went out."

"I'll handle it."

He shakes his head, turning to Harv, who smiles and shrugs. Harv thinks it's kind of funny: an old lady sitting on a roof, talking trouble.

"I didn't say she was in the way," Holly says. "That's only how she interpreted it."

"You *can't* think this makes any difference to us," Eddie says. "We're not here to settle your disputes. I'm gonna get back in that car and drive around the block and when I come back if she's still up there I'm gonna arrest you both and put you in that car and take you to jail."

Alison says, "Bye, guys. Thanks for coming out."

"I didn't call you," Holly says to Eddie. "I'm going back in the house. I have nothing to do with this. If you arrest anyone, you know who it'll be." She turns to look at her aunt. "You heard that, Fiona. I'm going in the house." She faces Eddie again. "I'm sorry she did this, Eddie, I truly am."

"Do I know you?" Eddie says. He's offended now.

"Eddie," says Alison, "try to let yourself go a little and be nice, huh?"

"I'm not moving," says Fiona from the roof, "until she apologizes."

Holly says, too quickly, "I'm so sorry, dear."

"She doesn't mean it."

Eddie says: "One revolution around the block, and if that roof ain't empty I swear somebody's going to jail." The two policemen get into the car and pull slowly away.

Alison gestures for Holly to go in the house and then stands facing the old lady on the roof. "You come down. Right now. I mean it. I won't have my little girl exposed to this kind of behavior. Do you understand me, Fiona? Right now." She doesn't wait for a response but goes on into the house. She's fairly certain that Eddie will return and she won't be able to stop him from making an arrest. Pathology. And there will be no one to watch Kalie while she goes to visit Oliver. Oh, how she hates it that Marge is gone, though, in fact, she never felt quite at ease when Marge was babysitting, either.

Holly seems amused, moving through the hanging plastic tarp to the back windows and peering through the curtains.

"It's fine," she says. "Here she comes. Everybody look busy."

Alison sits on the couch quickly, while Kalie simply stands in the middle of the living room and stares at the door. Holly has gone into the kitchen and is rattling dishes. "I'm going to cut up some fresh mozzarella," she calls. "We'll have Caprese. Fiona's favorite."

And here is Fiona, entering from the back door, straw hat still on. There's some shingle-grit on the palms of her hands. She's gotten a streak of it on her cheeks. "I dropped the ladder," she says. "It knocked over one of the tiki lamps out there. Broken glass on the patio."

"I'll get it," says Holly. "But right now I'm making Caprese."

"I've never been a fan of that," says Fiona.

"You always loved it. It's your favorite."

"We really have to go," Alison says, standing. She gives Kalie a look that lets her know she means business.

"My niece is stubborn," says Fiona with a little grin. "But don't go."

"Yes," says Holly. "Stubborn would be the word."

The two old ladies go into the kitchen together, and Alison watches Kalie stare after them with a dreamy expression of complete contentment on her face. In the kitchen, there's the sound of dishes being brought out, doors opening and closing. The two voices are soft and agreeable.

Fiona comes in, drying her hands on a small dish cloth. "Would they have arrested me?" she asks.

"Yes," Alison tells her.

"I would never do anything, you know. Though I was feeling pretty desperate."

"Fiona, please."

"He'll be fine," Fiona tells her. "I'm sorry. Will you forgive me?"

"I want you to do something for me," Alison says. "Then I'll forgive you."

"Anything, sweetie."

Alison points through the entrance to the dining room at the broken glass with its companion, lying there. "I want you to pick that up."

Fiona's face takes on the look of a caught child. She frowns, actually wrings her hands, partly turning away.

"That's my condition, Fiona."

"I don't know why it has to be me that gets singled out," Fiona says.

"Please," says Alison. "For me. And for Kalie."

"Well, for you two." Now there seems something like relief in the old woman's tone. She walks over, bends down, and retrieves the unbroken glass and the largest shard of the broken one. Holly appears from the kitchen with a washrag.

"Here," she says cheerfully. "Let me help you, dear."

5.

Oliver dreams he's in a dark place on a dark path leading to more dark. A terrible dark ahead, and there is ominous music all around him. It's a horror film, and he's both a character in it and the person watching it. He takes a step, and then someone else is there. Jesus. He realizes, it is Jesus. Actually. The Son of God. But then also, in the logic of the dream, this presence is Death, too. The terrifying thing itself. Jesus/Death approaches him reassuringly. "Don't worry," Jesus/Death says in a voice Oliver knows—intellectually, without quite feeling it—is the voice of hope, comfort, respite. "It's fine. It's going to be fine." Oliver looks into the human-shaped light of this companionate presence and abruptly does feel the peace that passeth understanding coming over him. He has the thought, feeling the sweet cessation of fear. It's going to be fine. The voice has told him, and the human-shaped light is standing there by his side. Pointing to the darkness ahead, he speaks to the shape: "Will you walk there with me, then?" And, out of the warm light, the voice says, "Are you out of your mind? *I'm* not going over there. Uh-unh. Not me. You're on your own."

And Oliver wakes up.

Early evening in the hospital. He turns his head slightly against the bandage on the side of his neck and looks to the entrance of the room. A nurse walks by the door, pushing a cart with something smelly on it. It's the dinner hour, and the malodorous something Oliver breathes is ten hospital-food trays, each of which contains a serving of broccoli. He hates broccoli. He has joked about how he never puts anything in his mouth that smells as though it has already been eaten and then brought up again, and never mind the health benefits.

In the bed next to him, Drew, with his phlebitis, groans softly, and then says, "What's that?"

"Broccoli," Oliver tells him.

Silence.

"What *is* that?"

"Broccoli."

Drew sighs. "Mary Kate."

Oliver's silent.

"Helena Marie. Baby."

"Dinner's coming," Oliver says. He's tired of the names.

"Did you say something?" Drew asks.

"I said din—" Oliver begins.

But then he can't say the word. This enrages him, though he knows somewhere down inside himself that this is not a reasonable reaction to the experience. The rage goes out toward poor Drew, who groans again and says, "I was dreaming something. Woman I knew. What're you telling me?"

Oliver manages to say, "Noth—ing. For—get it."

Drew's wife comes in. And Oliver listens to them talk—there's an irritability in their voices, though the words he hears are mostly endearments: darling, sweetie, angel. These are evidently terms that Drew and his wife have used so often and for so long that they issue forth even in expressions of mutual annoyance or impatience. Oliver finds himself thinking about love that has weathered everything, like a petrified old tree with thick roots churning up the ground at its base. He pictures the tree. His condition, he thinks, has made him philosophical. The thought amuses him. But it has been so many years since Mary's death. He has been alone so long, and now he has the desolate thought that Mary wouldn't have wanted him to be alone like this, in a bare room, with a television that now flicks on—Drew's wife, wanting to watch *Jeopardy!*—and a painting on the wall, of a sunny field full of unreal, yellow wildflowers and a fantastic blue, blue sky. He's lying here weeping quietly, feeling sorry for himself and then feeling sorry for all human frailty, the whole world of striving and worry, and all the children suffering everywhere. Life is infinitely sad.

Into this darkness, the nurse comes with the smelly cart. She sets the tray up, cranks Oliver to a near-sitting position. Takes a napkin and efficiently, off-handedly, almost roughly, wipes away his tears. "Dinner time," she says.

"No—broccoli," Oliver says to her.

She says nothing but takes the broccoli away. He eats slowly, nibbling—some mashed potatoes, already getting cold. There's turkey, too, thin slices, bland, so flavorless that when one part of it does taste like what he remembers as the taste, it's a shock, and makes him want to gag. He pushes the plate aside. A moment later, Stanley walks in, explaining that he asked at the front desk for him. "I stopped by your house yesterday," he says. "Alison told me."

Oliver stares at him.

"I was—I mean I saw a job I thought we might bid on, you know. It's a two-man job."

"I can't—do it," Oliver says.

"Well, it was just a shot. I wonder if there's anything you had underway that I could maybe help you with. See—the—well the truth is, I've got to catch a break with work. See."

"What—do you want—me—to—do," Oliver gets out. He can't help the impatience in his voice.

"I was just wondering," Stanley says, seeming a little lost now. He reaches for a piece of the turkey. "You're not gonna finish this?"

Oliver says, "No."

"You mind?"

"Help your—self." He watches the younger man eat what's on the plate. Stanley cleans it off, turkey, mashed potatoes, peas, cranberry sauce, and a small piece of vanilla cake.

"Didn't know how hungry I was," he says. "Damn."

Alison and Holly come in. Fiona is downstairs in the cafeteria. Alison is in uniform, having come from work. She tells him that the nurse on duty has determined that Oliver needs some rest before he can withstand the turmoil of children. Oliver wants to ask why they don't let him decide that, but the words won't come. Or they come in a garble, whose effect on Alison makes him stop. He touches her wrist and smiles, indicating Stanley, who says, "Hello again."

Alison introduces Holly. Stanley explains why he stopped by, and Holly says, "Actually, we do have work for you. You can help Mr. Ward with our house-partition project."

Oliver makes himself smile. A big chunk of thirty thousand dollars out the window.

Holly pulls a chair up and sits close. It's odd. She looks into him, with this pleasant, excited expression. "We'll increase the total amount, Mr. Ward, and you can give this young man whatever you deem necessary for him to continue with the project." She looks at Stanley. "You do this sort of work? You're good at it?"

"I'm a hard worker, yes ma'am."

"Well," Holly says. "There we are."

"I can start right away," says Stanley.

"Give him the—plans," Oliver manages, looking at Alison.

She seems worried and depressed. But she nods, and he feels his pride in her, like returning strength.

Holly says, "The sooner the better." She leans close and begins to talk about how it will be to have her own separate part of the house, as if this is a café and she and Oliver are having lunch.

"Can—I see—the children?" he says.

"Tomorrow," says Holly. "The hospital people insist."

He sighs, and Alison squeezes his hand.

PERDITION

I.

With the last days of October, as if to mark the time change, the weather turns quickly to the cold of midwinter. Oliver Ward has developed complications—a persistent fever—forcing a delay of his release from the hospital. The old ladies have been helping Alison with the children, and Elizabeth has taken on a project at the school, having to do with developing a new, programmed text for grammar.

And so several of Butterfield's evenings have been free lately.

Each time, he drove over to Macbeth's. Just to have a drink, he told himself. Each time. But, of course, Ariana Bromberg was there, and, on two separate occasions, he waited around for her shift to end. On the first occasion, they went to her car and necked like teenagers, steaming up the windows, but it didn't go further than that. There wasn't time: Shostakovich was picking her up that night. But the next time, they went to the railroad-depot parking lot. It was snowing, the kind of powdery fall that seems too thin to gather but does gather on every surface, making a deep quiet everywhere. He held her hand while she squatted next to the car to pee, and then they got into the back seat. Some part of him stood apart in amazement. He would never have believed this of himself. They had little, really, to say to each other—though they had talked in the bar. She made observations about the patrons of the place, and he talked about his mother and great-aunt, the process of dividing the house on Temporary Road. It was all rather humdrum and practical as talk, with no slight suggestion of flirtation in it. Yet, that night, in the back seat of her car, they were avid for each other. He suggested a motel in the next town, Strasburg.

"Maybe next time," she said. "We'll see." And she gave him that softly conspiratorial smile.

Oh, God.

Late at night, while Elizabeth sleeps, he sits at the window in the dining room, staring out at the next-door house, the lights there. Some lights are always on. Yet Shostakovich and his wife never seem to appear, going in or going out. It's just a house with lamps burning in the window all night, all the predawn hours, all morning.

Once Butterfield catches a glimpse of Ariana taking garbage out to the curb. She's in a yellow bathrobe, and her hair's in a knot at the base of her neck. She walks out and then back in, without looking at the street, without even seeming to watch where she's going. On the way out, she dropped a piece of paper—a wrapper of some kind—and she steps past it and back indoors without seeming to notice it.

Two weeks before Thanksgiving, Elizabeth runs into Ariana at the grocery store and ends up inviting her to dinner for that Friday night. "I didn't know what to say to her," she tells Butterfield, "and she kept hinting about it. They've been there for weeks and we haven't made any kind of gesture. I felt wrong about it. We did tell them we'd get together—or you told them."

"It's what you say under the circumstances," Butterfield says. "Jesus."

"Well, and that applies here, too. Right?"

He doesn't answer.

"What's the big deal?" Elizabeth asks him. "It's just dinner. I told you. I felt bad."

Friday afternoon, they both arrive home in a mood. It's cloudy and cold, gray, with a stiff wind, leaves blowing across the road, looking like live things fleeing something, stampeding in the direction of the houses across the street; there's the smell of burning coal in the air. All around them is the natural manifestation of their inner weather. Elizabeth has the beginning of a headache. She hurries into the house to take some aspirin. Of course, the unspoken tension between them stems from the fact that, for very different reasons, neither feels like entertaining Geoffrey Shostakovich and Ariana Bromberg.

Butterfield can't concentrate on anything. There's a chilly, dead hand at the back of his head. Getting through this evening will be nearly impossible.

Earlier today, Mark called him to ask what Elizabeth might like for Christmas, and he was at a loss, felt his culpability all the more intensely. The question seemed vaguely like a pretext. Mark has never asked before. Why would he call just now—was there a kind of emotional bad weather that even his children had seen coming?

He keeps going over all the aspects in his mind, and, still, in spite of himself, replaying the scenes of venery with Ariana. It's terrible how much delectation there is in the mental images of her body: over and over, he finds himself dreamily gazing upon it, feeling his blood quicken all over again.

How strange that a man can long for more of the very thing upon which his soul is turning in regret.

He finds it tremendously difficult now to imagine that every aspect of his failure won't show in the coming hours, like a pornographic projection on the walls. The long fretting and worrying, and the increasing weight of shame mixed with lust, have made him hazily irritable with Elizabeth. So strange, to have this incrementally expanding sense of failure be the core of his aggravation with the innocent party; he feels as if he has already let slip the fact of his indiscretion.

"Do you believe it?" Elizabeth says. "No Fiona. No Holly. They're so busy with poor Oliver Ward. I think it's terrible to be happy somebody had a stroke."

"Don't say that," he says. "Jesus."

"I'm sorry. I didn't mean it that way—not really."

A moment later, wanting to soften things, he says, "I can't get over how Fiona is with those kids. Holly, too. I never saw anything like it."

She doesn't answer. The headache is coming on. She goes into the kitchen and stands at the sink, looking out the window there. He pours water and sets it on the counter, then goes upstairs to the bedroom. When she comes in, a little later, she says, "I wonder if they'll really be any happier living in separate rooms."

"When I was fifteen," he says, glad of something far from his present life to talk about, "Fiona moved to the local YWCA, like a street person, and it was all to get under Holly's skin. All a snit of hers. She had money in the bank, and all that—and she looked like a bag lady for weeks. The goddamnedest thing. She stayed three weeks. Until the lady that ran the place found out that she had fifty thousand dollars in the bank every year from a trust fund."

"Why do they keep moving in with each other?" His wife seems to be peering into him.

"Did you take the aspirin?" he asks.

"Migraine medicine. Why?"

"Your eyes are scrunched up. You look like you're in pain."

"I am."

"I don't know why they do anything they do," he tells her, deciding that he can't really talk just now. "They were raised together. They can't take a step without each other. And they've always fought. I don't know whether it's gotten worse, or if my tolerance—and theirs—is just running out." His knees are tingling, his palms sweating. He goes into the bathroom, runs water, and washes his face. Anyone witnessing him in this instant would say that he's trying very hard to remove a deep stain. He pauses once and stares into his own eyes with precisely the expression of someone attempting to puzzle out an opaqueness, a mystery. There is only the watery blue stare. Then he's laving the soap and water over himself again, soaking his hair, emphatic and committed, the living cliché of a man far more interested in cleanliness than the average—and innocent—person. Elizabeth walks in behind him and fetches a small hand towel from the rack, and then goes back out, not quite noticing him.

They prepare, together, without saying much, for the evening. She cuts vegetables and he trims the fat off four thick pork chops. "I hope they're not vegetarians," she says. She puts music on—Van Morrison—and hums to it. It's clear that her headache is easing off. Elizabeth has perfect pitch, and her voice is lovely. Its loveliness pierces him.

Shostakovich and wife arrive promptly at six, carrying a bottle of cabernet that Ariana picked out of the admittedly limited cellar at Macbeth's. Butterfield takes the wine and uses it as a pretext to avoid eye contact. Ariana's wearing a black dress under her black coat. The dress looks more like a slip. It clings to her body and makes her dark hair seem a shade lighter. Around her slender neck is a small, tight strand of pearls. Shostakovich has donned a suede sport coat, pleated slacks, and a white shirt open at the collar. He and his wife look like a pair of socialites out on the town.

Elizabeth, in her jeans and tank top, explains that she and Butterfield have always been too casual. Shostakovich takes off his sport coat, talking about how Ariana likes to dress up in the evenings. Butterfield has moved to the kitchen area to open the wine. Ariana strolls in, arms folded, head tilted slightly. Elizabeth is talking to Shostakovich about Van Morrison.

"I picked this one because it's full-bodied," Ariana says, her voice completely without nuance. "I like wine to be jammy and fruity."

"I don't drink much of it," Butterfield gets out.

"I know. You're a whiskey drinker."

In the dining room, Elizabeth and Shostakovich are chatting politely. The music has stopped, but Butterfield can only hear the voices, not the words. The sense of this moment is so strange that he loses briefly the thread of what Ariana is saying.

"Pardon?" he says.

"You look guilty," she whispers. "Stop it. There's nothing for you to worry about."

His hands shake, putting the corkscrew to the wine. He works to get it open, while she watches him, standing there with all her weight on one leg, one hand on the outward-jutting hip. Elizabeth brings in the glasses, and he's finally got the bottle open. He pours a little in each glass. Shostakovich raises his and makes a great show of swirling it. He puts the lip of the glass under his nose and sniffs loudly, then drinks and makes a sound like someone using mouthwash. "A little too jammy, I'd say."

"Geoffrey," says his wife. "You wouldn't know the difference if it *was* jam."

No one says anything for a moment. "Just offering an opinion," Geoffrey says.

Ariana lifts her own glass and turns it up, drinking most of the wine with a single gulp. "Ah," she says. "Very well structured. Nice finish. Oaky. See? All you have to do is talk about furniture."

It's evident to Butterfield that she's completely relaxed. He marvels at this.

"Whatever you're making smells wonderful," she says to Elizabeth.

"Pork chops," Elizabeth says. "Nothing fancy."

Ariana looks around, as if Elizabeth has indicated the whereabouts of the pork chops. But she's just taking in the décor. She says, "I'm terrible at cooking. Mending. Cleaning house. Baking. All of that."

"My wife is most definitely not what you'd call domesticated," Shostakovich says, sipping his wine with another show of taking in its bouquet. "Useless for anything wifely except—well, heh, heh—you know."

Butterfield keeps his eyes trained on the wine in his glass. The pause following this remark is terrible.

"Geoffrey likes to talk about his fantasy sex life," says Ariana.

Shostakovich raises his glass. "Score one for the wife."

Butterfield moves to the living room to put more music on and to gather himself, feeling as though he's seeking momentary refuge. And again, Ariana is there. But Shostakovich has followed as well, leaving Elizabeth in the kitchen to finish preparing the meal.

"What do you guys like?" Butterfield asks and remembers, just in time, to add, "For music." He's got his back to them, picking among the confused mass of CDs in and out of cases. He can't clear his own mind.

"Not Shostakovich," Ariana says, laughing. She sits next to her husband on the couch.

Butterfield puts a Bonnie Raitt CD in and turns it down so that it comes from the speakers in a soft murmur of notes. Seeing Ariana's empty glass, he says, "More wine?"

"Sure." She holds the glass toward him with the slightest bending of her wrist, smiling that smile, her dark eyes taking him in—and in. He walks into the kitchen on weak legs, and Elizabeth glances at him, tending to the cutting up of a brick of gouda cheese. She licks a finger and says, "Pour me some more, too, okay?"

He does so, and pours more for himself. It's not quite numbing enough. He's thinking how implausible it is to be entertaining the idea of telling Elizabeth they have to sell the house and move—buy another dwelling elsewhere. Find a quiet little cottage by the ocean, on the other side of the continent, or across the Atlantic, the sunny hills of anywhere else. What he has become involved in is beginning to be nearly too much for him, as if some irrational element of his being has been let loose and is gathering strength. He feels he might begin raving any minute.

He opens one of his own bottles of wine—a cabernet from another winery—and refills his glass yet again. There's the whole evening to get through, the rest of his life in the neighborhood to get through. He gulps the wine, receiving the unbidden thought that while some men seem well suited to cheating on their wives, he's most certainly—and painfully—not one of them.

So, then how, he wishes to ask someone in authority, did this happen? How does a man whose life, as far as he can see, is quite smooth and even happy, come to such a pass? What unanswered hungers are in him? What excesses of behavior, what enormities await a man whose passions are not available to his consciousness until they explode from him?

He tries to recall other temptations—and there are one or two—but nothing ever went past the line he always drew across experience: that line the whole society accepts, past which one moves at peril, the stuff of novels and movies. Trouble of the most serious kind. He can't believe any of it, swallowing the wine too fast and feeling himself crouching, all too creaturely, under his own façade of polite interest.

The dinner is long, and finally a bad blur to him. For a long while, they all watch Shostakovich pick through the salad Elizabeth prepared, removing onions, mushrooms, cucumbers, green peppers, and cilantro leaves; he puts them all on the side of his dinner plate in a neat pile, and there's a deeply concentrating look on his face, a seriousness of intent and a single-mindedness that, in the dim light of the table, takes on an almost fiendish appearance, as if he were performing this little panto-mime with a kind of mad glee, eyes frowning over a strange, wide smile of premeditation. Finally, he becomes aware of the silence and looks up.

"Geoff, for Christ's sake," Ariana says. Then she turns to Elizabeth. "Ignore him, really. He's got the manners of a range bull and all the ob-sessiveness of a raccoon when it comes to food."

"Don't take it personally," he says, putting a large forkful of lettuce in his mouth. "I have allergies to these things. I like my salad greens and tomatoes and that's it."

"I'd've made it that way for you," Elizabeth says. "Really. If you'd said something."

"Wouldn't want you to trouble yourself." He stops chewing and takes something off his tongue. Part of a mushroom.

"For Christ's sweet sake Geoffrey," says Ariana.

Butterfield keeps his eyes trained on the pork loin he's cutting up and tries, with all his might, to eat heartily, though each bite makes his gorge rise. The wine hasn't helped his nerves at all, and he pours more, in pursuit of the calm that he hopes it might bring.

"More wine?" he hears Ariana say.

"Yes," he answers and holds his glass out, not making eye contact.

They all have too much of the wine. Elizabeth opens two more bottles of red and one of white. Shostakovich produces a little cellophane bag of dope, and they all partake of that. Ariana says with a smirk that they are all mellowing out now. They sit in the living room, listening to one of those heavy-necked jazz divas with a smoky, hard-experienced sound to her cigarette-gravelly voice; Butterfield can't recall the name. And he's too drunk to get up and look. Shostakovich talks about his time in the merchant marine. The women he knew. None of them were as beautiful as Ariana, of course. Ariana makes snide comments about his escapades overseas, and the tattoo she says he has on the back of one thigh—a little sinking ship. "It's ironic," she tells them. "Isn't it? Geoff's little sinking ship on his thigh?" Though Butterfield can't particularly see the irony, he laughs at her tone, as does Elizabeth. In fact, they all end up laughing a lot, in the kind of hilarity that comes of unfamiliarity breaking down in alcohol and cannabis. The evening begins to seem fairly pathological. Inwardly, Butterfield rides over caverns, terrible cliffs. He watches Ariana, who seems so impressively calm, at ease, talking now about some of the people she sees in Macbeth's. The bagpipes player is the Scottish ("Really," Ariana says) brother-in-law of the owner. The brother-in-law is a beer alcoholic. One beer is not enough, and twenty-four is also, um, not enough. They all laugh at this, Butterfield lying back on the couch, head in Elizabeth's lap—a thing that used to be natural as breathing and now feels like a stratagem, a gesture intended to hide things and therefore dishonest. He feels this as a desolation, a range of destruction. The others are relaxed and happy now, and he remembers his mother and great-aunt, his son and daughter. And then, once more, his mind presents him with an image of Ariana lying back on the floor of The Heart's Ease bookstore.

God. Help.

Ariana sips more wine, talking about the bagpipe-playing brother-in-law of the owner of the bar. Each night, she watches him get progressively more drunk and less able to play the instrument he's so proud of. There's a swift, humorous way she talks now, animated even more by what she's had to drink and smoke. She seldom looks at Butterfield, who isn't saying much. Elizabeth remarks this.

"I'm drunk," he manages. "Sorry."

"We're all drunk," says Shostakovich. He goes on to say that Ariana hides her drunkenness better than most people. She's very cagey and smart, and fast, and she knows it. Her wit is deadly, he says. But he has always, luckily, found that sexy.

Butterfield can't keep from glancing at the perfect shape of Ariana in that black dress as she crosses her legs and lets the high heel on one foot dangle almost off of it.

"Geoffrey married me for my mind," Ariana says. "He wants to fuck me for my deep thoughts. Isn't that right, Geoffrey?"

"Oh, baby," he says. He talks of meeting her in college, when he was about to graduate. He'd planned to go to graduate school, but got sidetracked by Ariana, who was tired of the college life. Ariana's an impatient sort of girl, Shostakovich tells them. She wants what she wants, and she just walks up and takes it. That was what she did with Shostakovich. He didn't have a chance, he says. But then he has always been drawn to unstable personalities, and for all her definiteness about what she wants out of life, she can be a bit flaky. Or people decide that she is. In the last nine years, she's held fifteen different jobs. He talks on in this vein as if Ariana's not there, and she simply watches him, a little half-smile on her face, almost of bemusement, the expression of someone observing unwittingly comic behavior in a child.

"Well," Elizabeth says, finally. "I've got to put some food away. Sorry for the wifeliness."

"I'll help," says Ariana. "Don't listen to Geoffrey."

The two women go on into the kitchen, and the two men are left alone. Geoffrey seems to brood a moment, sipping his wine. Butterfield breathes out with difficulty, unable to believe the badness of the situation. He tries to hear what the women are talking about in the kitchen, and can't. Shostakovich, the cuckold, smiles and nods, as if he's just told himself a joke.

"You usually do the dishes around here?" he asks.

"I do, yeah."

"Me, too, at home. Ariana's inclined to dark moods when she doesn't get her way."

They say nothing for a beat. Butterfield can't look at him. He stares into his wine.

"Do the cooking, too," Shostakovich says. "Most of it."

"I do some," Butterfield says.

"Pisser id'n it?"

He experiences an abrupt need to contradict the other man, as if being too agreeable might make him suspicious. "I like it, actually."

Shostakovich shrugs. "I like what I get out of it. Or *for* it."

Sex again. Butterfield wants to excuse himself and go upstairs and crawl under the blankets of his bed and bury his face in the dark of his own folded hands.

"You ever been around anyone who had a nervous breakdown?" Shostakovich asks suddenly, quietly, leaning forward.

There's a brief, awful silence.

"No." Butterfield waits.

"Makes you watchful."

Now the quiet seems to expand.

"You know what I'm saying?"

Nodding, he thinks of the other man spying on Ariana, following her, or having her followed, to The Heart's Ease bookstore, the parking lot by the train station. His mind races.

"Ariana's capable of some pretty zany shit," Shostakovich murmurs. Then: "I guess all of them are." Now it's as if he's seeking some sort of reassurance.

Butterfield can't supply it, and another bad silence ensues. The women are talking in the kitchen about the economics of running a house, specifically leftovers and how they preserve and use them. A perfectly practical conversation between two polite strangers. Wives.

"There's a price," Shostakovich says under his breath. "For all that high-strung sex."

Now Butterfield feels directly challenged, as if the other is indeed referring to the episodes that glare with lurid clarity in his mind. He feels the impulse to stand suddenly and deny that anything happened. But then he realizes that Shostakovich is drunkenly complaining about his own personal life with the woman on the other side of the wall. Now, the poor man drains his glass and picks up the empty wine bottle as if to be sure it is indeed empty.

Butterfield rises quickly and goes into the dining room for another. Elizabeth catches his eye and frowns, and he gives her a shrug.

Back in the living room, Shostakovich is looking through the CDs.

Butterfield opens the new bottle and pours two glasses, then asks the women if they want more. Ariana says she does, and Elizabeth, after a hesitation, says she'll have some, too. Butterfield pours the other glasses, then puts the bottle on the coffee table and sits down. Shostakovich is still looking through the CDs.

"See anything?" Butterfield asks him.

"You got any Led Zeppelin?"

"Somewhere."

"Ariana's messy, too."

The women are finished putting the food away, and they come back into the living room, where the men are drinking. They drink their wine, too, and, abruptly, the evening seems about to die. Elizabeth settles next to Butterfield and gives his wrist a small, caressive pat, which slices through him, then sits back and lets her hands lie open in her lap. It's the posture of someone for whom the evening is winding down, and there's even something pointed about it, so Butterfield glances at the other two, wondering if they'll take the hint. He sees Ariana gazing at Elizabeth, and he has the sickening realization that the woman must be having the same thoughts about Elizabeth that he has been having about Shostakovich, who now starts talking about catastrophic experiences in college, his bad early twenties, when life seemed so laden with anxiety and despair. Again he relates the story of when he met Ariana, and she interrupts him: "You're repeating yourself."

"I was gonna tell about my Brando experience, sweetie."

"Don't," she says.

But he goes on. Ariana had a flirtation with some kind of Buddhist feminism in her senior year, he tells them, and locked herself away in a house with two other women who were helping her seek Nirvana by renouncing all things male. She told Shostakovich that she wanted nothing to do with him anymore, and spent days and weeks in a big bed with these two women, who were, according to Shostakovich, heavy, large, and gross. They lived in this old house with a mansard roof and an ivy-covered wall. It was like a castle. One night, Shostakovich stood out on the lawn and called her name, like Brando in *Streetcar*, he says, over and over, until she got thrown out of the house by the two women. They made love that night, he and Ariana, in the downstairs closet of the fraternity house where he had been staying. "Ever make love in a closet?" he asks Butterfield with a wink.

"Not me," Butterfield says, trying not to allow into his field of vision the stare that Ariana sends his way. He can almost hear her say, "How about on the floor behind the counter of a bookstore? How about in the back seat of a car?" But her husband is going on with his story, how they were discovered in the morning, and how a wild fight broke out between Shostakovich and his housemates, with Ariana in the middle of it, swinging a frying pan she'd gotten from the kitchen sink. "I got beat up," he says. But it was worth it, for the eroticism of that closet all night. You get the smells coming right up at you, because it's such a closed-in space. Very romantic."

"You've got a pretty strange idea about what's romantic," Elizabeth says.

"Erotic, romantic. One."

"But they're different things, aren't they? Though I guess you can have them together. But for romantic, I like calm, and candlelight."

"How about you?" Ariana asks Butterfield.

"Calm and candlelight," he says as evenly as he can under the circumstances. Again, he hears *Not in a car, while snow covers the windows?*

A moment later, Ariana does speak, announcing that she has the munchies, so Butterfield hurries unsteadily into the kitchen to prepare more crackers and cheese, wondering if they'll stay all night. In his peripheral vision, he's startled to see the tall shape in the black dress. She's taken off her shoes, and he didn't hear her come in. It's as if she's a spirit, standing there. She takes a cracker from the plate and bites the edge off of it. "What was that?"

"Pardon?" he says.

"You looked at me funny. Don't do that. Everything's fine, you know. Nothing's changed."

He can't speak. Shostakovich is talking to Elizabeth in the other room about having seen Bonnie Raitt in concert two years ago.

"We could meet here while they're at work," Ariana murmurs, one exquisite eyebrow raised.

Butterfield drops the knife he has just taken from the silverware drawer, bends to pick it up, then sets it down and rests his hands on the counter, feeling the need to support himself. She takes a look at the doorway, then reaches over and pulls him toward herself by taking hold of his belt. He almost falls into her.

"I'm drunk," he gets out.

"I want you, bad," she whispers. "I've been thinking about you all day." Then she quickly steps back, folding her arms and checking the doorway again. "All day."

"We're almost out of cheese," he says, and his voice cracks like an adolescent's, one ridiculous falsetto note on the word *cheese*. He's holding on to the counter again. "Damn."

"That's all you can say? You're out of cheese?" She makes her own voice do what his has done. He understands that she's making fun of him. It's weirdly arousing. "Don't you want to play some more?" she says softly, staring at him, grinning.

"Jesus Christ," he says. "Don't do this."

"Are you turned on?"

No word rises to his mind. His own ribcage seems to be collapsing.

"I'm right next door," she says. "They both work all day."

"Will you please—" He stops. Then he picks up the knife, looks at it, no cheese to cut with it. He sets it down again and moves unsteadily to the refrigerator. He remembers Shostakovich's strange question: "You ever been around anyone who had a nervous breakdown?" Ariana sighs, then hums something indistinguishable but sultry-sounding, almost studiedly so. It's as if she's performing for him. In the other room, the talk is animated—all about different concerts, Elizabeth talking of having seen Arlo Guthrie in nineteen-ninety. Butterfield stares into the confusion of foods in his own refrigerator, and there isn't any cheese that he can see.

"Somewhere," he says. "Cheese. Where the fuck do we keep the—"

Ariana steps too close and puts one hand on his hip while leaning in to bring out a brick of feta. "How about this?"

"Okay, yeah—there. Thanks," he says, and takes it from her. She closes the refrigerator and walks with him back to the counter. He begins cutting slices of the cheese. She's standing so near; he looks at his own hands, trembling.

"Mmm," she murmurs. "Life just got pretty again." She leans in and kisses his ear, then reaches to wipe away any lipstick as he steps back from her.

"Here," he gasps, holding up a small slice of the cheese, looking at her as if at some primal force coming toward him. She takes his wrist and puts the slice in her mouth, licking his fingers. Butterfield has to move to sit down at the table. He does so, holding his hands to his head. "I'm so drunk," he says. "Leave me here, will you?"

"No," she says. "And I'm sober."

"Dizzy," he says. "Jeez. I can't stand up."

"Don't pay any attention to Geoffrey," she says louder. "He's stoned. He gets that way." She strolls to the other side of the room, to his right and in front of him. It's a sort of parading. He can hear Shostakovich going on in the other room, and then realizes, to his horror, that it's not speech. Shostakovich is singing. Ariana's looking at Butterfield, arms folded. "Christ," she says. "Here we go."

2.

Elizabeth sits staring at him, while he bellows the song, an old Sinatra standard, "One for My Baby." He's trying to use Sinatra's intonations and phrasings, and he's butchering it. It's terrible, not even close to being in tune. He wanders through several different keys, and she steals a glance at the entrance of the room, hoping for Will to show there, with Ariana.

It's as if she's being punished.

The squawk goes on from Shostakovich, and she stares, realizing that Will has indeed come to the entrance of the room, with Ariana just at his shoulder. They look like a couple. Ariana stands too close to him, gazing at him. And the expression on her face gives everything away. It's all there. Elizabeth believes it wholly in the instant that she attempts to reject it, telling herself without words that it's impossible, it can't be. She feels the nerves lining her abdomen. The nerves seem to be tearing apart. Her headache returns like a wave of illness.

Ariana walks around Will and into the room, crossing to stand before her husband, arms folded, one leg slightly extended. Someone impatiently awaiting an outcome, an answer.

Shostakovich slows and stops. "That's my favorite song."

"You murdered it," Ariana says. "Like all the other times."

"I'm stoned."

She turns to Will. "He thinks that excuses what he just did."

"I wasn't that bad," says Shostakovich.

"You were worse than bad." Again, she looks at Will. "We can go to the moon, we can send a rover to fucking Mars. You'd think we could invent a little implant for the ear that would sense the alcohol level in the blood and start emitting a little voice: 'That's not as funny as you think it is. You've already said that four times. You are not meant to sing this song, ever in your life, not even alone, and not even in the shower.' You know?"

Shostakovich looks around her at Elizabeth. "Was I that bad?" he says.

Elizabeth manages to say, "I'm tone deaf."

"So's Geoffrey," says Ariana. "I think we should go."

Geoffrey holds his hands out in a gesture of helplessness. "You guys just made some crackers and cheese, right?"

So, the four of them sit down again, like people in the middle of some shock, who can't find the strength to do anything at all. Will pours more wine. But no one has any, and no one touches the cheese, either. Ariana nibbles at a cracker. Her husband's talking about how he came to admire the artistry of Frank Sinatra. Elizabeth watches Ariana's face and works to imagine the Italian hillside where the grapes grew for this wine. There's a little illustration of the place on the label of the bottle. She places herself there, sunlight on vines, pristine blue sky. She has always believed that one manufactures at least again as many doubts and fears as are warranted in life, and she wants to dismiss everything she's presently feeling as the product of anxiety, the stress of the last few weeks. She watches Ariana turn the hair just above her husband's ear with her index finger and thumb, an easy, affectionate gesture. It's all been a mistake, Elizabeth thinks, all the product of anxiety, something she imagined out of the pressure of this evening she didn't want.

The talk has grown animated again, Shostakovich rattling on about how progressive jazz bores him, and Will agreeing with him about it all, in his strangely agitated state. He's not himself. But it's just that these people are essentially strangers, and the night is wearing thin.

She surfaces from these thoughts to hear Shostakovich say, "No shit, man I play the sax."

"I said only when he's drunk," Ariana says. "Right Geoff?"

He shakes his head. "You're confusing my sax playing with those times when I think you're interesting, sweetie."

Will looks at Elizabeth. "I'm drunk *and* tired." She can't read his face.

"Just kidding," says Shostakovich. "I'll be right back."

He rises and heads for the door. His wife watches him go. He closes the front door carefully, and, in the quiet that follows, Ariana sighs—luxuriantly, it seems—stretching her long legs and arms, lying back, gazing at the ceiling. The gesture is stunning in context; Elizabeth stares at her, half-expecting her to disrobe.

"I'm sorry about this," Ariana says. The little mound of her sex shows through the liquid cloth of the dress where it lies over her outstretched legs.

Elizabeth quickly looks at her husband, who seems also aware of the sight, and is busy staring at his hands. "It's so late," she manages.

"Do you have any aspirin?" Ariana asks, still gazing at the ceiling.

"I'll get it," says Will.

While he's gone, Elizabeth sits forward and takes the last of her wine, trying not to look at the other woman.

"Men," Ariana says. "If only they had their own vaginas."

"What?" Elizabeth says.

The other woman sits up. "You never heard that? I can't remember who said it. It's a bad joke, I guess. But Geoffrey's so transparent."

Will comes back with a glass of water and two aspirin tablets.

Ariana takes them, and drinks the water. "Thanks," she says, and smiles.

Elizabeth watches him leave the room with the empty glass.

"I shouldn't drink wine," Ariana says. "I'll be wide awake all night.

This whole thing now is ridiculous. We should've left an hour ago. I'm so terribly sorry, really."

The door opens, and Shostakovich enters, carrying a leather case, where his saxophone is sheathed in blue velvet. He has a CD with him. A recording of Coltrane's. He gives it to Will and asks him to put it in the player on track five. And he stands there in the middle of the floor, getting ready to play. Ariana's still lying back on the couch, eyes closed now, hands folded over her lower abdomen. "Bill Clinton, jazzman," she says. "Christ." The music starts, a saxophone—Coltrane's—and a piano. Shostakovich joins in. It's surprisingly good at first, if louder than the recording.

Elizabeth's headache is far worse now. She realizes that she's drunk, too. Drunk and stoned. And, she thinks, in some way, corrupt. She has a strange moment of sensing herself to be, on some profound level, a prevarication, a falseness. It's scary. As if her soul were drifting away from her body. She looks at Shostakovich fingering the valves on his saxophone, his eyes shut tight, the muscles of his face contorted, and then she turns to her husband, who's sitting with his head in his hands. Ariana hasn't moved; she might even be asleep.

The fears about this woman and Will are pharmaceutical, Elizabeth decides; it's all part of the paranoia of drugs. They've all gone over some line. Shostakovich plays on, faltering only a little, and, finally, the song ends. That is, the recording ends. But Shostakovich keeps playing, building to a terrible crescendo, losing everything, the notes failing, becoming an ear-splitting scratching. Track six starts, and this brings him, at last, to a halt, though at first he makes a stuttering effort to play along with that track, too. The tempo is too fast, the rhythms too erratic. He puts the sax down in the blue velvet of the open case, and sits, with an exhausted suddenness, on the sofa next to his immobile wife. "Damn," he says. "It's been a long time. I fucked it all up. I'm sorry."

"It was good, baby," Ariana says through a sigh. "Can someone turn the music off now?"

Will does so.

"I've got a blistering headache," she says, eyes still closed.

"I know what to do for a headache," Shostakovich says, and, with a strange, clumsy leap, he's standing on his hands in the middle of the room. Change, a wallet and a comb, a book of matches and a butane lighter fall out of his pockets. The coins clatter and roll in all directions from him, as if trying to get away from such a breech of decorum.

"Sorry," he says. "I'll pick it all up." He hand-walks a couple of paces toward the stereo, his legs surprisingly straight. But he's drunk, and, as he begins to topple, Ariana rushes to him and grabs him by the lower legs. "Wait a minute," he says. "Wait just a goddamn minute, will you?" They look for an instant like a dance team in the middle of a bizarre stunt gone wrong, and then he comes down with a thud and crawls to the couch, where he sits with his head in his hands. "Jesus, Ariana, we were just having fun. I played the fucking sax. I was a gymnast—you guys—really."

Elizabeth moves to the other room with the plate of cheese and crackers, thinking that the feeling now is exactly what it would be if they had all just witnessed an accident. She can barely draw breath, she's so weary. Now it's quiet in the other room, and she walks in to find that Ariana and her husband are both in the foyer, getting into their coats.

"I'm so sorry," says Ariana.

"My sax," Shostakovich says.

Elizabeth hurries to it, closes it up in its case, and, when she returns to the foyer, she sees that the tableau is unchanged; no one has moved. Ariana is looking at Will again, with that familiar, upsetting gaze. Elizabeth thinks she sees the other woman catch herself and look away.

"Thanks for dinner," Shostakovich says. "I'm really sorry."

The Butterfields say, in unison, "Good night." And Elizabeth closes the door. She leans into it, resting her head on her hands.

Will goes into the kitchen and runs water. She moves to the entrance and stands there, watching him. It's almost as if she were a biologist observing some separate species. There's an unappealing, vaguely raccoon-like way he washes his hands. Finished with that, he retrieves a water glass from the cabinet and, filling it, drinks. "Damn," he says. "That got strange."

She feels something shaking from its moorings inside her, a worrisome, unresolved pang. She takes him by the arm and leads him to the bedroom. They'll leave the mess for the morning. He flops down on the bed and stares at the ceiling.

She decides to say something light: "Boy, you can tell Shostakovich is no relation."

His face is a blank.

"To the Russian composer."

"Oh—right. I know."

"Well you looked like you didn't get it."

He sighs. "Weird." Then: "I think you were right about them being a nightmare. What do you think?"

She shrugs but doesn't answer. Then, quite suddenly, she knows she will find out the truth. And, as is so often the case in matters of love, she will have to tell a lie in order to arrive at it. "Ariana said she's stopped by the store a couple times."

He gives her a look, a quick glance, guilty as all the legions of hell. "Did she?" He nods, pretending a casual inability to remember the thing that is written across his face like a brand. "Oh, yeah. I guess she has. Not recently, though."

Elizabeth goes into the bathroom and closes the door, then washes her face and looks at herself in the mirror. She remembers how the first Elizabeth wrote on a mirror and disappeared. He's moving around on the other side of the door.

"You okay?" he says.

"No," she murmurs under her breath. Aloud, she says, "What?"

"Are you okay."

She runs the water again and doesn't answer. Finally, when she has mastered herself, she opens the door. He's standing there. "Everything all right?"

"Why wouldn't everything be all right?"

"You seem a little worried or something. It was such a weird night."

"I'm too tired to think."

"Too tired to make love?"

Bands of rage tighten under her heart. "A little," she says.

"Meaning?"

"Okay, Will. I'm too tired to make love."

He sighs. "Are you mad at me about something?"

It's all she can do to keep from striking him. "No. Why?"

"I guess we're just tired. It was kind of nice though, wasn't it?—no Crazies. A nice free-feeling night for a while."

He's trying to humor her. It's infuriating. Quite clearly, he was miserable the whole evening, and now she's glad of that, anyway. She removes her blouse, crossing the room, thinking that the Crazies, who have been such trouble, now seem entirely trivial as a subject for worry. The windows are open for the stuffiness of the room—she opened them upon first stepping in here, because of the sense of suffocation that had seized her—and now the whole chilly night seems to be screeching with life: the rush and whoosh of the city; the call and ruckus in the trees, birds in their continual predawn chattering, such a blind cacophony of procreation and increase. It sickens her to think of it. He's gone into the bathroom, and she hears him brushing his teeth. She gets in bed, pulling the blankets high. She knows, suddenly and with a sinking in her soul, that she won't get to sleep any time soon.

He comes out of the bathroom and flops down beside her with a deep sigh. It takes him a moment to get himself situated under the blankets, a lot of shifting and turning. Finally, he lies with his hands at his sides, very still, staring at the ceiling.

"Something wrong?" she says.

"I won't sleep."

She makes herself kiss the side of his face. There isn't anything else she can do. "Good night," she says.

"You mind if I read?"

"No."

But he doesn't move, and soon he's gone—the wine and the dope and the food, and whatever he's had to do to keep up his pretense of innocence, of life as it has been until now, shuts him down like an engine out of fuel. He sleeps, and snores, turns over on his side away from her. She reaches across him and turns out the light, and waits in the darkness for her own nerves to shut down. Nothing. She sighs, and then sighs again, and then leans up and looks at the shape of him lying there in the dark. She moves close and brings her knee up, hard, into his tailbone.

He comes out of his stupor with a cough. "What?" he says. "What?"

"Oh," she says. "Did you have a dream?"

"Jesus Christ," he says. "Did you kick me?"

"No. You woke me up."

"What the fuck," he says. "Elizabeth?"

"Honey, you're having bad dreams."

"You kicked me," he says.

"I don't think so."

"Move over will you?"

She does so. "I'm sorry."

He says nothing.

"Are you all right?" she asks. "You keep jumping."

"I swear I got hit. I think you're the one who's dreaming."

Now she's quiet, and, in a little while, he's asleep again, snoring again. She closes her eyes, feeling sophomoric, childish, remembering Holly with the saucepan of warm water and Fiona asleep in the hammock on the porch. Well, all right. There's a measure of relief in this kind of juvenile trick.

But she can't sleep. She lies still, crying quietly, listening to him breathe and gurgle and snore, glancing over at the shape of him in the dimness. The chain of thought leads her to wondering what she will do now, where she might go, how things might change. She thinks of being gone by the weekend, of moving out, or asking him to move out. She also entertains the thought of keeping what she knows to herself, giving him a chance to come back from it, to see the mistake he has made. But this idea fills her with fury. She wants to strike out at him again. How dare he? She turns in the bed and looks at him once more. The possibility occurs to her that she has misread everything, that he has only, so far, been tempted. It's entirely possible that he has warded it off and is, in fact, innocent. She wants to believe this because she loves him and because he has never given her cause to wonder before. And she has to admit that there's something unsettlingly forward about Ariana Bromberg, which would set any man's nerves on edge and might make any man act guilty. She feels a wave of contrition now for having kneed him, and she snuggles close, breathing into the curve of his shoulders.

But she can't sleep. The images go through her mind—the possible guilty scenarios.

There's light showing in the window from the next-door house. She gets up to close the curtain, and then stands there staring out at it. All the lights are on over there. Every one.

WINTER HISTORY

I.

Point Royal is a place where presidents used to come to relax from the stresses of Washington. Though it is only fifty miles south and west of the city, it is protected by mountains and sealed off by tradition from the incessant turmoil on the other side of the Potomac. The local joke about it is that every president has come to its remote-seeming hills and mountain-valley peacefulness to refresh and refurbish himself, except the two who needed it most: Abraham Lincoln and Lyndon Johnson. Lincoln, because he couldn't (although it changed hands a half-dozen times, it was usually in the hands of the enemy—or, as Lincoln would have put it, the rebellion); and poor Johnson because Kennedy had spent so much and such famous time there during his presidency, and Texas beckoned anyway.

Saint Augustine's is its oldest Catholic church, and one of the oldest churches in Virginia. Built in seventeen fifty-two as a small frame-building with a cellar and a steeple with a bell, and not much else, it was used for a time by Clara Barton during the second battle of Manassas, or second Bull Run, as it is called by the citizens of the area. A small, blue sign commemorates this event, and the little cemetery that flanks it contains some of the dead of that battle. One can walk among the stones and find graves as recent as last month (Mrs. Minnie Ellsworth, one hundred and nine years old), and as early as seventeen sixty-three (Thomas Hyatt, thirty-one, of the milk sick—that, too, is on the stone). In nineteen sixty-eight, in a misguided fit of flaccid, summer-of-love ecumenism, the name was changed to Our Lady of the Mountains, but it never took. Adults persisted in calling it Saint Augustine's, and their children kept it up, and, in nineteen eighty-two, the old plaque with its raised wooden letters and its bas-relief of the saint placidly scrutinizing all passersby was resurrected from the debris of old pews, falling-apart hymnals, and chipped icons in the basement. The parish was expanding—the new developments and the shopping malls spreading west from the glut of Arlington and Fairfax. An extension of the main building was erected in nineteen eighty-six, but then the expansion ceased—a casualty of the housing bust in nineteen eighty-nine—and so plans for a school that kept getting moved forward into what everyone called the "near" future were indefinitely suspended.

Since nineteen ninety-four, there has been no mention of it at all. And sometimes the present pastor of the church has the unpleasant intuition that his place here is only stopgap, that he represents someone to watch over things until a final decision can be made about the future. This morning, at breakfast, after the seven o'clock mass, he listens to his curate chatter happily about plans for the day. Father McFadden chomps his granola, slurping the milk like a child. In the afternoon, his father is coming for a visit, driving through on his way to Florida, where he spends his winters. The old man is a former pro soccer player, of which Father McFadden is quite proud. The young priest has got fifteen boys interested on his CYO football team, the Tigers, and his father is going to speak to them.

Brother Fire is fasting, waiting until he's through with the twelve-thirty mass, and he sits with his prayer book and makes notes on a yellow pad for the morning's homily. The subject is faith. He's thinking about Mr. Petit and his sad obsession, and he wants to put something in about how the whole universe is yearning toward God.

Father McFadden has placed two more of his poems on the table, and the older priest knows quite well what is expected. He can't bring himself to reach for them, yet knows that he will, that before the hour is up, he just will. Even the smallest lie gets you into trouble: he should've spoken truthfully to the younger man on first seeing his verse. But that would have hurt him; the poems are so important to him, and it is, after all, the sincerest expression of his faith.

"A Mr. Petit called for you, this morning while you were out for your walk," Father McFadden says now, slurping the last of the milk from his bowl. "I'm sorry, I forgot to mention it."

"Did he want me to call him at home?"

"He asked for you and when I told him you had gone for a walk, he hung up. He was really rather rude, I must say."

The old priest remains silent. On the table before him are the poems, and Father McFadden watches him.

"I'll be back," Brother Fire says and goes to the phone in the hallway. There's no answer at Mr. Petit's house. Disappointed, and feeling *that* as a failure, as part of his ongoing problem with morbid curiosity, he returns to the table, where Father McFadden sits reading one of the poems, murmuring to himself the syllables of his love.

Brother Fire, because he feels he must, picks up the other one.

LORD MY HEART IS FULL

I believe I'm capable
With the help of thy grace
To amend my commonplace
Life and change the face
Of my soul in the race
Like running from a bull
With my eyes covered by wool
To succeed in finding space
Against the devil's pull.

Good Lord.

Brother Fire realizes that there is nothing he can say about this, short of telling the other man to try his hand at, well, anything else. A phrase occurs to him: "Father McFadden, I believe it's best if you try avoiding language altogether." He can't control the little half-smile that comes to his face with the thought, and he turns away from the younger man, lest he see it. Father McFadden stares, a deep frown of concentration and worry on his face.

"What do you think?" he asks, offering the other poem. "Maybe take a look at this one before you say anything."

The old priest takes it and turns again. This is a revision of an earlier one:

> *There were no laughs at all on Calvary that day.*
> *That was when the devil had his way*
> *There were no children happily at play*
> *No warm songs in the merry month of May*
> *No pretty feelings parading on display*
> *No chance for any goodness to have its sway*
> *While all the cruelties of the nails and gray*
> *Spikes making wounds that evermore would stay*
> *Ran through*
>
> *Our Lord's hands. Oh now let us pray*
> *Forgive them Dear Father for not knowing what they*
> *Ever do,*
> *And forgive us too*
> *For all we do*
> *And say*
> *We are sinful creatures with our feet made of clay*
> *Who howl in the night like dogs that howl at bay*
> *And know that death is sin's poor meager pay.*

There are four more lines, ending in *nay, bray, gay,* and *neigh,* but he can't read further, or he will break out laughing. He has to fight the urge now. He stares at the blank bottom of the page, trying to keep the explosion back, feeling it rise almost like choking in his throat.

"As I think I told you, I'm experimenting with different rhyming patterns," says Father McFadden. "This one starts out just straight

AAAAA, and so on. But then I saw the B pattern in the middle of it, and made the shorter lines with this. The next stanza, which I haven't written yet, will be BBBB. Like that. And I hope it'll have a shift to CCCC with shorter lines again."

Brother Fire nods, concentrating all of his power of will in the effort not to giggle. He likes this young man. He also approves of his gentle belief in others, his enthusiasm, and his courage in battling his own perceived shortcomings. It's the simplest thing, to tell a truth, isn't it? But there's the expectation—and also the most tender hint of fear—in Father McFadden's eyes as he waits for the approval he needs.

"Do you read poetry?" the old priest asks.

"I have a Gerard Manley Hopkins book. Well, it's a biography."

"But do you read any poetry?"

Father McFadden shakes his head a little sadly. "No." Then, sitting up brightly, a new idea, something he can try. "I should, shouldn't I?"

"Well, I think you might find it helpful."

"Helpful." Heavy doubt darkens the younger man's gaze.

"The way all poets do, Father. They read each other, you see."

"Yes, of course. I see, yes."

"Well," Brother Fire says at last. "As I said, I don't know anything about poetry. But this seems very deeply felt." He sees relief in the other's eyes, and, so, he strikes the note again. "Yes, I'd say very deeply felt. Very sincere."

"Thank you," says Father McFadden. "But then, you know, Father, Hitler was sincere."

"I think that's being debated, isn't it? There's a school of thought that paints him as an evil opportunist."

"Well, but a sincere one. You—you see how I mean this?"

Brother Fire resists the impulse to be short with him. He feigns confusion: "Did Adolf Hitler write poetry?"

"No, I just mean that he was sincere. He believed all that. Opportunism or whatever, you know. I mean sincerity isn't necessarily a thing that would define quality in a poem. Do you—do you like the rhymes? Do they seem too much?"

"Well, there are certainly a lot of them and you certainly have an ear for them."

"Thank you. I don't use a rhyming dictionary, you know."

"Very impressive," says the old priest.

The phone rings—a blessed interruption. Brother Fire answers it. Holly Grey is on the other end, talking loudly to be heard over some commotion in the background. Fiona, she says, is doing dishes and isn't happy about it. Holly wants him to come visit Oliver Ward in the hospital, to help cheer him up. Holly goes on to say that he has always had the power to cheer anyone up, to make a person feel the essential gorgeousness of life, and Oliver Ward seems low these days, discouraged and sorry and maybe beginning to wonder if he'll ever leave the hospital alive.

"I'm so tired," Brother Fire tells her. "It's morning, and I'm exhausted."

"That doesn't sound like you at *all*," Holly says. "You sound like *you* need cheering up."

"As usual," Brother Fire says, "you put things in perspective for me."

"Now you're cheering me up. I don't need cheering up."

"I'm only speaking the truth," he tells her.

"Can we talk after mass today?" Holly says.

2.

Early Sunday night, at the end of her shift, Alison receives an emergency call—she and Roy are the nearest vehicle to the scene of an accident. They arrive only minutes after it happened. It's the coldest night of the fall, with a needlepoint rain being swept by gales. The American flag atop the car dealership down the way is blown straight out by the wind. The streetlights sway and shake and seem about to fly off their wires. And here, in this scene of a car askew in the road next to a broken streetlamp pole, is a man lying on his back, hands folded over his stomach, one leg up into the thrown-open front door. It looks as though he simply decided to lie down here and rest. The car is a Ford Taurus. A woman kneels at his side, crying and moving her hands back and forth over him in what looks like a frantic grasping at the rain falling on him. Alison moves quickly, gets in close, and ascertains that the man is breathing freely, though unconscious; then she reaches over and takes hold of the woman's arms, looking into her frightened eyes. "Don't move him, okay? Don't let him move, especially his head. Keep him still. Do you understand me?"

"Yes," the woman says. "Thank you."

Roy has already set out a couple of flares and is redirecting traffic. Alison moves to the squad car and pulls it around, lights flashing; she gets out the small first-aid kit, with its portable defibrillator and gauze packets, and pulls a blanket from the trunk of the squad car. The woman says something behind her, a plaintive note in her voice. Between them is the street, with its wet reflection of the red and blue flashes.

"Don't go, Clark. Please? Stay with me?"

Alison bends into this scene and puts the blanket over the man, who opens his eyes and looks at her and seems about to scream.

"Please, Clark," says the woman.

Alison puts part of the blanket over the woman's shoulders. The couple are enfolded, and the scene looks almost tranquil in the shifting light, a tableau of love huddled against the rain and the cold wind.

"Baby," the man says, gasping. "I love you."

"Yes," she says, crying.

"I love you, baby," he says, sighs, gasps out. "I love you." Then, with a little jolt along the muscles of his jaw, he's still. Gone. The eyes remain open, reflecting light.

Alison labors over him, uses the defibrillator, breathes into his mouth. Nothing works. The woman kneels, wailing, there in the highway, in the badly chaotic flashing. Alison embraces her even as she resists any contact at all. "No, no, no," she keeps saying, "no, no, no, no."

The ambulance comes, stops too slowly, it seems, inching forward with its weird, fragmented siren-sound, and at last two paramedics get out. They move quickly now, with their equipment, and soon they are bending over the man, working efficiently, steadily, muttering procedural words to each other. Alison hears, "No pulse." The woman has fallen silent, watching them. Every single thing about the night seems suspended now, locked in the moment, as if the wind has determined the seriousness of things and stilled itself, so that there is only the wild flickering, the vast, coldly drizzling dark above them, the little breathings of the medics, who keep trying and do finally get a pulse.

"Got it," one of them says loudly, with something of coaxing in it, as if he were addressing the man lying there under his hands. "Got another. Come on."

"Come on!" shouts the second paramedic.

And then they're quiet again, quite still-voiced, breathing heavily, working. Alison sees the injured man's hand move, and she almost cries out.

"Okay, pulse slightly below normal. Blood pressure rising nice. It's good. We can transport him now."

It seems a long time, a long wait. Alison directs traffic with Roy, while they get the man stabilized, ready to be moved. The man's wife waits in the ambulance, having been given something to calm her. She sits there trembling, crying.

Alison thinks about her father, in his hospital bed, trying to recover. For her, now, the whole world seems scarily precarious and darkly threatened. The wind has come back with force, a seeming conscious surge of cold air, as if nature has decided at last to comment angrily on the outcome. The paramedics place the injured man in the back of the ambulance.

She turns from them to see Stanley standing there. She experiences a strong urge to walk into his arms. He says, "I saw you from three cars back. I know you're on the job. Sorry." He begins to move away.

"Wait," Alison says, actually reaching for his arm, taking a hold of him at the wrist. "I was on my way to the station. I'm off now. Do you want to go have coffee or something?"

"Sure."

"Follow us?"

He nods.

In the squad car heading for the station, Roy says, "I love this job.

Where else can you see right away, directly, the good effect of what you've done? You saved that guy's life."

"*They* brought him back, not me."

"You know how it is when somebody tries to open a jar, and can't get it, and then the next person tries it and *does* get it? The first one got it started, right? You got it started and it was beautiful."

"He was stopped, Roy. And nothing I tried worked." She looks in the rearview mirror to be sure of Stanley's car.

"But you kept him going. You kept the blood moving to his brain. You saved his life. You must feel just terrific. I do for my little part in it. Really."

"Well, it's not supposed to be about what I feel, is it?"

"What's with you?" he says. "You feel whatever you feel. Damn."

Here's Roy, with his little eyes and his big frame, sitting behind the wheel of the squad car, worrying about her.

"It's okay," she says to him. "I feel fine."

And she does. She's abruptly filled with a sense of anticipation, an excitement she knows is perfectly unwarranted and probably even silly. Yet there is the car, following along behind her. She has a moment of recalling how it felt to be thinking of herself as sexy, looking forward to a date. It's ridiculous. She's in uniform.

They go to a Starbucks near the station. She has her car, so again he follows her. On the way, she uses the cell to call Holly and ask if she can be a little late coming home. Holly says things are fine, Fiona and Kalie are making Thanksgiving decorations and Jonathan is reading a book about dinosaurs. "Take your time, dear," Holly tells her.

The coffee shop is crowded, and they have to sit in the far window that looks out on the windy, drizzling street, with its entrance to Route 66, heading east.

Stanley goes to the counter to order, and she heads into the ladies' room, where she stares at herself in the mirror and decides that this is only coffee with someone who wishes to work for her father. She thinks of putting lipstick on, but then doesn't. Here is her face, her work face, under the police hat, small and smudged-seeming. She washes it, and then does apply a small touch of lipstick, hurrying. Her stomach aches a little. Outside, he's seated at the table, gazing out the window. His shape is decidedly less lean when he's sitting down: you can see the beginning of a paunch at his middle.

"That was something," he says to her when she's settled across from him.

"How much of it did you see?"

"I saw you working on him and then I saw them working on him. They're pretty efficient aren't they? They didn't even seem scared."

"They weren't. They see that kind of thing a lot."

"And you?"

"Pardon?"

"Well, you too, right?"

"I write traffic citations. I've been called on a few domestic disputes. One of them involving the ladies who are now my babysitters."

"They had a dispute?"

She smiles. "You can't find that hard to believe."

"They're so good-hearted, both of them. I mean, from what I've seen."

"They are. They've been great since Dad's trouble."

"You know," he says, "all those years ago, I used to look forward to working for your dad because I thought I'd see you."

She sips the coffee and looks at his hands. They're smooth-backed, almost feminine-looking. But now she can see the calloused palm of one of them, as he reaches for the little container of sugar packets on the table. Finally, she says, "I was still in school," and realizes almost immediately the banality of it as a response.

"I wasn't long out of school."

She decides to try a joke: "I seem to remember that you were late a lot. And missed a lot of days."

"Yeah," he says. "That was me."

"So," she says, deciding this, too. "You met my father again, after so much time, in the Point Royal drunk tank."

He nods carelessly, and then seems to come to his senses. "I don't usually drink," he says. "Gives me heartburn. Beer especially. I fell asleep in a phone booth after something like three beers. I'd been driving all night."

"Tell me," she says, "what you've been doing all this time?"

He looks down. "Working. I had a place down in Knoxville. I kept busy, you know. Just putting food on the table."

"Were you married?"

Now his gaze is directly at her. "Yeah. Didn't last long."

"I'm sorry."

"Well, I wasn't ready. And for that matter neither was she."

"How old were you?"

"Oh, I was married back then. Back when I worked for Oliv—for your daddy."

"And you moved to Knoxville—"

"She had family there. We lived with them for a couple years."

"You didn't want to live with her family."

"No—actually we got along. It was *her*—you know? We just weren't suited to each other, as they say. We tried though. I mean we weren't casual about it. We got this place, you know. Little house. I left her the house. You could say it was a mess from the start."

For a while, they're quiet, sipping the coffee, and the others in the little shop provide them with something other than each other to pay attention to. Alison experiences this as a relief, but then the silence grows longer and she begins to feel embarrassed. She says, "I didn't mean to seem to quiz you."

He smiles. "It's okay if you were."

"Another thing I seem to remember is that Oliver liked you back then."

But he has spoken, too, and stopped himself.

"You made him laugh," she says in the instant that he speaks again.

"Pardon?" he says.

"You did. You made him laugh."

"I'd like to take you to dinner one night soon, without the uniform."

She removes the hat and sets it on the bench beside her. "The uniform," she says.

"Right. Does it make you uneasy?"

"I don't work tomorrow," she says.

"I've got to finish roughing out the inside of the house, for the partition."

"Well, there's Wednesday."

"Okay," he says, and it's as though she has done the asking. She takes a slow sip of her coffee and realizes that her hand is shaking, that her own unruly emotions are running away with her. She wishes for calm, and for something other than his steady gaze on her.

"Well," she says.

"Wednesday it is," he tells her. "Good."

"I'll have to let you know for sure," she says.

"Of course."

They chat a little about the house on Temporary Road and about Oliver's slow recovery. He says quietly that she must remember it is all, still, recovery. Each day, right? he says, there's a little more progress. Yes. That's true. She tells him the story of Holly on the roof, how she came to know the two ladies, and how Oliver did, too, separately. They finish the coffee and remain for a spell, relaxing into their talk. It occurs to her that she's not so shaky inside anymore, that, in fact, she's enjoying herself. They part with a little surprising embrace, and he shakes his head, remarking, as if he has just now thought of it and it is original with him, that it is a small world indeed. There's something sidelong about his smile, a kind of self-deprecation: he's perfectly aware of the familiarity of the observation, and his tone and manner are purely for fun, to amuse her.

Later, at home, the children asleep, she gets a call from Marge, whose distance, since her departure, has only increased with time. Marge wants to talk about aspects of her pregnancy and her dissatisfaction with life in her mother's house. She wants news of her husband the champion asshole. Alison has no news. Or, rather, she has no news that she wishes to report. Oliver's recovering, yes, there have been minor setbacks. She's getting along, she tells her friend, who seems not to be listening, really. It's as if Marge is only waiting for a silence, a polite space in which to insert her next observation about life on the Great Plains, in a small house with her mother and stepfather. Her stepfather, Marge says, is embarrassed about the pregnancy and is making an effort not to show his embarrassment. The whole thing is exhausting. "But really," Marge says. "You can tell me. Greg's come over, hasn't he? He's hitting on you, right? You can tell me. He said stuff to me last time we talked. How he might be dating a cop before long. The bastard."

"I haven't seen him in a while," Alison says. "I think he might've gone north."

"Well, come on. Tell me how *you've* been."

"I'm fine. Really."

"You don't sound fine."

"I'm *fine*," Alison says.

"Well, I'm sick of this pregnancy and I smoked twelve cigarettes to-night and had four glasses of wine."

"Christ sakes, girl."

After a little space, Marge says, "You remember our chardonnay night?"

"Are you drinking now?" Alison asks.

"I'm drinking now."

"Marge."

"You try it out here in the house of the perpetually shitty."

"I have to go now."

"Are we still friends?" Marge wants to know.

"What do you think?"

"I think you're mad at me."

"I miss you, that's all—miss hearing from you."

"Do you love me?"

"Of course."

"I'll try to call more often."

"Just call *back* now and then."

"I will. You're all right, though."

"Yes," Alison says. "I'm all right."

"Because that's the important thing."

"I am," Alison tells her. "I'm fine. Really."

Yet, after they hang up, she sits crying by the telephone, holding a handkerchief in one hand and a book in the other.

Finally, she turns the lights off in the living room and makes her way to bed. Lying awake, she imagines that she and Stanley begin to see each other as a couple. It's clear enough that this is what he wants. She wants it, too. She admits this to herself in the same moment that she feels troubled by all the effort it will involve, the working out of schedules, the money, the two lives, the children, Oliver and what he will require—may require—with this stroke, her own inconsistencies, her own need, and whatever Stanley's needs and insecurities might be— all *that*. She doesn't allow herself to think about it more. Her own life seems so solidly fixed around her. She sits up, turns the light on by the bed, begins reading about the geological shifts of the centuries—and falls asleep. She dreams that she and Teddy and the children are together somewhere far away—the vacation they never took. They're all standing at the edge of a wide, beautiful canyon, very green, not stony, like the Grand Canyon, but green, verdurous, a canyon of brilliant plant life, lush vegetation, leaves the size of flags, all waving in a slow wind, wild growth unlike anything on earth. They stand there, and nothing happens, and she senses the strangeness of it, turning to look at Teddy. Then she stirs out of the dream with a fright, realizing that she has been asleep for more than an hour. How strange her own mind is. She turns the light out, settles under the blanket, and listens to the little sleep sounds Kalie makes, and then becomes aware that the child has crawled into the bed with her. Reaching for her, Alison snuggles close, and abruptly her mind presents her with the most vivid image of the scene in the middle of the highway, the man lying there and the medics working on him. She attempts to turn this off, concentrating on the child's soft shoulder, the little sighing breaths.

She won't sleep, and she knows it.

She thinks of Fiona and Holly, and Stanley. Of course, he won't really want permanent involvement with a woman who already has two children. The thought makes her stir, to want to shake it off. She *isn't* looking for anyone. There're the children to think of, and that's all. Kalie shifts, moans softly, and now Jonathan's moving around in the house. He comes to the door of the room.

"Mom? Do you have Kalie?"

"Yes," she says. "Go on back to bed, Son."

"I had a dream."

She can tell from the voice that he's been frightened by it, whatever it was. She's abruptly so weary in her bones. *Wait'll you know what's actually out there, Son.* She lets the words ride through her mind, then takes a breath and says, "Want to tell me about it?"

"I dreamed Grandpa was dead."

This rakes through her. She doesn't want to know more. "He's gonna be all right, Jonathan. It's just a little fever and some clotting in his leg. They're on top of it."

Kalie moans. The boy comes close, sits down gingerly on the edge of the bed. "It scared me."

Alison pulls the blankets aside. "Come on, sweetie. Get in."

He does so. He puts himself tight against her back, shivering. She reaches back and pats his hip, feels the sharp hipbone. Her little boy with his solidness there in the bed, and his dreams that take him far, his fear and uncertainty, and this small privacy, that he sometimes sleeps in his mother's bed for his night terrors. And she can do nothing about anything he fears, because the life they presently lead is full of this very uncertainty that troubles him.

"It'll be okay," she murmurs.

"I wish I didn't dream," he says, evidently a little louder than he meant to. He murmurs, "Sorry, did I wake her?"

No. Kalie sleeps on, stirring slightly with her own dreams, making little sighing sounds in the back of her throat.

"I love you," Jonathan whispers.

"Me too, you," says Alison, just able to control her own voice. "Go to sleep now."

"Mom?" he says.

"Please, honey."

He sighs. She can feel that he's tense, worrying over something.

"Your grandfather's okay, baby."

"Yes."

She tries to drift off. But he moves again and sighs again. "Tell me, honey."

"I don't know," he says. "Mr. Petit, at school. He's—he was real helpful, you know, for a while, and now he's being kind of mean to me. Like I did something wrong. And I didn't do anything wrong."

She waits for him to go on.

"I'm not good at the math. And he's not helping me anymore. I asked him if I could come see him after school again, and he acted like I'd insulted him or said something wrong. I don't know what I did wrong." He sighs again.

"He's probably just busy, sweetie, with the holiday coming and all that."

"But I was getting it when he'd explain it to me."

"He will again. You'll see."

"But it's like he's mad at me. And I'm falling behind in it."

"Do you want me to talk to him?"

The boy says nothing for a moment, then: "No."

She reaches over and pats his shoulder, and lets her hand remain there. He breathes, stirs very slightly, and she thinks perhaps he's dropped off to sleep. She takes her hand away and listens for him, but then she herself is elsewhere, dreaming.

3.

She wakes hours later, with a sense of something pressing on her chest. Kalie's head. Kalie is lying almost completely on top of her, hands flung up around her neck. She extricates herself, settling the child next to her brother, whose thrown-back face looks grief-stricken, mouth wide open, an aghast expression. This is indeed sleep that mirrors the end of life. She touches his shoulder and he stirs, closes his mouth, turns away from her. It will be time for school, soon. She listens for a while to the sounds of the early morning. The wind is still; the rain has stopped. Finally, she rises, looks out her window. There's a wide band of darkness sweeping across the morning, and she realizes it's made of birds, heading south, thousands of them. The sky is banded with high clouds, enflamed by dawn sun, the whole expanse a violet color, with a pink glow toward the horizon turning to brightest gold—a glorious sunrise, and here are the birds trailing across that splendor, as if they have brought it on somehow and are hauling it all across the perfect curtain of the sky.

She walks in her nightgown into her workroom to get her watercolors and some paper from the cabinet there, and returns to that window and spends a few minutes trying to render the sight, this apparently endless dark band of color crossing a magnificent firmament at dawn. Suddenly, gazing at it all, she's crying again, quietly, the tears running down her cheeks. This is the kind of sunrise people take pictures of and put on postcards to represent the promise and glory of a new day on Earth, and nothing about it is remotely sad—and yet she experiences it like grief, wiping the tears from her eyes and staring, aching with it. She thinks of Marge, all those miles away, and looks down at the painting, which is beginning to look smeared and wrong. Finally, she puts it all away and crawls back into the bed, having received a chill. Jonathan wakes with the change of her weight in the bed. He gets up and goes into his own room.

"Get ready for school, honey," she calls after him.

He coughs, as if to answer her with the reason he shouldn't go. But she hears him brushing his teeth, and knows he'll do as she asked. She wakes Kalie and dresses her, and then she makes breakfast for them both. Jonathan doesn't eat much. He kisses her good-bye, and she tells him again not to worry about the math or Mr. Petit. He nods, looking worried, and he walks out to wait for the school bus. She watches him, and watches the gigantic green-haired boy come from the house across the way. Jonathan stands a little to one side when the boy approaches; there's avoidance in it, though the tall boy doesn't seem to notice, but only stands there with his odd-colored spiked hair and dour, downturning face, holding his books with both hands, the way a person would hold a tray, so tall that he dwarfs poor Jonathan. The bus comes, and they get on. Alison watches it go, and then spends time tending to Kalie, who's restless and wants to know when they can go see Holly and Fiona. She takes the child out on the front porch and lets her play there while she works on her painting of the birds in the sky. The trouble is, she can't make any of them look like birds, quite. And the sky is now almost white, the birds long gone. Her efforts to be precise only end up making a muddier blur than before, and the painting is quickly becoming one she'll discard. She gets Kalie to come with her down in the basement room to bring up a doll she can work on. Kalie wants to help, a good sign. They go back up to the porch and sit out in the windless warm sunlight, and work on a doll's dress and bonnet. Kalie works the hat, having learned to stitch the brim and pull the cloth to make the wrinkle. It makes Alison very proud and happy to watch her do it. She looks out at the sunny world of her street and thinks of love, her love for Kalie, for Jonathan, for her father. If only it were enough. She remembers the carnal night she and Marge spent, drunk on chardonnay, and is momentarily light-headed, as if the effects of the wine have mysteriously returned. She feels a deep yearning in her abdomen, down into her loins, and her discouragement is almost complete. Kalie puts the little doll-bonnet down, comes to her side, and says she wants to try drawing the birds. Alison discovers there's another, smaller trail of them beginning in the present sky.

"When will Granddad come home?" Kalie asks. "Today, right?"

"Not today, but soon," Alison tells her, wishing she could believe it to be true.

4.

Oliver dreams of beaches, blue skies, white crests under sunlight, the swells of the oceans of the world. He's partaking somehow of all of them, from the North Atlantic to the Caribbean, over to the Riviera and on to the peaceful shores of the Mediterranean and farther, to India and Madagascar, the Far East, the coasts of New Guinea and Australia, New Zealand and Tasmania. It's as if the *idea* of shorelines has come to him in his sleep, made manifest by the imp of the unconscious. He wakes with a sense of having been transported to other realms, as though the dream were a kind of preparation. He lies quite still, wondering if he can move at all and trying to picture for himself all the beaches on which he has actually stood. He believes he can hear the sea banging the rocks off the coast of Maine, where one summer, when he was young, he stood with a friend, a boy so beautiful that Oliver himself used to tease about feeling a kind of lust for him. Mary's brother Thomas. He did not even know Mary yet. Thomas and he had been hired as captain's mates on a charter fishing boat, the *Ipswich*. Nineteen sixty-three, Oliver was visiting his aunt's family in York Harbor. Seventeen years old, a summer job at sea. Thomas was a native of South Carolina, and since Oliver was from Virginia, and they were two boys from the South, they became friends. Two other boys were working the same job that summer, both from New Hampshire, and they made fun of Oliver's and Thomas's accents. They also assumed things. During one visit to a boardwalk and beach, one of the New Hampshire boys pointed to a couple, a black man and a white woman, and said to Oliver, "I'll bet you never see that where you come from."

"Sure I do," Oliver told him. "I have."

"You're lying through your teeth."

"That's a pretty dangerous thing to do," Oliver said. "Calling a man a liar."

"I'm not blaming it on you," said the other. "You don't have to defend anything."

"What do you think," Oliver said, "I just came up from a holler and a shanty shack, with my mouth full of cornpone and a sheet over my head, shouting hee-haw?"

And then, later, he and Thomas stood at the edge of the pounding ocean and sang "Dixie," and harmonized the words "Fuck you" into the wind spray, laughing, a little drunk on beer. Thomas went to Vietnam, like Oliver, but he died there, a freak accident in a jeep on a street in Saigon. Nineteen sixty-eight. Mary never forgave the world for it. And it was all complicated by the fact that Oliver knew her because he had known Thomas and had been Thomas's friend. Mary was a steely person inside. Oliver loved her and failed her over and over, and she forgave him over and over, because she understood how it was for Oliver to have been there, too, in that war, how it all happened—how you went from a job riding the ocean in the sunlight of the North Atlantic in summer, catching the big fish, those spectacular flashes of blue and silver rising, caught, out of the waves, spiraling upward all the way to the tail and then plummeting to the surface again in an explosion of foam, a white shattering, and all the peaceful passes, too, the slow rocking and rolling of the boat, tying off lines, singing into the always-motion of the water, getting drunk in the nights, and feeling the sun still burning into you even in the dark, how you went from that to a war and to fearing the light, any light, and moving in a green terror, a terror of jungle deeps and sudden death and flames licking at you, and being in the terrible bloom of a mortar round that kills two of the men with you outright and leaves one knowing he'll die in minutes, a poor, frightened, wide-eyed twenty-three-year-old boy sitting in a muddy green ditch, holding his own intestines in his hands and murmuring that he doesn't want to be moved. Over and over, in the minute left to him, he said, "Don't move me, please. Don't move me, please." Over and over. Mary understood how all that played in Oliver's mind. And she tamped down her own sorrow and anger and tried to make a life, even after the damages of war, and she mostly succeeded, because she was strong-willed and brave and because she knew how to love a man through his failures. Oliver is that man. And all of it started with being at the edge of the northern sea with a beautiful, dark-haired boy, listening to the banging on the rocks and feeling pleasantly drunk.

Oliver remembers this, still hearing the roar of the sea—is it *that* sea, and is he still dreaming?—and, just as it comes to him to question it at all, he realizes the sound he has been hearing is Drew, snoring and sighing in the next bed. Drew's wife comes in. *Mildred?* Oliver can't remember, for all the *other* names. He nods at her as she walks by him. They turn the television on. Oliver stares at a pretty, blond woman, who speaks agreeably about coming warmer weather and rain. And, in the next moment, the nurse is there with breakfast—a hard-boiled egg, apple juice, a little fruit cup, milk. None of it appeals to him. The nurse, a girl with light blond hair and eyes the color of a midday sky in summer, frowns at him and threatens to spoon it into his mouth if he won't eat it himself. He takes a bite of the egg, thinking of her as the prig she probably is. It's all part of the stroke and the complications that have kept him here, this unsummoned rage, and he knows it yet can't control the feeling. He manages to say, "You go—to—church?"

She stops what she's doing with his IV and waits for him to continue.

"Well?" he says.

"I go to church. That has nothing to do with my wanting you to eat. If you don't eat, Mr. Ward, you'll die. That's not a matter for debate, is it? And I don't believe it's a religious matter, either."

"No," he says. Even as he appreciates her articulateness, the feeling of resentment toward her wells up in him. It's amazing.

"Eat your egg," she says.

A moment later, Holly walks in and takes a chair. "How are you this morning?" she says.

He looks beyond her, expecting to see Alison. But there's no one. The empty hallway, where a voice on the speaker system says the name of a doctor and then repeats it, and gives a room number. There's so much unexplained process in a hospital, so much surface matter that one is exposed to, it's like a laboratory for the production of paranoia: Oliver has found it impossible not to believe that every pronouncement on the intercom is about him, his condition, his situation. It's all in code, and it's all some bad development. In the nights, a nurse comes in and squeezes the bottoms of his feet; he has no idea why. He has simply let it happen, trying to keep the thin veneer of sleep, which is all sleep ever feels like here, even when it's deep and drug-induced.

"Fiona dropped me off," Holly says, evidently seeing the worry in his expression. "She's on her way over to pick up Alison and Kalie."

"Oh," Oliver says.

"Stanley's at the house. Working. It's noisy. I've decided we're all going to have Thanksgiving there." She thinks a moment. Then laughs into one hand. "Crazy, I know. But I think it'll lend a feel of the first Thanksgiving—the unfinished element of it, you know?"

He nods. "That's—good."

"You're not eating," Holly says. "Food's that bad, huh."

"Bad," he tells her, and wants to say more.

"You can't eat any of it?"

"Not—hungry," he says.

"But you've gotta keep your strength up," she tells him. Then: "Oh, God. What a cliché. What a stupid movie line. I don't believe I uttered it. Forgive me."

He smiles, or believes he does. He nearly asks her about it. *Did I just smile at you?*

But she's smiling, too, and she pats his wrist. "I take it that I'm forgiven."

5.

During the six-o'clock Monday morning mass, Brother Fire notices that one of the five people in the pews behind him is Mr. Petit. This is new. And, at Communion, the four others come to the railing, but Petit hangs back, hands folded in front of him, head bowed. It becomes nearly impossible for the priest to concentrate through the rest of the ceremony. The quiet in the church—the occasional sniffle or cough or throat-clearing, the soft, whoosh of traffic outside—begins to feel oppressive, weighted with something, some aspect of trouble. He wants to talk to Mr. Petit. But the mass ends, and Mr. Petit has gone off to his school.

Father McFadden's old man spent the night and is sitting in the small kitchen with the housekeeper, Mrs. Drake. He's drinking coffee and talking in a wonderful, charming brogue about what a hopeless student he was and how bright his son is. "Think of it," he says. "My boy writing poetry, like the Dean himself."

"Who?" Mrs. Drake says.

"Mr. Swift," says the old man. "They still call him that in Dublin."

Brother Fire missed being introduced to him, and so now he introduces himself. "Just in from the six-o'clock," he says.

"I never used to miss it," says the other. "I'm Sean. And people call you Brother Fire."

"Well, yes."

"Fine bunch of boys in this parish, Father."

Brother Fire feels remiss, because he hasn't been as involved lately. Father McFadden comes downstairs, wearing a sweater and jeans. He's taking his father to the mountains today.

"Look at ye," Sean says to his son. "A poet, and ye look like a raga-muffin. Doesn't he look a disgrace to ye, Father?"

The old priest deflects this with a genial wave of the hand but finds himself thinking about how it might have been for him had his own father lived long enough to visit him in one of his parishes. What might father and son have said to each other? Finally, he turns down breakfast and excuses himself. Today, he'll go visit Oliver Ward in the hospital, and then he's supposed to have lunch with Holly. There are a couple of other stops he has to make. This is the part of his life that has always pleased him the most, though, of course, now it's colored by this battle he's having with himself. Climbing the stairs, he thinks of Mr. Petit and feels the sense of frustration at not being able to speak with him.

6.

Elizabeth drops her husband off at the bookstore, and drives on to school. There are heavy clouds gathering in the lower quadrant of the sky to the west. It'll be another day of intermittent rain squalls. She pulls into the school parking lot, and then sits for a while in the car, cry-ing a little, watching the buses arrive and the parents' cars, dropping off students. Everybody busy with the business of the day, the familiar rou-tines. It all looks like the bustle and hurry, the busy activity, of a hive. She gazes at the old Briarly Building with its oak tree and its leaded windows and its little vanquished village of a graveyard, and thinks about sleep. On the ride to the bookstore, Will seemed distracted, ner-vous, drained. She didn't feel like talking, and, apparently, neither did he. She wonders now what his dreams might have been. Watching him limp around the room getting dressed, she felt bad again about kneeing him, and asked if he was all right.

"I must've slept wrong," he said. "My tailbone's sore as hell."

"Maybe I kicked you in my sleep."

"It does feel bruised."

Her own knee is, in fact, sore. She presses her hand to it, sitting here in the car and staring at the school, wanting to turn around and go home and get to the bottom of whatever this trouble is that has begun for them.

But there's the day's work. She wipes her eyes, does her mascara again, then gets out of the car and limps—her knee is indeed very sore—across the parking lot. And here's James Christ with his sour, unhappy, victimized expression and his way of sidling up to her. "I saw you sitting there in your car. You looked like you were crying. You crying?"

"No," Elizabeth tells him. "I was trying to decide whether or not to move to another town and change my name."

He's evidently at a loss. Moreover, he's depressed and, as always before, he wants company. He walks with her, talking about it all—his worries, his heavy woes, the problem of his low self-esteem. His difficult childhood and the fact that he has bad digestion; nothing he eats agrees with him. Every meal is a trial. And, on top of that, he can't find a stable relationship. He's a man capable of spilling everything in the space of a stroll across a parking lot—Elizabeth thinks this, and then momentarily feels sorry for him. She stops and says, "James, what can I do about any of this?"

"I don't know," he says. "I'm sorry. I've got to find another job. I'm tired of being unhappy. I'm always unhappy."

"Don't worry," she tells him.

"You're not feeling well and here I am complaining. What'd you do to your leg?"

"I have a trick knee."

In the faculty lounge, they drink coffee and talk a little about the day to come. He's low and sorrowful, and she senses that her own new situation makes her more readily accepting of his predicament—misery does indeed love company. She almost tells him about her night. But, instead, she just sips her coffee and pretends to listen. *What if a man who has been unfaithful, upon discovery, never does it again? What if the wife, who knows about it, never brings it up? What if the wife can bring herself never to imagine what it was, what was said, how it felt, how far from her the man of her house has gone? If the wife confronts the husband with what she knows, does that end the marriage? Did the first Elizabeth know something that caused her to go? But there were the two children. She left them, too. Can the wife find another life far away from the place where her once happy life was harmed? Can a woman pretend for the rest of her life that nothing happened?*

She makes her way to her classroom, trying to stop thinking of anything. And here's Calvin Reed, waiting by the door.

"What, Calvin?"

"Nothing," he says.

"Are you going in?"

"No."

She waits for him to explain. And, abruptly, he takes her by the shoulders. "Calvin," she says, "let go of me."

He moves his hands down to her wrists and grips them, bending toward her as if to listen to her whisper something.

"One more second," she says to him, "and you'll be in a lot of pain."

He lets go but remains where he is, hulking over her.

"Step back," she says through her teeth. "Or I promise you, you'll fall back."

He does so.

She enters her classroom and shuts the door on him. The disorder around her is no louder than usual, but this morning it's like an assault to her senses. She reaches to the first desk, which is empty, and tips it over so that its front edge hits the floor with an enormous crash. Several girls scream, and one boy says, "Oh, my God." Then they're all still. The television is already halfway through the morning school-news report.

"Sit yourselves down," Elizabeth says. "And be quiet."

They all obey. The morning is here, now, to be endured. She moves to her desk and sits, and puts her hands to her face. She can feel them all looking at her. Finally, she opens her lesson plans and begins. There are assignments to hand back, assignments to give. She writes on the blackboard and moves around the room during a written exercise, concentrating on each of them, keeping everything inside, not thinking.

At the first class bell, James Christ comes in looking like a portrait done by a Dutch master of disconsolation. The sharp light in the room contributes to this effect. He comes to her desk and leans down, to murmur, "I saw Calvin sitting in Mr. Petit's office." She nods. The students for this hour are already in their seats, talking and gesticulating and slapping at each other, the universal body language of teenage boys and girls in groups.

"Settle down," Elizabeth says, remembering all the times she interpreted a weary tone in a teacher as some discontent with herself or the class. How strange to have come this far in life and not to have reached an understanding of the truth that the personal life supersedes everything else.

The door opens now, and Jonathan Lawrence enters, moves quickly to a chair, and takes it, not looking at anyone. Elizabeth assigns a writing exercise and makes it a point to stop by his desk. The assignment is to write a series of sentences about fog on a mountain, to see how many different ways it can be said. Jonathan has written: "A veil of fog obscures the immensely pleasing mountain crags in the distance." And "The mountain is like a lady covering her stony countenance with white linen."

"How is your grandfather?" she asks him.

"Better," he says. "Thank you for inquiring."

"Can you try to write a bit less floridly?"

He appears horror-struck by the suggestion—and then she realizes he doesn't understand the word and is embarrassed by the prospect of being caught out in his nonunderstanding.

She says, "Fancy is nice. But simple is good, too. You know, 'You couldn't see the top of the mountain for the thickness of the mist.'"

"Oh, yes. I see. Oh, indubit—of course."

"Glad to hear about your grandfather's progress," she says. And finds that she has to fight back tears. She leaves him and returns to the front of the room, to her desk, where she sits and brings a tissue paper out of the top drawer, holding it to her nose, and surreptitiously dabbing at her eyes. She thinks about Will, about what he might be doing at this very minute. There's almost a half hour to go in the period. She makes herself concentrate on her lesson plans—the section on *The Great Gatsby*. The roil of possession and passion in the novel moves through her like a memory of her own recently lived life. She will have to explain Tom Buchanan's unfaithfulness to Daisy, and Daisy's unfaithfulness to Tom.

How could they? How could Fitzgerald write of it all so effortlessly? How can she talk about any of it, now? Her stomach does a little jolting turn, and she has to swallow several times fast. The hour is a slow progression of increasing anxiety.

7.

Butterfield endures an awful morning, fierce with guilt and with a frighteningly strong pull at his middle when he thinks about Ariana. He tries to look at everything reasonably. That is, he seeks detachment, the solace of the blameworthy: intellectual nicety, rationalization, what is happening is a small thing in the larger scheme of existence. The yearning he feels is both normal and unacceptable. He must put it aside and go on with his life. It will be possible to behave as if nothing has happened. It will be possible to forget it. Ariana lives next door and is talking about secret visits.

Oh, God.

The morning passes with almost no business—a man and his son, three elderly ladies. Butterfield's alone with his mind and the images there. When the elderly ladies come in, they remind him of his mother and great-aunt and the soon-to-be-divided house on Temporary Road. He's going to have to work through all that. He's growing shakier by the minute in the contemplation of everything. Sitting behind the counter, he imagines himself months past this day, with its lowering sky and its threat of rain, a threat which feels for all the world like the threat of devastation.

When the rain starts, he stands in the doorway and watches it—a slow, steady, windless fall. The eaves run. The street fills, and it still comes, agitating the surfaces of the puddles. As the water is displaced by car tires, it makes that soft swishing, that familiar sound, the cars going slowly by. Every common noise comes to him now as a kind of goad, as if the world means to tantalize him with its plainness, its imponderable separateness from his troubles. It's raining, dark, the sky looking poisonous, and none of this has anything to do with the darkness in his soul.

A little past ten o'clock, Mark calls. "What's wrong, Dad? You got a cold?"

"I'm okay," Butterfield tells him.

"You sound messed up."

"It's the phone, and thanks for the report."

"I'm calling to tell you Gail and I'll drive down from her place for Thanksgiving. I'm flying down the night before."

"Okay."

"Dad, something's wrong. I can hear it. Is Elizabeth—would it be better if we came on the Friday after?"

"Don't be ridiculous, Mark. Come as soon as you can. As soon as you-all want to."

"Well, there's something we have to ask you."

"Both of you?"

"Well, Gail."

Butterfield waits for him to go on. He sees Ariana pull up outside and stop. The rain is coming harder now. He's filled with the same measure of excitement as fear, an improbable balance of thralldom and dread. He can barely talk. "You—you want to t-tell me what it is, Son?" There's a seizing near his diaphragm.

"Well, I don't think she should surprise you with it."

"Okay." He hasn't even quite heard Mark. The muscles of his chest and abdomen seem to have tightened to the point of a cramp. His son says something he can't quite distinguish, so he asks him to repeat it.

"I said it's kind of heavy."

"Heavy."

"It's *very* heavy."

"Jesus, Son. Will you just tell me?"

"Gail's with a woman."

Butterfield waits for more. Outside, Ariana gets out of her car, taking her time.

"Dad?" Mark's voice seems to come from some far distance.

Butterfield watches Ariana Bromberg rush to the shelter of the entrance to the store, holding an open newspaper over her head. She pushes inside, and lets the newspaper down, running one dark, slender hand through her hair. He catches himself conjuring up a picture of the Mongol invasion of Europe.

"Did you hear me, Dad?"

"I heard you." He signals for Ariana to wait, and then tries very hard to draw in one single breath of air. She smiles; it is entirely, fatally inviting.

Mark's voice continues on the phone. "She was helping Gail search for Mom. They're in love, according to Gail. She wants to bring her to Thanksgiving."

"Christ," Butterfield says, meaning it in all the ways it can be meant.

"I don't think she'll come without her."

"Well," Butterfield says. "I'm—" He can't push air through his vocal chords.

"Dad?"

"—fucked if I can think of a thing to say, Mark."

"I think it's a bit rude and insensitive, of course."

"Of course."

"All right," his son says. "Sorry. This is Gail's thing—not mine."

Ariana shifts her weight, jutting one hip and resting her wrist on it, watching him.

"I've got to go, Son."

"She's worried about how you'll react, Dad. She asked me to—she wanted me to prepare the way."

"Look, I can't talk about this now, Mark. I've got a customer." This comes forth with unnatural speed, as if he's rushing through something he learned to recite.

"I know you'll have to clear this with Elizabeth. I know it's a big thing to have to tell you over the telephone."

"I'll talk to you later, Son."

Ariana stands there, arms now folded. She wears a tan dress with a low sweep at the neck, showing collarbones and the soft swell of the top of her breasts. There's a commiserating smile on her face, though now she raises one eyebrow, one dark, soft line, and he would never have believed there could be so much concupiscence in that simple gesture—so much of a conspiratorial invitation to venery. When he hangs the phone up, she crosses to the door and looks out, then turns. "Nobody on the street just now. Isn't it about lunchtime?"

"Early," he manages. It comes out of him at the level of a chirp.

"I still make you so nervous."

He can't utter a sound. Outside, the rain ceases, almost as if turned off, like a faucet. A car goes by, and she watches it, then turns to look at him again, still smiling that smile.

"I had fun the other night until Geoffrey got to be—well, Geoffrey."

"We can't do anything," Butterfield tells her. "Please."

"You're going on the old double standard," she says. "Right?"

"No."

"Sure you are. It's something I control. Isn't that how you see it?"

He can't help himself. He nods.

"And if I want to, you won't be able *not* to."

"No," he says.

"You're denying that?"

"I don't know."

"Want to?" she asks.

"Yes."

"Well?"

"No. I'm sorry. Please."

"Well, do you or don't you?"

"Want to?" he asks.

She smiles. "Oh, yes. *I* do. I certainly do. That's why I'm here."

"I was asking if you were asking did *I* want to."

"What?"

"Nothing," he says. "Forget it."

"But you want to."

"Yes," Butterfield says. "Christ. Yes. Goddamn it, yes."

She closes the door, turning the CLOSED sign around, then faces him and begins disrobing. He watches her and is filled with a sense, almost innocent-feeling, of purest wonder. It's weirdly as if he's a child observing a mystery of science unfolding in a beautiful presentation by experienced parental hands. Again he tries to call up the depredations of history. She walks over to him and unbuckles his belt. Her body is stunning. He looks at her breasts, her long belly, the tan line at the top of her thighs and across her lower hips. In a second, he's on his knees, the position for worship, arms wrapped around her hips. She thrusts her pelvic bone at him, holding him by his ears. The event is pornographic, and she wants to look upon it, gets him to move to the end of the counter where the mirror is, so she can observe them. He says, "Did you lock the door?"

"No."

And he stops, looks up into her face. There's a mad gleam in her eyes. She grins at him; it's almost a leer.

"You think I want to get caught?" she murmurs. "Geoffrey would kill me."

As with the other times, he feels astonishment exactly as strong as that of a man stumbling into a new and previously unseen world; and yet it's also as if he's standing apart from it all, watching his own actions. The quiet is unspeakable and thrilling. He's loose in it, like someone tumbling through space, and so when the telephone rings, loud as a fire alarm, he jumps back and scrabbles violently to his feet, hearing himself say, "Jesus Christ. This is a place of business."

"It's a telephone," she says, so matter-of-factly that it merely adds to the unreality of everything. He's up, facing her. She stands there, arms at her sides, quite at ease in her nakedness. The phone rings again.

Absurdly, he lurches to the door and separates the blinds with a metallic crashing, looking out the window as if the sound has come from there. The phone rattles a third time, pulling a sound of distress up out of his throat.

"Don't answer it," she says, as if this is a solution to his upset.

He topples toward the counter and picks up the receiver. "Hello!"

"Dad?" It's Gail. "What's wrong?"

He looks at Ariana. "It's Gail," he says.

"Is Elizabeth there?" Gail asks. "Are you all right? You shouted at me when you answered."

"Nobody here," he says.

"Who're you talking to, then?"

"You," he says. "I'm talking to you. Hello."

"But you told somebody it was me."

"I did. No, I don't think so."

"Are you all right, Dad?"

"What's up?" His voice quavers.

"You sound out of breath."

"I'm perfectly fine," he says. "Really. Christ Almighty."

"Did Mark call you?"

"Yes," he says, still breathless. Ariana bends to pick up her discarded clothes. She holds them, staring. "I just got off the phone with my son, yes."

"I know he's your son, Dad, what's wrong there?" Gail wants to know.

"Nothing. Nothing's wrong. Lord." He watches Ariana getting languidly back into her clothes. "I was moving books. Moving books. Jesus Christ. I'm out of breath because I was moving books."

"You don't have to cuss at me. It's upset you—Mark did call you."

"Mark called me."

"What did he say?"

Ariana gives him a look of playful ruefulness.

"He told me, Gail, okay?"

"I know it's hard to learn something like this over the phone."

Butterfield watches Ariana move to the door and open it. "Wait a minute," he says into the phone, then he covers the speaker part of it. "Don't leave yet," he whispers.

"Maybe I'll come back." Her lovely mouth curls up at one end, and once more she raises one eyebrow.

"Dad?" Gail's saying. "I don't know how else to do this. I couldn't just show up with Edie."

"Edie," he says. He's watching Ariana run her hands through her shining hair. The breath is returning to him, the ability to draw it in and hold it long enough for it to travel to the nerves and ganglia at the base of his skull. He can almost stand straight again. "Gail," he says. "Everything's fine, but I'll call you right back."

"She's anxious to meet you."

"I'll call you back."

She hangs up with a small, muttered curse, the first part of which he hears: "Motherf—" And Ariana starts toward him, grinning, but then he puts a hand up. "Please," he says. "We can't do this. We have to keep from doing this. I love my wife. Please."

"You want me to leave?" she says with an edge of incredulity. Something flashes in her eyes. "I don't mean anything to you, do I?"

He can only stand there, staring.

"Well, *do* I?"

"Ariana," he says.

"You don't love me."

He can't speak.

"This is it, then. We're over. Just like that. I was just a fuck."

"What?" he says. *"What?"*

"It's not that simple," she tells him in a thin, toneless voice.

"No," he says. "Of course. I don't—I didn't—you—we—"

"I get it," she says. "And we'll see. We'll just see." She opens the door and goes out, leaving it open. He watches her get into her car and drive away, brakes squealing.

For several minutes, he does nothing at all. And then the phone rings again, startling him once more.

"I didn't mean to hang up on you," Gail tells him. "Is your emergency—whatever it was—over? I was going to leave you a message saying I'm sorry."

"There was no emergency," he says. "I'm sorry, too."

"You sound awful."

"Thank you. So do you."

"I'm serious. What's happening?"

"Gail, why don't you just call back and leave me your message."

"Haw," she says.

They say nothing for a space. He thinks she might've broken the connection.

"Well, so what do you think?" she says. "Do you think it'll be all right with Elizabeth?"

"I don't know," he says, because he doesn't.

"She's been so much help trying to find Mom."

He draws in a breath and mutters, "You found her?"

"No, but I think we're close. I do. And so does Edie."

"And you're together."

"We're in love. Yes. I feel like myself for the first time in my life."

It seems to him now that something in his failures of the last few weeks has brought all this confusion on; it is precisely as if the unhappy elements of his whole life—the fatherless youth, the Crazies, the first Elizabeth's abandonment, and the years of a kind of stasis keeping a bookstore, living without ambition or much real energy on a trust fund, all that—as if these are swooping down at him from some height. Anyone walking into the store at this moment would see a man hunched over the counter in the posture of someone hulking against a very cold wind. But he finds that, indeed, he has the words to speak.

"Can you bring her down sometime other than Thanksgiving?"

Gail leaves a pause. "Well, I've sort of already asked her."

"Okay."

"That's the next visit, Dad. And I want you to meet her."

He says nothing.

"You and Elizabeth."

"I think you might wait until *after* Thanksgiving."

"She doesn't have anywhere to go and I'm not leaving her here, Dad. I—we'll stay here if that's what you want. We've *moved in* together. We're together."

He's quiet again, looking at the neat rows of books on the wall across from him. At some point in his life, he had procured these books and set them in order, just so. He had been a man convinced about the efficacy of his own efforts.

"Speaking of Mom, Edie's pretty sure she's in San Francisco somewhere."

"You know what, kid? I hate to bring up a sore subject and I don't want to be a sourpuss or anything, but *nothing* in me *remotely* wants to see your mom. I mean, not to say hello, and not to say anything else, either. I'm not even curious." He can't help his voice rising, though now he attempts to control it. "I don't even want to read her name in a phone book."

"I would still like to reestablish the connection."

"Gail. Go into your bathroom. Look in the mirror, look deep into your own pretty green eyes and say, 'What the hell?' Do that for me, will you?"

"She's my mother."

"She walked away from you."

Silence.

"Sweetie?"

"I'm here."

"Well, you *have* to understand how I feel."

"I understand it. I don't condone it."

"Condone?" Butterfield says. "Jesus Christ. What in the world have you been reading?"

"That's typical male-ownership talk, double-standard bullshit talk. This is the mother of your children."

Now Butterfield is silent. A moment passes, more breathing on the line.

"Edie says it must've been a combination of things that led her to do it."

"Well, she's certainly got a handle on it, having not been there for *any* of it. I can't wait to meet her."

"Male ownership again."

"Ownership," Butterfield says. "What the hell. Look, whatever you want to call it, as long as that translates to *you*, that with all my heart, all my *maleness* and my ownership and all I ever was or was not or could be or want to be and can't or can and don't want to be—you know? With all that, darling, I do not want to lay eyes on that woman again or hear her voice. I don't want to hear her breathing, walking, talking, snoring, whining, humming a tune. None of it. I don't even want to hear rumors about her. She's not dead to me, Gail— *She never was.* That's the closest I can come to describing how I feel about her. And, darling, I have to say that your expectations about this are a bit unreasonable. Not to say ridiculous and overbearing, entirely academic and—well—*silly*."

"I can't help it. I want to know her again." Gail sniffles.

He's appalled. "I'm sorry, sweetie. I know, I know. I understand. I do."

"And I understand your anger," Gail says.

His anger surges again like blood behind the eyes. "Is this a psychiatry lesson?"

Silence again.

He has an image of Ariana Bromberg glaring at him and saying "Don't I mean anything to you?" He has to call up the situation he is presently in with his daughter. Into the phone, he says, "Look, if you want to bring your new friend, that's fine, okay? But I don't want to spend the holiday talking about your mother. The fact is, my life's ambition is to go to my grave without ever catching the slightest glimpse of her. Is that clear enough? The only thing in my life that I'm more sure of is that I'm going to have to make that trip to the grave someday. All right?"

"All *right*." His daughter's voice, clipped and narrow and unhappy with him. He's heard it more often over the past couple of years.

"I'll see you and your new friend on Thanksgiving," he gets out as pleasantly as he can.

"She's not a friend, Daddy."

He says, "Better make friends. Even when there's passion, baby, it's all better if you're friends, too."

But she has hung up on him again. He hears the dial tone, and, for a little space, he listens to it as if to a scolding voice. Then he places the receiver in its cradle and goes and stands in the open door of his shop. The sky is lowering, not happy. He looks up and down the street, thinking, he realizes with a kind of shudder, about Ariana, half-expecting to see her car.

CONVALESCING

I.

Oliver walks slow down the hospital corridor with Alison on one side
of him and Holly on the other. It's almost time for lunch, and Fiona
and Kalie have arrived; they're down in the cafeteria, having a sandwich.
Alison's in her uniform, because this is another shift day. The hospital
hallway is bright, polished, sterilely designed to be warm and reassuring. There are other convalescents walking, and nurses and doctors hurrying past. With her gun in its holster, Alison bumps a tray with glass
vials on it, and their attempt to catch things only causes more havoc;
several of the vials fall and break. Blood everywhere. It looks like the
scene of an accident. A nurse hurries over and tells them to step back.

"Did you get any on you, Officer?" the nurse says.

Oliver knows that his daughter never has gotten used to being called
officer. He's aware that Alison doesn't know she's been addressed. He
takes her arm just above the wrist. "Sweetie?"

"Oh, I'm *so* sorry." Alison seems more upset than is called for under
the circumstance.

Oliver says, "Hey, kid. What is it?"

"I'm so clumsy," she tells him. And looks like she might start to cry.

"I'm getting out of here this week," Oliver says. "Nothing more to worry about, darling."

The nurse produces rubber gloves from somewhere on her person and puts them on with a smacking sound, bending to pick up the vials that haven't broken.

Oliver stands straight between the two women, being held upright by them. He's unable quite to believe that he'll ever be able to go home. In the window of a door across the hall, he sees a reflection of his own face, the look of a kind of fixed surprise in it and the incessant slow turning back and forth. It seems to him that the world is growing ever more dangerous, with its vials of possibly diseased blood. He knows these dark thoughts are part of his recovery, yet they discourage him. He looks over at Alison and has a moment of experiencing what a weight he must be in her still-young life. Alison's talking about how she has always been clumsy, and Holly tells about having knocked over a valuable scrim at a dinner party in a wealthy person's house in Florence, how the scrim toppled into a glass cabinet full of curios under soft light, the whole thing shattering like the end of the world. "For the longest time," she says, "everyone in that room stared at me. Complete stunned silent consternation and judgment, staring. And all I could say was, 'Whoops.'"

Alison laughs and thanks her for the solace, using the word.

"Well," Holly says with a touch of friendly sarcasm, "I'm glad it makes you happy."

"Did Stanley come to work at your house this morning?" Alison asks suddenly.

"I left so early," says Holly. "I haven't talked to Fiona."

Alison glances down at her hands. To her father, she has always looked small in the uniform, like a kid playing at being a cop, though she's, in fact, very good at her job and well respected by everyone with whom she works.

"Why the—interest in Stanley?" he asks her.

"I want the work to proceed." Her smile is cryptic.

"All right," Oliver says, and smiles back.

"Nice young man," Holly puts in, standing there with one hand on her hip and the other on Oliver's elbow, helping to support him. Oliver can move a little easier. In fact, things are improving—aches and all, setbacks and all. He can feel the returning strength in his legs as he moves again, shuffling along. It's so hard to make himself fully believe it.

"I never can get used to this equipment hanging off me," Alison says, moving the belt with her pistol in it around toward her middle. He thinks of touching the side of her face, a gesture he has mostly stopped making, but he brought her up with it from the time of her earliest infancy, the hand, open, lightly pressed to her cheek, and he would say, "Hello, little girl." He can do no such thing now, of course. Not now. He says an old joke between them: "How many guys went too fast today hoping you'd pull them over?"

She shakes her head but smiles and pats the back of his hand. It sends a thrill of fatherly pride through him: this grown woman.

Earlier, he and Holly talked a little about his time in Vietnam and her life in Scotland with Mr. Grey. Holly went on about Mr. Grey's temper and his sense of justice. Oliver felt strangely diminished by comparison, and he observed this feeling in himself, surmising it. Because he was uneasy, he began telling stories and was happily surprised at her obvious enjoyment of them.

He told her about a time when he and his father used his father's knowledge of electricity to rig a friend's television set with a circuit breaker—this was back when tubes were still in use—so that it would turn off when it reached a certain temperature, that of a normal television fully warmed up. The friend, his name was Clarence, was a Yankee fan and rather insufferable about it, because the Yankees were always winning, always beating the hell out of the old Washington Senators. So, Oliver's father, with the aid of Clarence's wife, rigged the television set so that it would shut off just as Clarence was getting comfortable with his potato chips and his dip and his can of sardines and his Senators-Yankee game. Oliver and his father sat on a little rise in the backyard and watched through the picture window of that house as poor Clarence railed and raged at his television set, which would act like any normal television set until the moment when he sat down again and was dipping one of his chips or picking up one of his sardines. And when it became clear that Clarence was going to give up and walk over to the neighbor's house to watch the game, Oliver and his father hurried in, to where his mother already had the television tuned to the movie of the week. Oliver and his father feigned deep interest in *Swiss Family Robinson*, and poor Clarence traipsed back across the lawns, followed in the dark by Oliver and his father. They sat comfortably in the backyard and watched Clarence struggle with his incredibly consistent television, which kept shutting down at exact intervals, just as the game was fully visible and the announcers were clearly audible. "That's how I got interested in electricity," Oliver said. Holly, who had laughed through the telling, went down into something of a fit at this statement. She coughed, and her eyes bulged, and Oliver put his arm around her and was happy in that way that feels as though it might change everything forever.

"God," Holly said. "I laugh at the story and then you said that and then I was laughing at my laughing."

"It just hit you that way," Oliver told her, liking her laugh while being faintly embarrassed for her.

Now, being helped by her and his daughter in the busy hallway of Point Royal Hospital, he has a surprising sense of comfort, even as he totters and has trouble getting his bearings. The two women are talking about other incidents of clumsiness, Alison telling about the time she fell asleep in a movie theater with a large Coke in her hand, and it dropped in her lap, so cold, and she laughed at it, and realized that the laugh had come at exactly the saddest moment in the film, and everyone looked at her as though she were some sort of psychopath. He kisses the side of her head, and then finds himself turning to do the same to Holly. Holly leans slightly to accept it, and then looks at him, this woman who has hired him to divide her house in two. And who seems, since his trouble, to be getting along very well with Fiona. He says, "I have a feeling the work on your house might not be necessary anymore."

She smiles. "That's the sweetest thing any gentleman has ever said to me."

He realizes with a start that she thinks he has offered some sort of gesture toward romance. The strangeness of this evidently shows in his face, because she seems to hesitate, her face flushing red, and then she seeks to recover the light tone. "I'm twenty years older than you are, at the very least you know."

Oliver's at a loss. He hears himself say, "You and your aunt seem to be getting along so well these days."

"Well." She has understood him at last. "Fiona's still doing things that drive me completely batty."

He squeezes her arm, once, lightly. "Maybe she'll surprise you."

"That's the trouble. All the surprises." Holly looks across at Alison and shakes her head. "This morning, we argued over whether or not to put a separate egg yolk in the scrambled eggs, the way I have been doing them for at least forty years, and with her watching me about thirty percent of the time. She swore up and down that I had never done it, ever, that this was a new development and I was adding cholesterol to her diet because mine is low and hers is high. I saw where she was going with it and left it alone. That is, I allowed as how it *was* new and said I wanted the eggs to have more body. But I threw them out and started over and then she didn't want any. Said she was never hungry in the first place and I shouldn't have wasted the eggs. That's life with Fiona."

"She's been so wonderful with the children," Alison says.

"She's always been that way, yes. With children."

They walk on to the end of the corridor and back, and they pass Drew going in the other direction with his wife. They're heading down to the cafeteria. They nod at Oliver, and Oliver nods back. It's like passing neighbors on a city street, so odd. He thinks about how it was in the war, and how he felt in that hospital, learning that he would live. "How am I doing?" he says to the two women, and, quite suddenly, something sinks inside him, far down, falling far, a great stone tumbling from heights into the little pond of his being. A desolation. Here is his daughter, whose life has been circumscribed, held back, limited to caring for a man like Oliver, with his needs and his amiable failures over and over. He can barely stand under the weight of this unexpected sorrow, a leveling force, so terrible. He was feeling so good only a moment ago. Holly and Alison look at him. They hold him up.

They all return slowly to the room, and somehow he gets into the

bed again. He knows that this that is going on in his soul is something
he must never tell them, never tell Alison or the old ladies or the children. No one. He will have to carry this, and try to find some way to
make up for everything without seeming to be compensating.

"You feeling okay?" Alison asks him, having, no doubt, seen something in his face.

He looks directly at her and then finds that he can't manage a smile.
So he pretends a gruff sarcasm. "I look okay to you, do I? You like me in
hospital blue?"

"Well, you look like something hurt you."

"Something did—remember?"

Stanley comes in for a little while and unwittingly provides Oliver
with something to concentrate on other than the devastation inside; he
has some diagrams for the wiring, which he wants to show Oliver. He's
also got sketches for another job, which involves building an enclosure
for a swimming pool. He and Oliver go over the diagrams, and Oliver
finds that he can muster the voice to suggest some changes. Alison and
Holly melt back into the hallway, but then Alison looks back in and
seems faintly agitated, removing Oliver's water glass and filling it up
and bringing it back.

"I have people to do that," Oliver tells her, hearing the gruffness
in his voice. It comes to him without words that his way of hiding his
sorrow over everything is to become surly and ill-tempered. "Really,
honey," he says, giving her a soft look.

"Nothing to it," she says, as if not quite thinking about it. She turns
at the door and asks if he needs anything else. Does he want the newspaper?

No. Oliver sees the way Alison's gaze trails toward Stanley and then
glides away. She goes back out, claiming curiosity as to where Holly has
gone, and it strikes Oliver that this is a pretext. He says nothing.

Stanley has watched her the whole time, quietly standing there with
his sketches in his hands.

"The ladies are having Thanksgiving on Temporary Road?" Oliver
says.

"That's the plan."

"We're not near—finished." It pleases him to be talking about it as though he's up and out of this white room with its institutional art on the walls.

"No," Stanley says. "And they know it, too. Doesn't seem to matter. Holly said she likes the idea because it'll be like it must've been on the first Thanksgiving. Actually, I don't think she's very peaceful with dividing up the house."

Alison comes back into the room and sits in the chair next to Oliver's bed. She's snacking from a small bag of potato chips. She offers the bag to Stanley, who thanks her and reaches into it.

A nurse brings Oliver's lunch. She's someone they haven't seen before, a thin, dark, narrow-lipped girl with acne-scarred cheeks and a look of discouraged efficiency, which reminds Oliver of the young woman who does the yearly inspections of automobiles at his service station. He thinks of that place, Carl's Auto Service, and wonders uselessly once more if he will ever look upon it again, ever worry about a thing as small as the inspection sticker on a truck.

Lunch is grilled chicken breast with red potatoes, corn, peach cobbler, coffee, milk—and broccoli.

Oliver says, "I've told this hospital five times I can't stand that stuff."

"I'm sorry," the nurse says, looking wounded. "I didn't know."

"Actually," says Stanley, "I'll eat it."

"Take it outside, then," Oliver says. "I can't stand the smell of it."

Stanley takes the dish and Oliver's fork and walks out into the hallway, where he stands, looking one way and then the other, like a man waiting to cross the street. He steps out of view. Oliver looks at what remains of the meal and moves the tray aside.

"Come on, Dad," Alison says to him.

"In a little while," he tells her. "I'm not hungry just now."

"Do you feel all right?"

"Sure."

They're quiet. They hear Stanley talking about the broccoli to a nurse out in the hall.

"Something—going on with you—and—and—Stanley?" Oliver asks his daughter.

She seems a little flustered, turning slightly from him, one hand going to her hairline. "Don't be ridiculous."

"And why, little girl—would that—be ridiculous?"

"I don't know." It's clear that she wishes him to drop the subject. He touches her hand.

"Daddy," she says.

Presently, Holly returns, looking as if she doesn't really know where else to be. She has been downstairs with Fiona and Kalie, but those two are playing Go Fish. She asks Oliver about his uneaten lunch, and Oliver, still reeling inside, tries to imagine that it is all a product of what he has been through. He would like to sleep. He would like everyone to leave, and he would like to go to sleep and stay that way for a long time. Days. He would like the black clouds to lift.

And now Drew enters the room, creaking along slow, on his cane, with his wife. There's a lot of rickety motion as he and his wife try to get the curtain drawn around him. He says loudly that he wants to watch television. His wife turns it on as Stanley comes back, carrying the empty plate. Stanley puts it down, sheepishly, on Oliver's tray. They all watch the television for a time—*Eyewitness News* at noon. A poultry truck has overturned on the highway south, and turkeys are scattered everywhere, living and dead, injured or simply wandering around in the road. Stanley remembers that he brought some pork rinds for Oliver, remembering that Oliver always liked them.

"He can't eat those," Alison says.

Oliver says, "Oh—yes—I can. Save—save them."

"We'll save them, then." She gives Stanley a look.

"I should've thought it out a little," he says.

"It's a thoughtful gift in its way," Alison tells him.

"Well," Stanley says. "Guess I better go do some more work on the house."

After he's gone, Oliver says, "Nice fellow," to no one in particular.

"I think that's true," says Holly.

For a moment, no one says anything. Oliver closes his eyes and breathes, and the despair begins to change, lessening slightly. He sees it now as despair, and it frightens him. He wants to fight his way out of it, away from it.

"Janice," Drew murmurs from the next bed. "Delores."

Oliver looks at his daughter and shrugs, pulling the bandages at his neck slightly. It makes him wince.

"Are you okay?" she says.

He smiles. "Fine—there, kid."

"Arletta. Carolyn," Drew says, sputtering.

"Wouldn't you love to know?" Alison whispers.

"I'm afraid I—do know," Oliver tells her.

She leans a little to look at Drew, slack-jawed and helpless-looking in his sleep. Drew's wife is dozing in a chair.

"I'm unreasonably afraid he's going to say my name," Holly murmurs. And then laughs.

A little later, Alison leaves to go to work, and Holly sits next to the bed. Oliver feels the oddness of this, even after all the warm attention. He wants to say something about it, and then he does. "I hardly—know you, lady."

She nods. "And here we are."

"I don't—under—under—stand." He has never felt a deeper need to be honest and straightforward. It's as if the very possibility of a mistaken idea about his relation to her is too much to risk, as if having experienced this awful inner collapse, he must strive to be exact and precise, for fear of the last strands of himself unraveling altogether—and now he wonders if this, too, is a result of the stroke, this sense of crisis in a simple, polite passage with this woman who has been so helpful and friendly.

"Do you want me to go?" she says. "Do I make you uncomfortable?"

"I'm a little—uncomfortable."

"I'll go."

"Wait," he says as she starts to rise. "I—didn't mean—that."

"It seemed pretty straightforward," she says with an edge of annoyance. "I've let my crazy aunt lead me to intrude, I'm afraid. Forgive it."

"No, don't—ask forgiveness. Please."

"Well." Holly clears her throat. "I remember when I was your age," she says, and laughs; she has amused herself. It's one of the things he finds charming about her.

"Dividing the house—wasn't—your idea," he says.

She looks over her shoulder and then leans closer. "I like to let her believe it was her idea. It's easier that way." This is spoken in the low tones of a joke between them, but then her eyes swim, and he realizes that she's hurting. It stops him.

"You know, she can be quite sweet," Holly says, controlling herself.

"I've noticed," he tells her.

2.

That evening, the Butterfields stay inside. She looks at student essays. Calvin's paper is disturbing, and she puts it aside, thinking about how it's one she would normally show Will, deciding not to in the moment of realizing that before this trouble of Ariana, she wouldn't have hesitated for a moment.

She feels more alone than she ever could've imagined.

For his part, he buries himself in a book—a biography of Winston Churchill. How strangely consoling are completed lives: the triumphs, travails, and failures done with. He's reading for the solace of other people's sorrows, and he's aware of her sitting near, the one he's wronged, the one he loves.

They do not speak.

After an hour of this, he forges the courage to ask if she wishes him to make something for them to eat.

"I'm not hungry," she says, feeling—as she has all day—that she's about to begin crying.

"I'm going to make a sandwich," he says. "Do you have another headache?"

"No," she tells him. Then she goes on precisely as he begins, so, they speak at the same time: she says, "There's a kid at school," just as he says, "Gail's in love."

She says, "Excuse me?" exactly as he says, "What'd you say?"

And then, just as he says, "Gail's gay," she says, "He's a psycho, I think."

He stops.

"You start," they both say.

Now she almost laughs, shaking her head, holding up one hand.

"No—you," he says.

"Wait a minute," she says. "Gail's what?"

So, he tells her. He has wanted to say something all day, and now he can. But because he learned of this in the company of Ariana, he feels harrowingly close to faltering through some sort of confession.

After a long pause, she says, "Jesus." It seems to him that all the color leaves her face.

"She's bringing her to Thanksgiving. I mean they're living together."

"Jesus," Elizabeth says again.

"I told her it was fine, of course. Though I did try to discourage it for Thanks-fucking-giving." He gets up and moves to the entrance of the dining room. He can't sit still, so he paces a little, thinking about the imposition, Gail bringing her new love home. He's aware of the essential ungraciousness of the idea: if it were a man she was bringing, there would be no such feeling. He looks at this in himself and is ashamed. "I just don't want any more to deal with on that day than the usual," he says softly, confidingly. Through the window on the other side of the dining room, he can see the next-door house. It makes him quail inside, and he steps back to where she is, on the sofa. "I love you," he says.

She hands him Calvin's paper, without quite looking at him. "This kid. Take a look at what he wrote today."

Butterfield looks at the paper and then reads it aloud, softly, almost to himself. "'The fog on the mountain is like the shirt covering your tits. The fog on the mountain is your—'" He stops. The word is *pussy.* There's another long silence.

"The hell," he says.

"I sent him to Mr. Petit when I got it."

After another pause, he says, "Jesus."

"It's nothing I can't handle," she says.

"Did you report it?"

"I just told you, I sent him to Mr. Petit."

"What else are you gonna do about it?" he asks. "Because I'll tell you what I'd like to do about it."

She shrugs. "It's a kid, Will. A fucked-up, confused, ugly, sorrowful mess of a kid."

He gives the paper back to her and sits down on the sofa. "God-damn," he says.

Shostakovich and wife appear at the door perhaps twenty silent minutes later. He's carrying a bottle of champagne. "This is to make up for the other night," he says. "And I'm not having the slightest touch of it, either."

"Well," Butterfield says, and then manages to stop himself from saying that he should help drink it. "Thank you. That's nice."

"We wanted you two to have it," Ariana says with terrible brightness.

There's a painful moment of bad quiet. They're waiting to be asked in. Butterfield does so, and the four of them go into the kitchen, where, out of sheer force of politeness and with trembling fingers, he opens the bottle of champagne. Ariana is a shape in the corner of his eye, wearing what she had on—and took off—this morning at the store. Shostakovich apologizes again for their last visit, scratching the back of his head and seeming puzzled that any of it could've taken place. "I think it might've been the dope."

Elizabeth stands at the counter, arms folded, her face a blank still-ness, neither smiling nor frowning. She seems to be observing everyone. Ariana begins chattering about Macbeth's and the fact that she doesn't have to work tonight. Finally, she says, "Why don't we all go out?"

"I've got too much work," Elizabeth says quickly but evenly.

"Maybe you can join us," Ariana says to Will.

He avoids responding to this by pouring the champagne. Three glasses, because Elizabeth hurries to say that she has too much work. This is true, but it's also rather pointed. Her tone is direct and matter-of-fact and not at all hospitable or inviting. She gives Butterfield a look that expresses her displeasure at the fact that he asked them in. A second later, he realizes that he's getting the same kind of look from Ariana, who lifts her glass to her lips and drinks, and then nods at him. "One of life's best pleasures," she says, also directly and matter-of-factly. "That first delicious sip of champagne." Shostakovich seems blissfully unaware of anything, drinking the champagne and talking about Coltrane as if Coltrane were a colleague of his. There are several things Coltrane does that could be better, he feels, and, in his opinion, a lot of the jazz masters have a way of messing with tempo. It's an indulgence, he says, precisely as though he knows what he's talking about. Butterfield swallows the champagne like something medicinal, barely palatable.

Shostakovich picks up the bottle and pours more into his glass. "We can't stay too long," he says.

3.

At the hospital, everyone's gone now from the evening's visiting. Dinner's over. Oliver feels that everything's over. Holly and Fiona came, with the children. A little later, Stanley, too, showed up. And Alison, after her shift, acting nervous around Stanley, and Stanley looking like a man with hopes for the evening. Oliver took his daughter's hand and looked love at her, and confidence in her, and approval, too. This made her smile. While Oliver's head went on saying no, no, no, every minute, and he kept looking yes with his eyes, wanting her to go now and find her way without worry about him. She didn't see it, talking about her day, which was uneventful, thank God, nothing like the terror of the other night, only three little traffic citations today. Small potatoes, and that's the way she likes it. Holly and Fiona tried to get Oliver to eat the asparagus that the hospital served, and he refused, and they had a little murmured argument about the vegetable, Holly saying she always hated it and Fiona saying that Holly always loved it. They came close to a full-blown argument and then seemed to remember themselves, turning to the task of trying to get Oliver to eat. It became something of a game they played: coaxing Oliver. And then they were all listening to Drew's sleepy murmuring of names. It was lighthearted, and Oliver felt that his body was on the mend. He wasn't in much pain, healing nicely now, the doctors said. He concentrated on the fact that good, hard work remained to be done, finishing the division of the house on Temporary Road. Holly murmured to him that Fiona had been on the roof again. And she had lunch with Brother Fire, who had said he was going to come see Oliver. Had he?

Not yet.

Holly shrugged. "He's getting a little dotty, I think. Today at lunch, he didn't remember that we'd ordered. There's something on his mind, do you think? It's hard to realize priests are people, too. But I know this one as a person."

Oliver said slowly that the priest could have come by while he was sleeping. "I do a lot of drifting off, you know."

Now, he lies in his convalescent bed, thinking of convalescence as something like a false front. He's in the hospital. It's serious. This thing, this trouble, has happened to him. But the real trouble is down in his soul. What he wants more than anything else is to get past this night. He's drifting in and out again, wanting so to sleep and not dream.

Rain darkens the window, sheets of it, looking far more severe than it is. It subsides rather quickly, and the window lapses into night. He can't sleep. In the next bed, Drew snores. His wife didn't come to see him tonight—probably because of the ridiculous recital of names. Oliver would love to ask him outright: "Listen Drew, what's the deal? Are these all women you knew intimately?" Through the snoring, here's the mumbling of names again. "Cassie," Drew sputters, then sighs. "Irene. Theresa. Jenny. Oh, Edith."

"Christ," Oliver says finally. "Shut up, will you? Will you just shut the fuck up? Or say one—just one goddamn name twice. Jesus."

"Agnes. Oh, Erin, sweetheart."

Perhaps he sleeps a little. But then he's wide awake and something dark is standing over him. He tries to shout in the fright that comes, but can't, and then the shape moves and he sees that it's the priest, Brother Fire.

"Hello," the priest says. "I was almost too late."

Oliver looks at him, feeling his head shake.

"I mean," Brother Fire hastens to add, "that visiting hours are almost over."

"I was—asleep."

"Holly asked me to come see you. I do not bring religion if you don't wish it." He grins. "Just to say hello, and to tell you I'm happy about your progress. The doctors, Holly tells me, say you're healing nicely."

"Slowly," Oliver says.

After a pause, he goes on. "Father, I haven't been to church in a long time."

"Don't worry," Brother Fire says. "Worry about getting better. Let me worry about that part of things just now."

Oliver watches the priest sit down and fold his gnarled, spotted hands in his lap. His eyes, deep set in their net of wrinkles, look sad, but he smiles and nods, and asks if the food is as bad as Holly says it is.

"Did Holly ask you to—come visit me?" Oliver asks.

"Well, yes."

"You didn't have to."

"Of course I didn't have to. I wanted to. I was here the day you came in. Fiona called me and I came right over."

"Fiona."

The priest nods.

"A—pair of—interesting—ladies," Oliver says.

"Yes," says the priest. And they both take a few minutes stifling the laugh that comes. They do not want to wake Drew.

4.

Alison wonders if Holly and Fiona will come in. They're all waiting in the car until the rain lets up. Stanley's going to come by tonight. She wants to be alone with him, and thinks of asking the ladies to take the children home with them, but then decides against it. That fact would announce all sorts of things about her plans for the night, both to the ladies and to Stanley.

One clap of thunder startles her—no one expects it this late in the fall—and the sound she made causes her to laugh. She feels giddy with anticipation and nervousness, and immediately marks this with a little

sour inward tremor of doubt about it all. Courage is necessary for looking forward to something, she decides, and she makes an attempt to find
that courage in herself—a feeling that, as a young girl, she simply took
for granted.

Holly says, "I used to dive under my bed during thunderstorms."

"That was me," Fiona says. "You used to make fun of me for it because I was older. Don't you remember?"

Another clap of thunder right overhead silences them. Alison tries to
think of something neutral to say. The children are watching her.

"I do remember," Holly says, "how you used to quail and cry."

"Well, I wasn't *that* bad."

"Nothing but quailing and crying. All the time. Quailing and crying."

Silence.

Kalie says, "What's quailing?"

And, smirking gleefully, Holly says, "Whining, sweetie."

Fiona sits with her arms folded tight, staring out at the rain. Alison
sees Kalie look at her and then look away.

"Quailing and crying," Holly murmurs in a singsong.

"We all got it," says Fiona.

When the rain lets up, they cross the wet yard and enter the house,
shaking the water from their hair.

"That first one really scared me," Jonathan says.

"It scared *everyone*," says Fiona.

Alison says, "Rain always makes me sleepy." She wishes she were
alone, just for tonight.

After Jonathan and Kalie are in bed, she makes tea for the two ladies, fearing that Stanley won't come and feeling abruptly glad of them
anyway, whether he does or not. She likes how vivid she feels in their
company. They talk about Oliver coming home soon. And Alison, with
her gratitude, worries aloud that there was something in Oliver's eyes
tonight. It's as though it hasn't registered until this instant.

Holly clears her throat and then recalls aloud the cold mists in the
morning in Scotland, how it could look, at first light, exactly like an
enormous flock of ghost sheep, sheep without legs, drifting across the
high grass.

"I was always cold in Scotland," Fiona says.

"It *is* a different chill there," says Holly. "Goes right to the bone with those cold, cold breezes off the sea. But I wasn't going to say that. I was going to say that appearances aren't always what they seem."

Fiona announces suddenly that she's tired and wants to go home. She gives Holly a look, which Holly doesn't acknowledge. "Holly?" she says.

Holly looks at Alison. "Are you all right now, dear? Do you need anything?"

"I'm fine. Really."

"I'm exhausted," says Fiona.

"Well, I want to stop by and see how Will and Elizabeth are."

"Now," says Fiona.

The two old ladies get up to leave and then can't, because of the rain: the clouds seem to be tumbling down the sky in windblown curtains of it. Stanley arrives, comes running to them from Oliver's truck, holding newspapers over his head. They all stand at the door and watch the storm, another lightning show. The wind sweeps the lines of rain sideways, and the rain can't seem to fall fast enough.

Alison offers more tea, and they accept. Stanley asks for a beer, and then Fiona wonders aloud if there's any wine. There is. A cabernet Alison bought for herself more than a month ago and hasn't opened. Stanley opens it and pours two glasses. Alison looks at the fluid muscles of his forearms, the way they ripple smoothly into his wrists. He has wide wrists, strong wrists, and his hands are big. He offers her a glass and hands the other to Fiona, then picks up his beer and twists it open, and takes a long drink of it. Alison can't believe how completely everything about him sinks down into her. It frightens her a little, and yet she keeps taking the opportunity to watch him move and talk, Stanley, with his brown eyes and sandy hair, his wide, boyish face, his thin lips and white, white teeth.

As they all sit down in the living room, Jonathan walks in from the hall, bleary-eyed, sleepwalking. In the silence that follows, Alison steers him back to his room. He begins to cry. It's an excruciating thing, watching a boy that age cry. Alison, afraid and heartsore—and puzzlingly guilty—gets him to lie down, moving him, really, without quite waking him. But then he awakens on his own and stares at her in the half-dark.

"Mom?" he says.

"It's okay," she tells him. "You were sleepwalking."

"Are they still here?"

"Yes. It's a storm."

He turns in the bed, so his back is to her, and he shudders.

"What is it?" she asks him.

"Nothing."

"Granddad's coming home. Things will get back to normal."

"Can I stay home from school tomorrow?"

"Jonathan."

"I don't want to go anymore."

"You're being silly."

"I don't want to go to Mr. Petit's class anymore."

"I said I'd talk to him for you."

"He keeps picking on me."

"How?"

The boy is silent.

"Jonathan, tell me how."

"I don't know."

"Talk to me," Alison says.

"I don't know. I don't want to go anymore."

"I'll talk to him."

The boy turns suddenly and seems almost alarmed. "No," he says.

"Well, what then? You can't stop going to school."

Again, he turns away.

"Tell me how he's picking on you, Jonathan."

"He's just not friendly like he was. He treats me like I'm—like I'm not there."

"Well, maybe he's got something on his mind. People—teachers have their own lives. They don't just come into being when you get to school."

The boy says nothing, lying there in the bed with his back to her, the blanket pulled high over his shoulder.

"Jonathan?" she says.

"I know. I'm quite aware of that fact."

"Oh, for God's sake, will you just talk to me as yourself and leave the high rhetoric behind?"

"I'm sorry," he says. "I didn't know I was doing it."

"It's impressive, Son—it's even charming. But not now."

"I said I didn't know I was doing it."

"All right."

He takes a deep breath. Then: "I'll go to school. Forget it."

She puts her hand on his shoulder and pats it softly, twice. "I realize you want to handle this yourself, Son. But you can't take care of it by staying away from school."

His voice is thin with annoyance now. "I said forget it. I'll go."

She waits, her hand still on his shoulder, still patting him. For a few seconds, it's like all those times when she sat with him and soothed him to sleep.

"I wish Granddad was home."

This stings a little. She rises. "Well, he's *coming* home. And you're going to school, like a strong young man. Right?"

"Okay," he says in the tone of someone who has been badgered into it.

"I'm just telling you what you already know," Alison says.

Silence.

"Good night, Son."

When he doesn't answer, she reaches for his shoulder and turns him toward her. His eyes are shut. He looks like Teddy, mouth in a stubborn, narrow line, that crease in his brow, that expression of renunciation and refusal. She makes herself lean down to kiss his cheek. "Poor boy," she says. Then she leaves the room, weighted down, as always, with worry.

5.

Brother Fire decides after the hospital, to go home for a time. There are several visits to make, but he determines that they can wait a day. He's tired. Poor Oliver Ward had to work to entertain him, and the priest's

help-call ended up being an indulgence. He likes Ward, likes his practical goodness of heart, and he understands that a part of the younger
man's attention to him was born of the simple wish not to have him feel
ill at ease: the sick man reassuring the healthy one. Brother Fire feels
put to shame, and he accepts the feeling as a form of justice.

It's still spitting rain, but, far off, there are openings in the clouds.
He is weary of not sleeping, and of being in this strange, gloomy state
of mind. He drives to the rectory and calls Mr. Petit's number. Too early,
perhaps—he could well be out having dinner. So, he busies himself with
the room and daily prayers, kneeling on the hard wooden floor to say a
Rosary and discovering himself unable to concentrate on the words, on
the fact of it as prayer. It's just words, sounds. He keeps trying. Words,
words, words.

Finally, he calls a physician's referral service and gets the number
of a psychologist with whom he and Holly briefly worked last year.
He writes the number down, then gets in his bed, lies with his hands
crossed over his chest, and drifts off to sleep for a time.

Later, he's up and moving stealthily through the house. Father Mc-
Fadden and Sean are probably still in the mountains, but he's taking no
chances. There's another poem on the kitchen table, awaiting him. He
missed it, coming home earlier. He picks it up out of a sense of obliga-
tion and also out of desire to be ready should the younger priest quiz
him about it.

> *The Lord is in the moon*
> *And the trains when they moan,*
> *In the cabs, too, and the loon*
> *And the grass and the tune*
> *You hear in the rains when they swoon*
> *And drop like coins upon the stone.*
> *The Lord is in so many things*
> *The diamonds on the lady's rings*
> *The robes they put on the royal kings*
> *Just all there is in the world of things*
> *The Lord indeed himself is in*
> *Except where there is evil and sin.*

He puts the paper down in its place and thinks about having to read this kind of thing every day for the next three or four years. He will have to say something. There isn't any use putting it off. Perhaps he can feign a dislike of poetry itself—so many people in America do dislike it. That's true.

Outside, he hurries to the car, not wanting to be caught by the return of the curate, but also mindful of the bad storm still roiling all around the valley and over the mountains. He drives to Mr. Petit's place of residence—a small bungalow flanked by tall trees and surrounded by shrubs that have grown far past their once-clipped shapes. The house looks as though it is sinking back into the foliage, branches hovering over the walkway—you have to part them to approach the door. He has said he might stop by this early evening, and so he believes he's expected. Yet he hesitates. It's very quiet. Nothing stirring. It's full dark now.

He knocks on the door and waits. Nothing. He knocks louder and waits again. He thinks he hears something on the other side, and he puts his ear against the wood, listening. Abruptly, the door opens, and Mr. Petit is standing there in an undershirt and slacks, without shoes or socks, holding a drink. "Oh," he says. "It's you. Come in." He walks away from the door.

The priest follows him. The room is surprisingly spacious for the appearance of the house from the street; it's full of clutter: books, papers, clothes, CDs, old newspapers. Petit shoves some of these off the low-slung sofa and flops down. The upholstery is of that cracked-leather kind that protests every movement upon its surface. "I usually stay pretty close to the bedroom these days," he says, indicating a doorway in the left wall.

Brother Fire leans slightly, out of reflex, to look in there. It seems from here to be much better kept than this room, though the bed is rumpled, unmade. "Were you sleeping?"

"No."

There's a flash of lightning and a bad clap of thunder. Both men jump.

"Thunderstorm, this late. Damn," Petit says. "Any talk from church people about the end times, Father? We *are* coming up on the millennium. Think of it. Could this be the last Thanksgiving?"

"I think it's probably better to worry about one's own individual end-of-the-world, don't you?"

"Been doing that, too, yeah—thinking about that, too."

"That way, one is, how do I put it, covered." He smiles at the other man, and experiences a sudden stir of concern, believing that he has said the wrong thing, misunderstood him altogether. "This isn't the end of everything," he goes on, feeling thick-headed and inadequate.

Petit indicates the chair to his left, also leather. "Sit down, why don't you?"

Brother Fire does so. Now, they are face-to-face in the sound of the rain and wind at the windows.

"I was going to straighten up," Mr. Petit says. "On the chance that you might show."

Brother Fire stirs and looks around the room, at the pictures on the walls—prints of Sargent, Vermeer, Homer, and other beautifully representational painters.

"You want something to drink?"

"What are you having?"

"Vermouth on the rocks."

"I'd like that."

Petit has some trouble rising. Evidently, he's already had several. He moves unsteadily to the sideboard, retrieves a glass, reaches into an ice bucket, the contents of which slosh with the melting that has taken place, brings out several half-sized ice cubes, and drops them in the glass. This is all done with a stagy carefulness, as if it were all very fragile. He pours the vermouth and brings it precariously over. Brother Fire takes it from him and raises it slightly, as if to offer a toast. The other man gives forth a little smirking laugh and clinks the glasses. He's still standing, and he drains his own glass, putting his head far back. He takes a couple of the nearly melted ice cubes in his mouth and chews them, moving back to the sideboard. "I had a problem student today, big as a horse. Green hair. I suspended him. Sent him home. I was less than professional in that there really wasn't a reason except that he's lazy and rather menacing to the others, including his teacher—Mrs. Butterfield."

Brother Fire sips his drink, nodding slightly, though the other man has his back turned and is pouring himself more of the vermouth.

"Sweet woman, Mrs. Butterfield. Nice girl. Lovely. In the old days I might've pined for her a little, you know? In the old days. Before I went pedophilic."

"That's no way to talk."

"I tell you the kid's grandfather had a stroke? A part of me was thrilled. Saw it as an opportunity. Think of it. I could step in and console him. Christ."

Brother Fire watches him sip the drink, and is silent.

"I'm sorry for that. Didn't mean to—*God*—take the Lord's name."

There follows a rather long pause. Mr. Petit crosses the room, then seems to hesitate, looking into the glass. He goes back and pours some more, and puts another ice cube in it.

"I—I thought we might say a Rosary together," the priest says.

"No, Father. That's not you and me."

Both men are silent. Petit rattles the ice in his glass, and then has another sip from his drink, sitting down and leaning back. The thickness of his lower legs makes him look weighted down, heavier than he is, probably. There's a space between his pants cuff and the top of his dark socks, which shows hairless, milk-white flesh; it diminishes him in some undiscoverable way. The priest looks to the other side of the room and has the sense that he's taking his eyes from a disgraceful revelation. The other man's dignity seems oddly to have been stripped away in that moment. Petit mutters something indistinguishable.

"Excuse me?" Brother Fire says to him.

"You probably came over to see if I've given in to my temptation."

He feels caught out. It takes him a moment to realize that the other man is merely talking from what he's ingested of the alcohol. He says nothing.

"Well, I'm waiting to see that myself, Father. I'm keeping the poor kid at a distance he doesn't understand."

Again, they're silent.

Presently, Mr. Petit says, "This must be strange for you."

"Not strange," says the priest. "You aren't alone, you know."

"You think so?"

"I *believe* so."

"An important distinction."

They drink quietly for a space, neither of them looking at the other.

"When I was first teaching," Petit says, "I knew a guy, maybe ten years older than I was. Nice guy—easygoing but a little sad all the time. You could just see it in him, see it in his eyes. Something brittle and hurt, a glassy something in the irises, like he'd already had a drink or two and it would be seven-thirty in the morning and you'd be drinking coffee with him and he'd be perfectly all right and cheerful, like anybody, you know, but there was something in his eyes. Something— Well, I said. Sad. Forlorn. You couldn't put your finger on it. And one day I was talking to him and in the back of my mind was the thought that I'd say something to him to get him to talk about himself a little. Because the thing I noticed was that he didn't ever really talk about himself. He was one of those types who seems so interested in everyone else, nobody ever notices that he's not really there as himself, not really telling anything. It's all about whoever he's with. And so this one day we were drinking whiskey and it was in a bar and the doors were closed, we had been with some others of us, everything just like you'd expect, you see, a bunch of coworkers out for a few drinks after a school function none of us wanted to go to, and because I'd had a couple of drinks I was about to ask him some question—something, anything to get him talking about himself. But before I could get it out, he swallows a big draft of whiskey, asks for another, and then starts telling me about his past—something so specific and so amazing that it explained everything about his sadness and his reticence, without his knowing it had done that. I don't know why he chose that time to talk, it was probably the booze—although we'd had drinks before and it never happened—I don't know why that time, or why, particularly, he chose me to talk to, but he did. He told me that when he was only six years old a friend of his father's came to visit, a nice man that he knew, too, of course, and always felt big and strong and happy to be in his company, this man, and so he wanted to impress him with how excited he was to see him.

So the man walks into the front door of the house, and this friend of mine, six years old, coming down the stairs in the front hall, completely happy and excited, and as I said wanting to impress him, comes halfway down the stairway and takes a leap into the man's arms. Well, the man wasn't ready for it, see. And so he falls back, tumbles backward from the force of it, and hits his head on the baseboard—and dies. You—you see what I'm telling you? This man I knew, when he was a perfectly innocent child, in pure enthusiasm and love, wishing only to show his excitement and his happiness, kills his father's best friend. The friend dies without a word. Silence. The kid is on his chest, stunned by the fall and the sudden stop, and under him, perfectly still and silent forever, is this friend. Of course the boy's father took him away from the scene and there was a lot of commotion, a lot of people arriving fast to occupy him. He remembered a—a crowd, a whole swirl of faces, and confusion and his father's friend lying really still, awfully still, in the front hallway of that house, and they all—all the adults, the family, the aunts and uncles and grandparents and older cousins—well, they all kept at him and at him, trying to distract him and then trying, over the days and weeks, to keep him from understanding what he did, and of course he did understand it, without saying it out to anyone, and he had carried it all those years, and it never, ever went away very far, was always just under the stream of whatever he had for thoughts, ever. The—the horrific silence that opened out, God it must've been just dreadful, after this—you see?—this harmless-seeming little stupid tumble in the foyer of that house."

"That's such a terrible story," says the priest.

"Yeah. Truly. But it's the world, right? It's fate. It's a freak accident. But, see, the guy—this guy, my friend—was never the same. Lost his boy's exuberance forever. And the truth is, he was never the same with me after he told me about it. Matter of fact he got mean. I couldn't do anything right. Nobody could. Nobody would have anything to do with him, before it was all over, you know? And when he took a job in Japan and went on his way everybody was real happy about it. Last I heard he was living on the street in New York. Somebody or other saw him lying in a doorway with bare blackened feet, and no shirt. Curled up, asleep.

Guy was a friend of mine, or as much of a friend as he could be, given who he was, and then this thing about him, this—this knowledge about him got between us, got between him and everybody else."

"There could've been other things, too," Brother Fire says. "Other causes."

Petit considers this, sipping his drink. "That was the cause."

"You never really know with people, though, do you?"

He looks at the old priest. "Hell, *you* do."

Brother Fire is silent.

"Right? You hear everybody's little dirty secrets, don't you?"

"It's not as clear as all that. Most of the time I don't know who it is I'm talking to."

"Isn't this odd?" Petit says suddenly.

The priest is at sea.

Petit sighs, and there's a kind of shudder at the end of it, as if he is fighting off the memory of what he has been telling. "Anyway. I figure that's me. Not long from now, I'll go over some line and it'll all come apart. Everything. Nobody'll ever hear of me again."

"Despair is the sin you must try very hard not to allow yourself."

"'Not, I'll not, Carrion Comfort, Despair, not feast on thee.'"

"I know the poem," says the priest. "Gerard Manley Hopkins. That's a willful beauty, that poem. A fight, a struggle. And do you know that when he died, his last words were 'I'm so happy, so happy.' He won, you see. He won through it all."

"Yeah. Well." Petit drinks, then nods several times, as if recounting some list to himself. His lips move. A man nodding in prayer? "Why'd you come here, anyway, Father?"

"You asked me to come here."

"Oh." He swallows still more of the vermouth, then sits back against the soft cushions of the couch, cradling the glass on his stomach, staring at the ceiling. "I'll tell you, it's not fair. It's too hard. Committing sins in your head. I mean, what if you can't stop thinking about something, Father? What if it keeps turning in your mind like a little merry-go-round. Round and round and round. Like it did for my poor helpless accidental manslaughtering once-friend?"

"There are medicines for what you're describing," says the priest. "That's an obsessive-compulsive thing and there are medicines that can help you, now. People that can help you."

Petit rattles the ice in his glass. "Prayer sure isn't helping me."

"You came to me, didn't you?"

His voice, answering, is chillingly devoid of feeling. "Oh, yeah. That. I did that."

"Let's say a Rosary together," Brother Fire says.

"I'm sorry," says Petit. "I'm facing the fact that I have to quit my job."

"Come on. We'll pray."

"I don't believe it anymore. Any of it."

Brother Fire puts his drink down on the side table next to his chair. "Son?"

"Do you really believe it?" Petit asks.

"Yes."

"No doubts?"

"Of course I have doubts."

"Do they turn in a little circle in your mind?"

"Yes, as a matter of fact, they do. They do that indeed."

"Do you take medicine?"

"I pray."

"You do."

"Yes. Of course."

"That's your answer."

"You asked what I did for my doubts."

"Prayer."

"Yes."

"Hasn't helped, has it." Mr. Petit sighs, and then laughs. And then they're both laughing. It goes on. The priest senses that this is an admission of a kind that can do no good, yet he can't keep from this silly chuckling now. It's appalling. And it isn't the drink, either; he's had very little of the vermouth. He looks across at the other man in his tremendous unhappiness, this man who is laughing hard, mouth open in an aghast expression, the laugh going up to the ceiling, and he decides to try suggesting that they take a walk—simply get out into the air. But, of course, it's raining buckets outside now, and they can do no such thing.

When, at last, the jag has ceased, they face each other. "A laugh is the saving thing," Brother Fire tells him, not quite believing his own words for having seen that look of open-mouthed horror on the other's face. "Don't you think?"

"Oh, try not to be pompous now," Petit says.

The older man feels justly chastened, but he had only been trying to point something out—trying to help, give solace, lessen the ache.

Mr. Petit raises his glass. "Here's to the laughs."

Now they are strangely awkward with each other. A few minutes of stumbling talk leaves them finally without much else to do or remark on. Brother Fire writes down the number of the psychologist. Mr. Petit thanks him, folds the paper, and puts it in a compartment of his wallet. They sit for a while longer and try talking about the late thunderstorm and the nightfall, always a bad time for Mr. Petit, all his life.

"I used to take a drink at that time, just to level the uproar."

"What was the uproar?" asks the priest.

"Hell," Petit says. And then seems to think about the word that he has just said. "Yeah. *Exactly* that. *Hell.* Me."

"But you never despaired, really."

He shrugs. "That comes and goes, don't you think?"

"I don't think true despair does that. True despair sits down on the soul, perches there like a fat dark bird and won't unperch."

"That's an ugly image."

For some reason, they laugh again. But it's past the ease that had come to them earlier; it's almost sorrowful now, and neither man can look at the other.

"Well, I've had some—uh, fly-bys," Mr. Petit says. "Yes, fly-bys, let us say then, from the—the bird."

"I know the feeling."

"That's comforting. Silly as it sounds."

Brother Fire stands. "Call that number for me?"

"I'll do that."

At the door, they wait a little for the rain to let up, and then Mr. Petit walks him out to his car. They shake hands. Brother Fire pats his shoulder and gets in.

"Thank you," Mr. Petit says.

6.

The disaster is upon him, Butterfield thinks. Shostakovich and wife are pouring the last of the champagne, talking about a fine Spanish red they have at their house. "I've got a headache," Elizabeth says.

"You get a lot of them, huh," says Ariana.

"I've got one *now*."

Ariana sidles past Butterfield, holding her champagne glass lightly, with two fingers, the little finger raised, the wrist bent just enough to suggest a kind of coquetry, and says to him, "How come you're not in a party mood tonight, sugar."

"Ariana, stop acting like a whore," Shostakovich says, but with a kind of merry smile, a proud smirk, really.

"I wanna dance, Daddy. Dance with me," she says.

So, they mince together and begin dancing in the middle of the living-room floor. Ariana's wildly enthusiastic, gliding against her husband, frenetic, playing to him, thrusting her pelvis at him. "What the fuck," he says. "I'm tipsy, darling."

Ariana takes him by the shoulders. Butterfield sees Elizabeth staring at him, and so he asks her if she wants to dance.

"Not just now," Elizabeth says evenly. "No."

Ariana's behaving exactly like someone trying to make a third party jealous. And Butterfield understands that this isn't lost on Elizabeth, who seems to be putting everything together in her mind, looking at him, brooding. Ariana throws a kiss at him, leaning back in Shostakovich's arms, saying, "Why don't you dance, Mr. Man. You've got somebody to dance with." Then she swings, letting her hair fly, and pulls her husband into another bending kiss. Because there's no music, you can hear the straining sounds they make in the room. It's far worse than last night; it's psychotic and scary. The Butterfields are, for the moment, fixed in a kind of flabbergasted, fright-stilled wonderment at it.

"Jesus Christ, honey," Shostakovich says. "At least put some music on."

Elizabeth actually does so, with a robotic motion, her face a complete blank, as devoid of nuance as a flat white sky.

Butterfield can't take another second of this. He steps out the front door for some clear air. He's having trouble breathing. There's a little wood-smoke-smelling breeze in the chill. The rain has at last moved off, and one side of the sky is gorgeous, washed, moon-bright, starry. He experiences no pleasure in it at all.

Elizabeth comes out and stands before him.

"They'll miss us," he says.

And she slaps him, hard, across the face. "I'm leaving you," she says. "And you know why, too." Then she just waits for him to respond, eyes narrow and tearful, hands on her hips, mouth drawn down at a perilously unattractive angle. It's a face full of hurt and anger, and he can't look at it. And, what's worse, he now finds—in the instant of trying to think of how to save anything of what his life has been with this lovely young woman—that he can't answer her at all, has nothing whatever to say. The power of this realization makes him begin to cry. She says, "Oh, Jesus Christ," and goes back into the house, without closing the door. He stands there crying, while the music plays behind him. There's a little span of time, how much he can't guess, that goes by, while the pair in the living room keep dancing, and he remains unable to do anything but sob and sniffle. Elizabeth has gone wherever she is in the house.

Shostakovich and wife continue to dance insanely, in their obliviousness, in the living room.

In the next moment—a further process of disaster—Fiona's little red car pulls up. The Crazies get out. Fiona leads the way, marching across the lawn, followed close behind by his mother. No doubt, they're arguing about something and want him to settle it. This would be comical if it were not so depleting. If he were not feeling the weight of his whole life collapsing around him. He tries to wipe his eyes with the sleeve of his shirt, and then he sniffles, pulling his arm across the lower part of his face, like a child at the end of a tantrum; he sobs like that and is astonished by the sound, a grown man blubbering on his porch, to music.

"What happened?" Fiona says. "Is Elizabeth all right?" She looks past him at the living room. "Who the hell are they?"

"Tell me the news, Fiona."

"There's no news. We haven't seen you for a couple of days." She moves to the door and then opens it and steps partway into the house. "What the hell?" she says.

"Go home," Butterfield says. "Both of you. Please."

"What's happened?" Fiona wants to know. "What the hell are they doing? What the hell are *you* doing? Are you—Have you been crying? Where's Elizabeth?"

"Bed," says Butterfield. It's all he can muster. "Please."

"You want these people to leave? Because *I'll* get them to leave."

"Just—please—go now. I'll handle it. Please."

"Will," his mother says. "For God's sake."

The music stops—is cut off suddenly. Elizabeth has pulled the plug on the stereo. "Go home," she says. "Both of you. Get the hell out."

There are mutterings, the specifics of which no one quite hears— harrumphs and rumblings of insult and umbrage. The two neighbors file out the door and on across the lawn, unsteadily, arm-in-arm. "Good night," Ariana calls. "Everybody sleep well, because I will."

It's like a challenge. Fiona and Holly are quiet, standing in the light of the stoop, staring after them. Butterfield has gained control of himself enough to say, "You all, too. Go home. Please."

Inside, Elizabeth is moving through the rooms, putting things in place with an emphasis, sniffling. Then she comes to the foyer and, without looking at them standing in the open doorway, she goes up-stairs.

"I was tired and wanted to go straight home," Fiona says.

"What is this, Will?" Holly asks.

"Please, Mom. Please go home now. I have to talk to her."

Fiona leans in and takes hold of his arm. "If you need us, call."

"Come on," Holly says. "They want to be alone."

"I was just saying we're here if they need us. You always do that. You always make it seem like I'm being inconsiderate."

"All the time," says Holly. "Every single minute of every day. That's me."

They go on to the car, muttering back and forth at each other. They get in, and Fiona drives them away.

Butterfield walks into the house and takes the phone off the hook. He hears his wife up there, moving around, closets opening, dresser drawers. She's packing. An icy wind blows through the heart of him; everything's crashing. He closes the front door and leans his forehead against it, listening. A silence now. His own breathing, the little hectic beep of the telephone off the hook. His mind presents him with an image of Elizabeth's face, only a year ago, at Wrightsville Beach, where they had gone for a brief vacation. She's closing the door of the bathroom, laughing at something he's said, her dark hair framing her lovely face, an easy, happy pass, her happiness in him. It rakes through him. "Jesus Christ," he says. Then he gathers himself and climbs the stairs.

7.

She stops for a moment over her open suitcase, sits on the bed, and begins to cry. But when she hears him on the stairs, she rises, rubs the tears away, and goes back to work. Out of the corner of her eye, she sees him come to the entrance of the room.

"Fiona and Holly," he begins. "Arguing."

She doesn't answer, moving to the closet and bringing out a row of dresses, work clothes. She folds them and puts them in, presses them down. Work. The idea of going there again weighs her down like a thousand years. She feels as if she can't even lift her hands to her face now.

"Please," he says. "Baby—don't. Don't go."

And the tears come again. She sits down and lets them flow, sobbing, resisting his embrace, throwing it off. He stands before her while she covers her face in her hands and wails. It's as if all the sorrows of her life are playing out of her now, unfolding from the deepest well inside: the lonely years in her parents' fortress of a house, the bad year of the first marriage, the deaths of her parents and the troublesome time attempting to adjust to Will's children, who missed their mother and wanted nothing to do with another one, younger, a usurper in their eyes. Everything, up to and including the complications of this summer with the Crazies, and her present unhappiness, which is, in its terrible way, harder now than everything else: her husband's unfaithfulness. It all keeps breaking over her, like an inner tidal wave, and he's standing right here.

"I swear—" he begins.

But she can't listen to it. She can't bring herself to sit still. She rises and goes on with her packing. He says nothing for a time—a minute, ten minutes. She doesn't know. It seems long; she can't be sure. She packs, crying, trying in her pain to think clearly about where she might go, whom she might stay with.

He asks the question: "Where'll you go, baby?"

And she lets herself down on the bed again, sobbing. "Somewhere—" she manages to sputter. "Away—from—you."

"No," he says. "Please. I'm sorry. I don't know what happened." He sits next to her and puts his arms around her. This time, she doesn't shake him off but puts her head down on his shoulder and sobs. A sound comes from her—it doesn't seem human—that he hasn't ever heard before, anywhere in his life.

"It wasn't—it didn't mean anything," he says.

"Please," she says. "Please. Please please please shut up."

So he does, holding tight, while she continues to cry. At length, she gains control of herself and moves from him. The suitcase is open on the bed, with its cargo stuffed in it. There's still so much to pack. She lifts one of the dresses and then puts it back.

"Don't go," he says.

She looks at him, and it comes to her in a rush, what she'll say. "Oh, I'm not going. *You* are."

He says nothing for a moment.

"*You* go. Get a room somewhere. I don't want to live with you anymore."

"Don't say that, baby. Please." He stands. "I'll do anything. Please. Anything you say."

"I know you will," she tells him. "And I just said it. I want you out of here."

Now he's crying again, following her around the room while she puts her clothes back. In her determination—and her rage—she's found a sort of hurting, cold calm.

"Baby, one indiscretion. One failure. Please. I'll make up for it. I will. It'll never happen again. Please."

She can hear the livid, composed, steely evenness of her own voice. "She lives next door. *Next door.* No. This is over. We're over. Please leave me alone now."

"Tell me you'll think about it, Elizabeth," he sobs. "I've been a good husband, haven't I, a little?"

"I don't want to talk about it now. Please," she says. She's almost thrilled by her own determination.

They end up lying quite still in their bed, far apart and sleepless. Restless, silent hours in the dark, in the faint glow of light from the next-door house. Sometime after midnight, a pulsing of bright emergency lights commences on the ghostly shapes of the trees in the yard. Will and Elizabeth rise, separately, without speaking, and go to different windows to look out. An ambulance has arrived, sirenless, parked half on the lawn; the quiet gives an ominous force to the spilled light. Two men go into the house with a stretcher, and, for a while, there's only the sinister pulse on the trees and street. The Butterfields watch in silence. Finally, the men emerge, with Ariana on the stretcher. Shostakovich walks beside them, holding his wife's hand. The men put the stretcher in, Shostakovich climbs in after them, and, in a little while, the ambulance pulls away. It looks as if the front door of the house has been left open, so, without saying anything to Elizabeth, whose silence seems only to express her wakefulness, he goes downstairs and out into the chilly night to look.

No, it's just the lights of the living room. The house is closed and locked. He waits a moment. His nerves are unraveling. The whole night is a dome of fright. The few leaves left in the trees make a susurration like the whispering of gathered witnesses. The sky has that rinsed look of a sky after storms; leaves litter the street and the sidewalk. The night sighs around him in the cold sparkle of stars beyond the roof, out of the glaze of light coming from the house. He has been a man who could make himself laugh riding along in a car, remembering. He has been a man who laughed in his sleep, and Elizabeth would wake him and ask him what he was dreaming, and he could never remember, except that it was funny, entirely and sweetly funny.

Back in his own house, he makes his way upstairs and finds her sitting on their bed. He walks over and very gingerly puts his arms around her and, for an instant, she relaxes into them. But then she shakes free with a small sound, almost of alarm, except that there's something wounded in it, too, a quality of injured rage, a creature caught and helpless in a trap. She moves to the other side of the bed and gets under the blankets, turning her back to him.

He's quiet, looking at the light on the walls of the room. When Shostakovich comes home from wherever they have taken his wife, what will he have to say and what will he want to do? What will he know, if he knows anything at all? Butterfield has an image of him coming to talk about whatever's happened—sees him sitting in the downstairs room, seeking to find commiseration. Perhaps it's something harmless—some household accident. But the way they went out of the house and the way they looked, it's clear that this was no small thing. Butterfield breathes an anxious sigh, lets it out almost without sound.

His wife isn't sleeping and is intolerably still next to him in the bed. Their bed. He can't believe any of this. He wants to say so, wants to find anything to say. He feels it as she stirs very slightly and is still again. A terror opens inside him, so powerful that he's sick, and has to rise and go into the bathroom. He runs water into his hands and lavishes it over his face, avoiding his own reflection in the mirror.

At last, after another hour of trying to drift off, he pads soundlessly downstairs, pours himself a tall whiskey, drinks it neat, and then pours himself another, standing at the kitchen counter; he drinks that one, too, to no effect. Except that it burns so badly all the way down. He takes the bottle and the glass outside. The chill shakes him. It's a moist cold. Sitting on the stoop, he pours still another drink for himself and swallows it, gasping. Then he gets up and starts over to the Temporary Road house. It's a kind of aimlessness, though he realizes there is something of the pull of his mother, too, and how strange, at this time in his life, with these troubles.

Shostakovich is sitting wrapped in a blanket on his own front stoop, smoking. Butterfield doesn't see him until he takes a draw on his cigarette: the little coal glows suddenly bright, and Butterfield nearly cries out from startlement.

"Hell of a thing," Shostakovich says.

Butterfield stops out on the sidewalk but says nothing.

"Late," Shostakovich says.

Butterfield recovers something of the resolve to keep up appearances. He walks toward the other, trying to look casual. "Not a good thing to be sitting out in this cold," he says.

"I took a cab back," Shostakovich says. "What're you drinking?"

"Nothing fancy. Old Crow."

"I like Old Crow." Shostakovich draws on the cigarette again.

Butterfield offers him the bottle. He takes a pull from it, then hands it back. Butterfield pours more in the glass, then sets the bottle within reach of the other. "I was going for a walk."

"Yeah," Shostakovich says. "I was sitting here shivering. But I didn't want to go inside. You know how it is."

"Restless," Butterfield gets out.

"You must've seen the ambulance."

"Yes."

"I took a cab back," Shostakovich says, as if for the first time. He's been drinking, too. "Ariana's had another—episode, we call them. Little trouble of hers that comes up. I guess I spoke about it."

Neither of them says anything for a moment. The night is as still as death now. Nothing stirring anywhere.

Shostakovich offers him a cigarette, simply holding the pack out. Butterfield declines.

"This my second pack."

"I didn't know you smoke," Butterfield tells him.

"Started again tonight. This my second pack."

"I'm sorry."

Shostakovich shakes his head and sighs, then seems to gather himself. "She's batshit, you know. Completely cuckoo. Unstable, we politely call it. Has been, too, long as I've known her. I don't know what gets into her."

Butterfield toes the ground and then becomes aware that he's doing it and stops. The other is smoking, sighing the smoke.

"I don't know, this time—don't know how much longer it can keep going on. You see, she—well, she—her illness usually manifests itself in the way of sex." Shostakovich looks at him and then looks away, drawing on the cigarette.

"Geoff," Butterfield says.

But the other man has begun speaking again. "I've lived with it so long. She gets it into her head that she has to have somebody. The other night I thought she might be starting on you, you know."

"No," Butterfield says, scarcely able to draw the breath for any kind of sound.

"Well—wouldn't surprise me. She gets this way. It's tough. It's been tough. She goes after people, and it's usually somebody not inclined to go along, even as beautiful as she is. She *appalls* people, you know? Sometimes I can catch it before it goes too far. But this time it went in a different direction. I mean she started painting the walls in the living room tonight. We were dancing here, or she was dancing. I know we looked crazy as hell. Nutty. I know. But I was just riding it, going along. Hoping it wasn't what I'd begun to think it was." He flicks the cigarette off in the grass, and lights another. "I took a cab home. Lonely in a cab after a thing like that. Wife sedated, sick that way. Absolutely the most exciting woman alive when she's okay. Then she takes it into her mind that she wants to go off all her meds, and pretty soon we're back to square one again."

"I'm sorry," Butterfield says, meaning it as completely as he has ever meant anything. He desires to find a way to express it adequately, and feels banked at the limit of the words. He needs another language altogether. He's sweating, even in this chill.

"She tried to hurt me this time. Threw things. Said things—nuts.

Quite mad. Accused me of sleeping around on her. I've never slept around on her. Never wanted anbody else."

Butterfield remains silent.

The other man smokes, thinking or remembering, staring off. A small sound rises from the back of his throat, but he seems to shake this off. Then: "Hell," he says gruffly, "she'll get back on the medicine and be herself and we'll have another wild old ride for a while. I signed on for this, you know? I knew all about it when I met her. She's crazy as a bedbug and completely unreadable and God knows what she'll do next—but it's a sweet ride when she's herself, and I'm no prize, as you might've noticed."

"I guess none of us is so much of a prize," Butterfield tells him.

"You know the odd thing?" Shostakovich says. "*She* is. She's a hell of a prize. Even painting the goddamn living-room walls."

Again, they're silent for a time. Shostakovich stares at him. "You all right? You're sweating like a fever or something. Look at you."

"It's the whiskey," Butterfield tells him, shuddering. He's sick to his stomach now, too. He waits a moment, wanting to find something reassuring to tell the other man. But there's nothing. There's the chill, and the sweating, and the fact of betrayal. Even so, Shostakovich has already been through the worst of his predicament as he understands it; he seems philosophical now, and Butterfield almost envies him: Shostakovich's wife isn't leaving him, at least not presently. In a way, it's clear that she needs him now more than ever. But then the whole sadness of it all comes through Butterfield in a storm, and he does reach out and pat the other's shoulder.

Shostakovich says, "You don't know anybody who'd like to sublet a house, do you?"

8.

After Holly and Fiona leave, Alison and Stanley sit on the couch in the living room and look through some photographs of the children when they were younger. This is Stanley's idea. He's plainly nervous, drinking another beer. Alison thinks of Oliver and *his* drinking, and it cools her sense of expectation a little. "You say you don't do that very well," she tells him.

He smiles. "I'm already a little dizzy. I won't have any more after this. I'm good for two, really." He takes a small sip, and then puts it away from himself.

Alison brings it back to where it was. "It's fine," she says. "Forgive me."

"Well, you're just thinking of me," he tells her, still smiling. "You don't want me to wind up in jail again."

This brings Oliver to mind for them both in a light that makes for uneasiness. They sit, gazing at the pictures, and Alison turns the pages very slowly, saying only the practical things for a time, where and when photos were taken and who is in them. This goes on for ten minutes or so, and then Jonathan wanders in, sleepwalking again. She leads him back to his bed, and, from the entrance of her own room, sees, to her dismay, that her own bed is occupied: Kalie crawled in and is curled there, asleep. Alison goes in and lifts her, and takes her back to her room.

"Don't wanna sleep here," Kalie says sleepily.

"Mom?" says Jonathan from his room.

She kisses the side of Kalie's face and says, "Good night, honey. You're fine here." Then she lightly pats the girl's back until she's gone to sleep.

"Mom?" Jonathan calls.

She strides in to him with the thought that, at almost fifteen, he ought to be able to be alone a little, ought not to be clinging so tightly to his mother. "What," she says, not quite keeping the annoyance out of her voice.

"I just wanted to say I'm sorry," he says.

She bends down and kisses his forehead. He feels feverish. She puts the back of her hand to the flesh there, and then takes his hands into her own. "Do you feel all right?"

He's gone back to sleep.

"Son?" Again, she kisses his forehead.

"I'm going out for a pass," he says. Then he sits bolt upright in the bed, and a belch issues from him. "I don't feel so good."

"Do you want to go to the bathroom?"

"No," he says, sitting there, holding on.

"Do you feel like you're gonna be sick?"

He shakes his head doubtfully.

"Come on," she says. "The bathroom."

"No." He breathes, then settles again in the bed. "I just had to burp."

"You're all right? You feel a little hot."

"I'm okay. I don't want to go to school tomorrow."

She feels his forehead again. It's still warmer than she'd like. "I'm going to take your temperature." She goes into the hall and opens the medicine cabinet. Stanley is still in the living room, with the book of photographs across his lap. He looks up. "Can I do anything?"

She shrugs at him and holds up the thermometer.

"Let me know," he says. "I'm right here."

Back in Jonathan's room, she puts the thermometer in the boy's mouth and sits waiting for it to beep, while Jonathan keeps his eyes closed and seems to drift. She holds the thermometer in its place. Kalie cries from her room, a little plaint but loud enough, and it continues. She's either had a nightmare or is sick, too. Alison starts to rise, but then Stanley crosses the hall, and she hears him soothing the little girl, hears him humming something soft to her. The thermometer beeps. She takes it out of Jonathan's mouth and looks at it. Ninety-eight-point-nine. So, there's no fever. Three-tenths of a point. Jonathan's asleep again. She gets up from the bed and goes to the door, and closes it quietly. Stanley is sitting on Kalie's bed, still humming softly. He looks up when her shadow comes to the entrance, and seems to question with his eyes.

"No fever," Alison murmurs.

He puts the back of his hand, quite gently, on the child's forehead. Then looks back at Alison and murmurs, "Cool as a cucumber."

She goes into the bathroom and rinses the thermometer, and then stands there, trying not to cry. What a wonderful feeling, having someone in the house again—a kindly someone. She starts back to the entrance of Kalie's room, but he's coming out, pulling the door to a crack, moving with the practiced stealth of a father.

They go back into the living room and are momentarily awkward with each other. She takes up the book of photographs, and they sit side-by-side again. He's being a good sport with it, paging through. There are images of Teddy with Jonathan, and of Alison and Teddy, and of Oliver, too, a family. Alison feels how it might pain Stanley to see her with Teddy, but he gestures to aspects of the photos, hills in distance, colors, shapes, formations of vegetation and stone, shifts of light, pretty sails in a harbor; he points out little details and asks about them, how it was to be in those places, and it occurs to her that, in the early years, she and Teddy did travel quite a bit. There's a photo of her and Teddy in front of Niagara Falls. She's got Jonathan in a little carrier on her chest, and Teddy's got his arm around her, her hand on his chest. Behind them, the wrack and mist of the falls stretches far. "That's not really us in front of the falls," she tells Stanley in a small, embarrassed voice. "They took the picture in front of a green wall. And then put the falls there."

"Mmmm," he says.

She turns the page, but he turns it back.

"I love to look at the falls. I went there once, about five years ago. It's amazing. You've been to the Canadian side."

"Yes."

"Me, too. You know what's strange about it? Here's this astonishing sight, this completely amazing thing, the falls, those fantastic walls of violent water, and all the way up Clifton Hill there's all these gimcrack cheap-assed places, carnival barkers and wax museums and arcades. 'Come see the *amazing* Guinness Book of World Records museum. *Amazing!*' And the thing is, they all make money, too. I mean what an amazingly funny species we are when you think of a thing like that.

How could anybody spend five minutes in one of those arcades with that gigantic sight only a few yards away? And they do. By the thousands, they do."

She turns the page. Here is Teddy, in the hospital after Jonathan was born, holding the baby. She turns that page. Stanley asks about Teddy. What was he like?

"A little boy."

"Oh, Lord."

"Why 'Oh Lord'?" she says.

"People say that about me, I'm afraid."

"Maybe it's true of most men."

"Well, we have to be boys first, anyway, right? And you have to be girls?"

"Yes."

They smile at each other and then go on turning the pages. They come to the many photos of Alison with her father and the children. Now and then, she reaches to point something out. Jonathan in soccer camp, hating it so much that his face took on a perpetual frown, and she had told him it would stick that way, and he went around with a stone-faced mask after that, for days. Stanley swallows the last of his beer and puts the can on the end table.

"Want another one?" Alison asks him.

"No," he says. "Thanks."

She moves the book from his lap and sets it on the coffee table. Then she turns to him, looks into his eyes, and waits a few seconds.

"Alison," he says.

And she moves to him, kisses him slow, deep, arms tight around his neck. His arms enfold her, and they go on. It's a long, lovely, luxuriant kiss. When it ends, he puts his hands on either side of her face. "I was so hoping that would happen."

She takes his hands and rises, and leads him into the bedroom. "The children don't think anything about joining me in the middle of the night."

"I'll go," he says kindly.

"I'll lock the door," she tells him.

"Do you think you should?"

"Yes."

She closes the bedroom door and then pulls her blouse up over her head, removes her bra, and stands there before him. How it charms her that he averts his eyes, looking directly into her own. "I want to take care of you," he tells her.

"Oh, yes," she says.

PART THREE

November

INCLEMENCY

I.

The week before Thanksgiving begins with snow. A rare storm that deposits almost nine inches on the town, making the angles of rooftops into soft, fat, pillow-like hints of themselves, forming little triangular thick wedges in all the windowpanes and burying the parked cars along the street. Everything seems padded, stuffed with white. School is canceled Monday, Tuesday, Wednesday, and Thursday, and Elizabeth keeps to her silence, grading papers, tolerating Butterfield's presence in the house because there's nowhere for him to go at present. She has made a bed out of the sofa in the living room. The Crazies call several times, and it's Butterfield who answers. Things are fine, he says to them, because he hopes things will be fine and because there could be nothing more disastrous than telling them the truth.

"Can we at least talk about it?" he says to Elizabeth.

Nothing. Not even a sign that she has heard him.

"It was a nervous breakdown," he says, for perhaps the fifth time. "She's in the mental ward. It's happened before. Shostakovich has been dealing with it for years."

Silence.

"Elizabeth, I don't know what got into me. She came after me. She wouldn't be denied, Elizabeth."

Still nothing. In fact, it's as if he's not there at all. So he goes out and clears the sidewalk in front of the house, laboring through the cramps that come, the stinging in his lungs, and the alarming pangs in his chest. He shovels the snow off the porch steps. The next-door house seems empty. The snow has encased its lower quadrants.

Holly calls Friday morning to say that Oliver Ward will be released from the hospital Wednesday, in time for the holiday, and she's taken the liberty of inviting him and his daughter and grandchildren to Thanksgiving dinner on Temporary Road. "You don't mind the extra faces at the table, do you? I've asked Brother Fire to join us as well."

"Not at all," Butterfield tells her, minding it very much. He doesn't even want to go. He says, "Did you know what's going on with Gail?"

Silence on the other end.

"She's bringing her new lover. Name of Edie."

"Is that what you and Elizabeth were so upset about?"

Because, for now, it's simpler to lie, he says, "Something like that, yes."

"Well, grow up."

"It's the timing," Butterfield says. "You can see that, can't you?"

His mother gives forth a little, knowing laugh. "Examine your own conscience."

"I think I'll barricade myself inside right here."

"Think anybody'll make it now, with all this snow? They're calling for more of it on Monday."

"Oh, they'll be here."

"Well, the whole thing ought to be fun."

"A laugh riot," Butterfield says.

Later, he walks into the living room, where Elizabeth is sitting on the sofa with a blanket over her knees, grading papers. "I don't know what to do about the holiday," he says.

She turns a page and stares at the words on it.

"How do we get through the holiday?"

She marks something on the page.

"Sweetie? Please."

"Do you want me to tell them?"

"Can't we come back from this, Elizabeth?"

Silence again.

"Honey?"

Nothing.

"Maybe I'll go, then. Find a place in town."

She won't look up.

"Will you be able to explain this to everybody?"

Still, she concentrates on the work before her, or seems to.

He walks upstairs and into their bedroom, and sits on the bed, hands folded in his lap. The wind hits the house, rams at the windows with a force almost solid. He gets up and looks out at the next-door house. Shostakovich is out there, shoveling his walk at last, wearing an open coat and a scarf, looking tired and discouraged.

The day passes. It grows dark, and the wind blows, and Butterfield sits in the living room and watches television news, where they talk about a warming trend—most of the snow will melt over the next day or two. The false cheer of the weatherman going on about the possibility of a white Christmas annoys him, so, he flicks the channel to another station. This one has its regular Y2K watch, with predictions about what sort of chaos might result from the computer glitch and the turn of the century. The idea of the turn of the century, the end of the millennium, seems too absurd for consideration now. And how strange it is to be here, in this room, under this bleak light, while a blandly handsome face on television goes on about the new century.

Elizabeth is upstairs somewhere, and then down in the kitchen. She makes a sandwich for herself and goes back upstairs, leaving the bread and lettuce and tomato on the counter. He desires to believe this is a consideration of him, a sign: she supposes he might want to make a sandwich, too. But it's probably only her low mood, the apathy that has settled over her. He can't break through the silence.

Shostakovich comes to the door a little after eight o'clock. He's bundled up, scarf wrapped across his face. Butterfield asks him in, hoping he'll refuse. He does come in, but only to stand in the foyer and talk a little. Ariana's still under sedation at the hospital. She'll be fine, though, once the medications start working. He's hoping she'll be able to go to New Haven with him to visit a friend, a former doctor of hers. They'll be gone through the holidays if she can go.

"Tough to travel on Thanksgiving," Butterfield says to him through an urge to gag. "The airports are so inhospitable."

"Actually, we'll drive up."

"Oh."

"I hope we can go tomorrow."

Butterfield nods and waits. The other man seems to be looking too deeply at him.

"I wonder if you'd keep a sort of watch on the house?"

He thinks of the fact that he's probably not going to be here. But he says, "Sure."

They shake hands, and Shostakovich walks on through the deep snow of the lawn back to his own house. When Butterfield closes the door and turns, he sees Elizabeth standing at the top of the stairs. A moment passes, in which they simply look at each other. Then she turns and is gone. He hears the bedroom door close quietly.

He starts up the stairs. "People coming in Wednesday, Elizabeth. Family coming in here. I'm not moving out. It's Thanksgiving, Elizabeth." He's outside the bedroom door. He puts his hand flat against it and then raps it once, letting the hand slide down the panel. "Elizabeth? How do you want to play this? People are going to look at us and wonder what the hell, baby. Can we decide something? You want me to leave now?"

Nothing.

"Elizabeth?"

He waits again.

"Honey?"

More silence.

He walks away from the door and down the stairs, into the kitchen, where the food is still out. He puts it all away gingerly, as if trying not to make a sound. Then he moves to the kitchen sink, puts his hands down on it, leans there, head between his shoulders, and begins to cry.

He wants to break everything in the room—make a huge crashing of everything. But, for a long time, he can only stand there weeping, and, when it's over, he lurches toward the sofa, her makeshift bed. He'll sleep here tonight, in the soft fragrance of her body, her nights here. It's agreed without having been spoken. He lies down, leaving the light on, and listens to the silence. When he turns and cradles his own head, the noise surprises him. So quiet. Even the wind outside has stopped. The world has stopped. He turns the light out, and stares into the darkness, waiting for sleep that won't come.

2.

Oliver's dressed and ready to go before the sun comes up. He sits on his bed, with his small bag of personal items: comb, brush, toothbrush and toothpaste, socks and underwear, and the two paperbacks Alison brought him, westerns, though he's tired of westerns. He's full of resolve now: he'll make everything up to Alison and to the children. He'll be better.

The doctor has spoken to him about a surgery that will correct the tic in his neck, and he's deciding against that, because he doesn't deserve it. But then he's aware of the essentially self-pitying nature of the thought, and, so, he begins mulling the idea over—how it might be, to have a few years without the continual denunciation of his shaking head. He's waiting patiently through all this spiraling in his mind. Alison will come get him, though she isn't due until eight-thirty. Another two hours. The corrective surgery will mean another hospital stay—a longer one, too, since it will involve the spine. A part of him doesn't want ever to see the inside of a hospital again.

Drew is sleeping behind him, for once without any sputtering or reciting. He's supposed to be released also today, sometime later in the afternoon. How strange it's been, with this man in the next bed and his quiet wife and his odd litany. Oliver still can't recall a single repeated name, and not one male name. Several times during the past two days, he's found himself glancing over there, stealing looks at Drew, trying to see him as all the named women evidently have seen him—if they are not indeed figments of his imagination, and the one time Oliver said to him, "I wonder who these women are that you're naming all the time," Drew looked at him, visibly mystified, and said, "What the hell're you talking about? I'm a happily married man." Either way, Oliver is unable to see more than the spindly-legged, squarish-faced, heavy-browed, graying man with the bulbous nose and the cloudy blue eyes. Nobody special. Deep creases on either side of a wide mouth, a turkey-wattle neck bristling with a two-day-old beard. An old man. Ordinary, ordinary. Like Oliver, of course.

He now looks over at Drew, who snores slightly, stirs, and then is still. Oliver finds himself thinking about the mystery of what draws one person to another. His Mary was a virgin when he met her, and, as far as he knew, she never loved anyone else. She loved Oliver. Oliver, static in a job that barely kept the wolf away from the door, and she used to describe their lives that way when people asked how she was. "Well," she'd say, "we've so far kept the wolf away from the door." Toward the end, there was so much lassitude in her voice, and she had been such a bright, happy, ebullient girl, with a lovely laugh and a sidelong way of looking at you that expressed trust in your good intentions. There are times when he thinks he'll see her again, imagines her watching over him. But he has seen the terrors of the world, too, and something in his soul bridles at the thought of her disembodied, diaphanous, insubstantial, in a spirit world, trailing from cloud to cloud like a thin veil. She was far too practical and earthy for such a conceit, would've laughed at him for entertaining it, or—as he has sometimes done—depending on it for solace. He carries her around in his heart, a memory, an instance, the dividing line of his life. Yes. There was a before Mary, there was Mary, and, for a long time now, there has only been afterwards. The long, blurring procession of days wishing he could have been stronger, steadier, more dependable. Finally, it seems now to him, sitting here waiting to get out of the hospital, that there are offenses in the world that the world refuses to punish. This depressing thought makes him sigh, and, behind him, Drew says, "What, Mary?"

The name on the other man's lips is enraging. But he's asleep, snoring lightly again. Oliver's careful not to wake him, even feeling the anger and the hurt. It's as if Drew has disrespected Mary. Oliver's Mary.

He rises from the bed and totters a little on his unsteady legs. He has always hated the way dead wives are portrayed in the movies—those dreamy, slow-motion images of soft light and glowing faces uncomplicatedly happy, glorious paradigms of love and acceptance. His memory of Mary is of her sorrows about him, her pinched face gone early to wrinkles. There were laugh lines and it wasn't all pain; yet Oliver remembers too many instances. He wishes it were different, wishes he could go back and find the beginnings of everything, wishes he could fix it, change it. And it wasn't ever really the war, either. He was drunk when he enlisted those years ago. No, Oliver's fault lines are older than the war. He's too honorable a man to use his wounds in Vietnam as an excuse for anything. Sitting back down on the bed, he puts his hands in his lap and thinks of Mary in the first spirited days he knew her. In important ways, Alison is a continual sweet reminder of Mary as Mary was then, except that, lately, Alison has been showing signs of distress, too. Oliver's mood is so black just now, and he bows his head a little, breathing in soft sighs. He sets about clearing his mind, and starts making the attempt to find something good in his immediate surroundings.

The window is coming to light, the sky all clouds, bruised and heavy-looking without quite being storm clouds—the kind of sky that is crowded with folds of gray but never yields up any precipitation. A traveling sky, Oliver thinks—it will move on and rain somewhere else, probably over the sea. There's snow on the windowsill and lining the panes of glass, and a thin coating of hoarfrost has formed along the bottoms of each one, perfect as all the pictures of winter windows. The clouds are visibly moving across the sky.

He thinks of this as of trouble that moves over the world, and something of his dire mood does begin to dissipate somewhat—the clouds *are* moving. The storms *have* passed. Like that, it is possible that trouble, too, may be moving on for a time. There'll be work for the winter. There's that. The rest of the work on the Temporary Road house.

Yes, he thinks. *Temporary. That's me.*

He smiles, mildly proud of himself for making the joke. He thinks of Holly and Fiona. New friends. He'll labor not to be sad just now.

A nurse comes in and is startled to find him sitting there. She emits a small gasp of surprise that wakes Drew, who sits up and looks at the room. "What the hell," Drew says. And Oliver waits for the name. But Drew lies back down and closes his eyes again.

"I didn't expect anyone to be up yet," the nurse whispers. Oliver's not seen her before. "Didn't mean to startle you," he says. And he sees that she's staring. His nerve tic has got her confused. He explains it, and the explanation is as automatic as the tic itself.

"Has the doctor been to speak to you?" she asks.

"Not yet."

"I'm supposed to check your blood pressure and take your pulse."

He holds out his arm, and she wraps the sleeve around it, competent, not even having to concentrate, her mind elsewhere, while he watches. Abruptly, he feels a sense of affection for her, so intent on her life, whatever it is, with whomever it is lived. Something's worrying her, because something is always worrying everyone. He believes anyway that he sees it in her eyes as she proceeds, measuring the diastolic and systolic matter of his living pulse, the intricate and mysterious signals of his heart.

"You're new," he says.

She nods. "Today."

"Hello," he says.

"Hi."

"This your first job?"

She smiles, letting the tightness go out of the sleeve. "This is my fourth hospital."

"You don't look old enough. How old are you?"

She smiles. "Blood pressure's very good."

"I'll live to be a hundred," Oliver says.

Then she seems to relent. "I'm twenty-nine."

He smiles. "I've got socks older than you."

3.

Friday morning. A light is on in the Butterfields' bedroom, made super-fluous now by the brilliant eastern sun at the window. Elizabeth wakes with a throbbing headache and pain around the eyes. The last school day of this week, and the schools are open. It takes her a bad little moment of darkness to remember herself. When she can manage to move at all, she rises and looks back at his side of the bed, which is, of course, empty. Last night, she packed the suitcase again, deciding that, with everyone coming next week, she'll be the one to leave. But she can't bring herself to do it. Now she takes a shower, puts fresh clothes on—it's all the motions of leaving—and changes her mind yet again: she *will* leave. She works to close the suitcase and has to turn around and sit on it, pressing down with both hands. The latch clicks shut just as she realizes that her toothbrush and makeup kit are in there, so she flips the latch, and the lid pops open. It's ridiculous. She puts her hands to her face, sits down on the bed, and begins crying again.

There's no time for this. She has to find something to say to the crowds of adolescents who are ill-tempered about not getting the one more little day off because of the snow, and who will want nothing to do with schoolwork. Everything's so strange now. It's all coming apart, and she can't master herself, can't stop crying. In the bathroom, she tries with trembling fingers to put makeup on. Perhaps Will has gone in the night. The thought occurs to her, and she puts it aside, an aspect of this trouble that will present itself in time—she can't think about anything just now but getting the makeup right, getting herself ready for the day's tasks. She stops a moment and stares at her own face, with its bleary eyes and its small, downturning mouth. Then she washes everything off and wipes the towel hard across her features, as if trying to erase them as well as the makeup. She starts over, slightly calmer now, out of the pure force of anger. But her hands shake, and she has to remove it all still once more. She gets that done, then brushes her teeth—nearly gagging on the paste. It's as if her body waits here, intractable, refusing to cooperate, inert as a doll, yet resistant, too. Obstinately showing the signs of her misery. She stands, weeping, in front of the mirror, while trying yet again to put on her makeup. It's preposterous. The mascara runs with tears as she applies it, though she continues to apply it anyway, stubbornly, angrily, sniffling. When it's at least marginally done, and her eyes are only dark-shadowed and red, she puts everything back into the suitcase and tries again to push it shut. It won't go. She lacks the strength to close it, and so she opens it and throws some things out, hurls them away from herself as if they are the cause of her sorrow. At last, sitting on the suitcase, she's able to latch it shut. And she lugs it downstairs.

Will is sitting at the kitchen table, with his hands folded in front of him, staring at the room, actually looking around it, a man who has found himself in unfamiliar surroundings.

"I have to go to work," she gets out. "I'll find a room for this weekend."

He rises, dazed-seeming, staring at the suitcase. "I'll take you wherever you want," he says.

"I'll take myself. And I'm taking the car."

"How will I get to the store?"

"You'll have to figure that out."

He looks down. "I have no excuse, Elizabeth. I'm sorry. Can we please not do this?"

"Do you want a ride to the store?" she says.

He sits back down. "Can't we please talk?"

"Oh, really—Will. What's there to say? She had a nervous breakdown and you fucked her."

"I don't know what happened," he says. "I'm still trying to figure it out."

"Well, you're gonna have a lot of time to do that."

"I love you, Elizabeth."

"Oh, Christ," she says. "Anything else?"

"I'm sorry?" he says. Then: "No—god. I'm—I'm so sorry, Elizabeth. Please."

"Those are words," she says. "Not much to them, you know?"

"I'll make it up to you."

"Words."

For a moment, he can't speak.

"Words," she says again, as if to herself.

"What—what do I say to Mark and Gail?"

She shakes her head. "Tell them—tell them I left you. They'll understand that."

"Oh, Elizabeth," he says, and his voice breaks.

"If you need something, call your mother."

"Please," he says.

For a few seconds, she simply stares at him, while he stares back. She tries to see the man she has known all these years as her husband. He's not there, it seems, not this hunched, pitiable figure in the kitchen, looking at her with pleading, dishonest eyes. Finally, he drops his gaze, and she goes out to the car with her packed bag, gets in, and heads to the school.

4.

Brother Fire has a dream of the house where he grew up. The rooms are eerily as they were then. The light is as it was on so many overlooked fresh spring mornings that he lived through, and they were common as air, as all the hours of his youth. The *hours*, yes, of being a devout boy, growing up in that fine old house, the last one before his mother died. This is a dream but not a dream; somehow, it is an actual *walking through.* Everything's complete, everything's itself, tangible, palpable as a stone held in his palm—the texture of a painted wall where the brush left its mark; the nicks in the wainscoting; the shadow path of heavy foot traffic in the hall; and the smells, too, of old wood, plaster, dust, washed clothes, floor wax, his father's sweetish tobacco. He stops and stares at the paintings on the walls: Christ in the garden, a flower-dotted field, blue mountains under snowy canyons of cumulus clouds, a shimmering lake mirroring an autumn scene. He looks at the hall table, with its little standing crucifix that his father brought from Italy when he was a boy, and here is his mother's chair by the front window, here are the baseboards with their gleam of white paint, the flat white walls, the shirts hung on the line across the kitchen, in the sun, where they can dry. It is all breathtakingly just as it was, and, while he's aware of this as a dream, he feels also the physical presence of these things, their corporeal reality. He's moving through the rooms, amazed and glad, even as the smallest part of him stands back with an odd admixture of something like alarm and aversion at the fullness of it all. It is as though he has died and—as people used to say when someone died—gone home. At the last second of the dream, he's standing in the doorway of the bedroom where, at fifteen, he first understood that he would not lead a usual life: here's the single, austere frame bed, his, with its sheets rumpled, and here are the books on his nightstand, the missal, *The Histories of the English Kings, Ivanhoe*, Shakespeare, *The Lives of the Saints,* and Aquinas. He's home.

Home.

The years of his traveling away, and away, seem to rush at him like a great gale, and he believes, in his sleep—and is not unhappy about it—that he's dying, that this is the last sight he will see of this earth, this ghost walk through his childhood home.

He sits up in his bed, hears his own steep intake of breath, shuddering, feeling, believing that something bad is unfolding out there in the stillness of the morning.

He thinks of Mr. Petit, and a sense of complicity rides over him, as if his own mind has produced some trouble the poor man must suffer. For a brief few instants, he lies there in the residual power of his dreaming and allows the occult thought to grow under his breastbone—it feels rooted there, like the painful area around a bruise or edema—that this is all a sign, or a summons, involving Mr. Petit.

He rises, dresses, kneels to say his morning office, tries to put the thought from his mind. He trudges carefully along the thinly cleared sidewalk across to the church, to say mass. There are three people in the dimness of the last pews, heads bowed. All women. He knows them, knows the effort they made moving old bones to get here. He can't stop thinking that he has been called by some power of intuition to seek out Mr. Petit this morning. The words of the sacrament go off from him like breath, no thoughts attached, and when there's the slightest movement, the faintest sound—a cough, the shifting of someone's weight on one of the kneelers, a sniffle—behind him, he turns and looks back, thinking it might be Petit. It's a sin to cater to such impulses. He gets through the mass, walks back to the rectory, goes up into his room and kneels to pray. This is not salacious interest anymore, he realizes, but a sense of having intruded upon a man's misery and started something. It's frightening. He says a Rosary, words, repetition; he starts again, head bowed, knees hurting on the hardwood floor.

His curate is moving around downstairs. The old priest lacks the energy to face him, while understanding with a pang that, of course, he must.

Last night, Father McFadden had a new poem. He seemed low and discouraged and rather lost, and it was palpable that the reading—and some form of approval—of the latest poem was required. The poem was full of references to Dante and bad rhymes of the name—Auntie, can't he, ante, vigilante, Monte (Carlo on the next line), and, worst of all, Constanti (nople on the next line)—and, of course, it was woefully far from anything like poetry. Bad, bad. *Bad.*

Deplorable, really. Brother Fire was tempted to say that it's unmannerly, too. Even aggressive. *God help me,* he thought, *I want to say that this man's talent is in not seeing himself as the fool that he is.*

The effort to be kind in such a state of affairs is draining on the nerves and generally exhausting. Brother Fire excused himself after some vague, appreciative remarks about the poem and a few comments about ways of dealing with spiritual dryness—this in response to the other's discouraged mood—and then climbed the stairs to his room, his evening prayers, the relief of solitude, and the balm of his bed.

This morning, with the sense of approaching disaster, he walks down to the kitchen and finds the curate sitting with hands folded over a bowl of Rice Krispies, deep in the saying of grace. He looks up as Brother Fire enters.

"Morning, Father," he says.

"Morning," says Brother Fire.

"We've been invited to Thanksgiving dinner. Holly Grey and her aunt."

"Yes."

"They called last night while you were away. I neglected to remember to tell you last night."

"There's no time pressure, is there?"

"Well, they want a response. I can't go. Won't go."

"All right."

"I'm thinking of leaving the priesthood," Father McFadden says abruptly.

Brother Fire walks over and sits down across from him. "I am, too."

For a long moment, they simply stare at each other.

Then they laugh. It comes loudly, like an involuntary spasm of the chest and throat, and then is quelled, so quickly that both men are embarrassed, and they move around each other in the small room, attending to coffee and the breakfast dishes, skirting the slightest contact, not even grazing shoulders. The phone rings, and Brother Fire picks it up. It's Petit. Brother Fire nearly blurts out his morning's foreboding to him, but Petit's talking. "Better come over to the high school, something's up. Come now." And then the line clicks.

"Hello?" the old priest says. "Hello?" Dial tone. He puts the receiver back and turns to Father McFadden, who avoids eye contact, seems purposely incurious. "I've got to go out this morning."

"I've been trying to write a poem about this thing itself," says Father McFadden. "Not Dante and not Jesus. This. This that I'm feeling. I haven't been able to. I've only got a few lines."

The other tries not to show relief. "Where will you have Thanksgiving dinner?"

"Here's the first verse: 'Sadness is the present feast/For this sad man who's not the least/Glad these days that he's a priest.' I can't get much more than that, Father. There's only this next half stanza—"

"I have to attend to something," Brother Fire interrupts a little brusquely. "I just don't have the time to hear more."

Perhaps he has never fully understood the word *crestfallen* until now.

Father McFadden, after a slight pause, says, "I'm staying here to supervise the sodality's charity dinner." He still makes no eye contact, his thick, dark brows stitching tightly together over his nose.

"That's taken care of," Brother Fire says. "There are plenty of volunteers for it. Why don't you come with me?"

"I volunteered also. You know."

The old priest moves to the doorway. "I do have to take care of this."

"I'm sorry, Father."

"You didn't do anything to be sorry for. We'll talk tonight."

Outside, he walks to his car in the chilly sun, the blinding brightness of the snow, feeling the expanse of air and dazzle around him like something to which he has escaped.

5.

At the high school, Elizabeth goes through the motions, attempting to pull concentration out of the ruin she feels in her heart. In the faculty lounge, before classes begin, she encounters Mr. Petit, who looks terrible, looks, she might say, how she *feels*. She almost does say it. There's a hollow cast to his face, the bones of his cheeks showing, and his complexion is gray, his eyes a shade of yellow. When he rests his hands on the table on either side of his coffee mug, she sees that his knuckles, too, are yellow. She wants to avoid him, but he follows her with his gaze, sitting there waiting for the coffee to cool a little.

"Waste of a day," he mutters.

She says, "Yep." She can barely keep her voice. She pours coffee and moves to the bulletin board, staring at communications concerning plans and activities for the day, the week, the month—the busy life of the school—without really attending to them. She doesn't want to sit down, doesn't want conversation. The room is too brightly lit. It makes the cloudy day outside the windows seem darker. The tables scattered around are polished and new, reflecting the lights above them. Nobody else is here but Petit.

But then James Christ comes in, hurrying, smelling of the outside, his coat collar twisted, his hair mussed by the wind, cheeks burnished by sunlight reflecting from snow. He squints at her and only glances at Petit.

"Got a job interview," he says. "Monday after Thanksgiving."

"Good for you," Elizabeth says.

"What's wrong?"

"Nothing."

He looks at Petit, shrugs, and then puts his shoulder bag down on the table with a thump. His lunch is packed in there, along with a thermos. He brings it all out with an attitude of someone removing fresh purchases, examining each thing as if to be sure it's what he bought, then setting it down next to the bag, like a display. "I'm finally going to get out of here," he says.

Without looking up, Petit says, "I have a headache."

"Sorry."

"You didn't do it."

"I'm so gone from here."

"You didn't give it to me J.C. but you can make it worse."

"Sorry. I don't know how many times I have to say I don't like being called that."

"J.C.?"

Christ sighs but doesn't speak.

"I'll try to remember," says Petit. "Tough to think just now."

Elizabeth sees Calvin Reed at the entrance of the room, and she walks over to send him on his way. Calvin's got his hands in his pockets, and there's a smirk on his face. "You didn't like my sentences about the mountain and the mist," he says in that unbelievable squawk.

"Go on to your homeroom, Calvin."

"You sent me to Petit."

Mr. Petit stands slowly, unsteadily, and moves to the other end of the room with his briefcase. He sets it down and takes a seat there. It's clear he wants to be far from the sound of Calvin's voice. When he sits, it's almost a collapse into the chair. He puts one hand to the side of his face, leaning the elbow on the table. He doesn't look up.

"Hey, Petit," says Calvin. "That you?"

"Go now, Calvin," Elizabeth tells him.

"Just want to talk to him."

James Christ says, "This is not an area for students, Calvin."

"Hey Petit," Calvin says. "You scared?"

Petit doesn't seem to have heard. He opens his briefcase, removes a folder, and opens it. His chin is lifted slightly, so he can look through his bifocals. The gray light from the windows reflects complicatedly with the room light off his glasses. You cannot see his eyes.

Elizabeth says, "I'll count to three, Calvin."

"Okay," the boy says. "Okay. I thought this was a free country."

She stands there and waits for him to move. It comes to her in her anguish that she never disliked a student as much as this one, and that a part of this feeling is indeed tied to his appearance: the trunk-heavy, lumbering solidness of him, that amazingly shrill voice. For an instant, she has a sense of how everything about him is determined by these unfortunate facts, but her own discouragement shifts inside her like a force kicking aside everything but the simplest sensation of aversion to him: she wants him gone, far from her.

He reaches into his loose jeans and brings out a knife, a switchblade. With a click, the blade is exposed, a long, thin shine.

"Uh," James Christ says. "Not allowed. Not—not—not allowed." His tone is nearly that of a boy calling someone on the rules of a game, except that his voice has a tremor in it. He's frozen where he stands.

Elizabeth says, "Calvin, you are in such serious trouble now."

"Take your blouse off," he says.

She doesn't move. In the tail of her eye, she sees Mr. Petit sit back and put his hands to the sides of his head. He looks like someone in the throes of a terrible headache, in the middle of shattering sound. She wants him to do something; she can't see James Christ, who has begun a sort of toneless muttering about this being completely out of line and against the rules.

"Come on," Calvin says. "Do it. Take it off."

"You go ahead and do whatever it is you think you're up to," Elizabeth says evenly, trying to control her fear and her rage. Finally, something snaps in her. She says: "Go ahead. You want to use it. Use it. You think I'm afraid of you? You think you've got trouble? Everybody's got trouble. And I don't care. Go ahead. Fucking *use* it. I don't care."

He's just inside the door now, holding the knife out blade-first, between his thumb and index finger, a pose.

Mr. Petit stands, holding his briefcase. "The world makes no sense anymore at all," he says. "And then it does." He reaches into the case and retrieves something in brown paper, unfolding it slowly, shaking his head. It's a revolver.

"My God in heaven!" James Christ says.

Calvin Reed sees it, too, and drops the knife. "I wouldn'a done nothing," he says.

Mr. Petit moves slowly to Elizabeth's side. She reaches for his arm, but something in his expression makes her pause. His eyes are wide, round, his mouth is agape, lips pulled back, a mask of pure fright, though his motion is steady and determined. "Suppose we go down to my office and have a little chat," he says to the boy. "You and me."

"I put the knife down," Calvin says. "Man, come on. I wouldn'a hurt nobody."

"Well," says Petit. "Turns out I would." He gestures for the boy to precede him out of the room.

The boy looks pleadingly at Elizabeth, who gives back a helpless expression. She can't believe any of this.

"Call the police!" James Christ says. "My God!"

Elizabeth moves to the doorway and watches Calvin's progress, slow, down the hall, followed by Mr. Petit. Several others are there, and they step back, move aside, startled and confused, too.

"Call them, James," Elizabeth says to the quailing man in the room behind her. "Do it. Call them now."

6.

Nothing happening on Alison's watch this morning but a backache and a feeling of having missed a night's sleep. Roy is out sick, and she's stuck with a man she hasn't ever worked with and doesn't know very well. His name is Rick. He looks like a high school kid. Blocky and overmuscled, and there's something about the crispness of his uniform that makes her think of his other habits; probably he keeps all his socks and underwear folded and accounted for. No one should be that perfectly creased and spit-shined. They have spent the first hour learning that they do not much like each other, arguing about the Clinton scandal—his opinions about it all are just too obtuse to leave alone. He's on the side of Congress, he says. Does Alison actually think she knows better than Congress? She decides to change the subject. But on other topics—children, schools, the international situation—he's also annoyingly tight-assed and dim. With effort that increases the wattage of her back misery, she manages, over the hours, to narrow the range of conversation to procedural matters. She can afford to be tolerant, too, because her father is coming home this morning, just as her night shift ends, and she'll go with Stanley to pick him up. She understands that she's at that place of anticipation where even with these irritations provided by the oblivious man beside her in the car—the smell of too much bay rum and the continual clearing of his throat—she feels glad, and the hours can crawl if they will. The end of it all is the welcome-home for Oliver.

The call comes in just past eight o'clock: something at the high school. Trying to put down rising panic, she turns the roof light on and the siren, and heads there, speeding.

"My son goes to that school," she hears herself say.

"Small odds," says Rick.

It takes her a moment to realize that he'd meant that her son is most likely not involved in whatever this is. It hasn't been characterized as an emergency yet.

Of course, she knows that this stiff, overgroomed, unsure half-boy is thinking, along with her, of Moses Lake, Washington; Dunblane, Scotland; Jonesboro, Arkansas; Springfield, Oregon; and, only last April, Littleton, Colorado: Columbine.

Just last month, there was a mandatory seminar and a briefing about high school shootings, characteristics that seemed repeated in the separate horrors—similarities between them.

"God," Alison says, without even quite realizing that she's said it.

Another squad car has preceded them to the parking lot, and the officers are out, standing with some teachers and people from the surrounding neighborhood. Children are coming rapidly but in an orderly way out of the front doors, and she sees Jonathan among them. Jonathan leaves the line of others and walks over to her. She grips his arms and looks into his eyes.

"What is it?" he says to her. "What's happened?"

"We don't know yet. Just go on over there with your class, and stay away from the building." She squeezes his wrist, and then watches him go over to stand with everyone, on the far side of the lot. Buses are lined up. Apparently, they never left from the morning's drop-off. Children are filing back into them, to be taken to another location, for precaution's sake.

The other officers are Eddie and Harvey. Eddie raises one hand as she and Rick approach.

"Hostage situation," he says. "We think. We guess. A teacher."

"A teacher's the hostage?"

"Teacher's holding somebody hostage. No kidding," Eddie says. "Petit. That ring a bell?"

Elizabeth comes from the main entrance of the school. She walks over to Alison. "I don't really know what we've got," she says. There's a darkness around her eyes, a kind of drained detachment, as if she's reporting everything from a distance. She tells Alison about Calvin and the knife, Petit and the revolver. "He wants everyone to go away for a while, or something might happen. That's what he said. Whole thing's—I don't know."

Alison can't speak for a moment.

Rick asks if Elizabeth got a good look at the gun, what kind of gun is it, what caliber? Elizabeth simply stares at him. Alison glances over at Jonathan moving along in the line of children and feels a rush of gratitude while worrying about someone else's boy, Calvin. She turns back to Elizabeth, whose eyes seem opaque, giving off no light at all. "Elizabeth, do you think he'll talk to me?"

"He won't say what he wants. Well—he says he wants quiet."

"Can you show us the way to the room?"

Elizabeth walks with them to the intersection of the two main hallways and starts down the right one.

"Just point, honey," Alison says.

Elizabeth shakes her head and then leans against the wall. She looks like she might fall over.

"Are you all right?" Alison says.

"No. Everything's—it's all in pieces."

"What is? Has he hurt anyone?"

"No."

"It's going to be fine," Alison tells her.

"Down there," says Elizabeth, indicating a door not twenty feet away.

"What's his first name?"

"Roger."

"And who's with him again? Calvin what?"

"Calvin Reed."

Alison and Rick make their way to the closed door. They listen for a moment, standing on either side of it. Behind them, Elizabeth murmurs to some others to go back, keep away.

Alison reaches over and knocks once. She starts to say the first name but then decides it's better to appeal to him as who he is in this place. "Mr. Petit?" she says. "Sir?"

Nothing.

She knocks again. "Can we come in there, please?"

"Go away," comes the voice, low but strong.

She hears a lividness in it—rage, and something else, too. She says, "Is the boy in there with you?"

Silence. Then, a murmur, another voice, impossibly high-pitched.

"Mr. Petit, is Calvin all right?"

Again, there are only the other sounds in the halls, the bustle and motion outside, more sirens. Rick starts to bring his piece out of its holster, and she gestures for him to stop.

He nods importantly, and she can't look at him.

She decides to address the boy directly. "Calvin, can you hear me?"

The voice that comes is the boy's. "This man's crazy. He's gonna hurt me."

"Okay, I want you to open the door, Mr. Petit, and come on out please. Or let Calvin out anyway."

"Go away, for a while." Petit's voice, now rather frighteningly calm. "Tell everyone to leave the building, please."

"Everyone's done that, Mr. Petit."

"You go, too."

"Let Calvin come out and we'll do that. Everyone'll go away for a time. We know you need time to think."

"You don't know anything about me, lady."

"Well, but I do. I know you're the beloved Mr. Petit. And I know you've got to give this up and come out."

"Calvin brought a knife to school," comes the voice. "What do you think of that?"

"Mr. Petit, does he still have the knife?"

"He's got a fucking gun," comes the boy's voice in a shriek.

Now Rick does pull his weapon out of its holster. "Mr. Petit? We're the police. We want you to open the door and slide the gun out on the floor, and then come out with your hands out in front of you."

"Go away, please, and no one important will be harmed."

"Mr. Petit, we can't do that," Alison says.

Again, there's an ominous quiet from the other side of the door.

"Mr. Petit?"

No response.

In the hall now, there's a stirring, and Alison turns, not without a sense of alarm, to find the old priest, Brother Fire, coming toward her with Elizabeth. "Go back," she tells them. "There's a firearm involved here. You can't be here."

"Can I talk to him?" says the priest, looking from Alison to Rick's gun to Alison again. "I'm his confessor."

She stares.

The priest, to her astonishment, shrugs.

Alison knocks on the door again, very lightly. "Mr. Petit, your priest is here."

Petit says, "You're kidding."

Now they are all quiet, looking at each other. Alison says, "Will you talk to him, Mr. Petit?"

"Through the door, yes. Just like in confession."

"Mr. Petit," says the priest. "I'm right here. Like you asked."

"You got here too soon," says Petit.

"Can you come out and we'll talk?"

"Make everybody else go away, Father."

"We'll just move down the hall," Alison says. "That's all we're allowed to do now. Okay, Mr. Petit?"

Silence again.

Alison gestures for Rick to move off, then indicates that the priest should stay to one side of the door. She nods and murmurs, "Go ahead."

7.

Brother Fire steps forward and pauses. "Everyone's gone now," he says.

"I've been thinking about it for weeks, Father. Thought I'd take care of it here."

"Mr. Petit, we are all in the hands of God."

"I don't believe that anymore. And neither do you."

For a horrible little space, he's unable to think of a response. Then: "Of course I do. We do. We both do." He feels a hot stirring in his gullet, an upsurge of stomach acid. He takes a breath and straightens, waiting for it to pass. He can't find words beyond the ones dictated by the present trouble; he senses the need to move past this, to the suffering of the other man.

The voice comes from the other side of the door: "Now we're in a B movie, Father. Aren't we. You're Pat O'Brien, I'm Jimmy Cagney. What the hell's the name of the movie?"

"Why don't you let the boy go?"

Petit's voice comes in a bad Irish brogue: "Oh, it's Father Flannigan, come to save the day."

"Mr. Petit, please."

Nothing.

"Mr. Petit?"

"I was just going to scare the lady," comes the boy's voice. "Somebody help me, please."

Brother Fire reaches to try the knob on the door, and is conscious, as he does so, that it's a ridiculous notion, given the situation, that it might be unlocked. But, to his astonishment, the knob turns, and the door rides open an inch, of its own weight, with a little squeak. Silence on the other side. Amazed, frightened, fearing the worst, expecting an explosion, a shot, he moves it a little more, saying, "It's just me, just me," and then he steps into the room—and takes another breath. Bright light blinds him from the opposite window. But then his eyes adjust, and here is Mr. Petit, seated at his desk, holding the revolver up, pointing it at him. Brother Fire raises his hands, out of reflex, and Petit shakes his head. "I won't hurt you. For God's sake."

The priest brings his hands down. They are shaking. He feels as if he should hide them in his cassock. He looks into the little, perfect, round darkness of the gun barrel.

Perhaps three feet to Petit's left, sitting on the floor with the bottom of his face buried in his upturned knees, is Calvin Reed, looking at the priest out of red eyes, his skin as white as the papers on Petit's desk.

"Okay, Calvin," says Petit in what is clearly the voice of the assistant principal, "you may go now."

The boy doesn't seem to believe it. He looks at Brother Fire and then back at Mr. Petit and starts to rise, then thinks better of it, pausing, eyeing Mr. Petit.

"Go on, son."

He stands now. Brother Fire cannot believe the size of him. Slowly, and then quickly, he moves past the priest and out the door. The two men hear his lumbering stride down the corridor.

Mr. Petit sits back with the revolver in his lap. "Shut the door, Father."

The priest does as he's asked, without thinking. He hears commotion outside, Calvin having walked into the gathering crowd, no doubt. More sirens are sounding now. Out the window, there's just gray sky with washed-looking white clouds scattered amid folds of darker ones, an intricate sky, and the thin snow dust rising in the wind—a peaceful landscape of snowfield and hollow, dips and drifts and ridges, swells; tall, bare, snow-laden branches of trees, all under the threat of more weather.

"I was thinking that Thanksgiving's coming," Mr. Petit says. "I didn't do anything much other than cruelty to be ashamed of. So I'm thankful for that."

"Can we walk out there now?" Brother Fire asks.

"No."

He waits.

Petit sighs, then lifts the gun and looks at it, turns it slightly in his hands as if to study the finish of it. "I've owned this since I was a kid," he says. "Lorraine hated it. I kept it in the attic for a long time."

"Let me have it," Brother Fire says.

The other shakes his head slightly, then smiles. "Really."

"You don't want to do this, Mr. Petit."

"No, but I do, Father. Right now I do. I've got such a blistering headache."

"There's medicine for a headache."

"True."

After a pause, Mr. Petit says, "Remember the joke about the man on the ledge, and the Irish priest trying to talk him down?"

Brother Fire indicates that he doesn't know the story.

"Priest says, 'Think of your mother.' And the guy says, 'I don't have a mother.' So the priest says, 'Think of your father.' The guy says, 'I don't have a father.' So the priest says, 'Your brothers and sisters.' And the guy says, 'No brothers and sisters.' And the priest says, 'Well for the love of God, think about the Blessed Virgin.' The guy says, 'Who's that?' And the priest says, 'Go ahead and jump, man, you're wasting everyone's time.'"

Brother Fire nods, smiling, trying to muster a laugh. "Mr. Petit, what should we do now?"

"You go on, Father. Really. Go on out and tell them all to go home."

"Will you come with me?"

Petit holds the revolver by its trigger guard and lets it dangle on the index finger of his left hand. "Not this time, Father."

"I won't go out there without you."

"You'll have to."

"Come on with me, son. And everything can end up right. Nobody hurt."

Petit smiles. "I think I made an impression on Calvin."

"Yes."

"Go on, Father." He grips the handle of the gun now and turns it on the priest. "Really."

Brother Fire stands there. "You said you'd talk to me."

"We've talked."

"I—I haven't heard your confession."

"Forgive me, Father, I'm intolerably alone."

"Loneliness is not a sin."

"Open the door, please, and go on out."

"You will give me that gun and walk out of here with me."

Petit stares at him for a few seconds and seems to be considering. Then he raises the gun to his middle and pulls the trigger.

8.

A hospital volunteer takes Oliver in a wheelchair down to the hospital lobby. She's been on the ward before, passing out cards and delivering mail, a nice woman whose children are grown and whose husband is retired and spends too much time, she says, in the house. She's not used to having him underfoot. She tells Oliver this on the elevator, joking about it. "I really don't need this wheelchair," Oliver says.

"Hospital policy," she says cheerfully.

"You like broccoli?" he asks her.

"Hate it," she says. "Always have."

"You have just made a friend for life," he tells her. "Pay no attention to the head shaking. I know it looks like I'm saying no. But I'm saying yes. I'm going home today."

"Yes you are."

It's a happy moment. The clouds in his soul are breaking up a little. When the doors open, here are Holly and Fiona, with Kalie. He sees the alarm in the child's face at the sight of the wheelchair, and he lifts her up onto his lap to reassure her. "There, baby," he says. "It's just how they let you go, here. They like to spoil a person—give him a soft ride out the door."

"We'll take it from here," Fiona says to the volunteer. "Bless you."

Holly explains that Stanley's working in the house, and the noise has driven them out. They wanted to join Alison on the joyous occasion, and Kalie especially wanted to be here. Alison isn't in the lobby. Fiona says they'll all celebrate by going out to dinner, perhaps. Oliver thinks he might even have a glass of cold beer. But then he dismisses the idea; there's so much to make up for. He'll make a gift of his abstention without announcing it as a gift—when asked if he would like something to drink, Oliver will say he wants mineral water.

They wait for nearly half an hour before it sinks in that something is amiss. The sirens are sounding, it seems, all over the city. Kalie cringes, holding onto Fiona, and then climbing into Oliver's lap again. He holds her, and they all gaze out at the gray day, waiting, watching the traffic out on the road with its piles of smudged snow in front of the hospital. It looks like a normal winter day, except for the sirens. Oliver thinks of nights when he heard sirens and knew Alison was out there, and it was always *her* siren he heard in the confused din of separate wails—there was always the sense that hers was there and that he could distinguish it. "Someone's getting the help they need," he would say to Jonathan and Kalie, seeing the anxiety in their faces.

Now Holly says, "We could all go in the Subaru. I'm sure she's just working past her shift."

"But what if we go," Oliver says more forcefully than he can help, feeling the rising alarm in the little body on his lap, "and Alison rolls in here five minutes after we leave." He pats Kalie's shoulder and kisses the top of her head. "I want us all to be there to celebrate."

Fiona says, "I can wait here."

After a moment, Oliver says, "Let's all wait."

So, they wait. The life of the hospital goes on around them where they sit, in the central high-ceilinged lobby with its bright blue futons and its low-slung plastic tables. The feeling of the place is of a tremendous human industry and busyness, all the goings to and fro and all the concentration in the faces. Two different men come in with very pregnant wives and sit at the desks in remarkable calm to register them. The wives look around the room, their gaze trailing up into the empty spaces near the ceiling. They, too, seem calm. Oliver remembers bringing Mary to the old wing of the hospital and waiting for a nun to come take her into maternity. The Catholics are gone now, having sold the hospital to the state almost twenty years ago. On the central wall over the admitting desks, you can still see the shadow imprint of the large crucifix that used to be there.

Oliver has a moment of terror at the mutability of everything. It's unreasonable. These little inward seizures keep hauling him back out of the sense of relief and gladness that he wants to feel going home. He straightens himself in the chair and watches Holly unfold part of a newspaper she took from her purse. She opens to the crossword and folds the page. Fiona sits with arms folded, nodding off a little, but then jerking awake and looking at everything and everyone. Kalie clings to Oliver and then falls asleep. Finally, he decides that they should go, mostly because he's sick of the hospital, tired of the bright light and the too-sweet air coming from the vents and the sourceless Muzak that seems to rain down from the high windows and then to come rising up from the very floor with its blindingly vivid blue carpet.

He asks Holly to go get the Subaru, and she obliges, Fiona following her, the two women finding something to argue about as they go, rattling back and forth at each other, crossing in front of the high windows toward the visitors parking lot. Oliver waits in the chair, with Kalie sleeping on his lap. But then she stirs and seems frightened, looking around. She wants down. Oliver lets her stand between his knees. Then he comes to his feet, and pushes the chair away. "Come on, sweetie," he says, and walks with his granddaughter out the double glass-doors to the entrance drive. The air is frosty; there's an icy breeze. He shivers, wraps his arms around himself, then reaches to gather the little girl to his side. She's wide-eyed. She doesn't like any of this. It's in the way she hunches her little shoulders and buries her chin in the cloth of her coat collar. And now Oliver sees, in the next drive over, at the emergency entrance, an ambulance with its roof lights flashing. He thinks he catches a glimpse of Alison, moving from the open back of it into the building. Was that his daughter?

Fiona pulls into the drive in the Subaru, with Holly in the back seat. Oliver helps Kalie get in and then leans in to look at Fiona. "I think I saw her. Can you wait?"

"Sure."

He closes the door and walks to the expanse of snow-covered lawn and across it to the emergency driveway, the entrance there.

Alison is at the admitting desk, filling out a form. He walks into the room and crosses to stand at her side. When she realizes he's there, she gives forth a sound very much of the same timbre and length as Kalie's earlier—it sounds so much like Kalie that Oliver can't help but say, "It's all right, little girl."

"Oh, look at you standing here," she says, kissing the side of his face. She's near crying.

"What's happened?" he asks.

"Poor Mr. Petit, at the school. He shot himself. They just admitted him."

"Alive?" Oliver says.

"He'll make it. But it's a felony, so I have to fill out a few forms."

"Whud he do—he miss?"

"Oh, he didn't miss. A twenty-two slug in his abdomen. They took him to surgery. Brother Fire is with him."

"Lord," Oliver says.

She looks beyond him.

"They're waiting for me," Oliver says. "Holly and Fiona and Kalie. We'll see you at the house?"

"Yes," she says. "Yes. Oh, you look so good, Dad. You do." She embraces him, holds tight. Oliver does, too.

THANKSGIVING NIGHT

I.

Stanley works the first two days of Thanksgiving week simply getting the living room ready for the gathering. All progress on dividing the house is at a happy standstill. Holly's will be done, he says cheerfully. He fashions a long table out of boards, sawhorses, and boxes, and covers the freshly plaster-boarded and partly open-framed walls with sheets of brown paper from a big roll, fastening it all with a stapling gun. The room looks like the inside of a package, until, with Alison, he brings Jonathan and Kalie over in the afternoon to paint and draw. Jonathan makes it a project, and Kalie follows his direction with surprising absorption and enthusiasm.

More snow falls that Tuesday, and the schools close again. They work all day on the room. By Wednesday, the walls are crowded with images of knights on horseback, wild animals—lions, mostly—quite well drawn, and mustangs with big black patches and flaring nostrils. And, of course, there are carefully rendered pilgrims, turkeys, Indians, a few cowboys, one unicorn, and a series of more abstract images (Kalie's) of houses whose front doors go all the way to the roof, whose windows contain round, threatening faces, even though they seem to be smiling.

Alison is kept very busy with work—has to take an extra shift because of the snow and because of poor Mr. Petit's failed attempt at self-slaughter. The bullet missed the abdominal aorta but did puncture the large intestine, causing leakage of fecal matter into his peritoneal cavity. And so there has been worry about septic trouble along with the wound itself, which was the occasion of serious blood loss and shock. Brother Fire has been spending most afternoons sitting by his bedside.

So, someone else is in the hospital.

Alison keeps reminding herself that her father's home in time for the holiday, and there's plenty for which to be thankful. This week, there's been some mildly unpleasant news for her: Teddy called to say that he's getting married again. This is not surprising, though it hurts, in its way. It's a cloud over the hours. Alison recognizes her feeling as bruised ego, and turns her attention to the good things around her, including Stanley. And then there's so much to do, finally, at work—what with the twelve storm-related accidents in the county. On the radio, some movie starlet says, with heavy seriousness, that the world is spinning at tremendous speed through space and it's a wonder the trees aren't lying flat. For Alison, even recognizing the shopworn nature of the observation, it feels true enough. In the nights, now, lying in Stanley's strong arms, she feels frightened of where everything is headed and can't visualize the days going by without breakage of some kind—can't imagine that what is presently happening to her won't end in heartbreak. She tells herself—and it is exactly like a murmured secret—that for this happiness, this calm, she'll find some way to weather whatever it does lead to. And just maybe it will lead to happiness. She hasn't mentioned Stanley's new status in her life to Oliver, and, since Oliver's return from the hospital, Stanley has stayed away some, wanting to give Oliver time to get used to things. The children seem to understand the whole situation—enough to keep to themselves what they do know. The fact is, they like Stanley, and, while for Jonathan there's been a certain edgy period of adjusting to the change, Kalie seems to accept everything as the natural flow of her young, changed life. The child feels at home. Oliver's back. Everyone's safe. The world looks mostly like itself again. Alison observes a kind of settled gladness in the little girl's eyes, and, drinking from those dark pools, she feels her own uncertain mood change for the better. The holiday, her favorite holiday, is here.

"I want to tell Oliver about us," she says to Stanley, who comes to have coffee with her on a break Wednesday afternoon.

"Not yet," he says.

"Aren't you sure?"

"Are you?" he says.

"I'd like to be."

"Me, too." He smiles.

It dawns on her that she likes his smile more than she can say. It's such a sweetly confiding expression, his eyes narrowing, and those white teeth.

"I don't want to upset him so soon after coming home."

"Do you think we'll upset him?" Alison asks.

"Maybe."

"Oliver likes you."

"Well—but this would be more than liking me. This would be son-in-law."

Alison puts her coffee down and looks at him. "Really," she says.

He seems to have become aware of what he has said. He considers for a brief moment, and then frowns, as though trying to solve some mystery about himself. "Am I proposing?" he asks.

2.

Brother Fire, attending to Mr. Petit, has discovered that aspects of his pastoral life are taking on the old urgency. It's as if the new purpose—helping this one unfortunate man in his journey back from the brink—has cleansed him in ways he could never have presumed or hoped for. But he tries not to think about it, doesn't want to indulge himself. Something has changed for the good. Life has the old flavor of work to do, and the hours are free of the monstrous appetite for secrets. At night, he recites the Lord's Prayer and remembers again that there are no real secrets in the Kingdom of God. He can pray now. The quiet is like honey poured into his soul.

Father McFadden decides not to stay for the Sodality Thanksgiving dinner, but to go visit his father in Florida, where he now lives. He tells the old priest this on Wednesday morning, while packing his bag. Mostly books. He'll drive all afternoon and most of the night. Brother Fire stands in the entrance of the kitchen while the younger priest prepares sandwiches for the road trip. "There's some fresh fruit in the refrigerator," he says. "Do you want me to put it in a plastic bag for you?"

"I won't eat it," the curate says. He sighs. "I always mean to. But I end up throwing it away."

"I do that, too," says Brother Fire.

They're quiet for a spell. The curate finishes making the sandwiches—peanut butter and jelly, ham and Swiss cheese—and puts them in a plastic bag. The old priest helps him put the mustard and mayonnaise, the cheese and peanut butter and jelly away.

Father McFadden thanks him.

"Do you want to talk about our mutual worry?" Brother Fire asks him.

"No." The other seems embarrassed now.

"Do you feel better?"

He leaves a pause.

"Because I feel a little better."

"No," Father McFadden says. "I'm just waiting for it to pass."

"And it has always passed, right?"

"Some times more quickly than others. You see, Father—sometimes I think—well, I think I'm probably a little ridiculous. I think I strike people that way."

The old priest can think of no form of response that would not be taken as pity, so he remains silent. He wants to reach over and take hold of the man's shoulder, or step over and hug him. But it wouldn't be appropriate, might even give away something of his recent thoughts, for which he now squirms inwardly.

"Of course it shouldn't even be a concern of mine. It's pride. Vanity. And then it becomes hard to think of myself as a true candidate for the spiritual life. I've been out of seminary five years. It's silly. I should've gone past these doubts."

"I've been having them, too," Brother Fire says to him, exhilarated at the chance to say something. "I have, you know. And how long have *I* been out of seminary?" He smiles.

"My heavens. You mean I can look forward to this terrible battle all my life?"

There seems to be nothing to say to this.

Father McFadden sighs and smiles. "Just a joke, Father. I'm sure it's always a battle for all of us all the time."

Brother Fire helps him pack the car and stands waving at him as he pulls down the street and away. He won't be back until after the holiday.

It snows all night Monday. And he spends sweet hours with Saint Thomas and his great book. Calls are few. Something about a big snow, it seems to the priest, makes everything quiet, even the souls of men.

Tuesday, though the roads are covered—the schools are still closed—he makes his way to the hospital to see Mr. Petit, who's conscious now and wants to talk. Mr. Petit apologizes, as if the action for which to be forgiven is nothing more than a failure of manners—getting drunk or being rude. He says he wishes he'd had a son. His trouble stems from that, and the loneliness he feels is only the loneliness of a father for an absent son. A son who was never born. He believes he can recall the face of every child he has ever taught.

There are so many different kinds of love, and don't they all, finally, come down to gestures?

The old priest reiterates to Mr. Petit that the province of sin is always self; self alone, to the exclusion of others. "And your whole existence has been other-centered," he says. "Look at it directly and you'll see that—anybody can see that."

"It's how much I *wasn't* ever like that, Father, that tortures me."

"But that's a sin of pride, isn't it? I mean it's perfectly understandable and human. But it *is* pride. And I might as well tell you, that's been my sin, too."

"I've got so far to go," Mr. Petit sighs. "Such a long way back."

"Don't go back. Go on."

Mr. Petit looks off at the windows, and a small smile comes to his drawn features. "I appreciate the deftness of expression, Father."

"I'm trying to tell you the truth as I understand it, son. As I *believe* it."

"I'm sorry, Father."

Brother Fire places his hand on the other man's wrist.

3.

Late Wednesday afternoon, Mark and Gail call to say they're less than an hour away. Elizabeth's still at school, and Will Butterfield isn't at all certain that she'll come home tonight. Each day of this week, she has talked about her dread of the holiday, her wish not to be here for it. Friday she came home, dragged the suitcase out of the car and back up to the bedroom. He thought she might be deciding to stay; but the bag remained packed and she remained distant and silent. The weekend was terrible in all ways, the two of them passing in the hallways of the house, and speaking separately on the phone to Holly, to Gail and Mark. Elizabeth gave no sign, let nothing of the awfulness of life now come out in her voice when talking to these others. This made Butterfield hopeful, until she would look at him again, with those measuring eyes, dismissing him, fencing him off. Monday, she lugged the suitcase out to the car again. He rode with her in silence to the bookstore, got out, and she drove away. He spent the long day there, mostly alone, sick with worry, looking for ways to keep busy, redoing inventory, rearranging shelves of books. When she came and picked him up in the afternoon, it was a surprise, it filled him with a brittle hope, but then they went home in the dreadful silence between them. She put the suitcase back once more. Still, she talked very evenly and matter-of-factly, all business, about checking into a hotel, and Tuesday morning she had the suitcase out, but school was canceled. The hours from afternoon to night, each day, have dragged on like a season in hell.

This morning, she left her suitcase on the cedar chest upstairs. She left it open, too, with clothes draped over its edges, as if she had been rummaging through it looking for something. Yet something about the suitcase being there makes him fear her leaving even more, as if, in the final stage of her going, she won't even take *that* with her. He tells himself this is panic thinking, and moves the suitcase into the closet, on the floor, closing the door on it.

Mark and Gail pull in with Gail's new love, Edie, who is short, squat, flat-assed—you can't help but notice it—round-faced, and with black hair cut so close it looks like stubble at the crown of her head. There is nothing remotely attractive about her at first glance, but, when she speaks, an animation comes to her small, round, hazel eyes. She has a stub nose and small, grayish teeth. She's thick through the chest and arms, but that may be that she's bundled in a heavy, navy-blue suede coat with fringe on the sleeves. Also, she wears tight, faded jeans, thick black boots. Her legs are muscular and slightly bowed. There are gold earrings in rows up her ears, all the way to the tips.

"This is Will," Gail says, indicating her father. She's dressed more like Edie, and Butterfield notices that she, too, has more piercings up the side of her ears. Gail's hair is also cut very short now.

"Oh," says Edie in a very pronounced New York accent, "how awe ye-oh," stepping confidently forward and holding her hand out. He looks down, into the palm with its rough calluses and at the cigarette-stained fingers, and he thinks, for some reason, about workman's compensation; there's something distinctly blue-collar about her appearance, except for the fringed sleeves of the coat—for that, she might as well be a country-music singer. He grips the hand, then eases his grip for the clammy inertness of it. She winces and then steps back, nervously looking up and down the street. He half-expects her to offer to shovel the sidewalk. Gail keeps studying his face, searching for signs that he feels what he, in fact, does feel—dismay. A profound, sorrowful consternation and disappointment. And do we not, anyway, wish normal life for our children? He allows himself the thought, ushering them into the house, determined to keep a pleasant front and to say nothing about this trouble with Elizabeth. He's not acting out of any rational plan or intention; it is pure cowardice and avoidance: he doesn't want it to come up. He watches them move through the house toward the kitchen with their bags. The two women are following Mark automatically, and Edie is remarking on the house. "Oh, *wuhn*derful," she says, lugging her own heavy bag to the entrance of the kitchen and then stopping and seeming faintly confused.

"Show Edie to where she's staying," Butterfield says to Gail. Mark is at the refrigerator, already unpacking his salmon, his sea bass and tuna. Gail apologizes for being a clod and leads Edie up the stairs.

Butterfield stands in the entrance of the kitchen, leaning on the frame.

"Jesus Christ," Mark says softly. "I think they must've consulted the magazines."

"Meaning what?"

"It's like they're *playing* to it, Dad. Gail told me that when they met, Edie was wearing a business suit, high heels, and had her hair long and permed. She looked like a—well, like an average middle-aged woman, in other words. This is some kind of coming out."

"You don't think this is a true expression of either one of them."

"Not my sister, I know that much. That lady's almost fifty, for God's sake."

Butterfield is surprised at the avidity he feels for this as a subject; it is far from him in its way—his son and daughter's private lives. The trouble with Elizabeth is a dark backdrop, and even that fraction of removal feels a little like surcease. But then the whole thing rides over him again, the weight of what neither of his children knows yet, the mess that everything will be in when Elizabeth gets home with her grievance and her intentions. Mark crushes the paper bag in which he had packed the fish. The noise itself is grating on the nerves. Butterfield discovers a desire to take a swipe at his son's complacency. "I've seen married women with their hair cut that short," he says. "Aren't you being a bit stereotypical in your reactions to them?"

Mark looks at him, having paused in the act of picking up his bag. "You weren't in the car with them. I felt guilty for having a prick. They kept going on like I wasn't even there."

"So, your feelings are hurt."

"Maybe. Yeah."

"Well, get over it," Butterfield says, and the urge to tell Mark everything rushes through him like a wave of fire.

"It's no skin off my nose," Mark says. "But the ride down here—Jesus. Edie's—that accent, too. I have never liked that particular accent."

"Happy Thanksgiving," Butterfield says. "You don't know the half of it."

His son stares, standing there holding his bag.

The two women are coming back down the stairs, and they are talking about the first Elizabeth. Edie has been in touch with the records division in San Francisco. It's best, she says, always to start with the person's actual name, though it's fairly certain now that the name is changed, has changed several times, first and last.

Without her coat, she looks rather less squarish of build. She's wearing a soft pink blouse and a belt with a large silver buckle, with darker facets in it, suggesting the look of the full moon at its zenith.

Gail pours a glass of milk and offers it to Edie, who politely refuses it. "I'm just fine." Gail drinks it down. They talk more about the house and the work Butterfield did on this kitchen—new ceiling, track lighting. Gail remarks that her father is good at track lighting. "He knows how to do that, don't you, Daddy?"

Butterfield sits at the table in the breakfast nook and forces a smile in response, folding his hands in front.

"Should I make coffee?" Gail asks.

"Not for me," says Edie.

"I don't want anything," says Mark, heading out to go up to his room.

Butterfield looks at his daughter, with her new earrings glinting in the light, and says, "Sure. Make some coffee."

She gives a little shrug at his tone, and sets to work. Edie stands at her side, talking to her about different teas she used to drink and how there's more caffeine in some teas. Gail takes this up and goes on about using caffeine to cut the effects of drinking, she never has a hangover, because she has a lot of coffee when she's drinking. They talk about caffeine and alcohol. They're both full of chatter, as if they don't want to allow space for the discussion of anything serious.

"Where's Elizabeth?" Gail asks finally, sitting at the table across from her father and setting his coffee down. "School let out a while ago, right?"

"Well, honey," Butterfield says, then stops.

Edie squeezes in next to Gail. Now they're both waiting for him to go on. He has the unpleasant thought that they already know everything, that Elizabeth may have called them.

"They're not doing afternoon-club stuff the day before Thanksgiving," Gail says.

"I'm gonna broil the salmon for tomorrow," says Mark, coming back in. "I brought some wine, too." He sets a cardboard carrier of three bottles on the counter and then makes a lot of noise reaching into the drawer under the oven, bringing out the broiler pan. He retrieves the salmon from the refrigerator, unwraps it, and then opens the refrigerator door again, looking in. "If a person wants not to be found," he says, "then it's pretty certain they won't be, unless it's the cops looking for them—and even then."

"Well," says his sister, "we weren't talking about that just now."

"Let me know when it's okay to talk about it again," Mark says with a smirk.

"I understand you own a bookstore," Edie says to Butterfield, with nothing like real interest. It's only to change the subject.

He wonders what kinds of disagreeable exchanges she had to hear in the car on the way down from Philadelphia, no one there with whom to change the subject. "Yes," he tells her. "Used books. Guy came in the other day and bought something like seven hundred dollars—" He stops, having received the image of Ariana Bromberg that day, walking into the shop, jingling her car keys. Did he know, even in that moment, where it was headed, where it would end up? It's hard to believe he didn't.

Edie says, "Books?"

He nods. Gail stares. "Claimed he didn't have any, never read any." He doesn't want to go on with it, but they're waiting. "He was starting from the beginning."

"How old was he?" Gail asks.

"Roughly my age."

"You okay?"

"Sure." Butterfield watches his son poke around in the refrigerator. At last, he brings out a stick of butter, tears the wrapper off, and greases the broiler pan, using it like a big crayon. The salmon he's going to prepare is an enormous pink slab lying in a crown of butcher paper.

"Salmon," Butterfield says. "On Thanksgiving."

"Don't alienate me," Mark says. "I'm on your side."

Butterfield looks at his own white knuckles. So, Elizabeth has spoken to them, he thinks. He looks across the table at Gail, who simply stares back. But then she shakes her head. "That was for our benefit." She turns her attention to her brother. "I guess you felt left out on the drive, little bro?"

Mark ignores her. "I put melted butter and lemon juice on it," he says, "and seafood seasoning. It's very good, actually."

Butterfield watches him.

Butterfield gets up from the table and crosses to the sink. He pours himself a glass of water and drinks it down. The whole sense of things now is of a deadening unreality. He looks at the napkin holder on the counter, the little wrinkle of green napkin falling from it, and tries to master his own breathing. He wants to sob, wants to move off, leave them here, retire to his room and sleep. Disappear. Lose consciousness. He pours more water and drinks it. Gail asks Edie to move, slides out of her place, and walks past him. "Bathroom," she says.

Edie remains standing, hands in the pockets of her jeans. Butterfield can't help picturing her with Gail in some sexual pass; he wonders what they do, has a flash of tangled limbs in an expanse of rumpled sheets, and then attempts not to think at all. His own mind repels him for its ceaseless grasping at everything, its stream of unwanted images, remembered and imagined.

They hear the door open, Gail's voice, the clamor of greeting. A moment later, Elizabeth enters the room with two bags of groceries. She hugs Mark, and then, to Butterfield's astonishment, she hugs him, too. It's mechanical, only partial pressure, but, for that one instant, her arms are around him. She turns to Mark, being animated for Edie's sake, and says, "My Lord. Fish. A fish for Thanksgiving?"

"I'm numb to teasing," Mark says. "Go right ahead."

Gail introduces Edie, who repeats, "How awe ye-oh."

Elizabeth shakes hands, then pats the other woman's shoulder. "Welcome to the family," she says.

Edie appears moved, looking to one side and stepping back. The little eyes show moisture. "I haven't been to a Thanksgiving—haven't been to someone's home to celebrate it in some—in some time," she says. Her demeanor is actually shy now.

Elizabeth pats her shoulder again and then busies herself with taking things from the grocery bags—bread and fruit and boxes of crackers and more wine. All reds, claret bottles with a ruby shine to them and rustic, brown labels. "Has your father spoken to you?" she asks Gail.

The evenness of her voice goes through Butterfield like a blade. Her face is completely without expression.

"Where do you want this to go?" he interrupts, holding up a bottle of the wine.

She hesitates, looking blankly at him. "Where do we usually keep it, Will?"

"Spoken to me about what?" Gail asks.

Her stepmother seems briefly perplexed, but she recovers. "Nothing. Your year. Your search for your mother."

"Marginally," says Gail. "We think she's living in San Francisco somewhere."

"This holiday is going to be fun," Elizabeth says. "A real treat." With the word *treat*, she sets down a carton of eggs with such force that it breaks open.

"What's wrong?" Gail says.

"Not a thing," Elizabeth tells her. Then she turns to Will. "Will you put the eggs away?"

Gail has interpreted things to be about her inclusion of Edie. She breathes a tired sigh and says, "I believe it'll be a wonderful occasion for family and for renewing ourselves as people."

"Gail," says Butterfield, "just when did you decide to live in abstractions?" He makes the effort of seeming to be joking, but she turns from him and takes Edie by the wrist. "I need a nap every five minutes in this house," she says.

"What?" Butterfield says.

"Happy Thanksgiving," Gail says with a brittle smile.

"Try not to assume that everything's always about you," Elizabeth tells her with the same kind of smile. "Just joking, sweetie."

"If you *were* just joking."

"Oh, well—I'm not that complicated, am I?"

"I don't have the slightest idea what anybody's talking about," Mark says. "So I'm going to have some wine and cook this salmon."

"I'm talking about having a good Thanksgiving," Elizabeth says.

Butterfield studies her face, and now she gazes back at him. They may as well have spoken the words: "Is this us finding a way to get past our trouble?" his eyes say. "I'm gone," hers say.

<h1 style="text-align:center">4.</h1>

The rest of the evening is spent in preparation for tomorrow. Mark broils the salmon, and his stepmother works around him, making deviled eggs. Then, finished with his fish, he works on cutting up vegetables, and his older sister, with Edie's help, makes broccoli casserole. Butterfield wanders through the rooms of his house, his once-happy house.

Shortly after dark, Holly stops by. She hugs everyone, including Edie, and she and Elizabeth talk for a time about the trouble at the high school, poor Mr. Petit. Elizabeth gives no sign that anything else is wrong. Mark turns on the television and spends an hour channel-surfing, so there's that noise, too. Holly and Gail and Edie start a game of euchre, and they want Will and Elizabeth to play. Butterfield declines, sits nodding off in his chair while a television special delineates what might be in store if the computer glitch isn't addressed, the apocalypse to come. It's all part of the unsettling knowledge of the turn of the century, and the millennium, too.

"Remember the great blackout of nineteen sixty-five?" Holly asks. "The whole Eastern seaboard, all the way north and into Canada went black."

"I remember," Butterfield says. "I was fourteen."

"Tell what happened to you," Holly says. "I bet these kids don't know it, do they?"

"I shot out a streetlight with a slingshot and everything went out. The streetlight went and in the exact same instant everything else went, too."

"We were in Richmond," Holly says. "Visiting my parents."

"Imagine me," Butterfield says to his daughter, who's getting into her coat. She and Edie are going to take a walk. "Running home thinking I'd shut the country off."

"Talk about guilt," Mark says.

"Let's not," says Gail, opening the door on the cold night. She and Edie go out, Edie again blocky-looking in her heavy suede coat. There's a residue of the icy air after the door is shut.

Elizabeth claims a headache and goes upstairs, without looking at anyone. Holly and Mark sit on the sofa in front of the television. Butterfield pretends to drift off, miserable and beginning to understand how Elizabeth will play this weekend out. Mark has wrapped the salmon and put it away, and poured a glass of beer for himself and red wine for his grandmother. They sip their drinks and stare at the roil of colors and images on the TV screen—commercials for a bank, a deodorant, a cleanser, a weight-loss shake, the new Ford Taurus, State Farm Insurance, and the next upcoming episodes of several sitcoms. It's all as if these appeals are spoken by someone referring to family members, and the voice comes in that infernal whisper: first names for everyone, familiar friends.

Butterfield rises, makes his way up the stairs, and comes to the entrance of the bedroom. Elizabeth is lying on her back in the bed, with one arm thrown over her eyes.

"Have you given any thought to where I sleep this weekend?" he asks.

She sighs but doesn't move her arm. "I don't know. I don't know anything anymore."

"What do you think of Edie?"

She looks at him, then covers her eyes again. "Are we having a conversation now?"

"Can we?"

Silence.

"You didn't tell them," he says softly. "Did you."

And she looks at him again. "No, I didn't."

"Are you waiting for me to tell them?"

She puts her arm back once more. "I have a headache. I'm exhausted. You figure it out and then let me know."

"Elizabeth, are you staying through the weekend?"

"I guess." This is uttered without conviction, with a sigh of exhaustion.

"You want me to go," he says.

"I want you to go just *now*, and let me sleep."

"Thank you for that—downstairs—" He himself isn't even certain how he means it. He stands there watching her. "I'm so sorry, Elizabeth."

She doesn't move, doesn't seem to have heard him; perhaps, she has drifted off to sleep. He waits another second or two, then sighs loud enough for her to hear him if she's awake, and takes himself downstairs.

Holly's in the kitchen, talking on the telephone. Mark's staring at the TV, though there's a magazine open on his lap. Butterfield takes his seat in the armchair and puts his hands over his eyes for a moment. Then he sits back and crosses his legs, hearing his mother going on about the ham she and Fiona are cooking along with the turkey—and how Mark has complicated things with his big piece of fish. Then it's quiet again, and there's just the television.

"What the hell is happening, Dad?" Mark says suddenly.

"Sounds like Holly doesn't know what to do about your salmon."

"That's not what I'm talking about. Come on."

Will Butterfield looks at his son. "When I know what's happening," he says, "I'll let you know."

Holly comes into the room with a glass of wine and a bottle of Bordeaux. She sits across from Mark, placing the bottle on the coffee table, on a coaster. She sips the wine. "Fiona's busy making the dinner," she says. "She's got her little mind made up."

"You're staying out of her way," says Mark.

"I wish we all could. God knows what Fiona will end up saying tomorrow when she gets a load of—when she sees Edie. Who seems like a nice person, by the way."

Butterfield reaches for the bottle and starts into the kitchen for a glass.

"Will?" Holly says.

"Pay no attention to that man behind the curtain," he says.

In the kitchen, he sees his own reflection in the dark window over the sink and looks away, as if having come face-to-face with a ghost. He pours a glass of wine and drinks it down, then pours another. Where will he go to sleep? He has more of the wine, finishes the bottle, then steels himself and heads out into the living room again. Holly has finished her glass and asks for another.

"Bottle's empty," he says.

"Open another one."

"Sure."

He goes into the dining room, retrieves another bottle from the rack, then walks into the kitchen, under the bright light, to open it. He's aware of the blankness of the dark window over the sink, as if it still contains his image. There's something almost spooky about it. The room is quiet; the house is quiet. Holly laughs at something Mark said.

Butterfield can't go in there just now. He pours his wine and drinks it down without really tasting it. The walls of the house seem too close; he goes to the back door and out into the chill, and across the crust of snow to the other house, which is dark now and looks abandoned once more, though Shostakovich and wife are only away. When the two of them were packing the car, Elizabeth stood in the upstairs bedroom window and watched them. He saw her there and tried to find something to say. Elizabeth stood quite still, staring out. She was aware of him, too, because, finally, she sighed and said, "She's very pretty."

"You're the most lovely woman I ever saw," he said. Then: "He was worried she wouldn't be able to go with him."

Elizabeth said nothing to this.

Now, in the dark, he tramps around it, a man stupid with grief. The snow gets into his shoes; his bones ache from the cold. It's a dreary night, lowering clouds. There's something primal-feeling about it, as if the planet had been through some nuclear storm and has come to rest this way, empty, silent, with just the wind tolling across the sloping, rounded, smoothed surfaces. The houses look abandoned, dead. No light anywhere. There isn't even the sound of distant traffic now, and the chasms of air above him are eerily devoid of airplane sounds. Off in the soundless dark, his daughter and her lover are walking. The ice bordering the sidewalk is melting, and so the temperature has at last climbed above freezing. He can't even say why he's out here. The wind tears at him. He feels it as something inimical, searching him out, getting into the folds and crevices of his clothing, leeching the warmth from his flesh. Holding his arms around himself, he looks at the windows of his house, the one lighted upstairs window where Elizabeth sleeps or broods. All of what he must bring himself to do in this holiday seems impossible and unlivable. Vast distances beyond him. He puts one foot in front of the other, moves across the rhomboid of light from the living-room windows, around to the back door again, and in. He takes his shoes off, knocks the snow from the soles, then pads into the living room with the bottle, shivering. Holly gives him a look.

"Where've you been?"

"Just stepped out for some air." He doesn't see Mark.

"You want to tell me what the hell's going on between you and Elizabeth?"

"No," he says.

She lifts her glass. "Give me some of that."

He pours it for her. "I'm taking a page from Fiona tonight. I might just walk home."

"I'll walk you," Mark says, coming back from the bathroom. "I'd like a little walk."

5.

When the blast of the pistol shook through the little room, Brother Fire stepped back into a chair and sat down, and the chair was on wheels, so it moved a few feet, as though he were trying to scoot away from the sound, from the catastrophe, Mr. Petit going down behind the desk with an enormous thud and shattering, one awful sound—the shot and the fall and glass breaking. And then there was the terrifying pause, the muffled-seeming aftershock of that sound, a stillness like no other on earth, the old priest hauling himself with some difficulty out of the moving chair and to his feet, lurching toward the other man where he lay on the floor in blood, a lot of blood, and Brother Fire had never seen anything like this, never anything remotely as dreadful, something so much itself that it took everything else and made it marginal, secondary in some way, the world outside the window and the sunny cold and the people, all of it gone, and there was just the solidness of Mr. Petit's arms, the bones in them under the skin, and the bleeding around his soft middle, the mess.

Brother Fire remembers crying out for help and scrabbling finally on his brittle-feeling knees across the hard floor, to the door, and opening it, or someone pushing it open on him, and his own voice saying please. Please.

Now he's unable to sleep, contemplating the dinner tomorrow. This holiday, above all, is the one that makes him long for a family, someone—brother, sister, cousin—to feel the necessity of visiting or calling. But he won't, won't, won't allow such thoughts. He dismisses the housekeeper so she can prepare the holiday dinner for her family. He hears confessions for two hours, concentrating on the miracle of forgiveness, and then he walks over to the rectory and makes himself a modest supper of canned chili and a glass of very cold beer. No one calls. He sits by the phone in case he's needed, and reads Aquinas's book. Such reasoned, calm determinations! It's restorative. And when the picture of Mr. Petit falling from the chair behind the desk goes through his mind, he strives to put it away—or, more accurately, he strives to dismiss the feeling that comes, the sense of an unspeakable futility. His failure with Mr. Petit is essentially a failure to see beyond his own despair—or even to recognize it as despair—and all of this constitutes a faltering, somehow, a subtle loss of faith itself. He's aware of this now, and now, when he prays, he asks for help with that, once more uttering the one prayer, over and over again: "Lord, I believe. Help thou my unbelief."

Father McFadden calls at nine o'clock with his poem. He wants to read it aloud.

"Of course," says Brother Fire. "Please."

"Nothing so tempting as hopelessness," the younger priest reads. "Nothing so happy as faith. Nothing so great as the sense of thankfulness. Not even Henry the Eighth, with all his earthly power and might, could ruin my glad tiding tonight, of Thanksgiving's happiness."

Brother Fire waits for more, and, when it doesn't come, forces a murmur of satisfaction. "I like that," he says. And, quite extraordinarily, in the instant that he says it, lying, it becomes true. He *does* like it; he admires it for its strapping, good-hearted conviction and trust.

"I had trouble finding a rhyme for *faith*," Father McFadden says.

"Well, it's a good one."

"And you are taken care of tomorrow, Father?"

"Yes. I'll say the two masses, and I'm having dinner with Holly Grey and her family."

"That's wonderful. And things are all right there?"

Brother Fire decides not to say anything about Mr. Petit. "Things are okay, yes."

"Well, that's wonderful. And you—you like the poem."

"Very much." It's possible, the old priest tells himself without words, to love the thought for itself, separate from the expression.

"I'm so glad, Father. It's been a wonderful year, serving with you. We'll look forward to more good works together."

"Yes," Brother Fire says.

"Bless you," says the younger priest. "I'll call again, see how your day went."

"Thank you, it's not necessary."

"God be with you," Father McFadden says.

"And with you."

After he hangs up, Brother Fire finds that he can't read. The quiet house creaks; there are sounds out in the winter night, the barking of a dog, a lone car horn, and then the combustive groan of several helicopters going over, doubtless the escort and lead chopper of the beleaguered president, on his way back to the White House from Camp David. The old priest kneels by his bed and prays for light, for warmth, for goodness, and for trust in God.

6.

In the middle of the night, Elizabeth wakes from a dejected, vaguely bad-dreaming sleep with a burning under her breastbone. She swallows several times, thinks of rising to take medicine, but is too sleepy, too exhausted and depleted; the image of herself getting out of bed is replaced by a strange, summer-calm light, beautiful but playing out in a kind of foreground over a blank screen of gloom; she hears, or dreams she hears, the trickle of water over stones, and now she sees flowers moving in breezes; it's all some lost picnic, and she has an overwhelming sense that she must open her eyes wide enough to take everything in, but then she receives another throbbing realization of the pain at her middle, another stream of intention to get up . . . and slips once more off the ledge of consciousness and is gone. An unknowable amount of time passes before she comes to with a shudder, experiencing still the pain under her heart—and her heart's pain.

She turns to her side and looks at the faint striations of moving shadow in the window, the shifting illuminations of the street, cars going by, and the clouds gathering and unraveling, breaking up in silver traces of lunar light, in glacial-slow procession across the wide midnight sky. She hears voices downstairs, or thinks she does. She sits up and sees that Will has settled in the chair on the other side of the room, a light-colored blanket over him—the tan one, she remembers, from the beach two years ago, Marco Island, Florida, and that morning they had wandered miles down the soft coast and filled a plastic bag with sand dollars, and, later, a man had sold them the blanket from a basket of them in a street market. How happy they were then. How good they felt to be walking alone on the shore of the gulf, as if they were on the first shore of the new world, before time and the thousands of years.

Will sleeps with one hand over his face, fingers spread, looking like someone fallen there in the middle of disaster; the hand covers the face in an aspect of surrender to some fate.

She sees herself rise and walk the four paces to where he is, imagines herself kneeling, reaching to take him into her arms, imagines his waking in the fright that he seems to express now, moaning softly and urgently in his sleep, stirring in little nerve-impulses, dreaming whatever he's dreaming. She loves him—loves even his failures. The thought comes to her and she rejects it, turns from it in her mind like someone refusing to attend to a pleading voice.

She gets out of the bed and moves soundlessly downstairs, to the kitchen, where she's startled—and dismayed—to find Edie, sitting with coffee in the breakfast nook. Edie seems discomfited to be caught here, seems to sense immediately that Elizabeth came down here thinking she could fix herself something in her own house in the middle of the night. For a little space, neither of them knows quite what to do. Finally, Elizabeth moves to the counter, acknowledging the other with a small, polite wave of the hand. Edie's in flannel pajamas, a flower-print terry-cloth robe, and slippers. She has glasses on, with those retro fifties frames everyone has been wearing. Her eyes are magnified to twice their normal size by the lenses; this gives her a mournful, overly expectant look—the look of someone who has suffered blows and believes more are coming. Elizabeth sees the blue veins of the other woman's ankles below the line of the robe.

"Couldn't sleep," Edie says. "I'm sorry, I hope I didn't wake you."

"I had heartburn," Elizabeth says. "That woke me." She opens the cabinet over the refrigerator and brings out a bottle of Maalox.

"I have it every night," Edie says. "No matter what I eat."

Elizabeth offers her the bottle, and she takes it, pours a few tablets out in her rough palm. Edie chews them like candy, and then sips her coffee.

"Coffee's not good for it," Elizabeth says.

"No, I know."

She doesn't feel at all like company, any other someone to contend with or consider, especially not a stranger; she wants to sit alone and wait for the heartburn to go away. But the coffee smells good, and she's come down here, and, since withdrawing would seem ungracious, she sits across from the other woman and takes three of the Maalox tablets herself. "I'm not much in the mood for feasting."

"Not with heartburn, no," Edie says.

"I don't usually get it—I've got it tonight."

"Gail made extra coffee."

"Where is she?"

"Bed." Edie sips the coffee. She doesn't look as strange out of her street clothes; there's something almost schoolgirlish about her, sitting here in the white flannels with the little flower pattern in them, wearing her glasses.

"I'm not up for this holiday," Elizabeth hears herself say.

"It's been so long since I celebrated Thanksgiving with anyone," says Edie.

Elizabeth looks at her.

"I don't have any brothers or sisters. My mother and father live apart, and in California. I'm adopted, anyway. They're—"

Elizabeth interrupts. "Gail's mother was, too."

"Yes, I knew that."

"Of course you did."

Edie smiles tolerantly, and then seems to catch herself. "You probably came down here to be alone."

"No," says Elizabeth. "You were saying."

"I was? Oh—right, my parents. I was saying they're good people but they didn't like each other. That's how I got into this work, you know, of helping people look for people. I spent several years looking for my own biological mother."

"Did you find her?"

Edie nods, sipping the coffee. "A perfectly nice lady living with her family in Provo, Utah, three girls, a husband who wouldn't understand an illegitimate child from another life. I left her alone."

During this speech, it occurs to Elizabeth that she's no longer so conscious of the other woman's accent, or, anyhow, she's not as predisposed to be annoyed by it. Indeed, looking into Edie's moist eyes in their amplified state, she experiences a sort of free-floating, detached affection for her, a little like that feeling she has had watching a celebrity on television, when an aspect of the real person showed through. There's something charming about Edie's accent now, something pleasing about the sounds resonating in her words.

"I'm sorry," Elizabeth says.

"No big," says Edie.

They're quiet for a space. And there's a component of this particular silence that seems freighted with their whole lives. They breathe. They are in this proximity to each other, two strangers in the kitchen of a house snug against wintry weather. Elizabeth feels an abrupt desire to say something defining in the moment. But nothing comes. Every thought embarrasses her.

Edie goes on: "I didn't have the heart to make her pay more than she already had for her mistake. She had me, anyway, and I don't suppose she had to, even then. I went my way, glad that I got to see her."

"Did you talk to her?"

Edie lifts her coffee cup and holds it with both hands, resting her elbows on the table. "We met for coffee at ten o'clock one morning. I got in touch discreetly, like they—like we tell people to. Better chance the person will agree to see you. And she did—she agreed. We met at a restaurant the next town over. Orem. Ever been there?"

"Never been to Utah."

"Nice country," Edie says. "Pretty country."

Elizabeth gets up and pours some coffee for herself, then she walks over and pours more in Edie's cup. It occurs to her now that she *does* want company. The windows are so dark; the wind moans in the angles of roof and gutter, followed by a metallic rattle, some part of the drain spout having shaken loose. She sits across from this woman, her stepdaughter's lover, such a strange thing to think of, under the circumstances. It's as if she has to remind herself that her marriage is over. "I think I'd like having a few Thanksgivings alone," she says.

"I probably should've stayed in Philadelphia," says Edie.

"No— I didn't mean that."

"I know."

Elizabeth sits back and looks at the room, the doorway, half-expecting someone to walk through it.

"But you don't need extra stress."

"My mother-in-law and her crazy aunt are causing most of it. It's all right."

"But there's other stress, too, isn't there."

"Yes," Elizabeth says, surprised at herself.

The other woman puts her cup down and looks at her out of those imploring-seeming hazel eyes, in which, Elizabeth sees, there is a kindly— even nurturing—light. Something in them, something beyond the fact that they are magnified by the lenses of her glasses, invites confidence.

"We're breaking up," Elizabeth hears herself say. "I'm leaving—or *he's* leaving. We haven't figured that part out yet."

The response comes quickly and without a trace of apparent doubt as to its appropriateness. "Why?"

"He cheated on me and I just found out."

"Is it still going on? The cheating, I mean."

"No. She—the one—she had a breakdown. She was—she was having a breakdown and she went to him with it and he cheated on me with her. I can't believe I'm telling you this. God. Mark and Gail don't even know it yet."

Now the response issues forth more slowly: "Has anything like this ever happened before?"

Elizabeth puts her face down in her hands and tries to fight back the tears that want to come. She has a tremendous urge to move across the table and be taken into the other woman's arms and held and soothed. "I don't know," she manages. "I don't think so."

"I don't mean to pry," Edie says.

And Elizabeth does begin to cry. "Not prying," she gets out. "Forgive this. I can't believe myself." She moves to the sink and runs water, dampens a paper towel and wipes her eyes and nose with it. "I'm sorry."

"He's confessed to it?"

She nods, crying. Angry at her own failure to keep it in. She returns to the breakfast nook and sits, holding another paper towel to her mouth. "He says she came at him, and he was weak. He says he doesn't understand it either."

The other woman waits for her to go on.

"I don't want to talk about this. Don't—I don't know why I said anything. Please don't tell Gail or Mark—"

"Of course I won't. But Gail thinks something's wrong. She said as much to me tonight."

"I just want to get through this day, you know?"

"You will. It'll be all right, you'll see."

Now, of course, it's only polite-seeming talk, reassurance that comes automatically.

But then Edie says, "Sometimes, you know—I'm—I'm just talking. But you already know this. Sorry. But a man is—a man can be susceptible to a thing, right? That kind of thing. Nobody talks about it because it sounds like double-standard sort of stuff. But I believe a man can be—well, as much as raped."

Elizabeth blows her nose, looking down, and she feels the other woman's gaze on her. "Everything's broken," she says. "It's all in pieces."

"I know the feeling," Edie tells her. "Believe me. My husband left me after twenty years."

Elizabeth stares, nearly dumbfounded.

"Sometimes finding out our nature is a journey we don't want to make."

There seems nothing whatever to say in response to this.

"God, forgive me—such a bromide. I don't talk like that, you'll have to trust me. But it's true that I got left after twenty years."

"I'm sorry to hear it," says Elizabeth.

"Don't be. He was right to. You see, the truth is, I didn't desire him, in the end. I never admitted that to myself while it was going on."

A moment passes, in which the only sound is Elizabeth's sniffling. Finally, she says, "I can't get past what he did. Can't get it out of my mind. Can't stop seeing it."

"That's the hard part of it," Edie tells her. "I know."

Again, they're quiet.

"I really didn't mean to pry."

"Don't say that."

"Well. You welcomed me to the family."

Elizabeth nods.

"Do you know how much that meant to me?"

"You're sweet. It was just a gesture."

The other woman stares down into her coffee, swirling it, as Elizabeth always does when it has begun to cool. She recognizes the motion as something that belongs to her own habits and attempts to put into words the feeling that this engenders in her. No words will come.

Evidently, the other is having the same trouble. The pause that ensues begins to feel awkward.

Abruptly, Edie says, "I had no idea Gail and I would—that we'd be together. I wanted to help her."

"None of this that is going on here is about you," Elizabeth says. "Or Gail and Mark."

"I know."

Presently, she changes direction: "Do you think you'll be able to locate their mother?"

The other ponders this for a moment. Finally, she shrugs and leans across the table. "It *is* true that someone who wants to disappear can do it and keep it that way. I'm afraid it's a dry trail right now. And I can't get Gail to admit it to herself."

"Gail gets things in her head."

"I do love that about her," Edie says.

"But there's even a chance the woman's dead, isn't there. And you wouldn't know it. Wouldn't be able to find it out, I mean."

"Yes," Edie says. "That's unfortunately true."

Elizabeth moves to the sink again and pours out the dregs of her coffee. The other woman is up, too, now. "Thank you," Elizabeth says to her.

"Thank *you*."

They embrace. It is as if they are sisters and have just spent a quiet hour catching up. There's a softness to Edie's shoulders, and she smells of lavender and vanilla and spices, fresh out of a bath before she came downstairs, hair washed and brushed. Elizabeth is aware that she herself must be wretchedly stale, still wearing the clothes of her long day and her troubled fall into heavy sleep and reflux, still carrying the dust of her movements, the traces of sweat and stress and the sour minutes and hours she spent clenched in the contemplation of her grief and anger. She steps back from the other woman and again begs forgiveness for involving her.

"No," Edie says. "Please. Please don't say that again."

"Well, then I'm sorry for repeating it."

They go upstairs together and depart in the upstairs hall, this time with just a passing touch of the ends of the fingers. "Good night," Elizabeth says, and watches the door close quietly on Gail's room.

Will is still slumped in the chair, still in that pose of desperate acceptance, fingers spread across his eyes.

She gets out of her clothes and into the bed, and thinks of waking him. But she can't. Not yet. The wound is still so fresh; it scrapes through her each time she thinks of it, and her mind won't let it go, keeps presenting her with the fact, almost as if to taunt her with it. Once, long ago, she had read that a quality of obsession is that the person suffering from it often *wills* the fixed idea into being, almost as if to test the mind with it, to grade the effect on the emotions. She lies quite still, thinking about *that* for a time, and then thinks about taking more Maalox. The body has its own will, too. She hears his breathing on the other side of the room, hears him stir, whimper high in his throat, and grow quiet again. It comes to her that in this present state of anguish, she can't believe in the passage of time; it's an intellectual construct, something she can hold in her mind, but viscerally it is as fabulous as the always-chilly weather on the surface of the moon.

7.

Alison wakes to her father playing his guitar. The chords are not quite sounding fully; there's something faintly tentative and halting about it, and she remembers with a jolt that he has come home from weeks of recuperation. It's as if she had forgotten this altogether in the good feeling of having him here. He pauses and then starts again. She's curled on her side, and behind her is Kalie, making a small, snoring sound. Alison carefully turns and cradles the little girl, until she grows sleepily irritable and moves away. Alison lies on her back with her hands behind her head and listens to the morning and is happy.

Oliver's playing "Blue Bayou." Such a simple, pretty song. She rises finally, puts her robe on, and looks out the window. A gray, late-November day; the sky is a pale screen, without a wrinkle in it. There's still snow on the grass and piled along the curb, but it's melting rapidly now. She walks to the entrance of the living room. Here's her father, sitting in his chair, fumblingly working the song, concentrating.

When he sees her, he says, "Oh, good morning," and puts the guitar down.

"Keep playing," Alison says. "Please?"

He picks it up and starts the song over. She leans on the frame of the door, arms folded, watching him. At one point, singing the chorus, he loses his voice. Then he laughs and finishes and puts the guitar down. "That song always chokes me up. That stuff about going back someday, you know, the yearning in it."

She walks over, leans down, and kisses him on the cheek. "You're back."

"Yes." His eyes well up. She hugs him. "Home," he gets out.

"I'm so happy," she says.

"Are you ready—for this—dinner?"

"Stanley wants to make something here, to take over there. Something his mother taught him to make with blue cheese and flour. Blue cheese chips, they're called."

"What're you making?"

"A couple of pumpkin pies." She can see that he's waiting for her to say more about Stanley. But she can't bring herself to begin.

"I didn't think I'd—ever play the guitar again," he says. And there's recognition between them, without words, of how well he's doing with his speech. "But it's—okay. I've got to learn some moves over again. But it's going to be—okay."

"It sounded wonderful, just now."

"Well, I'll have to keep it—simple, for a while. You know."

"How do you feel about Stanley?" she asks him. She's surprised at her own abruptness.

He doesn't hesitate. "Well—honey, the question is—how do *you*—feel about him."

"I love him."

"Well, then—*I* love him."

After a time, he says, "Are you *in* love with him."

She nods, though she isn't as sure as she supposes she ought to be. It raked through her to learn that Teddy is getting remarried, and that confused her. Still does. She sits on the arm of her father's chair and rests her hand on his shoulder. The sinews and bone there are surprisingly slack, and it makes her pause for a second.

"What," he says.

"Well, would it be—is it all right if Stanley moves in with us?"

"Hey, I liked—Stanley before you ever—knew him, sweetie. And this is your house."

"You live here, too."

"It's all right if Stanley moves in here. Really."

"Somebody you work with, though?"

"Stop—worrying," Oliver says. "Don't imagine more trouble than there is."

"But what trouble?"

"See?"

"Dad, you said 'trouble.'"

"Well, we've got this big Thanksgiving—dinner to go to, that we really would rather not go to. Our two zany—ladies. My trouble—all that."

"Think there'll be any roof-sitting?" she asks.

They hear Kalie in the other room, waking up. Jonathan, too, is stirring. "Go play with my—grandchildren," Oliver tells her. "And let me do all the worrying for a while."

"We won't do it if you think it'll cause trouble."

"Well, if it comes to—trouble, we could always—partition the house." He smiles. But then a shadow crosses his face. "Alison," he says. "I hope you'll ask—Stanley to come live with us."

"You mean that. Because Stanley won't do it if there's the slightest problem."

"What did I just—say?"

She hugs him again, feels again how much weight he has lost. "I love you," she says. "I'm so glad you're home."

8.

Late Thanksgiving morning, a mist forms, as if the sea itself, a hundred fifty miles away, had lifted and trailed in the currents of winter air over the gray mountains, to the shuddering trees lining the streets of Point Royal. The last snow-laden leaves drop heavily, so wet, straight to the sodden, melting ground, and the mist covers the surrounding hills, making the whole town look truncated, buildings seeming to disappear into the murk. Will Butterfield, having slept in a chair across from his wife in their bedroom, rises stiffly, with a catch in his neck and a bad tingle in his hands. He dresses stealthily, worried about the sleeping shape of his wife in the bed, and pads down the stairs, where he finds his daughter sipping a cup of coffee, watching television. VH1. A series of brooding images of a dark, willowy, frowning woman moving in wind and sun, while a song plays, female voices, and then one voice.

A plate with orange slices is on the end table at Gail's side, and she has a magazine open on the arm of the chair. "Happy Thanksgiving," she says without quite looking up. "Edie's still asleep."

Butterfield goes to the front door and retrieves the morning paper, then comes back to the sofa and sits down with it.

"What do you think," Gail says.

He only glances at her. Then turns to the paper, holding it open over his legs crossed at the knee. "Concerning what?"

"Come on, Dad."

And now he does look at her. "Nice person," he says.

"That's all?"

"What'd you expect exactly, Gail? She seems like a nice person. Damn."

"Elizabeth welcomed her to the family."

He looks at the paper again, snaps it straight to emphasize the gesture.

"I'm happy for the first time in my life," Gail says. "Doesn't that mean anything to you at all?"

"I'm glad you're happy. I don't know how else to express it, though. What is it that you find about me that's deficient?"

"Nothing, forget it."

"I said she's a nice person. I heard myself. And you did, too. Don't deny it."

"I'm so out of here." She gets up and makes a production of removing her magazine and her coffee and the plate of orange slices.

A little while later, Mark comes down from his room. "Did you sleep down here?" he asks Butterfield.

"Yeah," Butterfield says out of the side of his mouth. "Right."

"You going to the bookstore at all this weekend?"

"Why?"

"Like to see it," Mark says. "Been a while." He goes on into the kitchen. There he and Gail engage in a sort of muttering banter, not particularly friendly, more the back-and-forth of siblings, with their little ways of annoying one another and their ruthlessness in using every nuance. At one point, they both laugh, and Butterfield hears Gail say, again, sardonically, "Happy Thanksgiving."

Edie comes down wearing a pair of black slacks and a white blouse, with a red scarf at the collar, like a cravat. She has put makeup on—a little something to darken her lips, and eye shadow as well. She seems a bit sheepish, eyes down, murmuring "Good morning" to Butterfield. "How'd you sleep?" he asks her.

"Oh, ve-ry go-ud." That accent.

When Elizabeth comes down, preparations begin for carting dishes over to the house on Temporary Road. Everyone's friendly. Elizabeth even laughs at something Mark says about the fishy smell of a Thanksgiving morning. She keeps her gaze from Butterfield, and the busyness of the preparations makes it not particularly noticeable, though Butterfield thinks he sees Edie notice it—thinks, in fact, that Edie is in on things now. Gail, too, perhaps, and Mark. In the next moments, he catches Edie watching him and watching Elizabeth, too. What is it, he thinks, about strangers that makes them able to detect these subtle turnings away, when the ones who ought to notice do not?

He helps load the trunk of the car with dishes, and, at Elizabeth's request, goes back inside to make sure that the oven is off, the iron unplugged. Gail, Mark, and Edie leave in Gail's car to go pay a brief visit to one of Gail's old school friends; it's important to her—she takes the trouble to say to her father—that people from her childhood learn of the new situation regarding her sexual orientation. Butterfield walks out to his own car, where his estranged wife sits, arms folded, staring straight ahead. He gets in and starts it, then guns the motor and waits, watching the other car pull away. "I can't believe this," he says softly, not expecting an answer.

No answer comes.

They ride in silence over to the house on Temporary Road. As they arrive, they see that Brother Fire has just pulled up. He's getting gingerly out of his car, and he waves at them. Holly's standing out on the stoop in a bright blue housedress and green slippers. The street's enshrouded in mist, and the snow is melting fast, water running in dirty rivulets in the gutter, and there's an echo of it in the storm drains on the corner, the only sound, like the running of a river. The mist is now a kind of fixed element, water suspended on the air, neither falling nor rising. Butterfield looks at where he knows the roof to be. If Holly were sitting there now, she would not be visible.

"Welcome," she says, nodding at the priest and then looking past him at Elizabeth.

Butterfield begins to empty the trunk, and the priest good-naturedly helps, talking about all the nice smells and the London-like weather. Has

Butterfield, by any chance, read Dickens's *Bleak House?* The description of the fog in London in the first pages of that book portrays this very day.

Butterfield agrees, recalling the passage and feeling a sense of unlooked-for kinship with the priest. It's only in this moment that he realizes how much he has been envisioning, dreading him, as an adversary presence today. He takes Brother Fire's arm above the elbow and squeezes. "That's one of my favorite passages in all of literature," he says.

"Oh, mine, too," says Brother Fire.

They go into the house, which has an incomplete look and, even so, is festive, with its drawings on the sheets of brown packaging paper hanging from the framed-in wall, where the house will be divided. Fiona comes in from the kitchen, wearing a flowered apron over a white blouse and jeans. Her hair is pulled up in a tight bun on top of her head, which makes her seem a good deal taller than she is. She and Holly take the food from Butterfield and the priest, and then Fiona comes bustling back in, wiping her hands on the apron. She kisses Elizabeth and her husband and shakes hands with the priest, who seems more ill-at-ease every second. He moves to the paper wall and begins studying the drawings, like someone in a gallery. The room is festooned with Christmas decorations—strands of glittering white lights, and tinsel on the potted plant by the door, and candles on the tables, ringed with sprigs of holly and pine. Holly has already received several Christmas cards from far-flung friends, and these are taped to the frame of the entrance to the kitchen. The long table is already set: two bottles of white wine in an ice bucket, two of red in a small, wire basket. Platters of bread and cheese and fruit, water glasses, and a large pitcher of water at either end. Little flower arrangements have been set at each place, and there are names written on folded, gilt-edged place cards. Butterfield walks around the table, looking at the names. He moves slowly, for the aches and sore spots in his back. He looks at his wife, who is preoccupied with setting out the food she has brought for the meal—the casserole and deviled eggs, the cranberry salad. He and Elizabeth are to be seated next to each other at one end of the table. At the other end, next to Brother Fire, is Edie Proileux. Edie and Gail will be seated across from each other. Butterfield thinks of what his children do not yet know.

"You okay?" his mother asks him from the other side of the table.

9.

Elizabeth hears the question, even while Fiona rattles on about how the turkey and the ham will have to take turns in the oven, as they already have for most of the day, and how worried she is about spoiling the meat. Now there's the necessity of putting the salmon out, Fiona says, but she doesn't know who'll eat it. And Elizabeth hears Will say, "I'm wondering what the hell she's thinking, Mother."

This stops everyone for a second. But Holly seems unaffected. She smiles, glancing at the others, and then reaches over and touches his chin. Quite cheerfully, she says, "Well, you know, I think that's a question for Gail. But I wonder how you'd be if this were her new husband." She turns to the priest and asks him if he would like a little tea or coffee. "Or is it too early for wine?"

"I'd like wine," says Will, just as the priest says, "Perhaps one small glass, yes."

Holly stops her son from picking up the glass at his place setting. "Let's save those for the dinner, sweetie. Let me get you and Brother Fire some other glasses." Then she reaches over and puts her fingers, extended as though to catch rain, under his chin. "Lift here," she says brightly.

The old priest says, "I always think of the wedding feast at Cana whenever I have a glass of good red wine. It's one of my favorite passages. The second chapter of John."

"All we have is good wine," Holly says, heading into the kitchen. Elizabeth follows, not wanting to be alone with the others. The kitchen smells wonderfully of the cooking meats and the pies that are lying out on the table. There are biscuits in the oven, and two more casseroles sit steaming on the counter.

"Typical," Holly says. "We've got six things ready and three things not ready and it's all got to go on at the same time. And people are late."

"Can I help?" Elizabeth offers.

"Listen," Holly says abruptly. "You can tell me. Is something else going on? I mean I know Gail's thing—but I get the feeling something else is bothering you."

"Why do you say that?" Elizabeth asks, trying to keep the evenness in her own voice. "I like Edie, to tell you the truth. I have no problem with her at all."

"So you're not reacting to this. What *are* you reacting to?"

"I have no idea what you're talking about," Elizabeth says.

Holly frowns, then sighs, and then gives a faint shrug. "Well, I'm not going to pry." She retrieves the glasses and moves past Elizabeth to enter the living room, where she picks up one of the bottles of red wine and pours two glasses.

"I'm assuming you both want red," she says to her son and to the priest.

From where Elizabeth stands at the entrance to the kitchen, she sees that Oliver Ward and his daughter and her children are arriving, with some man she hasn't met. Holly and Fiona are like a force of nature, she decides; they go ahead with things, they go on. Nothing stops them. She hears Fiona introduce the man as Stanley. Stanley's carrying a large platter covered with aluminum foil. "Blue cheese chips," he says, holding them forward like an offering. Fiona takes the platter and sets it on the table.

"Look at this," Alison says to her father, indicating the drawings. "Kalie and Jonathan did these. Aren't they wonderful?"

Oliver Ward appreciates the drawings, with little whistling sounds and with questions to Kalie, "Did you do this one? And this one?" His head keeps its rhythmical, nerve-firing denial through it all. Elizabeth thinks to compliment him on his grandson, who is such a good student in her class. She starts toward him, but then thinks better of it. Jonathan's studiously avoiding eye contact with her, and now Oliver's talking to Butterfield about the drawings and about how this is his favorite holiday. The old priest chimes in that he has always felt exactly that way about it, too. Fiona says she has always liked Christmas better, and she'd bet that one of the charming things about Thanksgiving is really the fact that it represents the first flush of the Christmas season. "Ask yourself if you're not partly in love with the day because it means Christmas is only a month away."

"No," Brother Fire says, sipping the wine. "Actually, I always liked the thankfulness aspect of it."

"Well, you're thankful for Christmas."

"Oh, yes—well, that, too, of course."

"Which is more important, Father? Christmas or Easter?"

"Well," says the priest, "if you don't get Christmas, the birth—you know."

"My favorite holiday is the Fourth of July," Holly says. "I love the fireworks."

"I remember," says Will. Then, to the priest: "She used to get the real ones, rockets." He glances at Elizabeth, and it's as if he had momentarily forgotten himself and now has to realize everything all over again: Elizabeth and he are estranged, and she's in the process of leaving him. It all comes back to his features, the lightheartedness disappearing. Oddly now, she finds herself feeling sorry for him. For the first time in all this, she recognizes him, sees him as the man she has loved all these years. The fact sends something like a fright through her, a dread. She remembers Edie's comment about men being susceptible and rejects it with a shudder. It's no excuse; there is no excuse, she tells herself. The hours of this weekend go through her like a gale, the force of this occasion itself propelling everyone through the day—it's as though it all might weaken her determination. And then this worry turns into something else: a sense of it all as a threat to her pride. Once more, she can't think beyond the idea itself. She *has* to leave him. The future is a blank; tomorrow morning, the day after, all blank. She watches Oliver Ward moving slowly along the brown paper wall of drawings, his head shaking. No, no, no, no, he seems to be saying, with that tic of his. Alison stands with him; Jonathan and the girl wait with Stanley on the other side of the room. *Those people love each other*, Elizabeth thinks. *There is love. I'm looking at it.*

But then she watches Fiona and Holly working together to put the final touches on the dinner. She has never felt lonelier or more uncertain of herself.

10.

Brother Fire, feeling the mortal tensions in the room, steps outside on the porch. He is joined by Will Butterfield, who brings a pack of cigarettes out of his pants pocket and offers him one. The priest says, "Oh, no thank you." But then changes his mind, watching the other light up. "Well, you know that does smell good."

"Here, Father," Butterfield says.

They stand there, smoking. There's very little breeze now. The day couldn't be more dank, or colorless-seeming, though there are visible pockets of brown grass where the snow has melted, and some tints still show in the mist-shrouded trees that line the road. The mist moves, and the leaves seem washed out, drained of any vividness, like a memory of a street in the fall. Brother Fire thinks of Mr. Petit, staring out a hospital window at the grayness all around. It occurs to him to say that sometimes the soul can mist over like that, and one can so easily lose one's way. But he doesn't wish to spend the afternoon thinking about a homily.

Butterfield draws on his cigarette and gazes, tight-jawed, out at the street. Then he lets the smoke go and says, "Bad weather."

"It has its own sort of beauty, though, don't you think?"

"I suppose."

The priest watches him blow out the smoke. He seems about to say something else. But then he holds back, flicking ashes off the end of the cigarette.

"Getting colder," Brother Fire remarks.

"Feels like it," Butterfield says.

Brother Fire takes a drag of his own cigarette, and, having felt the enormous delicateness of the surface of this day, finds that he isn't slightly curious about the reasons for it. This, he realizes with a start, is significant. Yet he wishes also to help if he can—after all, it is usually a matter not much more complicated than a kind word or gesture at the right time.

He's suddenly visited by a sense of exhilaration so profound that it momentarily stops his breath.

It's as if the answer, the whole answer itself—to the puzzle of being, to the vast mystery bodied forth in the Fall and Creation and the immeasurable sorrows and horrors, the redemptive blood of Christ and every single human frailty no matter how trivial, and every triumph, too—were about to be laid open for him, standing here on this little porch in a little valley town in Virginia. He feels his own calling again, more strongly than he did when he was a young man, and he reaches over and pats Will Butterfield on the shoulder. "Things will be all right, son."

"I was more or less talking about the weather inside, Father."

Brother Fire pats his shoulder again. They stand there, smoking the cigarettes.

"You know how it is, Father, when the road looks clear and perfectly safe and dry and it's actually covered with black ice?"

No answer seems required, so he simply waits.

Butterfield flicks his cigarette out on the snow-patched lawn and says, "That's the situation we've got right here, right now."

Brother Fire experiences a knot of apprehension in the nerves around his stomach. He felt so wonderful only a moment ago, and he's aware of the threat and temptation of that kind of spiritual excitement, the fact that one can become attached to that for itself. Even so, he wishes not to have it dissipated in this fashion, with a sour confession of some emotional inclemency. "I'm sure it can be helped with prayer," he says with forced brightness, flicking his own cigarette.

"Will you say the Thanksgiving prayer, do you think?"

"Well—"

"Because I'd like you to talk about forgiveness."

I I.

Mark and Gail pull in with Edie a minute or so later. Elizabeth sees them from the living-room window, where she sits sipping ice water and talking with Alison about the trouble at the school—the trouble generally at all the schools. They come to the door, and Holly lets them in. There are polite introductions of Alison, and Stanley, and Oliver, the children, the priest, Fiona.

Edie has brought wine.

Holly takes it, saying, "Oh, good. I like Spanish."

There's a lot of confusion now, people moving about the little room, Fiona acting to get everyone seated. Dinner's about ready.

Brother Fire says the prayer—a simple expression of gratitude for the food, and the Lord's Prayer. Fiona says a word of thanks for Holly, for all the love Holly has given her over the years, and Elizabeth looks at the child's paintings on the brown paper hanging over the construction of the walls that will divide the house. She sees Edie looking at her, and gives a small smile. But no one says anything about the irony present in the room. Holly gives her thanks for Fiona and for Brother Fire and for her family. Gail stands to say she's grateful for her family and for her new partner, Edie, and for the hope of someday looking upon her mother, but especially for the love and nurture she has gotten from Elizabeth. Mark seconds this, and everyone toasts Elizabeth, who has the suspicion that they all know now, that Edie has told them. But Edie's smiling at her from her end of the table, and there's no hint of complicity in her face.

Surprisingly, the afternoon settles into an ordinary-seeming few hours of people sharing a feast. All the conversations are polite, calm, considerate; the children are charming, though they squabble a little, but they are both so happy that their grandfather is out of danger; Holly and Fiona seem perfectly in tune; Oliver and the priest talk sweetly about swing music, Ella Fitzgerald, and Benny Goodman; Will and his two grown children are civil. He teases Mark about his salmon, but then has some himself. Mark has a little of the turkey. The little girl engages Edie in a conversation about knitting, because she herself has begun, with Holly's help, to knit a scarf for her brother, and Edie remarks that this is such a kindly gesture, for one's brother, because brothers and sisters often have trouble getting along, and she wishes she'd had brothers and sisters growing up. Mark and Gail talk about their early conflicts good-naturedly, and the conversation shifts again, to the coming millennium, the resilience of the president, and the unfortunate Mr. Petit and his troubles. Gail speaks separately to Elizabeth about everything she went through searching for her mother and how it was, discovering her love for Edie. She murmurs, so as not to disturb the priest, who talks to Mark about the Redskins and how they might actually make the playoffs after such a spell of losing seasons. Gail is talking about Internet searches and private agencies and records. The others are caught up in it briefly, but then Stanley engages Oliver in discussion concerning plans for construction, and everyone starts in again about the drawings on the hanging brown paper and the festive look of the half-finished room.

Through it all, Elizabeth, hurting, feeling her own love like a wreckage in her heart, watches her husband move from conversation to conversation, apparently coming to some kind of ease, drinking the wine and pouring more, and drinking that, too, and it isn't until near the end of the meal that she realizes how much of the wine he's had. She watches him pour still another glass of it, to the brim, and drink it down. No one else seems to have noticed. The talk goes on around the table, and Holly brings coffee and desserts, and Elizabeth comes to see that all of it, all the talk and the whole afternoon of sociability, has been woven over a fearful tension, everyone carefully skating around or past the cracks in the surface, an amazing show of the ability of people to keep a cordial tone even in a room whose pathology is not quite known or understood, or even, for that matter, fully perceived. The finest line of amiability, held fast to, while the cold mist runs down the windows and the wind blows like a fitful argument, slamming itself at the casements as if to push everyone into an admission of what is lurking under the soft observations and meaningless exchanges. Finally, Alison announces that she should be getting the children and her father home. She has to work early in the morning. Oliver needs his rest. Oliver rises and offers a toast to everyone, especially to the hostesses, who nod and smile. "I wish to—thank you first. And to thank—everyone for their kindness. The—best thing in the world. A great—gift. I wish it for you all." His eyes brim and he loses his voice for a second. "I wish it for—you all as *I* have been—given it." It's Oliver's only glass of wine, and he sips it slowly, standing there. On the other side of him, Will swallows more of his own and then tries to stand. "I'd like to offer a toast, too."

"Don't," Elizabeth says to him. "That one was perfect. Don't ruin it."

"Right," Will says. And sits heavily down. He drinks the wine and pours more and drinks that, too. Seeing this, she catches herself feeling sorry for him, glancing now at Holly and Fiona, the people in whose company he had to try growing up. She turns her gaze back to him, thinking to give him an encouraging smile if he would only look her way. But he's watching the others, and now he stares down into his wine glass. Finally, he sets it down with a thump, then gets up and walks to the door. "Li'l air," he says, going out into the dimness.

"Let him go," says Gail.

Elizabeth follows him. He makes it to the end of the street, then stops, puts his hands on his knees, the pose of a man having run a distance. The mist is already darkening his shirt and pants. "Will," she says. "Come back inside. You're making a spectacle of yourself."

"Just needed a li'l air," he says. Not looking at her. "Happy Thanksgiving, dear one."

"Stop it," she says.

On the lawn where he's standing is a baby carseat. She sees it and thinks how strange, what a place to leave a carseat, lying out on a lawn in the falling mist. He sees it, too, and staggers on to it through a snow patch. It's sitting there in a little semicircle of wet grass. "Look at this," he says.

"Will. I'm going to leave you here if you don't come in right now."

"You're gonna leave me *here*?"

"Stop it, Will."

"Here, darling?"

"Will, please."

He sits in the carseat, or on it. The thing actually holds him up, like the base of a statue, and he folds his arms over his stomach, half-lying there propped by the seat. Elizabeth looks at the house, the closed windows, all the other windows along the street. There seems to be no one home anywhere.

She walks over and reaches down to take his hand.

"Naw," he says. "Here's me. This is me. This is my speed, right here, kid."

"Stand up," she says. "I swear I'll leave you here."

"Said that," he says. Then: "It hurts so much. I wish it didn't hurt you."

"Stop this, now," she says.

"I love you," he says. "Din do a very good job, I know."

"I'm gonna leave you here," she says. "Please."

"Well," he says, "then leave. Leave. Christ." He's crying. Sitting there perched, ridiculous, in the little seat, weeping, the tears running down his cheeks. "It hurts so much, Elizabeth. It hurts. I—I wish I didn't hurt you."

She takes a few steps away, then turns and stops. "Are you going to stop this and act like a man now? Please."

After a time, he gets to his feet, stands over the seat, and seems to salute it, faltering, as if he might topple over. "I'll come back and see you, there, baby seat." He wipes his eyes with the sleeve of his shirt, first with one arm and then the other, and now he wipes his nose that way, tottering, sniffling.

She waits for him.

"You go on," he says. "We just wanted a little air, right?" He sniffles again. "I was just going to offer a goddamn toast. Nothing bad, you know?"

"I'm going inside," she tells him. And she makes her way back to the house and up onto the stoop, where she turns to see him walking along, slow, ruminating, mumbling to himself. "You big baby," she says to him. Then she steps inside, where the others seem studiously to be avoiding watching her. Holly gives her a slight nod as she takes her place at the table. Edie is looking at her with understanding that she doesn't want—and then she does want it. She nods, and Edie's eyes glaze over. Will comes in and stands looking around the room. "It's cold out," he says. "But the snow is melting." Then he moves unsteadily to his place at the table. "The snow is melting. And it can't help itself, either."

For a time, everyone's silent. Alison remarks about Fiona's dressing, for perhaps the fifth time, and Fiona behaves as though the compliment has never come her way. "Oh, I just throw it together," she says.

"You only wear that when you don't care how you look," Will says.

"What is he talking about?" says Fiona.

Again, there's a silence.

"Matter of character," says Will to nobody in particular. "I accept full respons'bility."

The children want more pie. Alison relents and gives them permission, and everyone has seconds. Will has still more of the wine, then gets up and pours himself some coffee. Elizabeth keeps track of him out of the corner of her eye as the others go on talking about the pies, and Oliver says he's looking forward to Christmas this year, more than others. Elizabeth sees Alison put her head on Stanley's shoulder, and she wants to cry, holds it back, getting up to deposit some of the dishes in the sink in the kitchen. Holly stops her. "You sit down," she says. "Enjoy your coffee and dessert."

"I'm not hungry anymore," Elizabeth says to her. "I can't really enjoy another thing."

"Sit down anyway."

The windows have grown dark. The mist has become rain now, a steady, cold downpour on the glass. Alison stands and gets the children moving. The party's ending. Oliver and Alison and Stanley and the children gather at the door and express their gratitude for having been invited. It's been a fine feast, such a warm occasion—Oliver's words. Elizabeth feels only the deepest sense of oppression, as if all of it had been a show to hide sorrow, and now the falseness of the afternoon and evening causes her to reel inside, and falter. She feels spiritually sick. She can't look at the others.

She thinks she might begin screaming. "Have none of you seen what's happening between my husband and me?"

Edie murmurs something to Gail, who hurries to get her coat, and, expressing the same warm gratitude that Oliver and the others expressed, starts out the door. Edie comes to Elizabeth and murmurs, "What Gail said—that came from her. I haven't told her anything."

"Thank you," Elizabeth tells her.

Edie reaches up and kisses her on the cheek. "We'll be friends, you and I."

"Yes," says Elizabeth. "We already are."

Will is still at the table, his hands cradling another glass of wine. Fiona stands over him, one hand on his shoulder, watching the others leave.

Mark remains behind, with the priest, who, probably because he is so gracious and thoughtful, manages to seem oblivious to all of the tides of misery here. Elizabeth thinks this, and then strides over to thank him for coming.

"I wouldn't have missed it," he says. "And now I must go, too."

"Will you stop in on Mr. Petit?"

"Tomorrow morning, yes."

"Will you tell him hello from me?"

"Of course."

She wants to cry on his shoulder. He goes out, and she stands with Holly, watching him hurry in the rain along the walk to his car. "There goes a good man," Holly says, as if she has identified something quite rare in nature. "He had no idea what he was looking at today."

"Nobody does," Elizabeth tells her.

"Well, that was lovely," Mark says, starting to clean up.

"I'll take care of that," says Holly.

Elizabeth sits down, unable to believe how queasy she is. "I'm sick."

"You didn't eat much," says Fiona. "You coming down with something?"

"Here's to everyone," says Will from his end of the table. He drinks more wine; it's as though he's alone.

Holly says, "Lighten up on that stuff."

"Here's to you, too," he says. But he doesn't look at her.

"I feel sick," says Elizabeth. "I have to go."

"I'll walk," says her husband. "You take th' car."

She rises and puts her coat on and walks slowly over to him. She bends down and carefully takes his face into her hands. He seems almost alarmed, resisting slightly, but she holds on. "I forgive you," she whispers. She didn't quite know she would say it. And, having said it, she feels a rush of frustrated anger go through her. She speaks through and against it, with a bitter will, holding his face tight. "I'll be waiting up for you. Do you hear me? I forgive you and I don't care anymore. I forgive you, Will."

His eyes brim, but he says nothing. She has the realization that he himself must work to find some way back from where he has been. He gives the slightest, unconscious nod of his head, staring into her eyes. It comes to her that she has always felt something essential had been denied him from his earliest living, and, in her own way, she depended on that. She loves him. That's all she knows now, in this awful hour, after this endless afternoon of people trying to be kind.

When Fiona offers her a plate of leftovers to take with her, she gently refuses it, kisses the old woman on the cheek, and makes her way out into the cold rain. Mark comes with her, carrying what's left of his salmon on a big platter. The two of them move to the car, and she holds the door for him, then walks around and gets in, without speaking. The car groans and doesn't want to start, but then it does.

"You've been my mother," he says. "Nobody else."

She pulls out onto the road, sniffling. He's quiet on the seat at her side, with his enormous half-eaten fish in his lap.

"I guess this was a bad idea," he says. "This fish."

"No," she says. "It was just fine. It's all fine, Son."

12.

The two old ladies begin to squabble over the dishes, so he kisses them both, and thanks them, and then starts out. His heart is hurting him, a physical pang, like an injury to the chest wall.

"You okay?" his mother says. "What was all that about at the end of dinner?"

"Needed some air. A li'l damned air."

"You went out and got wet. Everybody got quiet. It was embarrassing."

"Just needed some air, Mom. Sorry."

"But you're all right."

"I'm flying," he tells her. "You can't have missed that, right?"

"You're going straight home."

"Where else?"

He has struggled into his coat, and he lets himself out and walks in the chilly rain to the end of the sidewalk. The snow's almost completely gone. Here's his mother's divided house. No lights on across one side of it. The two old ladies are bustling around in the one lighted window. They will, because they have started to, finish dividing their house in two. And then, whatever their new arrangement will be, they'll adjust, and, in the end, of course, they'll be whatever they will be, together or separate, it will be the two of them.

He stands in the dark, water dripping down his face and into his collar. Elizabeth has forgiven him, and he has come to this. Knowing how far there is to go now, to get back anything of what they used to have. And it's entirely probable, he knows, that they never will. And it's all entirely, only, all the way to the bottom of it, his fault.

Remorse comes over him like a fever; it stops his breath.

The years of getting used to everything, trying for faith again, for trust and peace, stretch before him, and he gasps, shoving his hands down in his pockets. Regret hurts more than anything he could've ever imagined in his life.

The street is so dark in the rain. He walks down the long declivity toward the old part of town, the train station. He hears traffic out on the interstate, beyond the houses to his right. All the houses are dark, with the occasional flicker of television. America in cold night. This night. At the station, he moves to the platform, under the one lamp whose circular pool of illumination seems to be producing the speeding drops that move in it.

The clock on the station wall shows that it's eight-thirty p.m. At eight-forty-five, the train from Charlottesville will come through on its way into Washington. Just out of high school, he worked here as a ticket clerk, and he knows that this train doesn't stop. It will come through at about forty miles an hour. He walks out of the light and on up the track a few yards, past the end of the platform. Something moves off in the bushes nearby—something scurrying away from him in the icy pelting of the rain. He isn't quite aware of himself as being on the edge of something. He knows he doesn't want to go home, and he knows he can't really go forward, either. He feels quite blocked inside, as if some inner wall is there, beyond which he cannot see or hear. He waits. Far off, through the patter of rain and the murmur of the wind, there are the sounds of night in the city—sirens, traffic, one dog barking, and then another. He can't hear the train yet. Looking back at the station, at the angles of cornice and ledge and beam, the boards with their age- and soot-stained surfaces, the frames of the windows with their leaded glass, and the signs advertising travel merchandise, he has a moment of understanding something of the intricacy and strength of order. This doesn't arrive as an intellectual thing; it enters his bones, a stirring, deep down, of panic. When he was a child, riding in his father's car, he would see tall, weathered, falling-down barns in the fallow farm fields passing by the window, and it would come to him with a little wordless shock that someone long before had labored to build it; abruptly, his imagination would take him back to the sunny days of work on it, the hammers pounding nails, men raising a barn, nothing more ordinary, of course, and Butterfield was for the time being one of them, a part of that force of human industry. This was all without words or even without much understanding of what it signified, other than that he, Will Butterfield, in a strange turn of a boy's mind, saw himself among others putting together something that decades of weather would reduce to this desiccated hulk whose appearance was a sort of a natural phenomenon, like a tree or an outcropping of rock.

He steps to the track, up the gravel bed, and along it for a few paces. The wind is still for a few seconds. There seems to be no sound now, anywhere. Thin moonlight has broken through the cloud cover to the east, and the rain trails off in the distance in two narrow reflections of the rails, smooth, functional. He turns and looks back at the pool of raining light under the station lamp. Then he walks a few more paces, marking how the bare treetops close over the tracks in the distance, dark, bordering fretwork, going off and seeming to meet at the vanishing point. The station is small now, in the distance, and he sits down on one of the wet ties and folds his hands over his knees. He picks up a piece of gravel and throws it into the bushes below. How bizarre the world is. And how outlandish to have come this far and not to have seen how unadventurous and ordinary one has been, how willing to hide in one's daily routines, avoiding things, living by keeping still. The first Elizabeth left him, and, in a way, he stopped there. He had kept himself in secret, lived in secret, nursing the wound, and the second Elizabeth had loved him through it all, loved him and searched for some way to bring him to herself, and then given up, let go of the idea of having children, spending her evenings with work and dope, and life was busy and empty, and Holly and Fiona came in and disturbed everything, because the two of them, old as the proverbial hills, are still passionately in the thick of life, still battering their way through the days, the days they understand are temporary, fleeting, and yet they are still agitated and hungry for everything.

He thinks of all this, sitting on the railroad tie in the dark. The clouds have covered the moon again. Slowly, he rises and starts to walk farther away from the station. But then he turns and heads back, toward the pool of lamplight with its lines of falling water. He can hear the train now at his back—it's a few minutes late. He steps into the very middle, between the two rails, and walks on, forcing himself not to look back. Elizabeth has said she forgives him. It's not real; he can't get his mind around it, can't process the information. The harm he has done to their lives looms over him, a dome, all heartbreak. The loneliness he felt when the first Elizabeth left seems small to him now, and again the fear spreads in him, like a cold vapor coming from his breastbone. The sound of the train is still far. He imagines it roaring over him. As another opening in the clouds gives forth the moon, he watches the little strands of reflection on the rails. He turns. The train is visible now, a big blackness, like the immense cold night itself shouldering toward him. Nothing ever the same. Nothing like it ever was. He waits, feels the thrill of the train's approach, the deadness at his heart, waiting, steeling himself. The wine is swimming in his head, and he's decided that he'll do this; he will, and why not? But then the air thrums at him, and, at last, he steps down into the gravel and away from the track, up onto the platform again. He steps to the edge and watches it come. It goes by in a rush, a prodigious blast of air, the horn sounding, he knows, off into the night, over his sleeping town. His own house, where his wife has said she would be waiting up for him, and he cannot address, or change, or lessen anything. The train recedes into the dimness toward Washington. He turns there in the light, breathing with effort, as if he has been running.

"Oh," he says, "goddamn."

The sound of the train dies away, and there's just his breathing and the stirrings of wind. It's getting colder. He walks out of the light and away from the station, heading back past Temporary Road, with its look of a place long-abandoned, windows shut, leaf-litter everywhere in the lawn, the hazy streetlamp shadow of tree branches reaching like skeletal, crooked fingers along the walls and up onto the roof, and he thinks of Holly sitting up there while the neighborhood gathered. Who can understand one human heart? He walks on, toward his own house, where he will have to be different, have to change himself somehow, for the woman who lives there, whom he has done such a bad job of loving. How he wants for her not to have escaped into the separateness of sleep tonight, this of all nights, the last Thanksgiving of the century. "Please," he murmurs as he turns the corner onto his street. "Please," he says aloud.

The lights are on, upstairs and down.

13.

Brother Fire comes home to a locked door and a key that, for some reason, won't work. It's the wrong key. He tries it several times, works it, jiggles it, but it won't budge, and all the while he's being rained on. Finally, he drives up the street to an all-night 7-Eleven store and goes inside, where he moves to the counter, soaking wet, and asks for a cup of coffee. The man behind the counter is a Sikh, a dark brown man with thick, black brows and deep lines on either side of his mouth, with a turban on his head and sleepy, yellow eyes. He indicates where the coffee island is, and the priest walks over there to pour himself a cup.

"You are very soaked," says the Sikh.

"Yes," says Brother Fire. "Locked out of my own house."

"Locked out how?"

"My key doesn't work. I don't understand."

"The temperature maybe. The metal contracts, you see."

"I couldn't turn it," Brother Fire says.

"It's cold out there, too."

"Yes."

"One never gets used to the cold."

He pays for the coffee and stands there sipping it, staring out at the rain. The road is empty; the street is empty. The only other car is this Sikh's, a beaten-up Plymouth with no hubcaps and with rust holes along the bottom of the doors.

"Where are you from?" the Sikh asks.

"Just down the road," says the priest. "Saint Augustine's."

"Ah."

They both watch while the rain slows and ceases, leaving a hazy mist, and soon even that begins to dissipate in the cold.

The Sikh says, "I would bet that it's the metal contracting. Or perhaps you tried the wrong one in the dark."

"Pardon me?" Brother Fire says.

"Your key. Locking you out."

"Oh, yes. Maybe. Yes."

"Have more coffee, it's on the house."

"Thank you."

"I believe in your god, too, you know."

Brother Fire regards him—his dark-lipped smile. There's something almost impish about it.

"I do. I believe all the religions are true."

"Yes," says the priest.

"Except where they say the others are not."

He nods, feeling the chill of his wet clothes but also warming himself in the friendliness of the other man. "I believe a version of that, too," he says. "Yes."

"Now, if we could only get the others to comply." The Sikh smiles, and then laughs, showing stained, small, uneven teeth.

"Well, thank you for the hot coffee," says Brother Fire. "It was good."

"Good night to you, sir."

"Good night. Yes." He walks over and offers his hand.

The Sikh grasps it and says, "Thanks be to our one god."

"Yes, my friend."

Brother Fire goes out to the car, gets in, waves at the other man, pulls around, and heads back to his church, the rectory. The rain is gone, but the wind pushes at him as he gets out of the car; it blows his coat back and exposes the skin of his belly where his shirt has come out. The icy band of air makes him shiver, and he hurries, muscles aching, remembering his age, to the door. The key won't turn, because his hand is shaking now. He takes it out, then puts it back, and tries one more time, and it slips, does turn, the door opens, a gift. The house is warm, the rooms quiet and clean. He goes upstairs and gets out of his wet clothes and takes a bath, sitting in the blessed quiet and replaying the day, the evening. He'll tell Mr. Petit about the Sikh. It's something to help him see the decency in things. After his bath, he puts a robe on and goes back downstairs. He's still full from the dinner, and he makes coffee, sitting in his kitchen in the robe. This coffee is good, too; he puts a drop of brandy in it.

He reads in Saint Thomas's great book, that wonderful book with its propositions and answers, and, outside, the wind lashes at the windows, winter rolling in, more snow before morning, say the television news people. The day after Thanksgiving. The last part of the last century of the second millennium. How strange. In the next instant, he has a sense of something gigantic approaching, unfathomable, unimaginable, and terrible. The new century. What horrors await? He gets down on his knees, shaking again as if he hasn't got out of the wet clothes, and begins to say the Lord's Prayer, realizing as the words go off from him that he can feel them; he can say them as they are meant, without a wandering mind. So he does say them. "Our Father, who art in Heaven. Hallowed be Thy name." The wind moans in the eaves of the house. The dark seems to lean in, colliding with the window glass like a spirit seeking entry. "Thy Kingdom come, Thy will be done, on earth as it is in Heaven." He closes his eyes, touches the tips of his fingers to his lips, murmuring the words. "Give us this day our daily bread, and forgive us our trespasses, as we forgive those who trespass against us. And lead us not into temptation, but deliver us from evil." He breathes and waits, and the wind keeps pounding at the walls of the house. Finally, he rises, creakily, putting the bad thought, the evil premonitory phantasm, the dread of events, of history itself, away from himself, striving again for thankfulness. He can pray again, and a man who can pray is not ever truly lost.

Father McFadden calls to inquire about his holiday feast (the young priest's phrase) and to read a little poem dedicated to him; how thankful to be remembering the goodness of God in November rain, he says, and the faith of the Lord in the storming sky; how thankful to be remembering the kindness of hearts in a day of feasts, when people feed family members and priests. It goes on in this vein, and Brother Fire admires it accordingly, and speaks with all the fervor he can muster about the year ahead, the grace of God, the abundance of good hearts, the joy of life working in the vineyards of the Lord.